I0590548

Ember in the Wind

AN EMBER IN THE WIND

Book two of the Leviathan's Call

Riley Knight

Copyright © 2025 by Riley Knight

All rights reserved.

No part of this publication may be reproduced, distributed, or transmitted in any form or by any means, including photocopying, recording, or other electronic or mechanical methods, without the prior written permission of the publisher, except as permitted by U.S. copyright law.

The story, all names, characters, and incidents portrayed in this production are fictitious. No identification with actual persons (living or deceased), places, buildings, and products is intended or should be inferred.

Cover Art by Natalia Junqueira

DEDICATION

To my husband, who always encouraged me to keep going, and to my brother, who helped me every step of the way.

MAP OF THRUINE

North Spire
YURI LLAQTA
Bruthine Mountains
Illia
Femora
Lavinia
SIGILUS
Southwest Spire
Creiv Lands
Valeria
SYLFESTRA
DRAGOS
Sunlit Bay
Clodia
Clodian Empire
Argiris Desert
ATHELSTAN
Piona
Eglisfelde
THUATIA
Fairborough
Trenowyth
Wardrieu
Gaevral Territory
ALTANBERN

BLINDED

Some time in the ancient past. . .

PRECIOUS FEW HELD dear a beloved home—a place of warmth and comfort, where they longed to return when gone. Seoras had never known one. And here he stood, seeking to build one anew in a place he did not belong.

A leaf tumbled from the canopies and landed in Seoras' palm. The trees here were utterly alien to him. Shades of deep greens and rich amber, growing endlessly under a sky whose sun never set.

Nor did it ever rise. What a wretched place this was. Why had the others chosen it? The country to their east sat under gentle night, reminiscent of the place from whence they'd come. Yet humans there had expressed fear of the unknown and swiftly pushed them out.

Seoras sighed. Here would have to do.

Snapping his palm closed, Seoras crushed the leaf and dropped its remains. There was someone he needed to see, alone. Boots sloshing through the dirt road, muddy from a fresh rainfall, Seoras trudged towards the tallest, broadest tree in the forest. Wind tugged at his scarf and tousled his steel curls. Wind that reached in every direction, brushing against every trunk and buffeting each falling leaf.

Seoras saw much through that wind. It was his eyes, his very being. Squirrels danced through the boughs above, pausing as a gale threatened to knock them from their perch. Songbirds huddled in their nests twenty paces back, and a creek trickled through the forest a mile to his north. Even the smallest insects crawling beneath the brush could not hide from him.

But something in this forest was wrong. Barely discernible in this great empty expanse of wilderness, something hid. The wind would buck as though striking a house or a wall and curve around something blocking its path. But no matter how Seoras strained to sense what it was, to outline its shape with the breeze, it eluded his grasp.

Trying to ignore the prevailing desire to flee, Seoras approached the so-called palace of the king. All that awaited him was a singular tree, tall as the sky and wide as several buildings strung together. When they first came to this strange forest, an unusual man claimed to be its king, building his palace where his kingdom would one day be.

Perhaps the man could see the future. Maybe he had a foolproof plan. Or perhaps he was merely a mad fool.

An arch carved into the trunk granted passage to the hollowed rooms within the colossal tree. The interior walls had been smoothed, and the floors were even, akin to paneled floors without visible slats. Space enough for a grand entryway was certainly here, but not one piece of decoration adorned the natural hall.

Curious and amused, Seoras craned his neck up to peer at the high ceiling, eyeing the bare walls and ominous halls leading to who-knows-where.

"There you are." A voice emerged from behind Seoras, though no one had been there a moment before.

Whirling around, Seoras found himself facing a mockery of a man, his face concealed by a bright red mask. A whimsical expression carved the surface: eyes perpetually closed, a mouth curled in a smirk. No strings bound it to the man's head; it was as though the mask itself was his skin.

Yet he was unremarkable in every other way. Plain brown hair gathered on his head, and a simple burgundy cloak draped his shoulders.

Seoras grimaced, trying to see where the mask met face. "Are you Ril?"

"The one and only."

Seoras had met someone named Ril before, but the 'king' before him bore no similarities to the lord of the fae.

"Sure," Seoras said doubtfully. "I hear you're the one we need to talk to."

"You heard correctly." The man passed uncomfortably close, his creepy mask an inch from Seoras' face. "Walk with me," the king of the Sylf forest bid. "I understand we have much to discuss."

Frowning, Seoras narrowed his eyes at the king's back uncertainly. The flap of wings caught his ear, and he glanced up to see a small songbird resting on a nook in the trunk wall, its belly a bright emerald. An insidious feeling raced through Seoras, and a shiver ran down his spine.

"This isn't much of a palace," Seoras observed.

"All things begin small." The king dismissed. "This way." He turned down a corner, directing them through one of the myriad halls.

Seoras bit his lip. Had the trunk been this wide from the outside?

"I think your request can be accommodated," the king said, "Assuming you agree to my rules." The strange man whipped around, mask glowing in the dark hall. The corners of its smirk turned down, and its eyes slightly opened, revealing a black void underneath. "But why did they send *you*?"

"They didn't," Seoras admitted, wincing. This king was more than a representative of the fae. He was one, himself.

"I thought not. Rash. Impulsive. Headstrong. A terrible negotiator." The fae king insulted Seoras with chipper glee. "They would not have sent you. But *you* would sneak off alone to talk to me in private. Ah, now that makes more sense."

"Why do you fae always seem to be three steps ahead?" Seoras asked despondently.

The king answered with a smile from his eerie mask and turned around.

Though it had seemed to stretch on for eternity, the hall came to a sudden end, pooling into a glade of snow-covered trees. A sky-less ceiling loomed above, a reflection of the world below. Thin and short trees reached down from the heavens, their powdered tips trickling snow over the room.

This was an aiceil. An overlap.

No footprints marred the snow where the man in the mask walked. Seoras stirred the wind with a shallow breath, feeling the man's edges. A breeze stirred the plain hair and the burgundy cloak. For all intents and purposes, the man felt utterly ordinary.

"So," The king named Ril said. "For what have you sought me out?"

"Who else is here with you?" Seoras asked.

"An interesting question." The masked man turned. His horrifying face shifted back to a neutral expression. "What do you mean?"

"Something else is here. Something only I can sense." Seoras explained. "I've pointed it out to the others, but they ignore me."

"Are you sure you're not hallucinating?" The king's mask shifted into a mocking smile. He waltzed away, plucking a flower from a pile of snow. "You are mortal, no? Fallible as the rest of your kind."

Seoras had no clue what this man was. And he hated that. Watching the king closely, he glanced up nervously. "I'm sure of what I saw. I need to know what it is lest we put ourselves in needless danger."

"Have I not expressed my joy at your arrival?" The king sounded offended. "More people under my boughs draw visitors, citizens. And my city will blossom as intended." He spread his hands. "We both have something to gain. I'll tell you what you want, so long as you can answer one question." He pointed the flower at Seoras. "What does an evoker forget?"

An evoker? That was the strange breed of magic bestowed upon humans. Seoras knew little of their mages, save they had perfect memories and could draw from their minds any spell they desired.

"That's a trick question." Seoras folded his arms. "They remember everything."

"I didn't ask you what they remembered. I asked you what they *forgot*." The fae king twirled his flower and paced a circle around Seoras. "You cefra have perfect memories of a sort. You share in everything, especially the mundane. You see every little moment; recall every stubbed toe. Every burned bread. Every lazy day where nothing at all happened. It solidifies that they are like you, and you are all one."

"I've only shared as much with a handful." Seoras pivoted, following the king, unwilling to let him escape his sight.

"But evokers do no such thing. They do not recall the mundane, even if they could. Humans see no cause for it. The tiny bruise is forgotten by tomorrow; the idle conversation is an unneeded memory. The information is in their mind, yes, and available for remembrance in perfect clarity. Yet they might as well have forgotten."

"Saint's winds. What are you getting at?"

The fae king stopped. His mask shifted. The eyes flew open; the mouth frowned. "When you lied to Diorbhail yesterday, she knew. Oh, you passed the fib well enough. But she dwelt on the memory. On the word. She thought through your sentence and concluded by the morrow that you might not have been truthful."

Seoras tugged on a loose hair. Ril knew about that? The lie had been utterly mundane, a wayward comment on her appearance.

Diorbhail was vain, sensitive. Her beauty mark *had* darkened, but why tell her so?

"But what if your lie had been perfect?" The fae king continued pacing, flower twirling faster. "She would think nothing of it. It would be mundane. Idle chatter. Never again dwelt upon. Forgotten."

Seoras froze. When he had expressed his concerns that something was stalking them, spying on them, or hiding out of sight, the response had never been, 'There's nothing there, Seoras.' The response had been to stare at him, confused, and continue the conversation as though he had never spoken at all.

But what did that mean? That he was lying to them? No, that wasn't right. Seoras was sure of what he saw. In all his life, his wind sight had never led him astray.

The mask on the unsettling man curled, changing as a terrifying smile grew and the eyes slammed shut. "But a perfect lie is impossible. For we are all fallible, aren't we?"

Seoras had enough experience with fae to understand he hated dealing with them. They were inexplicable. *Impossible.*

Was this thing he sensed the perfect lie? Indiscernible to all who tried to seek it out? Unnoticed to those yet unaware? Those who spoke of it, unbelieved? Did whispers dance through the forests, telling the others Seoras was merely seeing things before they could even respond to him?

And, if it did, they never remembered Seoras' words or the thing's response. Even Diorbhail, most brilliant of their number, had not noticed something meddling with her mind.

"I don't think we'll be taking your offer," Seoras said quickly, turning on his heel. "We'll settle elsewhere."

"Clever." The king stopped twirling the flower. "They don't give you enough credit. Still, I imagine one of you will be back." His smile deepened. "Safe travels. Who knows what hides in this forest?"

The chill in the air vanished as Seoras stepped back into the trunk's tunnel. His boots echoed in the dark hall. Desperately reaching out with his wind sense, Seoras brushed the walls, feeling for the exit.

The journey back was far shorter. Within a few paces, Seoras re-emerged into the barren 'palace' of the carved-out trunk. Hurrying outside, he exhaled in relief when leaves crunched beneath his feet and heavy canopies loomed overhead.

His reprieve was fleeting. No sooner had the breeze rushed through the northern forest than Seoras sensed it again—a blank space—a place the wind could not touch, reach, or feel the outline of, like the world had fallen away, leaving a void of pure nothingness in its wake.

Seoras sprinted through the forest, eyes closed, allowing the wind to see for him. The entity was moving north, slowly but surely. This time, he'd catch it. This time, he'd see.

Someone was moving toward him. A man. Tall, broad. Olbhreis.

"Woah, kid!" A familiar deep voice shouted as Olbhreis stepped into Seoras' path and grabbed his arm. "Where are you running to?"

Seoras' eyes snapped open. Olbhreis' face was always welcome: topaz eyes filled with roiling emotion, dark skin the color of rich soil. Neatly groomed hair piled on the shoulders of his yellow cape, delicate and soft compared to the thick leather armor wrapped around his muscular form.

"Kid?" Seoras balked, briefly forgetting his mission. "You haven't said that in a while."

"You haven't run around like a fleeing fugitive in a while," Olbhreis said. He tripped over himself as Seoras twisted out his grip and latched onto the scarf instead, yanking Seoras back. "*Wait.* I need to tell you something."

Choking as his scarf tightened around his neck, Seoras stared daggers at his friend. "Not now." He insisted, twisting out of the scarf and leaving it behind.

Olbhreis' eyes widened as he looked down at the body-less scarf he clutched as Seoras darted away again.

Their camp was just behind this glade, a collection of tarps and fires where refugees gathered, awaiting permission from the king to settle the nearby land. The void that should not be loomed at its edge, but for the first time since Seoras had sensed its presence, he saw something tangible.

A woman stood at the camp's edge, short in stature, clad from shoulders to ankles in a modest white gown. Red hair tumbled down her back, curled like rose petals. Youthful softness painted a pleasant face as she turned and looked at Seoras.

A human? Her eyes had those unusual, broad black spots called pupils, and their color was dull, lifeless, a shade of brown akin to barren dirt.

Yet, the wind slammed into the space around her, outlining the void it could not pierce, could not define. The breeze could not reach the woman, let alone feel her shape, brush her shoulders, and rustle her hair. How?

She was wrong. *Wrong.* Every fiber of Seoras' being told him so.

"Good grief." Olbhreis caught up to Seoras. "What were you doing, anyhow?"

"Talking to the king," Seoras said distractedly, staring at the woman.

Olbhreis followed his gaze, eyes narrowing. "We heard back while you were gone. He sent a messenger." Olbhreis nodded at the red-haired woman. "There's a plot of land not far from here we've been allowed to claim. Which means the hard part's about to be behind." The large man chuckled, slapping Seoras' back. "You're not cut out for hard labor. You can construct yourself a stage, be the jester that keeps morale up."

Normally, Seoras would laugh. But such a deep, unsettling feeling permeated him he could hardly speak. Grabbing Olbhreis' wrist, he pointed. "What do you see there?"

Olbhreis followed his finger. "That's the messenger."

"You can see her?"

". . . yes? Are you alright?"

Dropping Olbhreis' hand, Seoras cautiously approached. The woman had turned her back again. Gritting his teeth, Seoras extended his hand. The wind whipped around him, rising to a gale mighty enough to drive Olbhreis back and buck the smaller branches on the trees.

It slammed into something invisible, Impenetrable. But she was *right there.* Biting his lip so hard it bled, Seoras pushed and pressed, driving every ounce of air in this forest into that woman and the void consuming her.

Finally, it penetrated the void, rushing into tiny fissures like a great rock filled with cracks and crevasses from years of erosion. It found nothing resembling a woman, nothing whole, nothing human.

The ground beneath Seoras' feet heaved, tripping him up. Concentration broken, he yelped and tripped, landing on his knees.

"Talav shit, Seoras. I know you're crazy, but I thought you preferred flirting to murdering." Olbhreis bellowed.

Gasping, Seoras wiped the blood from his mouth. The woman turned around, hair flowing over her shoulder. Her visage was more terrifying than Seoras could have imagined.

Cracks broke her skin, like fissures in the earth. Black ichor hid beneath, streaking across her pallid being, tearing her gown, rending her perfect locks. A rift resided in her core, peering into more than mere darkness. It peered into nothingness—the void he'd sensed—a great swathe of unimaginable, incomprehensible *nothing.*

"Seoras?" Olbhreis grabbed his collar and yanked him to his feet.

Olbhreis' eyes briefly flashed with anger, and the ground drummed in response. But the frustration quickly quelled and was replaced with concern.

"I. . ." Seoras stuttered. "Can't you see her?"

"It's alright." The woman whispered. "He did not attack me."

Olbhreis' eyes glazed over. He looked confused, as though searching his inner self for something important. And then he spoke. "So eager to run over here. Your wife is right over there, you know?" He elbowed Seoras.

Seoras blinked rapidly, staring between the woman and his friend. Olbhreis' death grip on him slackened, and a calm demeanor returned to the man, though he had been alarmed a moment ago.

The woman chuckled nervously. Olbhreis quickly comforted her. "Oh, don't mind Seoras. He's a tease with everyone." Clearing his throat, he changed topics. "Have you met with the Lord Paragon yet?"

"No." The woman shook her head. "I'm still waiting."

"Let me take you to him." Olbhreis politely beckoned for her to follow him through the camp. "No cause to let news like this wait."

Bewildered, Seoras could only stand in silence, mouth agape. He snapped it close and watched the two depart. Olbhreis was a kind soul who could make anyone comfortable, and the woman gradually warmed up to him, though she seemed utterly intimidated by these strange people.

But. . . but that was not right. She was no innocent maiden.

Not a soul in the camp stared at her with anything but banal curiosity or disinterest, as though she were another of these stout, homely humans and not the monstrosity Seoras could see.

This time, the fae king did not manage to sneak up on him. Seoras felt something move under the breeze a second before the wretched man's voice apparated.

"Your people are unusually accepting of her odd mien." The fae king strolled around Seoras, hands clasped behind his back, mask smiling.

"What are you up to, fae?" Seoras demanded.

"I already told you. Planting the seeds for my people's future." His mask's smile widened. "It must be odd to feel so alone, no? Among people you can share everything with, at that."

"It's not wise to mock your future neighbors," Seoras advised.

"I'm not mocking. I'm observing. Which reminds me," The mask's smile fell into a thin line. "I have a riddle for you. How do you kill a fae?"

"You can't." Seoras snarled.

"Not so." The fae king leaned forward. "Fae die when unremarkable mortals become the opposite of that which they embody." He sighed. "Unfortunately for you, Leviathan, you are anything but ordinary." The fae stepped forward and vanished in a puff of smoke, but his voice lingered. "I wish you all the luck."

Coughing, Seoras waved the smoke from his face. He caught words, distant and quiet, the last he could hear before Olbhreis walked out of earshot.

"Forgive my manners!" The man's warm voice boomed. "I never caught your name."

The void-riddled messenger said something in return. But beneath the bucking trees and crunching leaves, the word slipped his grasp.

CHAPTER ONE

DISCORD

HE END WAS near. A mere stone's throw away. Fionn felt like she had been waiting for it her entire life, and now only a few weeks remained.

Taking a shaky breath, Fionn wrapped her cloak tighter around her arms. Her head had pounded ceaselessly since departing Yuri Llaqta. Every step shot paint through her knees and her fingers trembled. Was it nerves that frayed her being or something broken within?

A voice raged inside her head, a storm that never quelled. Seoras disapproved of the path she had chosen.

We're running out of time. The melodic voice in her mind snapped. *Change your course, or I will change it for you.*

Fionn flinched and stumbled into a tree. Rubbing her face, she looked up at the oak and the leaf pile gathered around its trunk. How far had she wandered from the boat in her daze?

It didn't matter. No matter how Seoras protested, her mind was made up.

From the forests of Sylfestra to the mountains of Yuri Llaqta, Seoras had guided her. From her own people, the Gaevral, and even the fae king, Fionn had stolen away her people's ancient jewels. After a great struggle, the final gem had been wrested from Kiylla, the Llaqtan's frighteningly powerful evoker.

Though the man was prickly and thoroughly unlikable, Fionn had grown attached to Arsene. And this attachment would not allow her to leave him to a wretched fate. The gems would go with him to Lavinia. Once he turned them over, won back his title, and reclaimed his life, their fate would be out of his hands.

In the night, Fionn would sweep them away from the Duke and his ilk and ferry them to their final resting place. She had succeeded thus far. She would again.

Leaves crunched under the footfalls of a familiar gait, heavy and deliberate. Fionn anticipated Wulf's voice before he spoke.

"There you are," Wulf called through the woods. "Wandered further than usual this time."

"I don't wander enough for you to have marked an average." Fionn protested, turning around.

The man sent a flutter through her heart. His beard was newly trimmed, though his hair had grown longer during their travels. Dark strands brushed against his forehead, above eyes the color of the ocean.

Many cefra found humans plain, stout. Ugly. Fionn saw something comforting in the black pools of their pupils. And it delighted her to see Wulf's widen when he gazed at her.

Wulf smirked. "I keep a record. Want me to recite it?"

"No."

"First instance, a night at camp in the Sylfestran woods. Two, the second day in Dragos. Three—"

"Alright, alright." Fionn rubbed her arms.

Laughing, Wulf reached out to brush back a loose strand of her wild curls, but Fionn winced and recoiled slightly. Frowning, he retracted his hand.

"You're. . .still not feeling better, then?"

Fionn swallowed. Seoras had been belligerent the night before they departed Femora. Wulf and Arsene had overheard, though Fionn could barely recall it.

"I'm fine." Fionn insisted.

"Hm." He didn't believe her. "I meant to say. Did you think I didn't realize you stole my dagger again?"

Touching her belt, Fionn wrapped her fingers around the hilt protectively. "You didn't mention it for *ages*. Finder's keepers.."

Wulf sighed. "Well, at least some things never change. Come back to camp before you wander into a bear's den."

Grimacing, Fionn glanced behind her and hurried after him. The sun emerged from behind the clouds, filtering through the branches and highlighting thin shadows beneath Wulf's eyes.

"Having more dreams?" Fionn guessed.

"Yeah." Wulf glanced at her. "Same as always, only. . . getting more aggressive, I suppose." He laughed breathily. "Dreams are just dreams. I probably sound crazy."

"No more than I do," Fionn reassured him, brow furrowing.

Seoras must have been the cause of those dreams. What Wulf saw within them, Fionn had seen as well. Memories that did not belong to her loomed at the back of her mind, just out of reach. Stray too close, and Seoras would pull her back.

Sometimes, an errant moment would surface in her mind: the face of the auburn-haired man and his kindly demeanor, the short, bitter laugh when the beautiful woman with hair of flame made fun of Seoras, a breeze stirring the air, a scarf fluttering wildly, and someone laughing nearby: a man with topaz eyes.

But so, too, had Fionn seen the black tower on the silver lake and the serene meadow of silver grass. The woman with rose-colored locks was known to all in the empire, though they had only seen her cast in marble. But when glimpsed in the flesh, cracks parted her porcelain skin, and what hid beneath. . .

Fionn believed she understood why Wulf repeatedly dreamed of her. Seoras was showing him. Because he could not simply be told.

Why him? Fionn wondered.

Seoras was silent for a moment, but a quiet hum responded. *Do you think it a vain attempt? We cannot tell him, but maybe I can help him see nonetheless. Should things go awry. . . an ally would be welcome.*

Are we truly the only ones who know? Fionn asked.

Seoras did not quite answer. *You cannot imagine what it has been like. Alone for so long. Screaming words no one else can hear.*

Resentful annoyance shot through Fionn. Maybe Seoras realized his hypocrisy. He knew well he was the cause of Fionn's lifelong isolation.

The rage must have shown on her face. Wulf raised his eyebrows. "Are you alright?"

"Oh, yeah." Fionn rubbed her arm. "I think something bit me."

Wulf smiled, mouth faltering as he frowned and turned away.

Fionn retreated back into her mind, bristling. *I thought you lost all trust when Olbhreis betrayed you.*

For once, she had said something to which Seoras had no response. The presence in her mind retracted, loosening its grip on her. Smaller, more diminished, it returned.

I know. Seoras said quietly. *A bard's duty is to weave tales, even if their meaning goes unheard.*

Wulf grabbed her arm and stopped her. "Listen. We need to talk, and this is the first moment we've had alone since boarding that cursed boat."

"It *is* a bit cramped."

"What's going on with you and Arsene?" He demanded.

A difficult question to answer. Fionn did not even know. "I'm not sure. I think he's worried I'm going to rob him."

"He always suspects the worst of people. *This* is something else."

"I could try talking to him, though I imagine he'll be more forward with you."

Wulf's mouth twitched. "He's never been forward with me." He shifted from foot to foot. "I can't help but think. . ."

"Think what?" Fionn chortled. "Arsene doesn't even like me. He revealed some. . . personal matters during our time in the Earth Father's domain. I think he resents me for knowing."

"That sounds like him," Wulf murmured, though he wasn't entirely convinced.

Nor should he be. When Arsene had leaned in that night when they were alone on the deck, Fionn had almost reciprocated.

"When we get to Lavinia," Wulf stepped closer. "Arsene will probably stay. I'll be down a partner."

Fionn grinned. "Are you asking me to join your little band?"

"Band? Hardly. It would only be me at that point."

"I'd love to." She looked away. "Though, we'd have to make yearly stops to Forsaidh."

"Maybe then we could have a ship cabin to ourselves." He gently touched her face and kissed her forehead. "If you need to talk, just find me."

Fionn stifled a sob, remembering the night in Femora when he'd held her. She had wept for the first time in years, a waterfall of emotions no dam could've held back.

When Wulf pulled away, she hugged him tightly, burying her face in his gambeson's thick cloth. He returned the embrace, running a hand gently down her back.

Releasing her, Wulf guided her back to shore, head tilted, listening.

Voices carried from the riverbank, where their ship had been moored for the night. Bleating drowned out the words, a sound Fionn had grown accustomed to. Feeling a bit more cheery, she raised her head.

Eckart stood with his back to them, watching the rushing water. That blue surcoat he wore was alien to Fionn's eyes. The man she knew was always slightly disheveled and smelled of dirt. The appearance of a noble Athelstani lord did not suit him. The sun caught in his eyes, reflecting the ice of his pupil-less irises as he turned around.

Relia knelt by his boots, chatting away. Rose-colored locks hid within her bonnet, nary a strand displaced. One hand tugged on her cloak while the other scratched beneath the goat's chin. It bleated again happily.

"Taking your dog for a walk?" Wulf asked loudly as they joined the others.

"That's not a bad comparison," Eckart admitted. "She needed to stretch her legs."

Tefnut was a cute little thing. Fionn had never thought much of goats; they did not live in Forsaidh. But the tiny spotted creature had sweet eyes, impossible to resist. Spellbound, Fionn knelt and ran a hand down the goat's spine. Her eyes met Relia's soft brown gaze, and the girl smiled.

A kinship had grown between Eckart and Relia, in no small part due to the girl's belief they were long-lost siblings. Would she be disappointed when she learned the truth? Everyone had agreed to allow the Duke to handle the delicate affair, but there was a chance she would resent them for keeping quiet.

Perhaps a chance remained that her appearance was an odd coincidence, and Relia was but a commonplace nobody.

"Seen Arsene?" Wulf asked, folding his arms over his dark gambeson.

"Is he missing?" Relia questioned. "I thought he was still brooding in the hull."

"Not when I looked." Wulf nudged Fionn. "For once, you're not the only one I'm trying to track down. Don't tell me you rubbed off on him."

"I can't think of anything less likely," Fionn said earnestly.

"Mm," Eckart grunted, fishing through his pockets. "Fionn." He handed her a wrinkled scroll.

"Oh." Fionn unrolled the poem Leo had given her. "You're finally ready to hear it?"

"I'm in a good mood. Read away."

Chuckling, Fionn glanced over Leo's farewell poem. "When midnight calls, stars brush the land, and heavens fade to night. Pain and dreams dull to sleep, and flowers bloom where warmth has fled. And in that place of silent reprieve, I'll see again the one I seek."

Eckart narrowed his eyes. "It's just a plain farewell."

"No!" Relia blurted out. "That's what you got from it?" She scrunched her brows, thinking over the deeper meaning.

"I understand it." Fionn tucked the poem in her pocket. "You're telling me you don't know what his riddle means?"

"Spirits." Eckart shook his head, looking to Wulf for help, who shrugged in response. "I'll figure it out eventually. I just don't understand why the man can't speak plainly."

"Relia," Wulf ordered. "Call for Arsene."

"Why me?"

"You're a woman," Wulf answered, striding away. "The sound attracts him, like moths to flame."

Relia stuck out her tongue and stood, dusting off her jerkin as she scanned the river. Eckart chuckled and scooped up Tefnut like she was a lap dog. "We're heading out soon. Stay put," he said.

"No, I think I'll swim." Fionn joked halfheartedly.

Eckart pursed his lips. He loitered, probably wanting to say something. Nodding awkwardly, he walked away.

Sighing, Fionn leaned against a tree and watched the shore. They could not leave without Arsene. She could steal a few more minutes of solitude. Wrapping her cloak around herself to ward off the encroaching winter, she watched the crewmates carry the water stores onto the deck and lead the grazing horses back into their pens.

A figure on the deck caught Fionn's eye: a man dressed in dark blue robes laid over steel armor. Ciprian, the evoker who had been chaperoning their journey. Beside him stood a woman in black, raven hair bound in a tight braid with a vibrant blue flower tucked into its ribbon.

Johanna glanced at Fionn, and Ciprian followed her gaze. Noticing her staring back, they both looked hurriedly away. Curious.

Fionn had not spent much time with the half-Llaqtan evoker, but Eckart seemed to trust Johanna. The two had spent weeks together during the campaign and its subsequent failure. But Eckart was not known for his ability to read a room or glean a person's intent.

An unusual surge of confidence bloomed in Fionn's chest, and she took a step forward, guided not by herself but the leviathan within. Marching to the riverside, she addressed the pair.

"I saw you staring. Something you want to tell me?" She questioned.

"Yes," Johanna answered surprisingly quickly. "Er, no. I have Arsene's account of your entrapment by Kiylla, but I would like yours. So, a question."

Brief confusion flitted through Ciprian's pale eyes. So, that was not what they had been discussing.

"I see," Fionn said. "Surely an evoker's recount is more reliable than mine."

"Still, I'd like to hear it." Johanna waved Ciprian away. "Leave us."

Bowing, Ciprian walked away, granting them solace. Johanna leaned on the railing, watching Fionn across the lapping water. Arsene would have written an academic report focused on essential details. Maybe Fionn could give her a proper story.

Johanna tucked her hands in her pockets, deep brown eyes gleaming with genuine interest. "Start from the moment you stole the gem from Kiylla's grasp."

Summoning the last shreds of her enthusiasm, Fionn wove a quick tale against the backdrop of the verdant woods. From their heist beneath stormy skies in the mountains of the Qoyllan camp to their sudden plunge into the unknown world, she spoke of the sinkhole that nearly swallowed them and the shadows moving in chasms at the center of the world. Fionn painted an exaggerated picture of their struggles in the moving land's domain but left out the tender moment where echoes of old memories had made Arsene spill secrets of his life.

Johanna listened, face blank. Not until Fionn finished the tale on the not-so-truthful details of their flight from the angry swarm of talav did she speak.

"Fascinating," Johanna said. "Your story matches Arsene's. Though, you included more details."

"What did he leave out?"

"Most. The part about the shattering mountain, the herd of tarbe. . . Arsene glossed over it." She chuckled. "Probably because it made him look bad."

"He was pathetic." Fionn agreed. "But in all fairness, so was I."

"I suppose." Johanna bounced on her heels. "So it's true. Kiylla merely extrapolated a new use when the original intent was anything but."

"Huh?" Fionn asked, not understanding her meaning.

"It's a door. Arsene claimed those were the fae king's words." Johanna smiled slightly. "Thank you." She said, leaning off the rail and returning to the rooms beneath the deck.

Fionn shook her head, confused. What an odd woman. Maybe that was why Eckart got along with her. Shoving her hands in her trouser pockets, Fionn strolled down the riverbank and crossed the bridge onto the deck.

Noise startled her out of her reverie. Wulf shepherded a distracted-looking Arsene onto the deck, gripping the evoker's arm and wearing an amused grin. Typically well-kept, Arsene looked frazzled this morning, his auburn hair unbrushed and his hard amber eyes flashing between jubilance and distress.

Noticing Fionn, Arsene straightened his coat and raked back his hair. Their eyes met, and she found herself victim to an intense, accusing glare. Whatever was on his mind, she could not discern. And then he threw open the doors and fled down the stairs.

"Someone's grumpy." Relia's voice emerged from behind Wulf as she joined Fionn's side. "Must not be a morning person." She laughed awkwardly.

"I think he's mad about his hand, still," Wulf suggested. "It's not healing right."

"Oh." Relia looked sheepish. "I'd forgotten. He never talks about it."

Arsene never spoke of himself to anyone. But Fionn had seen how the lingering wound on his hand pained him—a parting gift from Kiylla.

"I'll ask him." Fionn said. Flying down the steps, she caught up to Arsene in the hall and grabbed his arm. "*What?*" She demanded.

Halting, Arsene raised his hands dramatically. "Why the accusatory tone?"

"I saw that look you gave me." She folded her arms. "What's bothering you?"

"Nothing." He snapped, turning to go. He made it one step before whirling around. "*You.* You are bothering me."

"What have I done?"

"Nothing." Arsene spat. "And that's the problem." He stormed away, slamming the cabin door behind him.

Human men were confusing. At least Fionn could glean cefran men's memories and understand their thoughts. And with so many people crammed onto this boat, they would not get another moment alone.

Testing the knob, Fionn pulled out her hairpin and lock-picked the door. Slipping inside, she found Arsene waiting for her, hand on his hip and foot tapping.

"I should have known." He muttered. "Degenerate thief."

"Talk," Fionn ordered. "I have you cornered."

"It's that damn song." Arsene strode up to her, jabbing an accusatory finger into her chest. "About me. You meant for me to hear. You, or. . . or Seoras."

". . . So?"

"So. . . so everything." Arsene stepped back. "I don't even know why it troubles me so. But it does." His eyes narrowed. "I'll be staying in Lavinia, with Marius."

"I assumed so."

Arsene swallowed. "Wulf will take the news hard. You'll be there for him, yes?"

Laughing breathily, Fionn shook her head. "I'll comfort him. He'll be mourning you for some time."

Nodding, Arsene turned away, staring out the cabin's tiny window. He had not said what was truly on his mind. Fionn had come to know him all too well.

"Arsene?" She asked. "Why did you always avoid my gaze?"

He winced. "You noticed that?"

"Hard not to." She looked down. "I'm not sure why you hated looking at me, but I'm glad that's changed. You met my eyes for the first time, a few nights ago."

"I never hated looking at you," Arsene insisted. "You just reminded me of myself. And. . ."

He hated himself. Fionn knew what he meant to say, even if the words had not emerged. Touching his back, Fionn squeezed his uninjured shoulder and stepped away. She heard him turn, contemplating saying more or reaching for her, but he never did.

Another week remained before this boat reached Lavinia. One night would be spent therein before she needed to enact her heist. Arsene carried all the jewels save one. He would hand them over to his brother. Fionn would take them. She retraced her plan as she drifted into the women's cabin and felt Seoras' fury that she was willing to risk their fate for foolish sentimentality.

I don't wish to control you, Fionn. But I will. Seoras warned.

Fionn searched the sky outside the window for the brown songbird. *You're supposed to be the god of freedom.*

One life is nothing compared to what could be, and I'm willing to sacrifice yours.

You picked me. Why don't you trust me? Fionn bit her lip as she strained to get through to him.

It was supposed to be her mind, but it often felt like his. Now, he threatened to wrest control of her limbs and voice. His words lingered with her, an uncomfortable reminder that her life had never been hers.

The cefra believed in reincarnation, at second chances. Fionn wanted to believe them, too, but. . .

She doubted any second chances awaited her, where she might live as herself. What might that Fionn have been like? The Fionnuala who never would have taken this nickname because she never would have known Seoras' attachment to it. Would that woman have been a mere cook dancing drunkenly beneath the boughs of the Aeourant's forests?

The dagger that was not hers hung heavy on her hip. Should she return it before slipping away? No, maybe she would keep it and pretend. Pretend this week would not end and that something more awaited her, as everyone else on this ship believed.

The others were in high spirits, thinking the danger had passed and a reward awaited them, even if that reward was simply release from this arduous task. But Fionn had one more step to carry out.

One final trip south, and then she could rest. Part of her had longed for this. But now, part of her yearned to remain. She touched the dagger on her hip. The blade she had thoughtlessly stolen back in King Ril's chambers.

Cefran lovers in the Aeourant clan took something from one another to express their feelings. Should the feeling be mutual, something would be stolen in return. She held Wulf's dagger, and he, hers.

But she ought to return this before the heist. Release him from this bond. A dagger stolen on the night of their first heist and slipped back before the last.

CHAPTER TWO

PARTNERS

THE RIVER RUNNING past Lavinia city was the only spot of life on an otherwise barren land. Mountains towered overhead, shadowing the world and sheltering the sprawling city in their embrace. Massive drakes carved from volcanic rock greeted anyone who entered.

Lavinia was not to Fionn's taste. Far too colorless. Hostile. And the endless stairs were a sin on her knees. She fidgeted in Tipple's saddle, already dreading the ascent.

The great gates were always open, save for times of war, and decades had passed since the last. Arsene led the way, riding into the first-tier courtyard. Crowds channeled around the center stage, a stone platform cheerily decorated with pyres for executions. Charred remains of convicted criminals or heretics remained bound to two. Fionn grimaced at the unpleasant sight.

Drawing them away from the crowd, Arsene turned to address the group. "Johanna, take Eckart and find our accommodations. I have business with the rest."

Eckart pulled his hood up, obscuring his eyes. Johanna nodded. "Where are you going?"

"The Duke deserves better than to be visited by these peasants." Arsene pointed at Wulf and Relia. "We need to see a tailor."

"I see." Johanna chuckled. "Not staying at the manor, then?"

"Not like this. Reserve the Flaming Lake if you would." Arsene gestured for Relia and Wulf to follow him.

Their venture sounded entertaining. Fionn tapped Tipple's flank and trotted after Arsene. Wulf rode protectively alongside her, though she doubted anyone could see her vibrant features beneath her heavy hood.

Lavinia's markets were a sight to behold compared to the rest of the city. Packed stone buildings crowded wide streets, their windows lined with goods aplenty. Ash-crafted pottery cluttered one window, and heavy fur mantles hung in another. A display of specialty soaps crafted from ashfall remains caught Fionn's eye, and she stared longingly as they passed.

A smaller building than Fionn expected awaited them, where Arsene motioned for them to dismount and tie up their steeds. A bell on the door rang as he pushed it open and ushered them inside.

Dragosi people preferred heavy coats and layered dresses, with scarves and head-wraps to protect them from the ashen air, but Arsene's chosen tailor displayed far more than its city's fashions. Silk gowns from Sigillus hung in one corner, while floral doublets from Eglisfelde rested on a shelf near the counter.

As Arsene pulled Wulf toward a rack of stately coats, Fionn paused beside a dress tucked into the corner of the building. Her breath caught. This was a Forsaidh-style gown, the kind she had worn for her reitath: a two-piece dress with a generous midriff, the skirt thin and flowy. Golden thread patterned the black cloth, tracing wings and feathers across the hems.

It reminded her of home. Fionn glanced down at her simple trousers and jerkin and longed to dress up for a reitath again. To hear the Aeourant bards sing.

"Why do I need fancy clothes?" Relia asked across the room.

"You were my partners. You need to be there." Arsene insisted. "Ah!"

Fionn turned to see a woman emerge from the back room. Quite the character, her brown hair was bundled in an enormous bun, and her hook nose sported a beauty spot just above her bright red lips.

"Romanitza," Arsene said with respect. "I need your help. We have a meeting with the Duke."

The woman raised her eyebrows and glanced between her clients. "Oh dear." She smoothed down her gown. "Let me see what I can do."

Fionn smiled as the seamstress descended upon Wulf like a hawk, aggressively turning him around and taking his measurements. Leaving her to her work, Fionn turned back to the lone dress in the back corner.

Footsteps echoed just below the chattering voices. Glancing to her left, Fionn noticed Arsene staring at the dress. "You like this one, then?" He guessed.

"Yes." She said. "It's just like what we have back home."

"Romanitza sews all styles. Or, most." He cocked his head. "I didn't know she'd taken up Forsaidh fashion. It's too cold here to wear such thin fabrics. And they would scandalize any devout Viridian within thirty paces."

Fionn chuckled. "These are hardly scandalous. This is high fashion for an evening of import. Imperials understand nothing of my home."

"Can you blame them? It's an ocean of hostile waters away."

"I took a boat to the Altanese harbor. It wasn't that far, actually."

"Fionn. . ." Arsene shook his head and pointed at the dress' midriff. "Do all Aeourant members paint the exposed skin, or only important sorts?"

"Everyone does."

"Does that mean you also never bathe?" Arsene scowled at the thought. "How awful."

"And here I thought we finally agreed upon something."

"We never will." He assured her, turning to watch Romanitza work. "Don't you want to watch? She's going to turn Wulf into a prince."

Fionn chuckled. "He doesn't have the manners to be a prince."

"Neither do I," Arsene smirked.

Pulling her hood down, Fionn waited for the others to finish. They did not have time for personal tailoring, so the seamstress picked out clothes she had on hand. Thorough and passionate, she treated Wulf and Relia like a canvas and the clothing, her paint.

Wanting to be surprised when they emerged the following morning, Fionn looked away when they wrapped their purchase into parcels and paid. The hook-nosed seamstress glanced at Fionn curiously as Arsene laid a pile of coins on the table. Swallowing, Fionn glanced down sharply.

"Don't be a stranger anymore," Romanitza said, shooing Arsene away. "I expect to see you again before winter ends."

"Don't worry. I mean to stay." Arsene bowed his head as he tucked his coin purse into his satchel. "Wishing you the clearest of nights, dear lady."

Important business concluded, they departed the shop and remounted, navigating the increasingly packed streets to their inn, the same building they'd slept in upon their last visit. Fionn kept her head down, thinking. Dragosi businesses shuttered after evening meal; the streets would be dead come nightfall. Sneaking to the manor should prove easy.

Eckart waited for them outside the inn, a cloaked figure leaning against the wall. He grabbed their reins as they dismounted, happy to stable the horses. The man had never liked crowds. He probably preferred the company out here to those inside.

The red-bricked interior was as cozy as Fionn recalled, though the common room was more packed than before. Several tables sat Dragosi guests, olive-skinned and bundled in fur-lined coats and cloaks. Johanna sat alone at a table decorated with a metal sculpture of flowers and beckoned them over.

Wulf sat heavily in a chair, and Fionn leaned on its back. Johanna crossed her legs and looked at Arsene. "Ciprian is informing the Duke. We should have a meeting tomorrow."

"Good." Arsene placed a hand on a chair but did not sit. "And rooms?"

"Taken care of."

A sour expression crossed Arsene's face as the heavy-set bartender sat a tray of mugs on the table—mushroom ale—the greatest enemy of Arsene's days.

Lush foliage covered every inch of Forsaidh soil. Fionn could not imagine growing up where the infertile land killed any crop not grown underground. A fate even a prince could not escape, it would seem.

Eckart returned earlier than expected, adjusting his hood as he sat beside Wulf. "Want to play a round of Hart's fold?" He asked, grabbing a mug.

"Sure." Wulf reached into his satchel and pulled out a deck of cards.

"Deal me in." Relia leaned forward eagerly.

Stuck on a boat for weeks, they had huddled around cots in the cramped, dim hull, playing round after round of cards as Eckart and Wulf raised the stakes. Fionn had long grown tired of it.

As had Arsene. He waved a hand dismissively. "Count me out."

"You're just sore about that last loss." Wulf chuckled.

Tapping the table, Johanna requested a hand and tucked her cards beneath the table. Glancing at the bar, Fionn scanned the shelves for a drink not brewed from fungus and tapped Wulf's shoulder to inform him she was walking away.

The bartender nodded at Fionn as she scanned his shelf of bottles and returned to cleaning his cups. Most of the labels were unfamiliar to Fionn, but maybe she would be lucky enough to find a foreign import.

"Your efforts are futile," Arsene said, joining her at the bar. "But I can take you somewhere we might have more luck."

Fionn's eyes darted to the table. "I—"

Arsene cut her off. "We need to talk anyway." He grabbed her arm and steered her toward the door.

"Would it kill you to ask nicely?"

"Yes."

It felt colder outside than it had before. Burying herself in her cloak, Fionn stared curiously at Arsene. "Talk about what?"

"Not now. I'm thinking." He said curtly.

"Cacmun," Fionn murmured. At least she would get a decent drink out of this.

Silence accompanied them on their walk. Arsene guided Fionn to the dizzying stairwell leading to the second tier and began the ascent. Huffing to herself, Fionn considered the possibility he was shepherding her to the peak so he could push her off the mountain.

Fionn could not deny she relished the thought of pushing him instead.

Thankfully, Arsene remained on the second tier, bringing her to an establishment pressed against the sheer wall that dropped off to the tier below. A bar, judging from the sign. He held the door open for her, only to cut her off and walk in first.

Balling her hands into fists as the door slammed in her face, Fionn took a deep breath, steadying her anger. Calming, she raked her hair behind her ears and stepped inside.

The increase in quality from the Flaming Lake was apparent. Though plain gray stone outside, the bar was garnished with dark wood walls and flooring, a rarity in these parts. Higher-brow customers sat at the tables, their hair and faces' cleaner, their coats well-tailored. A middle-aged woman worked the bar with her husband, a handsome couple in burgundy attire.

"There you are. What kept you?" Arsene pointed at the display of bottles behind the bar. "Imports from Athelstan and Sigilus. My savior in troubled times."

Fionn chuckled and stepped closer, taking care not to show her eyes. "I tried Sigillite wine once. If they have it—"

"I take back what I said. We have *one* thing in common." Arsene approached the bar and ordered for them, carrying back two glasses of white wine. "This way."

A back door in the tavern led onto a patio whose edge hung over the drop-off. The first tier sprawled below them, and great drakes carved by the gates stood at eye level across the city. Stepping forward, Fionn tested the stone banister, checking its stability.

Arsene handed Fionn her glass and leaned on the rails. Gratefully accepting, Fionn looked at his dominant hand. A shard of metal had torn through it during the battle in the shrine. "You didn't drop the glass. Hand healed?"

"No." Arsene turned over his dominant hand, scowling. "The bone hasn't mended right. It aches something terrible and is deathly stiff. But I didn't bring you here to talk about me. There's one unresolved matter I haven't decided upon."

"And you want to talk to me rather than Wulf?" Fionn asked, closing her eyes in bliss as she took a sip. She could not recall the last time she'd had a decent drink.

"Wulf's reliable but simple." Arsene's eyes darkened. "We found a cult living in a creepy cloister amidst a forbidden aiceil. Tettiena belonged to them. And she reappeared in Femora."

"She did."

"I knew her. Passingly. She was a quiet woman, kept to herself, kept the gossip about her to a minimum. But my mother was her dearest friend. So was Beau Rosa. And who showed up just before the catastrophic wave that would have flattened the Third Legion?"

"Beau," Fionn answered. "Then, you think your mother is involved, too."

"I'm worried she is," Arsene confirmed, swirling his wine.

"Then so is Marius," Fionn suggested.

"*No*," Arsene said harshly. "I know my brother. Perfect. Saintly. I've listened to him talk, heard his woes, his desires, his fears. To wipe out a legion of our own? He would never." He paused. "But I don't know my mother."

"What's the problem?" Fionn turned to watch the flickering torches below. "You've done as she asked."

"That's never been enough for her." Arsene leaned on the banister, staring down. "You're going to disappear, aren't you? After tonight. But my curiosity hasn't been sated." He turned to look at her, hard amber eyes boring into hers. "The one who lingers in your mind. . . was I right?"

Fionn rolled her tongue in her mouth. Arsene had guessed correctly the night he'd overheard her song. "Yes."

He won't believe you anyway. Seoras whispered.

"And you've been trying to tell me something. Something I can't hear. I feel like I'm walking into a room full of vipers, blind." He stood straight. "So, here I am, open-minded. Tell me something you think I need to hear."

"You're that worried?"

"Only when it comes to Marius."

She tilted her head, gesturing with her glass. "Is this about what I said? That evokers cannot remember what they don't believe?"

Arsene sighed. "I'm a natural skeptic. But I'm trying." He spread his arms to reinforce his offer. "So tell me all there is to tell."

Grasping her glass with both hands, Fionn tried to think of something to say. "My road takes me to Fairborough, so I can't bring Wulf."

"What for?"

"For the aiceil there. For the plane it touches."

"Interesting," Arsene muttered. "Why?"

"So my kin will be safe. So you'll be safe. Whatever fears you have for Marius will vanish with me."

There remained a place out of reach where the jewels could be hidden away. And there they would lie, untouched, until this world crumbled into dust. Fionn only had to reach it.

But once she stepped inside, there was no return path. She would seal the door behind her, preventing anyone from finding the cefran gems again.

Arsene's brows knit. "You should tell Wulf. You'll break his heart if you vanish in the night."

"Would you tell him? For me? Not until after tomorrow night. Then, it will be too late to catch up."

"Hm." Arsene tilted his head back and forth, countenance shifting as he deliberated. "Fine. But indulge me. What's special about Fairborough's aiceil?"

"That's where I'll find the shadow's eye," Fionn said. Seoras delighted at the cryptic words, the first hint of joy he'd expressed in weeks.

"Helpful." Arsene rolled his eyes. "How about this? Those things, those jewels. They'll give the empire an idea. And while I don't much care if they crater Yuri Llaqta, I *do* care about war because I'll inevitably be involved."

"You're a hero now; they'll want your aid."

"Precisely. So if you need help on your little heist, a bit of inside aid. . . I'll see what I can do. And then," He flicked a hand at her. "Disappear as you promised."

"Wulf might not agree, but I don't think you're so bad."

"Don't say it so loud." Arsene paused, thinking, then raised his glass. "Well, we've been ill-fated and ill-paired partners since the first day we arrived in Lavinia. Today marks the end of that arrangement. It concluded alright, I suppose."

"Partners." Fionn agreed, raising her glass to clink against his.

Arsene chortled as he toasted her. "We're not celebrating the arrangement, but rather the finality." He idly swirled his glass again, starting over the city. "I'm surprised you came. You don't think Wulf will be jealous?"

"Of you? Not a chance."

"True. He knows I have a more refined taste." He laid his glass on the banister, staring into the night.

Fionn tilted her head, studying him. "So what's next for Arsene?"

"Hm?" He seemed surprised to hear her voice again. "I, um." He furrowed his brow. "I haven't thought about it. Normally, I'm a man with a plan, but. . . But I've been so focused on surviving I've forgotten to consider it."

"What did you want before you switched to surviving, then?"

"To be important," Arsene answered. "To be looked at the way they look at Marius. Not because of my connection to him, but because of. . . me."

Fionn reeled in surprise. Not in a thousand eras would she have anticipated an honest response. Was he such a lightweight the wine had already intoxicated him?

"What about Fionn?" Arsene asked. "Where will she go after Fairborough?"

"I. . ." Fionn half-smiled. Her life would end after reaching Fairborough. "I think I'll turn in for the night."

"Typical." Arsene turned away. "Flighty and dodgy. The woman of mystery." He rolled his eyes. "And Wulf calls me dramatic."

"You are."

"Not as much as you." He set his emptied glass on the stone banister. "You owe me. By Sigillite customs, you've dealt great offense."

"I owe you?" She repeated, exasperated. "Everything I do offends you."

"While that's true, this particular slight has been stewing for months." Arsene extended a hand. "In Sylfestra, you never danced with me."

"At the soiree? We never got a chance. It wasn't part of the plan." Fionn raised an eyebrow. "Besides, I thought Dragosi men hated dancing."

"We do. But, even the coldhearted tyrant sings lullabies to his daughter."

Fionn stared at his hand. "There's no music."

Arsene's brow wrinkled in concentration, and a moment later, soft violin danced over the night. A quiet memory of music. "There." He offered his hand again.

Accepting, Fionn was surprised when he pulled her close and danced with the confidence of one well-practiced. She should have known. Smiling, she tugged on his uninjured hand, pulling him into a quicker, lighthearted waltz.

Her attempt to trip him up failed. Arsene kept up with her.

"I should have known." Fionn said. "Of course you know how to dance. Who taught you?"

"Self taught." He said smugly.

"Gods, I wish I could have seen you dancing by yourself in your room."

The smug smile vanished. Arsene pushed her away, changing the subject. "Stop leading. The man's supposed to lead." He flicked his wrist, and the music shifted to a gentle, romantic ballad.

Seoras offered his opinion. *You do have a bad habit of leading.*

Lolling her head to the side, Fionn made a show of going limp. When Arsene took her hand and guided her into a slower waltz, she resisted the overwhelming desire to choose her own steps, and instead followed his.

"Much better." Arsene paused, glancing away. "Have you ever wished a moment could last forever?"

"Occasionally. One time, when we visited Aoife, my mother bought me this little cake—"

"You ruin everything." Arsene sighed.

"If you wanted me to say something specific, you should have given me a script."

"Look me in the eyes and tell me you don't improvise all your roles."

He had her there. "Start over." Fionn ordered.

Arsene cleared his throat, and tried again. "Have you ever wished a moment could last forever?"

Hiding a grin, Fionn tilted her head down. "I have. I'd clutch it to my heart for the rest of my days." She said with a theatrical flair.

Arsene tilted her chin up. "That's the wonderful thing about memories. They last for eternity."

As Fionn opened her mouth to respond, he yanked her towards him, cupping her the back of her neck as he kissed her. Desperate and harsh, everything unlike Wulf's gentle touch.

Surprised, Fionn's eyes widened. Letting them flutter close, she leaned in, but he pulled away.

"There." He stepped back. "Now you can leave." Dropping her hand, he dismissed the memory of the music. "I'm getting another drink. Want one?"

Disappointed, Fionn touched her bottom lip. "You stole that! I never said—"

"You owed me, remember? For the night on the boat." Arsene smirked. "But I'll take that as a yes." He slipped through the door.

Seoras spoke up, lighthearted for the first time in a while. *It would have been smooth had you not floundered your part.*

Sighing, Fionn leaned on the banister and stared over the city blanketed in night. Serenity always preceded a storm. But if all went as planned, the storm would be gentle. And it would be nice to see that black tower and its beautiful sea in person for the first time.

Fionn took a breath. She'd bid farewell to the others tomorrow. If only she, too, had perfect memory and could hold their images in her mind forever.

CHAPTER THREE

REVELATION

Three weeks ago

THE SHRINE OF the Earth Father was a sight to behold. Cracks splintered along the cavern ceiling, filled with golden fog. Topaz light peered from within like a gemstone sun hid behind the rock. Against the cavern's far wall rose thick pillars supporting a vaulted ceiling half-buried in the earth. Broad steps led to an open archway, and deep chasms cut through the rock to either side of the stairs, where underground streams rushed. A thin path of stone between the moats ushered them inside.

Leofric stared in awe at the otherworldly cavern. If Johanna was to be believed, this was an aiceil, the forbidden dwelling of the goddess. Yet, it differed greatly from what he had seen in Athelstan and what he had read in religious texts.

"Give me a moment to make a mental map," Johanna said, approaching the temple steps.

"How old is this place?" Leo marveled, rotating to take the space in.

"Ancient." Wulf guessed. "Watch your step. Would be a shame if you fell into a hidden chasm."

"In that case, I advise you to be exceedingly reckless." Leo retorted.

"People might actually miss me, Leo. I can't say the same for you." Wulf jabbed.

Tall and broad, the temple's stairs weren't sized for humans. Wulf carefully climbed them first, and Leo followed. Thin air stifled his breathing, and dust crumbled from the ancient stone. Four pillars, several paces wide, held up the looming ceiling, and a dais supported a stone statue at their center.

This statue depicted a man—tall, muscular, imposing, yet with a warm expression etched on his timeless face. An eagle perched on his shoulder, and he clutched an orb radiating with topaz light while the other rested atop the handle of a war axe, its head pressed into the ground. This must be the Earth Father.

Sweeping stairs rose to his left and right. Johanna trotted up the left, and Wulf approached the right, but Leo remained rooted to the spot, gaze fixed on the statue.

The crystal orb in the statue's hand flashed violently, blinding Leo. Stunned, he raised his arm to shield himself from the unexplained light. The searing pain faded, and he lowered his arm to see a terror far more grave.

The sinkhole that swallowed the First Legion stretched before him, a gaping maw of darkness. Leo blinked, noticing shapes at the chasm's base. A city waited below. Ornate buildings, painted with colorful yet unfamiliar murals, lined packed streets carved along the chasm walls and floors.

Gentle light illuminated the area, white and soft. Twin moons hovered in a black sky, as large as the great white orb of Athelstan. But this was not home, nor was this the same sinkhole as had swallowed the First.

"Leofric, was it not?" A booming voice shook the very earth.

Spinning in panic, Leo found himself face to face with a man who resembled the statue in nearly every regard. Only. . . only he was alive, his dark skin not like those of Sigilus, but the color of stone. At a loss for words, Leo stepped back and teetered on the sinkhole's edge.

"You were assigned to the First." The man continued. "You did not want to serve, but you supported the campaign against Yuri Llaqta. Did you not?"

Regaining his balance, Leo only managed a few words. "I did, but—"

"Then shall I show you what you long for?" The man did not give him another chance to speak. He waved his hand, and the earth moved the way Llaqtan soil changed shape.

The sinkhole collapsed, filling in as the flat plains surrounding it rose into ledges and plateaus. Soil hardened into rock, shaping into streets and buildings of hardened clay. This was Femora, yet its roads were whole, its structures bereft of fractures. Was this what the town had looked like upon first construction?

Overlapping voices burst into being, deafening Leo. Disoriented, he stumbled over himself and felt his back slam into a wall. Imperial soldiers in steel armor and green tabards flooded the streets in equal numbers to Llaqtans in strapped sandals and short tunics. Deep unease stained the Llaqtans' bearings, and the Imperial soldiers resembled those in the Third: tired of the war and eager to return home.

Was this a hallucination? Leo rubbed his eyes until they ached, but the voices and sights would not fade.

A commotion drew Leo's attention down the street, where a mother and daughter in simple tartan gowns argued with an Imperial soldier. The man grabbed the younger woman's arm and yanked her away from her mother as the older woman wailed.

Gasping for air, Leo pushed off the wall, spinning as he searched for the man from before: the statue come to life. But he was gone. Changing course, Leo reached for the soldier's arm, but his hand passed through as if he were a ghost. The Imperial continued unhindered, dragging the girl down the street into a building and slamming the door heavily behind him.

Stunned, Leo froze, watching the crowd around him pass through him, unaware of his presence, walking down streets of intact buildings he recalled as being destroyed: barracks for the soldiers, homes for the families, and brothels.

Searching for an escape, Leo ran until his path reached a crossroads, passing an empty plot of dirt. A Viridian priest clad in green robes emblazoned with a golden laurel stood just ahead, directing Llaqtan men as they constructed a new building. A young boy labored with them, lagging behind the rest as he dragged a heavy stone into place.

Had this chapel ever been completed? Leo did not remember seeing it.

Forgetting he was but a ghost, Leo moved to help the kid, but something behind the empty lot caught his eye. The foundation for the city walls was there but otherwise unbuilt. Leo could see the plains beyond Femora's bounds; disturbed dirt lay in loose mounds as far as the eye could see—shallow graves for the dead in the war's final battle. Leo remembered reading about it.

The cleric struck the boy's back, sending him sprawling. He dropped the heavy stone and landed atop it. Leo reached for the kid, but his hand passed through the ghostly figure.

The booming voice shook the earth behind him. "This chapel was destroyed." The man said. "Torn down by the insurgents."

"What is this?" Leo spat, whirling around.

"Femora. Forty years ago." The man glanced away. "And war will again blanket its streets when the Llaqtans lose their one hope of salvation."

Leo's mouth twitched. He felt no sorrow for warring against the Llaqtans and their champion, Kiylla. Too many had died by her hand. The sinkhole would haunt his nightmares for the rest of his life.

But should they succeed in subduing Kiylla, the war would renew. And who could say if he and Eckart would emerge alive?

With a wave of his hand, the man changed the world. The people vanished, and the buildings collapsed. Clay melted and reformed with the earth into a barren plain of ashen earth, lifeless. Dead.

Corpses littered the area as far as the eye could see. With open eyes, they stared at the cloudy heaven. But they were not human. Not one corpse had pupils in their irises, and each shone with colors far more vibrant than any human's.

The godlike figure joined Leo's side. "But I have more kin than merely the Llaqtans."

Wrenching his gaze away from the bleak scene, Leo stared into the man's luminescent, topaz eyes. "Your kin are dead?"

The man shook his head and silently pointed to a corpse a few paces away, lying face down.

Dread filled Leo's heart as he knelt and flipped the body over, revealing a familiar face. Brunette hair and icy blue eyes. Eckart. The imagery was so vivid, so real. Desperate, Leo felt for a pulse but met only frigid skin.

"This one carries Floraidh's Ice." The man continued. "It will lead to this."

"Like. . . like the tidal wave?" Leo questioned. "But Eckart protected us from it."

"But can he protect himself?"

"What are you trying to tell me?"

"Only that which I fear. Though, I may be wrong." The man said unhelpfully. He rested both palms on the handle of his massive double-bladed axe. "Leofric von Trenowyth is a romantic. Rashness takes hold when guarding his own. My kind of man." The stern exterior cracked slightly, and grief poured through his eyes as he gestured around them. "I foresee this end."

Leo leaned back on his haunches, thinking. Eckart had been imprisoned while Beau endeavored to convince Consus the cefra were plotting something untoward, something catastrophic.

If. . . if the jewels were weapons, and Kiylla's was captured and taken to Imperial lands. . . then, the Empire would surely use them instead. But not solely on the Llaqtans.

No nation could hope to match the might of the gems. Altanbern, Forsaidh, even Sylfestra would fall.

The Earth father's brilliant topaz eyes gentled. "You are like me in many ways, I feel. You would be his shield."

"Aren't I already?" Leo blurted out.

The man chuckled. "I don't think he sees it that way. As I once shielded another, I ask you to do the same. Watch for that which hides in the dark. Douse the growing fire where you can."

Pinching his hand, Leo tried to wake himself from this hallucination. It stung, as did the pain of gazing upon the lifeless eyes of his friend. This was all real. . . and yet it shouldn't be. But what could one man like him do when he was unaware of all that was happening around him?

The large man moved to stand at Leo's side. "I must do what I can to aid my people. Though he may see it as betrayal, it is not." The booming voice paused. "Asking this of you is my way of holding that shield before him once more."

Who the man spoke of, Leo could not guess. And what was meant to be gleaned in this vision, Leo could not grasp. But one thing became clear.

"You—" Leo struggled to find what he wanted to say. "You're him, aren't you? The Earth Father? Olbhreis?"

The commanding voice changed instantly, its deep tones becoming warm and boisterous. "You're as daft as Eckart claims. But sometimes foolishness can work in one's favor."

The imposing and severe aura melted instantly, replaced with warm air. The Earth Father's broad smile was welcoming as if inviting Leo to enjoy a mug of ale.

"I'll keep him safe," Leo vowed. "Somehow."

The god spread his muscular arms wide. "Then why are you still here?"

The dream vanished. Leo tripped as the world shifted underfoot, and his breath returned. Gasping, he fell onto his hands and knees, catching himself painfully on the cold, stone floor.

This was the Shrine. He was back in the world of the living.

"Leofric?" A woman asked.

Looking up, Leo saw Johanna and Wulf staring at him in concern and confusion. Brushing himself off, he stood and looked up at the lifeless stone statue one last time.

They had not seen him, not heard him? But Leo had. As real as this moment. But he believed in Viridia and had been devout all his life.

What, then, was he supposed to make of this?

CHAPTER FOUR

SHIELD MAIDEN

LEO WANDERED THE streets of Femora in a daze, remembering the vision he'd seen in the Earth Father's shrine. He slammed into something metallic and reeled, surprised. Raising his head, he peered into dark eyes on a sharp face of pale skin framed by short hair.

Thurston von Wardrieu never looked pleased to see Leo; the sentiment was mutual. Dropping his gaze, Leo stared at Thurston's blue surcoat, and the crest stitched onto its fabric: twin moons hidden behind the cloud, just like in the vision.

"Are you alright?" Thurston asked. "No, don't answer that."

Leo frowned. Soldiers surrounded them, hurrying up and down the fragmented ledges. Word had come that the Third Legion was to strike out and unite with the Fifth before surrounding the camp the Vira and Qoyllan tribes shared.

The routine mockery in Thurston's voice was oddly comforting. "Helpless without your servant?"

"I'm fine," Leo said. "I'd gotten comfortable, is all. I'm not eager to march."

"Come with me, then." Thurston turned away.

Leo followed him without question but halted as they passed the field where the melee had taken place. "Wait."

Pausing, Thurston glanced around. "What?"

"How can we be sure the Vira don't have a Kiylla of their own?"

"Where did that come from?"

"Someone must have considered it."

"Of course they have," Thurston said. "But she's detained, and her weapon is on its way to Lavinia. If there were another, now would be the time to step up, yet none have."

"We should tell them to delay longer." Leo declared. "Or. . . or pull out. Why the rush?"

"Why are you so worried?" Thurston asked quizzically.

"Are you so eager to wander into another sinkhole? Or worse?"

Thurston shrugged. "Unfortunately, we aren't of high enough station to alter plans. Your father wanted you to see real action, did he not? Now's your chance. Think on the bright side."

Shifting from foot to foot, Leo paused before he spoke again. "I never asked. Were you at Fairborough?"

"You never asked for *good reason*." Thurston scoffed. "Shadows, Leofric. What's come over you?"

"I. . ."

Thurston grabbed Leo's collar and yanked him closer, checking his head for injury, and Leo pushed him off.

"Quit it," Leo said. "I'm fine."

"Then act like it." Thurston turned away but quickly spun around. "Or better yet, learn to be as silent as you have these past few weeks."

A few choice words came to mind, but Leo clamped his mouth shut and glared.

"Good, just like that," Thurston said, tone lightening. "Now quit stalling. Consus is waiting."

Leo stumbled after him, clumsily raking his blonde locks together and tying them back.

General Consus Parnesius was not far; he stood before the meeting tent, overseeing its disassembly. The man was striking as ever, his silver armor engraved with a golden tree and adorned with a deep green cape.

Standing here now, Leo felt foolish for never noticing Consus' resemblance to Eckart. Both had inherited their mother's almond skin and brunette hair. Even their high cheekbones were identical.

Consus pivoted as they approached. "There you are. I have news." Pulling them away from the tent, Consus found a spot on the side of the broken road where none could overhear. "We're to board a ship and return to Clodia."

Leo breathed a sigh of relief. "Why?"

"The Chamber of Lords demanded Kiylla be brought to the city for detainment, questioning, and execution. We are to escort her. The remnants of the First will formally join the Third." Consus explained.

"Even me?" Thurston raised an eyebrow. "Well, I suppose I won't complain."

"Perhaps they recalled the remaining officers," Consus suggested. "I cannot say. Orders are orders." He looked at Leo. "The ship will moor to the south. Pack your things and be ready to leave on the morrow."

"They sent a ship?" Thurston questioned. "Truevan shallows aren't known to be safe."

"We face choppy seas or Llaqtan ambushers," Consus said. "They chose the former." Nodding, he returned to his duties.

"Well." Thurston turned to face Leo. "Happy day. Now excuse me; I have something to take care of."

"Fix that ugly mug of yours while you're at it," Leo muttered.

"Better. Still lacking any wit, but better." Thurston called over his shoulder.

Breathing out heavily, Leo turned in a circle, trying to remember where he was and where he ought to be. Deciding to check on his horse first, he wandered down the hill toward the pasture.

Temple was a fine steed from a reputable pedigree. Father had bought her for Leo upon his fourteenth birthday. Though not half as sentimental about animals as Eckart, Leo was still glad the cefran lunatic had raced back into the Qoyllan camp to retrieve Temple and Dilsaeth.

The white mare dropped her head as Leo approached and bumped his shoulder. Absentmindedly rubbing her neck, Leo leaned on her flank as he tried to steady himself. It felt like fog inundated his mind, obscuring anything he reached for.

Memories of the shrine surfaced instead. A man had stood before Leo, a man the Llaqtans called their god. Had that truly been who he'd seen? Proof that all he'd been raised to believe was false?

Whether the Earth Father was a god or something masquerading as one, his message had been clear. The danger pursuing Eckart was not confined to Femora, and he was not safe now that he'd departed the war front. If anything, Eckart was in more peril now than ever, but Leo had no means to aid him. He felt like an idiot.

Gasping, Leo looked up sharply. He *was* an idiot. During their confrontation, Kiylla had spoken heavily accented Imperial common, and while her pronunciation was clumsy, she had been perfectly understandable.

A devoted worshiper of the Earth Father might have answers for Leo. But such questions need be asked in confidence.

Thurston was right. They did not have the rank to influence the war. But Leo's name carried enough weight for prison guards to heed him. Patting Temple goodbye, Leo leaped over the pasture fence and hurried back to his quarters.

He needed to pack. And to think.

lll

When Leo first came to Yuri Llaqta, the moving land startled him when the dirt so much as twitched. Now, he hardly paid mind to the trembling road as it slowly sank a few inches, carrying him down with it.

Stepping off the sinking stone, Leo glanced behind him. At this time of night, most soldiers were abed. Quiet blanketed the town, save for the crackling fire of torches and the groaning road as the earth settled into place a hand's length lower than before.

Pushing open the prison door, Leo stepped into a cramped, dim room where a weary guard sat on the bench against the back wall. The man did not budge, and a soft snore escaped him. Sleeping on the job. Perfect.

Quietly closing the door, Leo held his breath as he passed the sentry and descended the stone steps into the basement. Another guard sat on a stool by the holding cells, watching the prisoner.

This one was awake. The young soldier glanced up as Leo entered and quickly noted the crest emblazoned on Leo's tunic.

"My lord." He said inquisitively.

"Any changes?" Leo asked.

"None. She hasn't said a word."

"Take a break," Leo ordered. "I'd like to try again before we depart."

"Of course, my lord." The guard said, rising and bowing his head before walking up the stairs.

Watching to ensure the man ascended the entire flight, Leo grabbed the stool and pulled it to Kiylla's cell. A ragged woman was held within, brown hair tangled and packed with dirt, her tunic torn and stained with blots of blood. Her sharp brown eyes stared intently at Leo from behind the bars.

"I know you speak my tongue." Leo started, voice hushed. "But you've said not a word since we detained you."

Kiylla had no interest in breaking her silence. Her lips pursed tightly, expression unchanged.

"Maybe you remember me." Leo continued. "I've run across you a few times now. Eckart spared you. Let you escape."

If she recalled, Leo could not tell. Evoking could addle minds, cause a poor soul to fall into a world of illusion, where they could not discern the past from the present. Was she trapped there after conjuring unheard-of feats of magic?

"Listen." Leo lowered his voice to a murmur. "I was there in the Shrine. I saw the statue of your god. The one you think gave you that gem. The Earth Father."

These words elicited no response, but perhaps his next question would.

"Could you tell me about him?"

Kiylla tilted her head slightly, though she did not answer.

Waiting for a response, Leo folded his arms and glanced behind him. No sounds came from above. "You're the shaman's daughter. You probably know more than most."

Her mouth twitched, but she said nothing.

"Stubborn, aren't you?" Leo leaned forward. "You see, I saw him. Your Earth Father. I think he spoke to me, but his message was not entirely clear."

The shackles binding Kiylla's wrists behind her back clinked as she reclined on her cot. Her mouth opened, but a few seconds passed before she answered. "You speak true," she said, voice choppy and accent thick.

Leo knit his fingers together, a nervous bead of sweat dampening his brow. This was heresy. "I do. It has troubled my nights for days. You're the only one who could tell me more."

Rising from the cot, Kiylla approached the bars and lowered herself onto her knees beside them, voice but a whisper. "You are from the south land. Why would *you* hear him?"

"I don't know," Leo admitted.

She chuckled. "The Earth Father is a kind soul. Not like your red goddess. There is no punishment, no. . ." She rolled her tongue, searching for the word. "Smiting. He is kin. Family. Home. In all its forms, for all its people. And there, in his place, where the land lives, we go when we die, to become one with the dirt that nourishes our descendants."

"His place," Leo repeated. "You mean where you took us? The place with the golden mist, with the stifled air?"

"It was not meant for the living."

Leo did not believe that place was the afterlife, but he did not wish to antagonize her. "I don't know why he called to me. But I caught a glimpse of it. Of him. I think he was warning me."

Kiylla shifted, dragging her bare feet through the dirt. "Of what?"

"The jewel you had." Leo tapped the bars. "The Empire holds it now. They'll learn how to use it. And there are more."

She laughed again, leaning her head against the bars. "Your empire would go unchallenged. If I am lucky, they will target enemies within their walls and be no more."

Biting his lip, Leo watched her bitter smile fade. "Why did you agree to turn yourself in? You must have known this would happen, that Arsene was tricking you."

"He was not. The Earth Father did not punish him." Kiylla said. Her faith was unshaken, even now. "Arsene may have thought his words a lie, but there was promise in them. I can do more for my people there than here."

"Do what?"

Kiylla gazed at him silently. She blinked slowly and spoke. "Tarbes are led by a first runner. He gallops to their destination, and all follow in a line. Shoot the first runner, and all behind panic, their goal lost."

Furrowing his brow, Leo looked away. Intelligence had never been his forte, but he'd read enough romances to understand a metaphor. Her intentions became clear.

Pulling the stool closer, Leo spoke urgently. "You must know of the tidal wave that nearly swept Femora away. There are people who would target their own. The cefra. You. Us."

Kiylla inclined her head, one eye glaring at him between the bars. "South lord. . . are you suggesting something?"

Leo opened his mouth, hesitating long enough to wonder if he was mad. Maybe the Earth Father had read him like a book when he'd proclaimed Leo rashly leaped to decisions concerning his own. He had rescued Eckart and Johanna from the Qoyllan camp and broken Eckart out of this prison with Wulf, but both plans had been ill-conceived with nary a thought put into them. Only luck had seen their success.

"Yes." Leo blurted out. "I am. . . considering something."

"Then answer this." Kiylla dragged herself upright. "Who orders this war?"

"The Emperor."

"What for?"

Leo glanced away. Rumors swirled about that particular question. The Emperor had never been particularly popular, most in the Chamber of Lords thinking him weak. Coupled with the loss of his heir, most wanted to replace him. Father had thought this was a bid for success, something to secure a positive legacy.

And Father had supported it, seeing a chance within it for himself. If Leo could win glory in battle, the Trenowyth name might rekindle its honor.

"The clergy preach that we must bring the seed of Viridia to all nations, to enlighten all people." Leo answered.

"I know." Kiylla spat. "Why?"

"People hate Yuri Llaqta. Many had family who died in the last war, or the insurgency."

"You are daft." Kiylla insulted. "I mean, why did the Emperor choose *now*?"

"Ah. . ." Leo wrinkled his face, trying to think the way Johanna would. Or Eckart. Or anyone, really. "The situation is tense. The Emperor has a final chance to add his name to annals of history before the Chamber of Lords replaces him, or he dies."

"Yes." Kiylla found the answer she sought. "Our spies thought it a war of glory, one unpopular with the people. You recall how our people shoved you out of our lands after the last war?"

"I've read of it."

"I have given your kind reason to *fear* again." She said. "Let a curse fall on the heads who begin this futile charade."

Leo stared at her blankly for a moment before a gear in his head clicked. Was that why she wanted to be captured? Knowing she would be taken to the capital, brought before the Emperor, and given a fleeting chance to assassinate him?

She was nothing if not a martyr; Leo had to give her that. Not a selfish bone composed her body. Such a feat would assuredly end in her death.

And maybe Leo was a heretic, traitor, and worse for considering helping her.

But he would say no such thing tonight. "Can I ask you one last thing?"

"I don't see why not, south lord."

"I have a name. It's Leofric."

Kiylla looked at him wearily but did not correct herself.

Sighing, Leo continued his earlier thought. "Why do you think your god showed me what he did?"

A curious air surrounded Kiylla as she studied Leo's being, from his boots to his face. "You say he warned you. Not that he threatened you."

"Yes."

"Curious." Kiylla breathed. "Maybe there was a reason you survived that sinkhole. Perhaps he saw something greater for you. Only time will tell." She stood and limped back to her cot, sitting heavily. "I'm interested to see."

Rising from his stool, Leo stared at her through the dim flame of the torchlight. Part of him loathed her for the death she had wreaked on his company. Innocent souls, some but young boys, snuffed out in an instant.

But he could not deny that another part of him respected her and the lengths she had gone to for her people and for sparing Eckart when she could have killed him.

In the romantic stories of his youth, the world was black and white. And as often as Leo tried to pretend reality was the same, he found it challenging. Standing there, straining to hate her again, he failed utterly, and a confused ball of butterflies fluttered in his stomach.

Giving the woman one final glance, he walked away, ascending the steps with baited breath. But the guard on the bench was still dozing, and all was quiet. The soft sound of crickets greeted him as he pushed the door open to see the young guard enjoying his breath of fresh air.

"Did she talk?" The guard asked.

"No." Leo lied. "Stubborn one."

"Tell me about it. The way she stares, though. . ." The guard shuddered and bowed his head. "Good night, my lord." He bid as he returned to his station.

The night was fair, but Leo shivered. He had no idea what he was doing, and no one he trusted remained. If only Eckart had stayed. The cefra could have beaten sense into Leo and reminded him that this was blasphemy and his life was not a price worth paying to play some kind of hero.

Or, in this case, some kind of renegade.

Maybe clarity would come in the morning. Perhaps the dreams would cease. Shaking his head, Leo tried to toss away the murmurs in his mind and the ceaseless thoughts, but they followed him back to his room and into his dreams.

CHAPTER FIVE

THE LEVIATHAN

FIONN FASTENED THE bow on the back of Relia's gown and laid the fur mantle around her shoulders. Spinning hesitantly, Relia examined herself in the tall mirror on the far wall, mouth shifting between a smile and a thoughtful purse.

"Do you think this suits me?" Relia asked, tugging on the shawl. "It's so. . . dark."

"Dragosi fashion prefers muted tones." Fionn grabbed her hair tie off the bedpost. "Brown is in fashion."

"If you say so. . ."

Biting the hair tie, Fionn gathered the girl's red locks into her hands and tied them into a mannerly updo. Her hands trembled as she worked, but whether the tremors stemmed from nerves or the lightheadedness she felt, Fionn could not tell.

Seoras had been silent since last night. Perhaps he'd accepted Fionn's plan and trusted her. Or maybe he intended to wrest control of her when she least expected it.

"There." Fionn pinned the bun into place and stepped back.

Turning her neck to see the back of her hair, Relia grimaced. "I don't want to go. But Arsene insists."

"I thought you liked dressing up."

"For Ril's ball, sure. I got to wear something exciting then." She smoothed down the thick wool skirt and sighed. "I need to poop before we go."

Fionn snorted, watching the girl wander toward the latrine. What a princess she made with her noble steed, the lame mare named Butter.

An image of the fae king, Ril, flitted through her mind. His horrible red mask twisted into a sneer, and she stepped back, frightened.

Another vision followed. An auburn haired man stepped in front of her, shielding her. In his golden eyes gleamed an apparent, and familiar message: I will protect you.

Confused, Fionn shook her head. Had that been Seoras' memory? It didn't seem familiar. . .

Stepping into the hall, Fionn listened for noise from the boy's room and heard rustling and a muffled curse. Chortling, she trotted down the steps into the main room and found a seat by the crackling hearth. Hoping warmth would soothe her troubles, she held her hands against the flames, but they quivered without pause.

Fionn wobbled in her seat, losing her balance as the room spun. Pressing her hands to her face, she rubbed her eyes, hoping to clear out whatever haze had plagued her these past few days.

Taking a shaky breath, she steadied herself. Was she ill? These ailments felt too present to be mere nerves.

"Fionn!" Arsene called playfully.

Lowering her hands, Fionn turned. Arsene's appearance matched his title for the first time since they had met. The usual brown coat he wore was finally gone; a heavy black mantle draped his shoulders, edges seamed with gold. A spot of crimson lit up the ensemble, the cravat tucked into his doublet—Dragosi colors.

And his hands were tucked secretively behind his back. Frowning, Fionn tilted her head, trying to see, but he swiveled just as quickly.

"What's that?" She asked.

"Guess."

"Poison."

Arsene rolled his eyes. "Poison would suit Wulf; I can't take him in a straight fight."

"What do I warrant, then?"

"I prefer not to dirty my own hands. A hired assassin." Arsene set a small black box on the table and pushed it toward her.

A gift? Fionn sat upright, curiously eyeing the box. Looking up for approval, she grabbed the parcel and opened it. Inside lay a gown of thin black fabric stitched with gold—the dress from the tailor's shop.

Grinning, Fionn pulled out the gown and held it up to herself. It looked to be a perfect fit.

"Sorry," Arsene said. "I couldn't help myself. You always look like a begging pauper, and I couldn't stand it any long." He waved a dismissive hand. "Consider it a parting gift."

The gown was like a younger sibling to Arsene's outfit, his fabric thick, the golden borders wide, unlike the delicate stitching of wings along hers. Folding it in her lap, Fionn smiled at him. "You only liked it because it's in your colors."

"They're good colors." Arsene fussed with his cuff. "The only nice clothes you have are those. . . undergarments you wore to the ball."

"I wanted to show off my paint." Fionn protested. "Too bad I can't wear this here."

"You haven't changed your mind? Marius will see that you're rewarded."

"It was always your quest to begin with. I doubt they remember me. And, should they require me for any reason, I'll be in the city. It's just. . . I don't much like nobles."

"Now you sound like Wulf." Arsene shrugged. "Coffee?"

"Please." Fionn watched him walk away before looking at the clothes in her lap. In all likelihood, there would be no opportunity to wear them. Perhaps she could humor herself and wear them on the day of her final task.

You should. Seoras spoke up for the first time in a while.

Nobody would see. Maybe that didn't matter. Fionn recalled a rare day when Seoras had encouraged her, insisting she think not of others' opinions but only her own.

Leaning her head against the chair's back, Fionn watched Arsene. What was going through his head? He hummed to himself as he waited for their mugs of coffee, yet his hand quivered as he hesitated to pick

them up. Part of him was undoubtedly satisfied with their success, yet.
. .

Fionn shot from her seat as Arsene returned and set the cups down. "Hey." She said.

"What?"

Every muscle in Arsene's body stiffened as Fionn hugged him. She could practically feel his eyebrows shoot up and the dead stare as he was stunned into silence. Eventually, the stupor broke, and he returned the embrace.

Familiarity and warmth surged through Fionn as she caught a glimpse of orange where his auburn hair brushed against her face. Memories swirled through her again of the golden eyed man with the overbearingly affable presence. A friend, a protector, maybe. Someone from Seoras' memories.

But were her feelings for Arsene her own, merely alike? Or did the echoes of Seoras' life drown out anything that might be hers?

Fionn quickly stepped back. His hand remained fixed on her waist and prevented her from escaping. Surprised, she glanced down then back at his face.

Facial expression unreadable, Arsene seemed to be in an entirely different world, eyes fogged as he stared at her. Placing a hand on his chest, Fionn tilted her head. "Arsene?"

Snapping back to reality, Arsene hastily stepped back. "What?"

"Thank you." Fionn said. "For the gift."

"Oh, so she does have manners after all." Arsene teased as he picked up his cup. "Don't mention anything about that." He paused, mug at his lips. "Or last night."

"What? Did something happen last night?" Fionn twirled a strand of her hair.

Smirking, Arsene joined her at the table, and they silently basked by the fire. Little noise disturbed the inn, and few guests came and went. Stiff footfalls descended the stairs, and Wulf emerged, rolling his shoulder uncomfortably.

The mercenary looked like an entirely different man. Arsene had combed his hair and fitted him in a slightly too-tight silver doublet with a stylish blue overcoat. Quite noble in mien and a look Fionn doubted would ever be glimpsed again.

"This is miserable." The gruff man announced as he joined them.

"I think you look dashing." Fionn smiled at him.

The compliment bounced off Wulf's thick head. His scowl did not lessen. "Dashing like a noble idiot, maybe. This looks like something Trenowyth would wear."

"That's why I picked it." Arsene pulled out his pocket watch and flipped it open. "Where in Bruthine's name is Relia?"

"She's taking a—" Fionn caught herself. "Taking care of some things."

Wulf chortled and pushed Fionn aside, sitting in the same chair. Arsene rolled his eyes and watched the stairs, fingers tapping impatiently on the table.

Swirling her coffee, Fionn stared into the warm mug. Had she fallen for Wulf, but Seoras' personality preferred Arsene? Or was it the other way around?

There was no way to know. And it didn't matter. She would never see them again nor learn who she truly was.

Thumps on the stairwell drew her attention. Teetering from left to right, unbalanced by the heavy wool skirt, Relia looked exhausted when she reached the bottom of the stairs.

Disbelief and disdain swept over her countenance when she noticed Wulf. "Why does he get to wear colors?"

"I told you, Relia." Arsene rolled his eyes. "You're wearing a Dragosi gown. Romanitza thought Athelstani style would suit Wulf."

"Hmph." Relia snatched up her skirt and waddled over.

A cold breeze swept over the common room as the door flew open, and Johanna walked in, black coat swirling around her. She slammed the door behind her, the wind half-yanking it closed. Shivering, she approached Arsene.

"I'm ready whenever you are," Johanna said.

Setting aside his drained coffee cup, Arsene rose. "Relia?"

"I'm ready." She assured him, fussing with the bow on the back of her gown.

Groaning, Wulf rose, and Fionn shot up after him. He cast her a quizzical glance when she grabbed both his hands. "You look like a prince. Try to make the most of it."

"I better get an accolade. A medal." Wulf paused thoughtfully. "Maybe a plot of land."

Trying to hide her feelings, Fionn stood on her tiptoes and kissed him on the cheek before reluctantly releasing his hands. She must have masked her sorrow well, as Wulf did not sense anything unusual.

"See you tonight." He picked her hand back up and squeezed.

"Enough already." Arsene placed a hand on Wulf and Relia's backs and steered them toward the door. "Let's go."

Frigid air blanketed Fionn as the door swung open, and Arsene ferried the others outside. Johanna paused in the archway and glanced over her shoulder at Fionn one last time before following them.

Fidgeting, Fionn knit her fingers together and played with the strap of her satchel. Her lute was upstairs. Maybe she could play away the hours of the day.

A shadowy figure in the corner of her eye startled her, and she quickly spun toward the stairs. The silhouette looming in the hall became apparent, and Fionn's shoulders slumped as she marched over to it.

"Why are you creeping back here?" She demanded.

Eckart tilted his head up, and his eyes gleamed from beneath his hood. "Watching. I don't like it here."

"I thought you were a mountain man."

"A southern mountain man. There's no dirt here. Only rock." He pulled his hood down and folded his arms. Sometime in the past two days, he'd acquired a simple tunic and leather vest. Much better. He looked more like his old self.

"Intending to loiter here all day?" Fionn asked, leaning on the wall beside him.

"I dunno. Maybe I should go home. Or maybe I should rejoin Leo."

"Go home and face Tamhas?"

"I have to eventually."

Fionn tapped her wrist. "I found a decent place for a drink with a nice view. We could wile the hours away there."

"What's wrong with the drink here?" Eckart asked.

"I should have known you'd say that." She tugged on his arm. "Come on."

"Hey, hey. I don't want to go anywhere without a human escort."

"We're not forbidden from Imperial lands." Fionn insisted. "Just disliked." She tugged him one last time, and he relented.

"Fine. But they better have something strong." He muttered before pulling the heavy door open.

Saint's winds, it was cold out here. Forsaidh never experienced weather half this frigid even in the worst winters. Half-running to keep herself warm, Fionn ducked through a narrow side road, hoping to avoid the crowds.

"Wait!" Eckart called.

Skidding to a halt, Fionn backtracked and peaked around the corner. Eckart walked in the opposite direction, heading for the inn's small stables. Typical. Fionn shook her head and followed him. Might as well stand near the warm horses if Eckart needed a moment to kiss his goat goodbye.

Sure enough, he went straight to Dilsaeth. And his goat was curled up beneath the black stallion, head nuzzled against its white hoof feathers. Grabbing Tipple's reins, Fionn leaned against her stalwart mare, listening to Eckart softly cooing at Tefnut.

She supposed the drinks could wait.

A BROWN SONGBIRD perched on the roof sill, bright green eyes watching the pair below. Maybe it was a coincidence, or perhaps Seoras had stilled the freezing wind, granting them respite from winter's chill.

Fionn flipped a page, thinking, pen tapping against the table. The view from this tavern's balcony was not half as majestic during the day, but Eckart enjoyed watching the bustling crowds going about their day. His eyes were glued to the city beneath the banister, mug clenched tightly.

Taking a sip from her wine, Fionn tried fruitlessly to write. Her pen hovered over the page. Eckart noticed. "Still stumped?" He asked. "I would think this little adventure an easy tale to adapt."

"It should be." Fionn agreed. "But I can't seem to find the inspiration." Sighing, she set the pen down. "Bah."

Eye narrowing, Eckart set down his mug and folded his arms on the table. "So, um. . ."

"Yes?"

"Do you want to talk about your love life?"

Fionn snorted. "I don't have one."

"Everyone's noticed, I mean. . ." Eckart shifted in his seat. Saint's Winds, he was bad at this. "Everyone's noticed." He reiterated. "But Wulf seems like a nice guy. He's *Altanese*."

Fionn laughed. She would miss Eckart, too.

"We Altanese, we're reliable," he continued. "Dragosi princes, on the other hand. . ."

"Are nothing to worry about," Fionn interjected. "He's regained his place in his brother's court. And I, a wandering bard."

Eckart nodded, relieved. "Good. You should seal the deal. Humans are fickle."

"What do you mean?"

"They aren't loyal like cefra. They move on quickly."

"Speaking from experience?"

"Speaking from Leo's experience." Eckart corrected. "He waited too long to confess."

"I see. I'll keep that in mind." Fionn assured him.

He moved to ask another question but glanced up sharply. The songbird's wings fluttered wildly, and it took off. Worried, Fionn stood, eyes glued to the tavern's door. Heavy footsteps thudded inside the building, and deep voices boomed, though Fionn could not make out the words.

Seoras' voice hissed inside her mind. *They're here for you. Run!*

Tripping over her chair, Fionn slammed into the balcony and looked down. A lethal fall greeted her, but one she could mitigate with the right spell. Reaching into her satchel for a flute, she spun around when the doors slammed open.

A broad man in a high-collared cloak stood in the doorway, his thick beard and rugged face painting an imposing countenance. To his sides gathered a cluster of men in dark armor and black tabards: Lavinia city guards.

Eckart rocketed to his feet and grabbed his bow, pushing Fionn behind him.

The man in charge spoke with a deep timbre, his Dragosi accent quick and heavy like staccato notes. "Fionn and Eckart, I presume?"

"Who wants to know?" Eckart asked warily.

The light Sigillite accent in Eckart's voice surprised the Dragosi man. "I have been ordered to bring you in for questioning. You will not be harmed if you cooperate."

"Questioning? What for?" Eckart demanded.

Steel scraped as the guards drew their weapons and encircled the small balcony. "You have nowhere to go," the large man said calmly. "I would like to avoid an altercation."

Fionn could see Eckart considering every possible option. His eyes flicked back and forth, searching for an escape. Slowly, his stance relaxed, and he moved to drop his bow.

The songbird darted over Fionn's head, plunging the free-fall to the first tier. Following his lead, Fionn whirled around and heard the chink of metal as the soldier closest to her lunged. But his sword slipped through the air rather than flesh.

A gale burst from the stone balcony, sweeping the guards away and knocking them into the walls and banister. Eckart slid back, catching himself on the railing, his eyes wide with shock as a tornado manifested at his feet.

The first time Fionn had adopted Seoras' form, it had been painless. Now, tearing agony ripped through her being as her flesh was torn asunder, and the Leviathan burst from her remains: a creature of swirling wind, booming thunder, and crackling lightning. Lunging forward, she swept Eckart up in her midst and shot away.

A thousand questions raced through her mind as she strained to focus; her vision blurred as she darted through the skies above Lavinia's city—buildings swam into view, and the tall walls of mountains.

Why had the Dragosi attacked? Were Wulf and the others in danger? Or had they always planned to detain the cefra?

Fionn did not know. But she had to get them to safety.

Screams echoed below, faint, like they were trapped underwater. Shapes moved, people scrambling, pointing up in fear. Where was she? The first tier or the second? A mount's peak came into view as pain jolted through her being, and everything briefly fell dark.

A voice screamed at her. Familiar. Seoras. But even he was muted.

Safety. Where was safe? Beyond the mountains? Straining to regain focus, Fionn tried to find them, but blackness flickered over the fuzzy images of mountains, and she felt herself losing balance. The leviathan had not been entirely under her control the first time, and now it felt like she had no agency to direct its movements.

Air wooshed over her as she began to fall. Pushing forward, straining to put distance between them and their pursuers, she propelled herself forward, though she knew not where they were.

An impact followed. Stone shattered and broke as the magic keeping her together waned. Something slammed into her chest, and she felt the strange, esoteric form vanish entirely as the wind stitched back together into a mortal shape. Cold ground rose to meet her, and she rolled over herself several times before finally stopping.

Gritting her teeth, Fionn shakily rose and looked around her, vision still blurring. Gray stone buildings, rubble scattered on the street—screams and retreating figures. And Seoras' voice finally pushed through to her.

I should never have taught you that. He shouted. *You were not meant for it.*

"Fionn!" Eckart staggered to Fionn's side and helped her up. Something hurt, sharp and biting, and she winced, pressing a hand to her side. Crimson flowed down her jerkin.

More shouting drew her attention down the street. Specks of black grew clearer as they approached—guards.

Yanking her satchel off, Fionn tore her scarf from her neck and pushed it inside. "Go. Take it and run."

"Not without you." Eckart protested.

"We'll not get away if you have to carry me." She pushed the bag toward him again. Sentimentality overtook her, a foolish, pointless notion. Grabbing Wulf's dagger from her belt, she shoved it into the purse.

Cursing, Eckart grabbed the bag, glancing over his shoulder at the oncoming guards. His grip on her arm slackened as he realized he had no choice but to leave her. Fionn's vision faded, but she felt his touch slip her shoulder and heard pounding footsteps.

Shouting replaced the steps, words of caution and fear. Then someone grabbed her, and everything fell to black.

Chapter Six

RECUSANT

TEN YEARS HENCE, when Wulf had watched Lord Barron Trenowyth execute his father, he never imagined he would step foot into a royal palace, save to be executed himself.

Dragos' palace reminded Wulf of an imposing fortress more than a foppish noble's abode. Constructed of black stone, it stood out from the gray buildings in the city. Smaller drakes guarded its iron fence, looming over the promenade protectively.

Pulling at his itchy doublet, Wulf looked up at the stone dragons as they walked beneath them. He supposed they suited the people's standoffish, unfriendly attitudes.

The Dragosi people were not fond of cefra. Of all Imperial nations, their history with the other race was the most raw. Wulf hoped Fionn and Eckart kept their heads down.

Ciprian led their group, his boyish face hidden beneath an unfittingly imposing steel helm and dark blue cowl. Bowing his head, he pushed the manor doors open and beckoned them inside.

The Dobrescu manor resembled fire. Obsidian-colored tiles and crimson carpets, the walls lined with gold-tinted crown molding. Yet the layout was simpler, smaller than Wulf had expected of a palace. A thin stairwell led upstairs, and Wulf could see the halls to the parlor and dining room. Hardly the maze of pointless chambers the Sigillite palace was said to be.

Ciprian dropped them off in the parlor and bowed. "I'll return for you when the Duke is ready."

Arsene paced the length of the couch, nose scrunched distastefully. Wulf sat in the armchair, eager for a break after the arduous climb up the mountainside. "Not happy to be home?" He asked.

"I never am," Arsene muttered, stepping aside so Relia could collapse on the couch. His hard amber eyes flicked to Wulf, wanting to tell him something, but he looked down sharply and bit his tongue.

Why was Arsene so nervous? Wulf had thought his partner would be overjoyed upon achieving their mission, returning with his prize in hand, though doubtless his overseers had expected him to die. Yet only apprehensive worry plagued him, like a child who did not wish to open the door for fear a monster hid in the shadows.

"Wulf." Arsene finally said. "No, Relia." He changed his target. "Was Fionn acting oddly?"

"A little, yeah." Relia sat up. "I think she might be sick."

"Yes, I suppose that must be it." Arsene knit his hands together, wincing when he brushed the ragged scar on his dominant hand.

Narrowing his eyes, Wulf stood in front of Arsene. "What are you hiding?"

"Nothing." Arsene insisted.

Their conversation was cut short. Ciprian returned and guided them down the hall into a meeting room lit by glowing candelabras in the corners. A map of imperial territory covered the polished table, and the Duke awaited them before curtained windows.

Wulf had met Marius once, and even then, they had not spoken. Arsene mentioned his brother rarely, but Wulf could tell the two were close-knit.

The Duke matched his portrait in the aiceil's cloisters. Long wavy auburn hair, olive-skinned with a thin nose and high brow. His amber eyes were soft and kind, and with hands knit together before his burgundy mantle, he gave off an inviting and approachable aura.

Arsene bowed his head and kicked Wulf's shin, instructing him to follow suit. Coughing when he realized his error, Wulf dipped his head and caught Relia hastily mimicking him out of the corner of his eye. Unmoved by the display, Johanna walked around the table, trailing a hand on its edges as she stood on the western side.

With a chuckle and a wave, Marius instructed them to rise. "It's only me, Arsene. No Vasille or Rasvan are watching."

"Thank the goddess," Arsene muttered, straightening out and standing opposite the table from his brother. Wulf stepped forward, joining his side as Relia drifted uncertainty to the eastern side of the room.

"You must be Wulf." Marius smiled at him. "Arsene had much to say about you during his brief stay."

"Really?" Wulf raised an eyebrow.

Arsene coughed. "Shall we get to the matter at hand?"

"He spoke flatteringly of you," Marius smirked briefly before regaining his calm demeanor. "I've read Ciprian's report. Those present are the ones you attribute to the success of your venture, with an honorable mention to the young Lord Trenowyth."

"Correct." Arsene swallowed. "This is Relia, a young woman we met in Sylfestra."

The girl's eyes widened when the entire room looked at her. "Um." She curtsied awkwardly. "Pleasure to meet you."

Marius seemed to find the clumsy reaction endearing. "The pleasure is all mine. Ciprian mentioned the cefra we sent you would not be coming."

"Yes," Arsene said. "We worried that, with tensions between our people still high, the citizens would not take kindly to the news."

"Good." Marius seemed distracted momentarily, but then the fog in his gaze cleared. He opened his mouth to speak again, but his eyes darted to Arsene's hand. "What's wrong with your hand?"

Arsene tucked his injured hand into his mantle. "Nothing. Just an injury I sustained during the trip." He shook his head and pressed his good hand on the table. "We need to discuss what happened in Femora. Nothing in the report we reviewed before departure could have prepared us for that."

"So I've heard," Marius muttered, tucking his hands behind his back and looking down. "You speak of the wave?"

Johanna pursed her lips and folded her arms, casting her eyes down. Wulf expected her to say something, but she remained silent.

"Something threatens us from within." Arsene continued. "It should be everyone's highest concern. The war cannot continue while those stationed with our soldiers seek to destroy them."

Marius hesitated a while before responding. "I agree. Recount to me what happened from your perspective."

"From mine?" Arsene glanced away. "Perhaps Wulf should tell the tale."

"Why?"

"I. . . was not present for much of it." Arsene cleared his throat pointedly and stared at Wulf.

"It might be a dry tale." Wulf leaned on the table. "I'm not much of a storyteller." Retracing the events to their beginning, he recited the tale of Eckart's imprisonment, the wave conjured from the sapphire gem, and the aftermath.

The room listened quietly, and Arsene quickly interjected when the tale ended. "Odd, isn't it? That Lord Rosa appears in Femora just before the travesty? That he wanted Eckart moved for some reason?"

Marius stepped away from the table and began slowly pacing its circumference. "One could see it that way, I suppose. But Arminda had been tasked with the jewel's study. She conjured the wave."

"She could not have been working alone." Arsene protested.

"Still, Arsene. You're making a grave accusation against a powerful and well-respected man with nothing more than a hunch." Marius pointed out, passing behind Relia.

"Well, Johanna?" Arsene swiveled to stare at her. "He's your father. You would know better than I."

"Father is well-respected." Johanna agreed. "He attempted to convert the Llaqtans after the first war and departed when the plan was annulled. I doubt he would sympathize with them now."

"There's more." Arsene's gaze darted to Relia. "Another appeared there. The evoker who attempted to kill Wulf and Leofric. We heard her name. Tettiena Parnesius. Someone we both know well."

Marius froze behind Wulf. "She has not been seen in over a decade."

"And now we know why." Arsene nodded at Relia. "Look at her, and tell me you don't recognize that hair."

Marius' eye twitched as he pivoted. Nothing in his face changed; no surprise nor scrutiny marred his serene countenance. "So the rumors are true. Tell me, Arsene. Why did you not present her when first you came home?"

"Why would I?" Arsene asked, stepping back. "I had no proof but her hair. And she might have simply been part cefran." He paused. "Cinders, some Sylfestrans have red hair. How was I to know?"

"What are you talking about?" Relia blurted out.

"You haven't told her?" Marius asked incredulously. "Oh, I see. You thought I would handle it better." Approaching Relia, he pressed a hand to his chest and bowed his head. "Your true name is Lady Renata, heir to the Imperial throne, inheritor of Viridia's will. And we have long thought you lost to us."

Relia blinked, stunned. She knew little of Imperial customs and less about the appearance of their nobility. Hailing from Altanbern himself, Wulf had not connected the dots until Arsene had spelled it out. Who would think to find the missing heir in the forbidden glades of the goddess? A perfect place to hide her, in the end.

"Seventeen years ago, the newborn heir was robbed from her very cradle by an unknown assailant." Marius continued. "No trace was ever found until now." He rose. "Much of your tale must be documented, but for now, it is imperative we return you to the capital and have the proper authorities confirm your identity."

"Wait, back up." Relia raised her arms as though defending herself. "Arsene has known this all along?"

Arsene shrugged and looked away. "I had no proof. I already said as much."

A half-decent lie. Wulf knew Arsene had feared retribution, especially after they'd offended the Sylfestran king. From what Wulf understood of the Empire, they would be eager to pin the crime on someone's head and set them ablaze.

"There's nothing to fear," Marius assured her. "I'll have servants prepare you a room and begin travel preparations. If you have any questions, I'll, of course, be happy to answer."

Pressing a hand to her head, Relia walked away. Poor girl. Many would be exuberant to receive the news, but Wulf did not think Relia among them.

"Now that's settled," Arsene said. "We must consider what's to be done about the looming danger."

"Take what time you need," Marius said to Relia before turning around. "Let me see the gems."

Assenting, Arsene pulled out a small leather satchel and carefully laid the jewels on the table: the ruby of Bruthine, inlaid with fire; the sapphire rain, reflecting an endless ocean; and the earthen topaz, which hid a golden world of shifting land.

"These," Arsene said firmly. "Are exceedingly dangerous. They should be treated as such."

Johanna stepped forward. "They should be studied. Carefully. The way Kiylla used hers was not its intended function."

"Perhaps they should be destroyed," Marius muttered. Wulf had to agree.

"No." Johanna spat. "They are much too valuable to be thrown away."

Surprised by the force of her refusal, Marius' eyebrows shot up as he regarded the woman. "No decision will be made here by me alone. But I must consider where to keep them in the meantime." He lowered his brow. "Maybe, where they have already been."

"Oh, lucky me." Arsene lamented.

Wulf shifted from foot to foot, waiting for Arsene to bring up an important point. As he had yet to voice it, Wulf stepped in for him. "Duke Marius. You have connection with Lord Rosa, yes?"

Surprised, Marius stood straight, the light from the windows dancing on his cloak. "Beau Rosa? He's. . ." He hesitated. "He was acquainted with my mother, yes."

"According to General Parnesius, Lord Rosa gave him a grave warning," Wulf said. "A warning that the jewels were cefran, which is true, but also that the cefra meant to wage war on the Empire with them. And soon."

"Concerning, if true."

"But it's not. The cefra cannot use them the way Kiylla could. Only an evoker can do what she did." Wulf stepped forward, waist pressing against the table.

"Such a threat would be an apt excuse to begin a new war," Marius concluded. "War on the cefra would be easy to make popular with the people. Unlike Yuri Llaqta, their tribes are an easy target."

"And-" Wulf cut off as the room rattled.

What sounded like a veritable hurricane from the lower tiers shook the air. It raged for several seconds, growing louder with each passing moment. Relia roused from her stupor to look up, and Marius darted to the window, pulling back the curtains to look outside.

A tremor shuddered through the ground, vibrating the table. And then the commotion ceased.

"What was that?" Johanna asked.

"I don't know." Marius breathed. "Ciprian," he ordered.

The young evoker bowed and left the room. Wulf stared after him, considering following. Arsene grabbed his wrist and pulled him closer, silently shaking his head no.

Pressing his hand to his eyes, Marius suddenly seemed exhausted. "Where were we?"

"Discussing your under-reaction to treason?" Arsene suggested.

"I'm afraid it's simply out of my jurisdiction. I will, of course, bring up the concerns when we arrive in Clodia."

"Good enough, I guess," Arsene muttered. "So, what about me? After Mother and Vasille's threats, I half expect to be exiled again."

"No." Marius sounded earnest. "No, whatever they think, I don't care. I never wanted to force your hand. I knew you'd agree, regardless. As far as I'm concerned, you've more than earned your place again."

Relief flooded Arsene's face, but there was also disappointment. What was going through his partner's mind? Wulf had never managed to get Arsene to open up, and he doubted anyone else had received the privilege.

"In that case, I suppose we are done here." Marius collected a couple scrolls from the table corner. "Johanna, if you would-"

Relia whirled around. "Why was your portrait next to mine?" She demanded.

"What?" Marius said, surprised.

"I understand now why my portrait was hung behind Viridia." Relia continued. "Because I'm the heir. Her kin. So, why, then, was yours there, too?"

Arsene flinched with every word. Wulf tensed, wondering if he should intervene, prevent the girl from slipping up and revealing their heresy. But he did not. More of him wanted her to get the answers she was owed, and he wanted to hear the Duke's response himself.

Over and over, Arsene insisted he knew his brother. But did he?

Silence prevailed as Marius searched for an answer. "You speak of the Viridian sect you found in Sylfestra. Arsene told me of it."

"I think you already knew about it. And I think you're evading Arsene because you know." Relia's face twisted into anger. "Viridia stands alone at the altar because she is without equal. No temple hangs the Archbishop's portrait. To display mine implies status equal to hers."

"That's true." Marius agreed.

"So tell me. Why was your portrait there?"

"Relia," Arsene whispered harshly. "He did not know. Be reasonable."

"This was where you found the ciphered text?" Marius asked, and Arsene nodded in confirmation.

Relia relaxed and spoke calmly. "Mother attended a church, though she never brought me there. She and her comrades lived around it and passed letters in ciphered text."

"You're saying this entire group conspired to steal you?"

"Yes."

Marius closed the curtains, sealing off the light. "The Emperor must be informed of this and the dangerous magic they practiced. To say nothing of the iconoclastic location they chose."

Arsene looked up sharply, his face paling. He opened his mouth, shut it, and opened it again. "She did not say anything about where the church was."

Wulf saw Marius' face flicker with panic. It was oh so brief yet unmistakable, and with it, Arsene's heart visibly sank.

"You did know." Arsene breathed.

The room's atmosphere shifted instantly. The man across the table became an enemy, and as Wulf dwelt on those Marius must have called allies, his gaze darted to Johanna. She was a quiet, unassuming, cooperative woman. Yet she stepped closer to the Duke as Arsene's stance tensed.

"So why is your portrait there?" Relia repeated.

The door burst open, and Ciprian dashed through, out of breath. He doubled over, straining to breathe so he could speak. Alarmed, Wulf stepped back. "Lord Duke, Rasvan says they were attacked but have safely apprehended her." He stood, catching his breath. "But there are significant damages. Many are injured."

"That was the noise." Marius realized. "Take me there."

The Duke darted around the table and followed Ciprian outside. Wulf's hand fell upon the spear on his back.

"Attacked?" Relia repeated. "By who?"

Not a thought crossed Wulf's mind, but his feet moved. Running, he took off after them.

"Wulf!" Arsene called, reaching out to grab him but missing.

Surprised servants ducked out of Wulf's way, and a guard called for him to stop. Ciprian and Marius dashed through the doors, and a commotion from outside caught his ears.

Bursting through the palace doors, Wulf thundered down the promenade, dodging the royal knight who tried to stop him as he exited the gates. Marius had paused by the waist-high wall guarding the overlook to the city below.

Seeing smoke rising from the second tier, Marius dashed left, and Wulf pursued him. Several footsteps thudded behind Wulf. Royal guards, most likely.

The royal barracks sat down the road from the manor, a gray building festooned with black banners. Their general approached its doors with a unit of men in tow—Rasvan, the broad-muscled evoker with the bushy mustache Arsene had mentioned.

In his grip, he clutched a woman swathed in a dark gray cloak, a few shades darker than her silver curls. Blood streamed down her side, and a gash cut across her forehead. Her emerald eyes hid behind drooped lids, and her throat was guarded by the blade of Rasvan's sword.

Seeing Marius coming, Rasvan tensed. "Careful, my liege. She's dangerous-"

"She's injured." Marius interrupted. "I told you to take her alive."

The nerve to plot against them while laboring under the pretense of a civil meeting. They had been betrayed from the first and had not even known.

"She. . ." Rasvan shook his head. "She's too dangerous to keep alive, Marius." He dug the blade into her throat, drawing scarlet blood.

The rest of their conversation faded into muted silence. Wulf felt Arsene bump into his back and touch his arm before walking to Marius' side. He heard the soldiers pursuing the prince gather around them. His hand drifted again to his spear.

His father's spear. Jorn had thrown it at Wulf's attackers, saving his son's life and condemning his own. Wulf had lived his remaining days knowing full well that he would have died in Fairborough with his father if not for that final act.

How dare these men attack an innocent woman? Any man who believed in his father's creed would have intervened: do what seems right in the moment, no matter the consequences.

But so had Wulf's father impart another lesson, one that took precedence over the first: protect those you love, for nothing in this world matters more.

Yanking his spear from its holster, Wulf stared at the man holding Fionn, listening to him advocate for her death. And before Arsene realized what was happening, before his partner could stop him, Wulf acted.

The spear flew across the road, landing squarely in Rasvan's shoulder, ripping through his cloak and sundering his mail. Buckling, Rasvan dropped his sword and released Fionn, staggering back to grab his wound while his captive slumped to the floor.

Two heavy bodies slammed into Wulf from behind, driving him into the stone road. Everything flickered black as his head collided with the rock, dazing him. Fighting to stay awake, he saw Marius rushing forward, pointing and yelling. Ordering the men to bring the woman to the knight's infirmary for treatment along with the general.

The soldiers behind Wulf hauled him to his feet and bound his arms, dragging him away. Away from the barracks and the manor and down to where Wulf knew the dredges of the city's dungeons hid beneath the mountain.

He glimpsed Arsene's horrified face one last time before he was forcibly turned around.

CHAPTER SEVEN

AMBUSH

THE SMELL OF salt on the breeze heralded the appearance of the ocean shore. Clodia's beaches were gentle cascades of white sand into sparkling waters. Athelstan's western shore met the sea on sharp piles of rocks scattered in turquoise waves.

Trueva's southern coast was hostile by comparison, a gathering of slick cliffs rising from dark buffeting waves crowned with thick foam. Leo watched their ship bob on the restless sea, dreading the weeks he would spend captive in its hull.

A narrow path winded down from the cliff to the shore. Leo guided his mare down the steep ascent, watching the choppy sea, reflecting on Eckart's tale. The other world he described had been composed of naught but water, fathomless yet alight. Had it been rougher than these waters?

Men of the Empire awaited them below, dressed in dark green coats and brown pants rather than armor and tabards—seaman's uniforms. Leo's boots sank into wet, coarse sand as he dropped off his horse. One of the sailors saluted Consus and invited them on board.

Hesitating, Leo glanced back at the two men escorting Kiylla. Shackles bound her wrists and feet tightly, inhibiting her steps. She stumbled on the rocky shore as they pushed her forward.

"Excited?" A monotone voice asked.

Turning, Leo noticed Thurston had joined him. "Overjoyed," he answered.

"I've never been sailing before, save on a lake. This should be interesting."

"Here's hoping you fall overboard."

"Glad to see you're feeling better," Thurston observed, leading his steed across the planks onto the deck.

Leo examined the mast rising into the cloudy sky. Furled sails still fluttered under a relentless breeze. Would he be able to sleep at night, or would he be too busy heaving over the side of the ship?

Handing his horse to one of the sailors, Leo accompanied Kiylla's escort as they brought her aboard and led her into the brig. The first flight of stairs brought them past the crew cabins, and the second brought them to a cramped, claustrophobic room with four tiny iron cells, her home for the next few weeks. Leo did not envy her.

Pulling a cloth from his belt, the guard blindfolded Kiylla before opening the cell door and pushing her inside. Fiddling with the keys, he found the right one and locked the door. A faint click echoed through the brig a moment later, and the cell door swung back open.

Stunned, the guard stared at the open gate before looking to Leofric for help. The poor lad was young, no more than seventeen. Stepping in, Leo closed the door and fastened it shut again, ensuring it was fully locked.

Useless. A click sounded moments before the door swung open again as if by magic.

Leo gasped softly. Because it was magic. Somehow, she recalled the door's locking mechanism, though the blindfold should have prevented her from evoking it.

"This won't work," Leo said, handing the keys to the guard. "She can evoke her way out."

"But the blindfold-" The guard stuttered.

"Inform the captain and Consus. I'll wait here with her."

The two young soldiers bowed and walked upstairs. Pursing his lips, Leo stared at the woman standing in the cell rigidly, her eyes glazed over. Kiylla had acted dazed, confused, and disoriented to accompany her silence. The symptoms of overexertion, of an evoker trapped within the phantoms of their memories. Consus had wondered aloud if her mind had shattered.

But Leo had heard her speak lucidly. This was but an act.

"You're good," Leo muttered.

Kiylla did not answer, but a thin smile crossed her face. Shaking his head, he turned as Consus thundered down the stairs and stared at the open cell. The general took a deep breath and shook his head.

"How did she?" He murmured to himself.

Leo snorted. "Maybe she's seen this ship?"

"Impossible. It's Clodian." Consus stepped closer, scrutinizing the woman. "There's nothing to be done about it. She's been harmless so far. But I'll have to assign a rotating watch."

"Down here?" Leo asked.

"Yes, down here," Consus affirmed. "Well, you and Thurston. Not me." He paused. "I'll have Gaius take the first shift. Wait here."

Sighing, Leo watched Consus walk away. Guard duty—how fun! Leaning his head against the cell, he stared at his charge, wishing she would at least acknowledge him.

Thurston returned quickly with the young guard to relieve Leo. Patting the young man's shoulder for luck, Leo happily followed Thurston back above deck. The bridge had been pulled from the shore, and the ship was abuzz with activity as they prepared the vessel to make sail.

A heavy breeze slammed into the newly unfurled sails and threw Leo's long hair ragged. Grabbing his bow to keep his hair from falling loose, he waited for the relentless breeze to pass before speaking.

"Is there food?" He asked.

Thurston raised an eyebrow. "You're in luck. A new pot of slop was just prepared in the kitchen."

Leo groaned. "Great. And here I hoped they might have better than camp rations."

"We're Athelstani." Thurston reminded him. "Backwater nobles like us are used to living on scraps of porocks."

Thurston clapped Leo on the back as he walked away. Dragging his heels to the kitchen, Leo worried less about the daunting meal of slop and more about finding a means to get Kiylla to speak with him again.

NIGHT SHIFT. Why the night shift? Leo blinked rapidly, trying to keep himself awake. The waves churned gently tonight, rocking the boat like a lullaby. Even this cramped, hard cot seemed like a luxury bed in these conditions.

Rubbing his eyes, Leo looked at the cell across the hall, where Kiylla sat in her unlocked cell. Occasionally, she would glance at him from behind tangled strands of dirty hair, but she kept silent.

Bored, Leo figured he could keep himself entertained by pretending to have a conversation with the woman. Leaning his head against the wall, he stared into the darkness of the cell he occupied.

"I'm a fan of poetry." He said. "Reading was my favorite pastime back home." Pausing, he waited for an answer before continuing. "Do the Qoyllan's have theatre? Maybe you don't know that word. Plays? Acting?"

Kiylla sat on her cot and side-eyed him. "Yes."

"I guess-" Leo cut himself off. She'd responded. Clearing his throat, he continued. "I suppose you don't have stages. They must be simple affairs."

"Stages? No. But many people participate," Kiylla said quietly. "We gather in a circle to watch those in costume. Though I don't think our tales are like yours."

"Chatty tonight. I guess you aren't crazy after all."

"I've decided you don't mean to tell the others I still have my mind," Kiylla answered.

"I'll let you know when I've figured out why." Leo folded his arms and shifted to face her. "You must be as bored. Tell me one of them."

Kiylla stared at him with a deep frown, deciding if she wished to share. Pulling her knees up onto her cot, shackles rattling, she leaned her chin on her knee and spoke. "We speak of tales from our ancestors, when the Earth Father walked the land when great gods of other peoples clashed." She hesitated. "I only acted in one. The tale of Virnya, patron of the Vira clan. Johanna and I played the twin sisters in the story."

"Right. You grew up together." Leo furrowed his brow. "Then, share that one."

Brushing the hair from her eyes, Kiylla thought intently before beginning. She kept her voice low, a harsh whisper. No dramatic flair colored her voice, but she told the fable with passion.

To Leo's ears, accustomed to Sigillite romances and chivalric Athelstani epics, the story was odd. Twin sisters, born from a dragon's womb, led their people to safety from the hostile southern lands. They shared the same soul, one piece fractured into two. Upon their dying day, the soul fragmented a final time, leaving a piece of them behind. And from those shards, the three great spires arose.

A far-fetched tale. Leo wondered if the Llaqtans really believed it.

"You'd make a half-decent bard." Leo commended her.

"Do not mock me, south lord," Kiylla said.

"I'm not mocking." Leo insisted, leaning toward her. "I can't imagine Johanna acting. She's so. . . detached."

"Maybe now. Once upon a time, Johanna never stopped talking. Like a bleating baby goat stuck to her mother's skirt."

"Really?" Leo chuckled. "You must have known Beau and his wife. What were they like?"

"Necalli was too much," Kiylla said fondly. "Curious about everything and eager to share. She did not get along with my mother; it was no secret she was not pious. The other side captivated her, though. She yearned to find it.

"Did she?"

"Shortly before she died, she thought she made a breakthrough." Kiylla furrowed her brow. "I remember her excitement. But then she was gone."

"What happened?"

"I don't know," Kiylla admitted. "She would visit the thin places. You call them something. . . ai. . . aiceils? She raced off to one in the night and never returned." Kiylla leaned forward. "She taught me Imperial common, not Beau." Distaste wrinkled her nose. "I never liked Beau. He charmed many, but I always felt he looked at me like. . . like refuse."

"But. . ." Leo glanced up the stairs. "We think Arminda made an agreement with you and suspect Beau ordered it. They'd destroy Femora if you gave him the jewel."

"Close." Kiylla turned her head, eyes narrowing. "Maybe I will answer your questions. But I'll need to trust you."

"How?"

"I want to see the waves. Take me up to the deck."

Leo grimaced, standing and peering up the stairs. There would be no satisfactory explanation for his actions if he got caught. But this late at night, most sailors were abed. The lingering sensation from the shrine still ate at him; he needed this feeling assuaged.

"Alright. Let me take a look around." Leo said, creeping up the stairs.

Pitch black blanketed the deck, save for a couple of torches burning where the night watch was stationed. A man stood off to Leo's left, watching the port side, but the path starboard was clear.

While he puzzled over how to silence the jangling of Kiylla's shackles, she appeared behind him and pushed him away from the guard. Leo stared agape at her before shutting his mouth and hurrying around the bulk of the cabin building. A thin rail wrapped the starboard side, and it was blissfully empty.

Once Leo felt sure nobody could overhear, he leaned toward the now-free woman. "How did you-?"

"I heard them be shackled," Kiylla said. "I only kept wearing them for the men's sake."

"How in shadows do you do that?"

"Study locks enough, and you can lock pick blindfolded," Kiylla said, leaning over the rail. "Do not worry. No one will know come morning."

Sighing, Leo joined her. Water reminded him of Eckart, even if these waves were far darker than the pristine lake an hour's walk from his family's manor. Eckart had loved that lake. So, too, had his little sister.

"You," Kiylla said, thick accent slurring the word. "Are not very bright."

"I know," Leo said. "You could so easily push me overboard if you wanted."

"Then, perhaps you will trust me after tonight." She said.

Leo tightened his grip on the railing. He was walking a dangerous road but had no inkling where it might lead. "So, you like the ocean?"

"I do not get to see it very often." She stared wistfully into the dark waves. "Yuri Llaqta is vast, and we rarely travel to the shores."

"Mm." Leo agreed idly, remembering the lake his sister had been obsessed with taking Eckart out to.

"You look sad," Kiylla observed. "I know that look. You are thinking of home."

"Perceptive, aren't you?" Leo muttered.

"Anyone can see. But, no one does. They think their home is the only one that matters."

Standing straight, Leo stared at her. For the first time, he saw past the piercing stare of maddened eyes, the tangled locks of a violent and dangerous witch. He saw Kiylla, the way her clanspeople must have seen her.

Chimes of a bell rang above Leo's head, and he looked up sharply, trying to find their source. A second bell joined the alarm, ringing with rapid urgency. The watch were alerting the ship of an approaching vessel. Leaning over the railing, Leo strained to see the oncoming ship but could detect nothing in this darkness.

Sounds of movement erupted in the cabins as the sailors roused. Leo grabbed Kiylla's arm. "We need to go."

Several men burst through the doors as they flew to their stations. Throwing Kiylla behind him, Leo waited for the rush to pass as the unmistakable sound of a ship cutting through the waves carried across the still night.

A resounding boom shook the sea, and something landed in the water. A great splash surged over the railing, showering Leo with water. Had that been a cannon?

A second boom followed, accompanied by the crunch of wood and cracking of steel. Leo felt the deck beneath him quake, and he was tossed forward onto his hands and knees. Reverberations shot through his jaw as he tried to steady himself and stand.

Cursing under his breath, Leo scrambled up and drew his sword, finally noticing the enemy vessel. Bright spots of fire lit up their deck, and cannon balls arced through the night.

Did they intend to board? Spinning around, Leo reached for Kiylla, but she was gone. Running down the deck, Leo scanned the men for the woman he'd lost, flinching with every cannon ball that flew overhead or sank into the sea.

Inevitably, one found its mark. A canon tore through the starboard deck, shaking the boards beneath Leo's feet. With a horrible crack, they split apart, and Leo lost his footing as he tumbled to the deck below, landing in a pile of debris.

Rolling over, Leo found his sword and tried to rise. Blood trickled down his elbow and streamed from his knee.

A hand grabbed his collar and yanked him to his feet. Consus stared at him with wide green eyes. "Are you alright?"

"Fine." Leo gasped.

"Did you see their colors?"

"No."

Consus shoved Leo. "Then make yourself useful." He whirled around, grabbing a cannonball from a nearby pile.

Maybe Consus had naval training, but Leo certainly did not. What in Scael's name was he supposed to do?

The only thing he could: find the prisoner who had been under his care.

Racing up the stairs, Leo burst onto the deck to see the enemy ship now within boarding distance. How had they managed to gain ground so quickly? It was as though magic itself guided their vessel.

Men in unmarked gambesons threw planks between the decks and raced across them, clashing with the men aboard the Imperial vessel. Dashing forward, Leo attempted to interpose himself between an enemy and one of the sailors, only to feel a gust of wind slam into him with the force of a charging bull.

Tossed backward, Leo landed on his back and choked as the wind was stolen from his lungs. Someone grabbed his collar and yanked him up, a familiar sensation.

Thurston dragged Leo behind a mast, taking cover from the battle. "That was cefran magic." He hissed.

Cefran? Leo felt ice run through his veins. He had never clashed with one before, not in a real bout to the death. Leaning around the mast, he searched for the one who had thrown that spell.

Two men charged him, faces covered by simple metallic helms. Darting out of cover, Leo raised his sword and blocked the oncoming axe as Thurston intercepted the other. More concerned about the cefra amongst them, Leo shoulder-checked the man before him and slammed his sword into the side of the man's helm.

Pushing the dazed axeman aside, Leo ran forward and locked eyes with shining purple beacons in the night. A cefra's eyes glaring out from behind its helm.

Lunging, Leo attempted to skewer the cefra, but it darted out of his way with ease. An electric charge surged through the air, wrapping Leo's arm and reverberating down his sword. Lightning rattled Leo's gauntlet, paralyzing his arm and burning the skin. His sword clattered to the ground, and he grabbed his shaking hand.

Time slowed just before you died. Or so it felt. The eternity between losing his weapon and watching the cefra draw its axe seemed to last forever.

The man with blazing purple eyes buckled, losing his balance as quicksand opened beneath his feet and dragged him down. Forgetting Leo, he floundered, struggling vainly to pull himself out.

Kiylla ran to Leo's side, fingers glowing with sand-tinted light. She raised her other hand, and a block of stone rose from the deck and slammed into the cefra, throwing him overboard. Leo flinched. She had used that on Eckart, too.

Using his off-hand, Leo picked up his blade and saw something whistling toward them. Sweeping his sword through the air, he broke the arrow before it hit Kiylla, and the shattered pieces struck the deck at their feet.

"Get down," Kiylla instructed, kicking Leo in the knee.

Buckling, Leo opened his mouth to protest, but his eyes widened when he saw her hands consumed by fiery light. Ducking, he pressed his hands to his ears as a cannon erupted beside him, the boom temporarily deafening him.

Kiylla's evoked mortar struck the enemy ship head-on, splitting their main mast. With a creak, the most prominent sail collapsed into a pile of splintered wood and tattered sail as fire raced down its edges.

The interlocked vessels jolted apart as the enemy slowed, and the Imperial ship flew forward. Planks slipped and fell into the water as enemy boarders desperately leaped back onto their ship. One caught an arrow in the back and plunged into the depths.

Relieved, Leo caught his breath, but the respite did not last. He heard steps thundering towards him and turned, dazed by the smoke and darkness. A shadow bolted, spear-first, at his chest, and Leo hastily raised his sword.

Someone collided with the attacker from behind, throwing them to the ground. Thurston spun his spear around and knocked the man's weapon from his grip before pressing his spear tip to the man's throat.

With no time to loiter, Leo grabbed Kiylla's cloak. "Forgive me." He breathed, shoving her to her knees and pressing his sword to her throat. She cooperated, the glazed look returning to her eyes.

Thurston wrangled with the spearman as he pressed his knee into the man's back and held him still. "You wear no colors." He breathed. "Mercenaries? Pirates?"

Half-concealed behind his helm, the man's brown eyes darted between Leo and Thurston, but he held his tongue.

Consus raced to their side. "You captured one? Good. Take him to the brig." He helped Thurston drag the man to his feet. "This was no mere raid." He whirled around, noticing Kiylla. "What is she doing here, unshackled?"

"I. . ." Leo gasped. "I was worried she would drown."

Leo had never been a liar. His parents had effortlessly seen through him, and Eckart always knew when even the tiniest fib emerged. He could not fool Consus.

Yet the general did not question him. "Good. That's good." He breathed. "Heavens rays." He cursed, looking at the pair of holes in the deck and the smoke drifting from the dying fire.

"Why do you think it was not pirates?" Leo asked.

Consus stared at him with concern. "The watch spotted a ship following them from Clodia's harbor. They lost sight of it before reaching Llaqtan soil, and thought it was gone."

Thurston paused. "But it wasn't."

Leo balked. "This was a Clodian ship?"

"And no coincidence." Consus breathed. "Not after what happened in Femora." He grimaced, glancing around as though traitors hid among them even here. "The Empire is being attacked from the inside."

CHAPTER EIGHT

INCIPIENCE

ARSENE'S ENTIRE LIFE had been a lie. His mother and brother led a double life they had carefully excluded him from—a life they had never given him a chance to be part of and never trusted him to know about.

To what extent had they gone? What acts had they taken, and what lies did they keep? Whatever they planned, Arsene had no inkling.

Yet one thing stood out to him in crystal clarity. The promise made had been broken. The vow their deal would be honored had been but smoke to force them to war, only to descend upon Fionn like vultures when she returned.

Arsene leaned on his door, playing with his bracer, staring at his childhood bed of crimson sheets. Would he be next? The attack on Rasvan had absorbed much of the manor's attention, and he had been ushered back into the estate for his safety.

Feeling like hot coals lined his shirt, Arsene ripped off his jacket and rolled up his sleeves. Bursting out of the room, he stepped into the hauntingly silent hall and searched for any doors with lights flickering beneath their gaps. Most were quiet, dark, the same color as the walls.

Candles burning in the parlor below decorated the stairway with dancing flames. Arsene had not ventured from his room, gripped in a paralysis. Maybe others were still awake. Quietly padding down the steps, he paused when he heard voices drifting from the meeting room where everything had gone wrong.

Fixing his hair, Arsene marched down the hall and nearly ran into Marius as he darted out of the room. Even with distress writ on his face and his hair disheveled, Marius looked composed and regal.

"We need to talk." Arsene spat.

"I can spare a moment." Marius agreed. "This way." He turned and strode away.

Arsene glanced behind him, catching two voices in the meeting room: one feminine and breathy and the other nasally and unpleasant. Mother and Vasille. A contemptible room better left untouched.

Marius brought Arsene outside onto the stone courtyard. A rare rainfall graced the Bruthine mountains tonight, and light drops clinked on the metallic roof. Exhausted, Marius leaned on one of the tables.

"So." Arsene folded his arms. "You caught your prey. Rasvan's wound causing you that much trouble?"

"No," Marius said. "Her companion escaped."

Companion? That could only be one man. Arsene had thought Eckart a wildsman, incapable of navigating a city like this. Maybe his upbringing in Clodia as an undesirable had taught him a few tricks.

"Why is he a target? He's a no-name fletcher."

Marius did not deign to answer. "Are you alright?"

"Oh, I'm fabulous." Arsene walked around his brother to the edge of the courtyard. "Where's Relia?"

"She's been given quarters."

"I'm surprised I haven't heard her knock. She's known to be stubborn."

"We decided to confine her. For her safety."

"I see," Arsene muttered, watching the rain fall from the dreary sky. "I'll make this simple. What is this about?"

"Arsene," Marius said softly. "You saw what happened in Femora. Heard the stories of the sinkhole. We have good reason to believe we know who's orchestrating these events. The Empire can not sit on its hands while such grievances against us stand."

"I see. Take the cefran weapons so you can wipe out the Llaqtans and maybe the cefra along with them. Blame the cefra for taking the Imperial heir and unite the people in a holy war?"

"It was never about wiping anyone out." Marius stood straight. "Imagine a Yuri Llaqta whose land is still. A Dragos whose sky does not rain fire, where crops can again flourish."

"I can imagine it. Doesn't make it real." Arsene looked over his shoulder.

"But it is." Marius approached him. "Let me see your hand."

Unfolding his arms, Arsene studied his injured hand. Marius grabbed his wrist and gently cradled the hand in his own.

"There's something I want to tell you," Marius said. "But I don't think you'll hear me. You never did believe in anything you couldn't see."

Arsene furrowed his brow as Marius raised his free hand and closed his eyes. The world felt strange and fuzzy. A whisper grazed his ear, its words unintelligible. Shutting his own eyes in discomfort and confusion, Arsene tried to grasp what he heard but lost it.

Feeling Marius drop his hand, Arsene opened his eyes and raised his injured arm. The bumps where the bone had mended incorrectly were gone, and the ragged scar had vanished. No pain troubled him, and the fingers curled freely. He was healed.

Such a thing was impossible. Evokers could not cast upon a living being nor draw a living being from their memories. Many scholars of eld had tried fruitlessly to remember a wounded arm when it was still whole, but never to any effect. Nor could any cefra heal. The one problem in the world magic could not solve.

"How did you. . .?" Arsene asked, stunned.

"I heard something when I was still very young," Marius said softly. "A voice. With time, I began to understand it. Someone was calling me. Choosing me to carry out their will."

Arsene knew what Marius would say before he continued. His brother had tried to tell him once before, and Arsene had been unable to accept it, unable to hear.

"You understand our need for secrecy." Marius joined Arsene, gazing at the rain. "There are many clergymen in the Empire who would rejoice at the news and many more who would accuse us of heresy. For not all who wear the cloaks do so because they are devout."

Arsene flexed and fidgeted with his newly healed hand. "And she's ordered you to do this?"

"To save our wayward Empire? Yes." Marius said, holding out a palm to catch the rain. "Even on this night, we are graced with a rare rainfall." He dropped his hand. "The mercenary you traveled with, he was at Fairborough."

"He was," Arsene confirmed.

"Then you know its tale. A bishop ranked below only the Vicar turning his chapel into a reign of terror." Marius' mouth curled in disgust. "It was not the first. Nor would it be the last."

"Does that surprise you? One chat with Vasille taught me those who preach the loudest are the last to meet the goddess."

Marius sighed. "War after war. Yuri Llaqta, Forsaidh. Altanbern, inevitably. Corrupt clergy who have forgotten the way. They need to be set straight."

"And Relia is your ticket in." Arsene guessed. "Why did you never tell me?"

Another's voice answered. Mother's. "Because we cannot trust you."

Arsene whirled around. Mother was her queenly self, an elegant portrait in her voluminous black gown. She needed no tiara; the perfect blond ringlets around her head formed their own.

"You decided that when I was just a child?" Arsene asked, stepping away from Marius and folding his arms.

"*She* did," Aurica said, glancing at Marius.

Oh, the goddess herself had deemed Arsene a rat? The notion was ridiculous, yet with a single act of healing, the kernel of possibility had wormed into Arsene's mind.

"What we do is delicate." Marius reminded Arsene carefully. "The best way to shift someone's course is to push them so gently they do not realize the wind has stirred. And all will fall into place."

"Assuming," Aurica said, voice like a razor's edge. "We can trust you."

Arsene turned around and stared at the mountain face. Why did this bother him so profoundly? What did he care who ran the Empire, who they named their enemies? All he cared for were the comforts of a wealthy life and books aplenty to sate his curiosity. His family could do as they pleased.

"Why not?" He turned around. "I don't intend to aid you, but neither will I stand in your way. Someone must remain home and pretend everything is normal, no?"

Marius seemed both unhappy and relieved. Aurica strode towards him, eyes narrowed. She usually gazed at him with disappointment but rarely genuine anger like this. "We will see. I will be watching."

"In that case." Arsene shimmied around her. "I'll be turning in." He hastily walked away, eagerly opening the door and re-entering the manor.

Now, Mother's favoritism made sense. Marius had been the better child, the better student, the better person, and the one called to by the goddess herself. Ash and cinder, Arsene must have seemed like the sole rotten crop in a perfect harvest.

Rubbing his eyes, Arsene walked past the meeting room, but only one man remained inside: the evoker who had been tasked as his chaperon. Compelled by something unseen, Arsene stepped inside.

"Ciprian. Got more than you bargained for, I presume?"

Ciprian whirled around, eyes already lined with bags. "There was always a chance for this to go poorly. I had not expected it to go *this* poorly."

"And how fares the hunt?"

"Poorly." He repeated. "We've had no leads thus far. The men are scouring every tier."

"Right. And what about the prisoner?" Arsene prodded.

"You mean your old partner?" Ciprian guessed. "He's been safely confined. Once the other fugitive is captured, Vasille intends to hold a joint execution."

"Oh, that one will attract quite the crowd." Arsene whistled. "Best of luck." He turned around, gritting his teeth. Somehow, he needed to delay their search. What for, he was unsure. The end was inevitable.

Trotting up the stairs, Arsene searched the upstairs for the room Relia was confined to. If he knew the girl, she would still be up, pacing, maybe trying to break out to no avail. Arsene had never taught her the simplest evoking trick in the book. Lock-picking.

Footsteps echoed in one of the guest chambers, and Arsene knelt, peering under the crack. He caught a glimpse of feminine feet charging across the rug in a frenzy. This was the right place.

Glancing up and down the hall, he reached out and recalled the door unlocking. The lock clicked inaudibly, and Arsene let himself inside.

Hair the color of roses flew in an arc as Relia whirled around and thrust her hand toward him, fingers glowing the color of steel. A spear manifested midair, leveled at his throat, and Arsene quickly threw his hands up.

Seeing a familiar face, Relia dropped the spear and it dissipated before it hit the ground. Pushing him aside, she shut the door. "What are you doing here?"

"What do you mean? Can a man not walk around his own home?"

"I thought I was confined," Relia said, eyebrows shooting up when she noticed the door was unlocked.

"What are you planning?" Arsene asked, pressing a hand against the door.

"What is that supposed to mean?" She huffed, fidgeting with the shawl around her neck. "They threw Wulf and Fionn into the dungeons. They're going to execute them."

"And what do you intend to do about it, exactly?"

"I don't know. Something." Agitated, she yanked off her shawl and tossed it across the room, retreating from the door.

"There's good news," Arsene said. "Eckart got away."

Relia's eyes lit with relief. Snarling, the softness faded, and anger flared to life. "You. Lied. To. Me."

Arsene made light of the comment, shrugging his shoulders and rolling his eyes to the side. "I did not lie, Relia. I had no reason to think you were the princess."

"You *knew*." She insisted. "I thought for sure you would turn me in, win great acclaim for recovering me."

"No. The Empire needs, first and foremost, a great evil to pin the crime on, to choose for their next crusade. I did not want to risk being tossed in with that lot."

Relia's anger subsided when she saw his point. "I guess nobody knows what I look like."

"No. I assumed you were long dead. Maybe sold to an exotic brothel." He took a deep breath and walked to her window. "Here's what you're going to do. Marius will see you escorted to Clodia. You'll be confirmed as the heir and given a nice, comfortable life in the finest palace in the world."

"You say that as if you expect me to do otherwise." Relia dropped onto the bed despondently. "Mother kept me hidden away to reveal me at the right time. But I ruined that plan, I guess. What would have happened, and when?"

Brushing aside her curtains, Arsene peered outside. Several black shapes moved in the night, soldiers running to and fro amidst the crisis. Fionn had destroyed a few buildings in the second tier and panicked the populace. Arsene did not envy their task.

"The right time was when their other pieces were in place." Arsene supposed. "The jewels, I'd wager. That's why your mother searched for the fae king's treasure. And now they have nearly all. Once they catch Eckart, I imagine they'll have everything they need."

"Weapons?"

"Or doors," Arsene muttered. How exactly did Marius intend to seal off the plane's overlap? The ashfalls had existed since before Dragosi history began. Every regions' border had been drawn where one realm's effects transitioned to another.

"And what about you?" Relia asked. "What are you going to do?"

"Take stock of the situation." Arsene closed the curtains.

"Take stock?" Relia's jaw set. "We sit in comfort while Fionn and Wulf rot in a dungeon?"

"What would you have me do? Throw my life away?"

She looked away, anger burning in her eyes.

"All I wanted was my title returned." Arsene said. "As the prince, my duty is to my Duke."

"Then, I suppose I'll take stock of *my* situation." She glared at him.

Did she intend to do something rash, or would she realize its futility? Nodding, Arsene slipped out the door, relieved to see an empty hall. Running back to his room, he grabbed his coat off the floor and pulled it on.

Placing a hand on his belt, Arsene grabbed Death Knell's holster as he flew down the steps and out into the night. Nodding to the royal knights on watch, Arsene exited the manor gates and strode down the road.

Myriad figures passed, heading to the lower tiers or the barracks. One grabbed his arm, pulling him to the side of the road. "Arsene. Where are you going?"

A hint of blue appeared inside the woman's cowl, the petals of a flower. "Johanna," Arsene said carefully. "I take it you're looking for the fugitive."

"I've been instructed to, " she said, pushing back her hood so Arsene could see her eyes. "Cefra are dangerous. Marius wants our evokers on hand."

"Hm. Tell me, did you know about all this?" He gestured vaguely. "About Marius and Beau and-"

"Yes," Johanna answered readily. "I work for my father. He and Lady Aurica have been close for decades."

"Interesting." Arsene ground his jaw. "Well, best of luck." He moved to walk away, but Johanna pulled him back.

"Wait." She said. "My father told me to watch Eckart, to try and learn the cefran's plans. But I was never told of executions without cause."

"I'm supposed to believe that?"

"He asked for my judgment. And my judgment was that the jewels are doors. To cefra, at least. Nothing more."

"Is that right? Seems your father found his answer without you. . ." Arsene trailed off.

Johanna had been there, in the northern cliffs above Femora, miraculously safe from the devastating wave. Yet, she had not attacked Arsene when Arminda ordered her to.

"Tell me something." Arsene leaned closer to her. "Why didn't you kill me when your master ordered? When Arminda called to you for aid?"

Johanna blinked, her brown eyes widening. "I did not know what the jewels did. I requested to study them." She stuttered over her words. "Studying was my life, uncovering history, truths about the planes, their effects. . ." She shook her head. "Now I understand why they forbade me."

Arsene looked down. Johanna's hand slid off his arm. "I see. You were your father's lapdog, not his confidant." He chuckled cruelly. "Fits you. The woman I knew never cared for the details, only chasing her theories."

Her nose flared, and her mouth twisted, but she said nothing.

"How about this?" Arsene suggested. "Marius mentioned something about the plane's vanishing. Yuri Llaqta's earth going still, the ashfalls of Dragos ceasing. Were you tasked with finding a means to sever the plane's connection?"

"No. . ." Johanna looked away. "Thank you for telling me."

She turned on her heel, but this time, Arsene called her back. "What *did* you know?"

Johanna stopped, hands in her coat pockets. "I knew Father was part of a coup—one for the better, one they believed would steer the Empire back on course. He wanted my aid, and I gave it." She glanced over his shoulder. "That's all." Pulling her hood back down, she marched away.

Rolling his tongue in his mouth, Arsene resumed his course, weaving past a cluster of knights outside the barracks. Mountains loomed overhead, guarding the stairwell to the lower tier in their shadow.

A woman walked by him, one of countless many. But she turned her head just as a lantern flickered, illuminating her face—a face Arsene had seen before.

Green eyes, the color of jade, almond skin, the same shade as Eckart's, a wisp of brown hair curling out from her hood: Tettiena Parnesius. She did not notice Arsene in the darkness, or maybe she merely paid him no mind. Without stopping, she continued on.

Freezing, Arsene watched her go; enough torchlight lit this street to trail her figure to the barracks. She stepped off the road and merged with the mountain's shadow. Where exactly she intended to go was unclear, but her direction was apparent. She headed toward the manor.

For a moment, Arsene considered following her. Forcing his head away, Arsene trudged down the stairs. Maybe he could find Eckart himself, get the half-breed out of the city and waste the searching evokers' time.

A pointless gambit. Any number of atrocities could have befallen Fionn and Wulf, helpless in the dungeons. Their fates were sealed.

CHAPTER NINE

SEORAS

ANCIENT WALLS WELCOMED Wulf into their halls as he entered the dungeon. Buried within the mountainside, these corridors were pitch black, lit only by the rare sconce glowing dimly against the oppressive pall.

The cells lingered in infinite shadow. Wulf could hardly see them as he passed their iron gates. Shadows moved behind the bars, prisoners muttering to themselves, others banging on their cell as they heard life in the hall.

The knight guiding Wulf drove him down a slope, deeper into the earth. The cells here were larger, spaced further apart. Stopping before a flickering sconce, the knight unlocked an iron gate and shoved Wulf inside. Slamming the creaky gate closed, he locked the cell's heavy padlock and strode away.

Footsteps retreated down the hall, and Wulf was alone. Narrowing his eyes, he strained to see in this shadow, noticing a stone bench and a bucket. Lovely. Were these cells designated for criminals soon to be executed?

A man would go mad, confined to this cramped darkness. Wulf doubted he would stay here long enough to crack. A pyre assuredly awaited him.

Pressing his back against the wall, Wulf took a deep breath. What idiocy had compelled him to attack Rasvan? Part of him had no regrets, yet the other half knew the act had been pointless. No one had been saved.

In hindsight, Wulf should have seen this betrayal coming. And yet he had trusted Arsene's word. He felt a fool; warnings had appeared along the path, yet he'd overlooked them without a second thought.

The recurring dream Wulf saw each night resurfaced in his mind. Someone had been trying to tell him something. A message hid within those images, the sensations, and the fractured woman. But Wulf had awoken each morning and dismissed the dreams as odd coincidences.

Sliding to the floor, Wulf fretted over Fionn. She had been injured, though he knew not how. Had Marius kept his word and tended to her? Restrained and half-conscious, she could not defend herself. But Wulf doubted he could have saved her even had he restrained himself.

New footsteps approached, and Wulf leaned forward. Had they returned for him already? Scraping echoed against the walls, like boots being dragged across stone. Shadows appeared before his cell as someone unlocked the bars and shoved a new tenant inside.

Wulf gasped and lunged forward as Fionn collapsed onto her knees. A clumsy dressing covered her side, dotted with blood stains. Hoisting her up, Wulf carried her to the stone bench and sat her down.

Glowing green eyes met his with fury. "What were you thinking?" Fionn demanded.

"What?" Wulf asked, taken aback.

"Attacking the general. What good did that do?" The intensity in her voice vanished as she winced in pain and doubled over.

"I wasn't going to let them get away with this," Wulf said, tightening his grip on her arm.

"And, what, you get to be executed now, too?"

"It was the right thing to do."

"It was the stupid thing to do."

"Would you rather we go back, and–"

"Yes!" Fionn stared at him furiously. Then she looked down and choked out a laugh. "I can just imagine what Arsene would say."

"Yeah, me too," Wulf muttered. "Did they hurt you?"

"No. They didn't take much care patching me up, though." She winced and sucked in a painful breath. "Everything's been a blur. I don't even know how I was injured." She sat up, eyes widening. "Where's Eckart?"

"Let me see," Wulf laid her down. "Were you two together?"

"Yes. I gave him my stuff and told him to run." She bit her lip nervously, wincing as he lifted her shirt and pulled back the gauze.

Wulf studied her wound, flinching. Something jagged had torn into her side, like a chunk of rock. "Marius said he didn't want you harmed. What happened?"

"The general, the big man." Fionn held out her arms to display his size but flinched and pulled them back. "He wanted us to surrender peacefully. I didn't give him the chance to explain."

Wulf sighed, carefully reapplying the dressing. "It doesn't matter now unless you're an expert at breaking out of dungeons."

"I've only ever broken into places, not the reverse." She closed her eyes. "And I don't think I have the energy for it."

Pulling off his coat, Wulf wrapped Fionn in it. "It's freezing down here. You're going to die of frostbite."

"And you aren't?" She murmured into the fabric.

"You think a temperate autumn day is worse than winter."

A soft whistle hummed through the cell, eerie. Warm air followed its melody, blowing across Wulf's face and sifting through Fionn's curls. "There." She said. "That's all the magic I can spare."

"Should you spare any at all? You look pale."

"Maybe not. But it's too cold in here." Fionn said weakly. Sitting up, she shimmied closer to him and timidly laid her head against his shoulder.

Relieved, Wulf pulled her into his arms, This was the first time she'd been affectionate with him since their argument in Femora.

Static shock reverberated up Wulf's arm, and he flinched in pain. Violet crackles of lightning flashed in Fionn's eyes. She set her teeth in concentration, gasping heavily as the surge of magic calmed.

"What was that?" Wulf asked, concerned.

"He doesn't like prisons," Fionn said, trance-like.

"He?"

Leaning away from him, Fionn looked up into his eyes. "We need to escape. And. . . there's something I should probably tell you."

Fionn fell silent. Only water dripping in the distance broke the stillness until something scraped against the ceiling. A familiar songbird shimmied through the cell bars and landed on the bench, the same bird Wulf saw perched above his head nearly every day on their boat.

Fionn offered her hand to the bird, and it climbed onto her palm, little feet off balance. "I need a map." She whispered, noticing how the creature quivered. "You're not shackled. Calm down."

The bird shrunk, eyes squeezing shut, wings wrapping around itself protectively. Its little body convulsed as lightning crackled through Fionn's body, and she shivered in pain. As the electricity snaked through Fionn, the bird settled, unwrapping its wings and opening its eyes, and the magic assaulting Fionn ceased.

Tapping Fionn's finger with its beak, the bird took off, wings flapping silently as it disappeared into the hall. Exhausted, Fionn slumped against Wulf's chest.

"Fionn?" Wulf asked, confused.

"Do you remember the night I tended your wound, in Sylfestra?" She asked softly.

"Of course. You did a mediocre job."

"That's not the point! I told you of our gods there. You asked me about my patron. I admitted that I was scared of him."

Wulf remembered. She had spoken of her patron with strange reverence yet with palpable fear. A patron who had ordered her to collect the cefran relics, items that, when placed in the wrong hands, could wreak unimaginable havoc. Items that the world had all but forgotten.

Everything snapped into clarity. Fionn had lain beside him, beneath the solitary tree, tracing the painting of a dragon on her skin while sharing the tale of Seoras, the god of storms. Above Femora, that very dragon appeared, its limbless body composed of the wind.

"My patron," Fionn said. "I think you've figured out his name."

Time was difficult to measure in the dark, but Wulf imagined at least two days must have passed. Guards would stop by occasionally to pass water through the bars, but never food. The pain of hunger had long passed into gnawing weakness.

Wulf's eyes fluttered as he leaned back against the frigid wall. Running a hand through Fionn's hair, he strained to stay awake. For hours, she had slept like the dead, curled up in his lap. An illness beyond the wound on her side afflicted her, but Wulf wasn't sure what was wrong.

Was it fever? Her skin was pallid; her breath came in short gasps. But she was cold to the touch; no sweat dampened her brow. Worried, he ran a hand down her neck and felt her pulse. Faint. Too faint.

Trying not to panic, he lingered on his dreams. A black tower. Silver waters. The imagery had to mean something. Fionn claimed to have seen it in memories but knew not what the dream giver meant to impart. Only one thing from the recurring dream stood out: the blackened sky, darker than ordinary night. Athelstan's sky.

A shiver ran up Wulf's spine as he gave up trying to think. All they could do now was wait. Fionn believed the best chance to escape would be when guards arrived to remove them from their cell. When they would be escorted to the pyre.

The songbird had mapped the dungeon for them, returning with news of a winding maze with a singular entrance. Each time the bird returned, it would quiver in fear. Lightning would pulse through Fionn painfully, and she would soothe the creature with gentle words.

But it was more than a bird. Cefra called him the eyes of the wind and claimed he spoke with the voice of a god. Wulf knew not how to feel about the revelation. To no gods had he prayed, not even his homeland's spirits. No evidence of blessings from deities had manifested in his lifetime.

Only one option remained: this Seoras was something, but no god. The proof lay in its quivering feathers and jolting lightning, for no true deity would fear a mere cage.

Fionn sat upright, bright eyes flying wildly around. "Someone's coming." She warned.

Leaning forward, Wulf saw fire approaching their cell, growing brighter as footsteps approached. This time, more than a single guard ferrying rations appeared; several knights escorted a man of higher standing, one Wulf instantly recognized.

Arsene had called the Chancellor a worm, offering no further details of his appearance, yet Wulf could see the resemblance clear as day. Bald-headed, the man's beady eyes stared hungrily, his mouth curled in an unpleasant smile. This was Vasille, the man who had cast Arsene out of his city.

Crimson robes danced like flames under the torchlight as Vasille stopped before their cell and waited for the guards to pull the prisoners out. One grabbed Wulf by the neck, holding his head forward so he could not glance back at Fionn. He heard her yelp, and resisted the urge to smash his head against the man holding him in a bid to escape.

The procession returned via the same halls Wulf had first entered this place, heading up a slope and diverting down a western hall. They passed the door Wulf remembered as the entrance, instead walking into a small room on its opposite side.

Ciprian waited inside, dressed in his formal armor and dark blue cowl. He bowed his head as Vasille entered, and the Chancellor barked an order. "Take the girl to the next room. An evoker should handle the cefra lest she become violent."

"Yes, my lord." Ciprian rose and stepped outside.

Wulf strained to turn his head, managing to glimpse Fionn entering the next room in the hall. Propelled forward, Wulf was placed on an uncomfortable stool beside a heavy stone table. Vasille walked its perimeter, seating himself in the high-backed chair opposite Wulf.

How feasible would an escape attempt be? Wulf glanced around, counting the guards in the room with him. Two had accompanied Fionn, leaving three with him and the Chancellor. All wielded blades and wore black steel armor, but if he could wrest one of their weapons away. . .

No good. Wulf had never been talented with swordplay; the weapon was inferior to a spear.

Chancellor Vasille folded his hands on the table. "You were instructed to escort the heir and jewel back to Lavinia. One of your company was a half-breed mercenary, no?"

Wulf stared at him silently. He must look a fool, arrested in this ridiculous doublet Arsene had insisted was of the highest fashion.

"His name is Eckart." Vasille continued. "A fletcher from that Altanese clan."

"Yes," Wulf answered.

"Rasvan claims to have seen him in the company of that girl, but when they caught up to her, the fletcher had mysteriously vanished." Vasille leaned forward. "And has been all but invisible since. You were friends, no? Perhaps you know where he might have fled?"

If Wulf had a singular talent, it was stubbornness. And he could dance with the best of them. Sealing his lips shut, he returned to staring silently at the Chancellor, biting his tongue to hide his expression. Eckart was still free. They might have a chance.

"Playing the silent game?" Vasille asked. "From what the guards tell me, you and that girl are always quite. . . *close*, in your cell. I need not hurt *you* to extract answers." The Chancellor smiled, the threat plain on his face.

"You'll have to give me more details," Wulf said. "I was with the Duke when the chaos erupted."

"Smart man. No need to make this difficult." Vasille encouraged. "The citizens' and soldiers' accounts speak of something also seen in Femora: a veritable dragon of storm flying above the city, tearing apart a few buildings in a crash landing. Familiar?"

"Yes."

"The half-breed was last seen just before that girl. . . transformed. And never again."

Wulf remembered Arsene saying he had ridden upon the leviathan's back, describing it as tangible, if esoteric. Eckart must have done the same. Upon crashing, Fionn passed Eckart her bag and bid him flee. Could he have escaped the city from the second tier without being seen?

"If I were him." Wulf leaned forward. "I would have run for the gates."

"Our city watch are vigilant. Had he departed the gates, they would have seen him."

"Well, he was unfamiliar with the city. I doubt he could have found any crevices that slip outside." Wulf suggested. "But with each hour that passes, it's more likely he's left city bounds."

Vasille's face fell, unhappy with Wulf's answer. "You two were acquainted. And I imagine you conspired. So tell me your plan, and you may return to your cells, no more damaged than before."

A door slammed nearby, shaking dust loose from the ceiling. Eyes darting around, Wulf listened as a female voice sounded next door, though he could not make out the words. Vasille sat upright, watching the far wall, before slowly returning to Wulf.

"You are speaking with me." He reminded Wulf.

Turning his head away from the wall, Wulf searched for something to satisfy the Chancellor. In truth, he could not guess where Eckart was. The man was sharp and talented. The Gaevral clan had been known in Altanbern as peerless hunters, expert trackers, and ambushers.

But Leofric had claimed Eckart fled back into the Qoyllan camp to rescue his horse and goat. If the madman was willing to risk his life for animals, Wulf doubted he had abandoned them. But did he dare hope for outside aid?

A harsh response brewed on Wulf's tongue, but he swallowed it for Fionn's sake. "We had no plan. The arrests came as a surprise. I can't say where he might have gone."

Annoyance bloomed in Vasille's eyes, but he looked at the door instead of Wulf. A woman in a dark cloak entered, boots rapping on the stone. A hood covered her head, but Wulf recognized the intense green eyes beneath the fabric: Tettiena, the woman who had pursued them through the Sylfestran woods.

"She's resisting," Tettiena said. "I may need help holding her down."

"Pah." Vasille stood. "Give her to the men then. Try again once her spirit has been broken."

Wulf shot to his feet. "If you so much as touch her-" A gauntlet slammed into his head, sending him reeling.

People spoke around him, and shapes moved. Struggling against the drowning fog, Wulf shook himself from his daze. When his vision cleared, he saw a gleeful expression on the Chancellor's face. "Better yet. Bring her here."

Wulf winced, glancing back as Ciprian guided Fionn into the room, her feet dragging on the floor as she struggled to keep pace. Vasille approached her, grabbing her collar and roughly yanking her necklace off. The cord snapped as he pulled it loose.

Returning to the table, Vasille laid the crystal down and gestured to someone behind Wulf. Cold steel pressed against Wulf's neck, drawing a single speck of blood. Another soldier handed Vasille a hammer, and he held it aloft above the necklace.

Wulf's breath caught. That was Fionn's connection to her maevruthan, the only link between her and the memories stored in her homeland. The blade digging into his neck seemed trite by comparison.

"I presume," Vasille addressed Fionn, "You should be sufficiently motivated now. Behave, and I won't slit his throat nor smash your pretty little necklace."

Eyes wide, Fionn stared at Wulf in horror. Her voice emerged as barely a whisper. "Fine."

Ciprian positioned Fionn against the wall, and Tettiena knelt beside her, placing a hand on Fionn's shoulder. Their interaction was brief, too short for Wulf to understand what was happening. And then it was over.

Tettiena stood, breathing deeply, staggering as though disoriented. Ciprian offered her an arm, and she took it, hobbling to the table for support. Catching her breath, she nodded. "I have what I need. We're done here."

Wulf's muscles tensed. Tettiena had slipped into Fionn's mind, and read her memories.

Pleased, Vasille lowered the hammer, and Wulf felt the sword retract from his throat. His relief was short-lived. Vasille suddenly raised the hammer again and brought it down upon the necklace, shattering the crystal to pieces with a horrible thud.

Fionn's eyes shrunk and dimmed. She slumped against the wall like a lifeless doll. Tettiena whirled around, mouth agape. "What did you do that for?"

"She'll be harmless this way." Vasille set the hammer down. "Better safe than sorry with a monster like that."

An irritated scowl ripped across Tettiena's mouth. She barked at Vasille. "You overstep your bounds. I should-"

Unbothered, Vasille interrupted her calmly. "You should know your place."

Snarling, Tettiena snapped at Ciprian. "Rescind the order for the man's execution. He is not to be harmed."

Surprised, Ciprian glanced at Wulf. "For what reason, my lady?"

"Rescind it." Tettiena ordered. "Take them back. Now."

The young evoker scrambled to pull Fionn up, but it took all his strength to drag her limp body. A second guard hastily pulled Wulf to his feet and propelled him from the room. Stunned, Wulf locked eyes with Tettiena as he was hauled away, and a terrible truth struck him.

Eckart's mother was here, hunting her own son.

And, she wanted Wulf alive. Why?

Ciprian paused outside the interrogation room to pick Fionn up, and Wulf felt his breathing quicken as worry overcame him. The trudge back to their cell lasted an eternity, the time for Ciprian to unlock the cell and deposit Fionn inside even longer.

Wulf did not wait for the guards to close the cell behind him. Dropping to his knees, he felt Fionn for a pulse and exhaled heavily when he found one. Metal crashed as the gate closed, and the guards departed.

What happened to a cefra whose necklace was smashed? With their link to their memories destroyed, did they simply languish? Pulling her into his lap, he stared at the wall, defeated.

Footsteps heralded someone's return. A tap on the cell drew Wulf's attention. Ciprian stood there, pressing a small bundle through the bars. "Quickly." He insisted.

Gently setting Fionn down, Wulf took the parcel. Even concealed, he could tell what was inside. The distinct texture of bread and mushrooms hid beneath the thin cloth. Surprised, he eyed the evoker curiously.

"Toss the remains into the bucket, and they won't know," Ciprian whispered.

"Why?" Wulf asked.

"You've suffered enough." Ciprian turned on his heel and marched away.

Maybe the evoker had grown fond of them on their long boat ride. Grateful, Wulf returned to Fionn's side, hoping to shake her awake. Her eyes flew open as soon as he touched her, and she sat bolt upright.

"Fionn?" Wulf asked cautiously. "Do you. . . remember me?"

"Of course I do." Fionn barked, eyes darting to his bag. Her voice echoed as though another's overlapped hers. "Is that food?" She asked.

"Wait." Wulf grabbed her shoulders. "Tell me what happened."

Fionn stared into his eyes, her emerald irises brighter than before. "The girl's memories have been severed. But I might save us yet." She snatched the bag from him and pulled it open, tearing the hunk of bread in half and offering it to Wulf.

Overwhelmed, Wulf tentatively accepted the offering.

"They have their answers." Fionn hissed. "The execution will come soon. Tomorrow, if the whispers I've heard are true. We will have but one chance, and we must take it."

"You're. . ." Wulf shook his head, gathering himself. "You're the patron."

"Wise, aren't you? Only took a thousand dreams."

This voice did not belong to Fionn. The inflection was different, airy, and melodic as if every sentence were a poem. Wulf gritted his teeth. "Yeah? Some help you were. Would it have killed you to send a clear message rather than cryptic nonsense?"

"The images were nonsense only to a fool." Fionn, or rather, Seoras hissed. "You cannot glean what we face." She stood, freezing, eyes locked on the iron bars.

A shiver ran through her, and lightning streaked down her arms. Hollow horror dimmed her eyes. Wulf rose, reaching out to her, but Fionn walked away from him, choosing an isolated spot in the corner.

"Rest." Seoras ordered. "You will need it."

Sliding the remaining food to her, Wulf retreated to the bench, eyes glued to the woman across the cell. Her blazing green eyes darted about for a few minutes, never landing on Wulf. Then, they abruptly faded, and a bird darted out from the shadows of the ceiling and squeezed out into the hall.

"Fionn?" Wulf asked again.

The girl's eyes lit with panic. Wrapping her arms around herself, she shrunk against the wall. Rising, Wulf rushed to her side, but she flinched from him.

"Who are you?" She asked, terrified.

Grimacing, Wulf stepped back. He wanted to answer, but she buried her head in her lap, arms trembling. She must be overwhelmed. What would it be like to suddenly be stripped of all memories? To be a hollow shell?

Kneeling a few paces away, Wulf watched her, waiting for her to calm down. He felt pathetic. Weaponless, born without magic, there was naught he could do for himself, let alone her.

Wulf was nothing. He was useless.

CHAPTER TEN

BLOOD OATH

CLODIA WAS THE picture of divinity. Piercing light descended from the clouds, illuminating the white-marble buildings huddled around the crystal-clear sea. Leo shaded his eyes as he searched for the sun responsible for such intense light.

The Emperor himself awaited them across the bay. In another life, he might have been Leo's father-in-law. But the course of history had seen the Trenowyths be held at arm's length from the Imperial families they once courted.

Sighing, Leo lowered his hand and closed his eyes, shutting out the light. Their ship arrived late, its hull tattered where quick repairs had been made. Luckily, nothing critical had been damaged in the battle, but the two holes torn by cannons had slowed their pace considerably.

Consus snuck up on Leo; he did not hear the general's footsteps. "You Athelstani's have weak eyes." Consus teased. "I, for one, missed this."

Squinting, Leo looked up at Consus. "It's not my eyes I worry for." He turned over his hands, imagining the white skin turning beet red.

"It's cold. Wear gloves."

Shaking his head, Leo tucked his hands beneath his arms. Once they reached land, an envoy would greet them and take custody of their prisoners: one, a despised Llaqtan responsible for the death of thousands, and the other, a mercenary who claimed to have been following his captain's orders, ignorant of the details.

"It's been some time since you last visited," Consus noted. "Returning like this is almost nostalgic."

"I disagree," Leo said. "You always won our sparring bouts. The memories only serve to make me feel sore."

Consus chuckled. "It's hardly my fault you preferred reading to training."

"I'm going below deck." Leo sighed. "Who knows how long we'll be stuck outside."

"Good idea." Consus teased, hand running along the inside of his collar. Nerves had been disrupting the general's otherwise calm demeanor, and Leo could hardly blame him. If they were right, and that ship had been hired by Clodians, who could say what enemies awaited them within the city?

Trotting down the steps, Leo paused in the crew cabin's hall before continuing to the lowest level. Gaius, the youngest of their number, had the final shift before landfall. He looked up as Leo entered the brig.

"Take a break," Leo suggested. "I'll watch them until we arrive."

"As you say," Gaius bowed his head and hastily departed.

Watching him ascend the stairs, Leo first looked at the man sitting in the cell closest to the doors—a rugged-looking fellow with dark skin and short-cropped hair. Kiylla inched closer to her bars, eyeing Leo curiously.

"What is the Imperial dungeon like?" She asked.

"I don't know," Leo admitted. "I've never been inside."

"You're unhelpful."

"And you don't know how to start a conversation," Leo muttered, staring at the mercenary. He claimed to be ignorant of who hired his captain. But was that true? The bruises and cuts on the man's face spoke of the interrogation he'd been through, but perhaps his loyalty ran deeper than most.

"I made you a deal," Kiylla said, drawing Leo's attention back. "But I never made good."

"I'm listening." Leo leaned against her bars, recalling the question he'd asked before the mercenary ship had struck, one she claimed she would answer only once she trusted him.

"You wished to know of my deal with Beau? I received a message from him shortly before your failed city fell under attack," Kiylla explained, shimmying closer to him on her cot. "He warned me a pair were coming to steal my gem: one cefra, one man. He would ensure the Imperials retreated if I captured the jewels they carried."

"Did you believe him?"

"No. But, sure enough, the pair arrived. And neither of us was prepared for the other."

A useful confession, but it did not come from a mouth any imperial would acknowledge. Leo bit his bottom lip, thinking. If he continued his current course, Kiylla would be presented before the Emperor, and she would strike. When the man died, she would be killed, and the war on Yuri Llaqta would waver while new leadership was established.

But would they demand retribution or call a retreat? Beau would go unpunished in the chaos, his quiet scheme hidden away. Leo had yet to guess the extent of his plan but had no doubts the lord was connected to the vision he witnessed inside the shrine.

Kiylla read his expression. "You're worried about Beau."

"Of course I am."

"Hm." She stared thoughtfully at the other prisoner. "One of yours, the fire-hair, he tried to read my memories. I had not realized evokers could do such."

"I didn't either." Leo agreed, brows wrinkling. "Fire-hair? Do you mean Arsene?"

"If that was his name. Give me a moment with him," she nodded at the mercenary. "You know not where enemies hide. He might disappear tomorrow when the Imperials claim him."

Backing up, Leo checked the hall before closing the brig's main door. Kiylla let herself out, unlocking her cell with a spell and pushing it open with her shoulder. Sitting upright, the mercenary looked between them with widened eyes as Kiylla approached.

"What are you doing?" He demanded, fear illuminating his face as Kiylla unlocked his cell with another quick flash of magic. "Keep. . . keep that witch away from me."

"I might," Leo said, "If you tell me who hired you."

"I already said I don't know."

Shrugging, Leo nodded to Kiylla. The mercenary squirmed to the back corner of his cell, desperate to escape her. "Fine. Fine." He panted. "I only know a little. We were paid more gold than I'd ever seen to ensure the ship sunk."

"Our ship." Leo figured. "But who wanted us lost to sea?"

"He must have been someone powerful. But I don't know who. Captain met him in private."

"Not good enough. The men would whisper. You had an idea."

Glancing in terror at Kiylla's intense face, the mercenary swallowed. "Yeah. We had ideas. The helmsman thought he saw a priest-looking fellow talking with the captain. But I can't promise that's true."

Leo studied the man's face, dirty forehead covered in beads of sweat. He glanced at Kiylla, silently asking her opinion.

Her sharp eyes met his, and she backed away. "I believe him."

Relieved, the man pressed his back to the hull. Leaving him be, Kiylla walked back out, locking his cell with another quick spell before returning to hers. Grabbing her cell door, Leo prevented her from shutting herself in.

"Wait." Leo blurted out. "Someone in the city wanted us dead. And none hold more power than lords who join the clergy. I can't find them alone."

"Yes, I doubt you could." Kiylla agreed dryly.

"Think," Leo whispered. "You have one chance. What if you fail?" He grabbed the bars. "Your Earth Father spoke to me. I cannot ignore it any longer."

Kiylla tilted her head. She understood what he suggested. "I misjudged you, south lord, when first we met." She stepped closer, face an inch from his. "Ask yourself. Who wishes you dead?"

Leo's mind reeled. The men of this ship had been sent to bring three lords and the prisoner home. Whoever hired the mercenaries bid them follow and attack only once those lords had boarded. No crew members could be the target.

So, did they seek Kiylla's head? The prospect seemed unlikely. But Leo could find no cause for anyone to murder himself or his allies. He stared at Kiylla desperately, wishing he were more clever.

"I've learned a few things about you, south lord," Kiylla said quietly. "The people who want you dead *will* succeed." She breathed deeply, tilting her head to whisper in his ear. "Do you recall the place I brought you and the other evoker to? Where we negotiated a surrender?"

"Yes," Leo recalled the golden landscape of towering mountains and the stifling air.

Kiylla smirked, and the air in Leo's lungs vanished. Choking, he staggered back, hand pressed to his throat as he struggled to draw breath. A vacuum surrounded him, following his steps. Suffocating, he backed toward the door, grabbing the handle and pulling it open before losing his balance.

An impact shattered the hull, and wood splinters flew overhead, digging into his arms and legs. But sound dimmed, and the world blackened as he passed out.

"Leofric!" Someone called from beyond.

Light flashed into his eyes, and Leo sat bolt upright, gasping for breath. Air flowed freely into his lungs, and he regained his senses. Pressing a hand to his aching chest, he blinked, trying to remember how long he'd been out. It had only felt like a few seconds.

Water lapped around his ankles. Water? Stumbling, Leo shot to his feet. The sea poured in from a hole in the hull, dragging the ship into the deep. Metal moaned, and wood creaked as the boat heaved, throwing Leo across the room and slamming him into the cells. His vision blurred again.

In the darkness, something grabbed the back of his shirt and yanked. Bewildered, Leo's vision returned in time to see Thurston hauling him from the flooding brig. "What happened?" he shouted.

"I don't. . . know," Leo said honestly, head still swimming.

Cursing, Thurston dragged Leo up the stairs as a stream of sailors hurried into the brig to patch the damage before the ship sank. Casting one last glance over the room, Leo finally registered where the holes were: Kiylla's cell. And the woman had vanished entirely.

"What happened?" Leo asked as they trudged up the stairs.

"We heard something explode," Thurston explained. "Or sounded like it. Then the ship started rocking, and water poured in."

"Huh." Leo's eyes darted around. He breathed in as they returned above deck, chest still aching from suffocating.

Doubling over, he caught his breath. Something dug into his chest, and he stood, grimacing as he pressed a hand to his breast, searching for a wound. He felt a circular bump beneath his tunic like a scrap of wood had been sewn into the fabric. Digging at his chest, Leo found the loose threads and severed them, yanking out the strange item.

His mind froze when he held it up to the sun. It was a small wooden token, a couple of inches across, with a beautifully intricate pattern carved into its surface. Unfamiliar text ringed the exterior, framing a constellation of stars gathered around a rocky spire. This was a Llaqtan familial print, the same kind Johanna had used to gain them entry to the Qoyllan camp.

This piece must belong to Kiylla. Turning it over, Leo found new words scratched into the back: *The southern woods. Tonight after dark.*

Far cleverer than he, Kiylla had escaped while relieving Leo of blame. Now he had but meet her. Closing his fist around the token, he felt the wood between his fingers slip loose. Opening his palm, the token was gone. Merely an evocation.

Leo looked up as Consus ran to his side. "Are you alright?"

"I will be," Leo said. "I think I was attacked, but it happened so quickly. . ."

"You're bleeding," Consus observed. "Snap out of it and tend to yourself." He ordered.

Blood trickled from Leo's arm and knee. The explosion must have reopened the wounds he took during the battle. Pressing a hand to his gash, he watched someone fly up the stairs.

"General!" Gaius called as he raced to their side. "The prisoner. She's gone!"

The Parnesius estate stood alone on a quiet road west of the palace. Leo had visited it countless times in his youth, unaware of the half-breed who hid away in its crevices. Light snowflakes fell through the golden shafts of sunlight, landing in the frigid water of the courtyard fountain.

Following Consus through the gates, Leo slid off Temple and allowed a steward to take her to the stables, though Consus kept hold of his steed. Wrapping his cloak around his shoulders, Leo watched the groundskeeper trim the hedges surrounding trees that matched the family crest: white flowered, their blooms dying with winter's arrival.

"Consus," Leo asked, catching up to the general. "Do you trust your Father?"

"Of course," Consus answered. "He will take my concerns to heart; we can count on him as an ally."

Thurston side-eyed the general, less convinced, but he kept his thoughts to himself. Before they reached the manor doors, a woman emerged. Consus' stepmother, Leo presumed, though they had never met before.

The newer Lady Parnesius resembled the first: tall, stately, dark hair swept into a braided bun. She must have been freezing in her thin, silken brown gown. Hiking up the skirt, she flew down the steps.

"Consus." She had a heavy Sigillite accent, rich, the words almost too thick. "You arrived later than expected."

"Where's Father?"

"Called to the palace." She answered, beckoning them inside. "Come. I'll have rooms prepared for you and our guests."

"Thank you, my lady." Leo offered politely, happy to step into the warmer mansion.

Consus remained outside. "I have dire news I must deliver in person. I should return shortly." Offering a polite bow, he turned and remounted.

"Dire?" Lady Parnesius questioned as she ushered them inside and closed the door.

Leo glanced at Thurston, and with reluctance, he explained. "We transported a prisoner. I'm sure you heard. She escaped, hoping to take our ship down with her."

"Heavens." The lady pressed a hand to her chest, noticing Leo's bandages. "Let me get you something warm to drink." She hurried away.

Sighing, Leo walked into the foyer. A fire raged in the marble mantle, warming the pristine, white home, but it did little to make the room feel cozy. Sigillite abodes were stately with sharp edges, lacking the homeyness the simple wooden structures in Athelstan imparted.

"What a mess." Thurston sat in the armchair behind Leo heavily.

Tapping his fingers on his chest, Leo remembered the token Kiylla had temporarily given him—an evoked message. He smiled at the lady as she returned with a tray of tea and happily accepted the hot drink. Sipping it by the fire, he deliberated over his next move.

Leo knew what he needed to do. And he hated how little he resisted the notion. Draining his tea, he shouldered his bag.

Thurston raised an eyebrow. "Have somewhere to be?"

"Tell Consus I went out if he returns before me."

"You two have all the fun."

Slipping out the manor doors, Leo jogged to the stable. Temple had settled into a warm pile of hay and snorted unhappily when Leo urged her to rise. Quietly apologizing, Leo ran a hand down the mare's neck as he saddled and mounted her.

Pretending he was heading out for a leisurely ride, Leo nodded at the manor guards as he departed the gates and clopped down the road. Nervous, he leaned forward, watching every corner of the lane.

The southern woods. . . Clodia bordered the sea to the south, save for where the shore met with a thick forest. Roads curved far around those dense woods, leaving miles upon miles of uninhabited wilds. How was Leo to find a lone woman within?

Maybe she would find him. Settling his nerves, Leo tried to enjoy the ride through Clodia. It was a beautiful city, after all. Even when sunlight faded, the marble buildings shone like white gems under the torchlight. Golden roses still bloomed even in early winter, clustered in planters against the walls or poking out from between decorative rocks.

The buildings fell into disrepair as Leo approached the southern gate, and weeds poked from the mounds of dirt instead of flowers. Pulling his hood up and pressing a hand to his sword hilt, he navigated the slums with a watchful eye.

Only a lumber mill awaited beyond the southern gate, and a muddy road led to the forest before tapering off. Checking for onlookers or pursuers, Leo passed it by and dove into the woodlands.

Kiylla would have hidden deep within the trees. He had no doubts a talented evoker like herself had enough tricks up her sleeve to ferry her safely from the ship to the shore. Clutching his sword hilt, he scanned the packed trunks for the woman he sought.

The further he rode, the louder the laps of the ocean grew, though he could not see the shore beyond the dark woods. Minutes flew by as he departed civilization and entered the unchecked wilderness.

Figuring she would keep to the shore, Leo did as well. Deep within the underbrush, he caught sight of a flickering fire. Riding toward it, he leaned forward in the saddle, spotting a woman curled up by a trunk, nearly camouflaged in her brown cloak.

Kiylla watched Leo approach, eyes glued to his person as he slid off Temple's back and walked to her side. "He lives. Good."

"No thanks to you." Leo rubbed his wounded arm. "You could have warned me."

"I saved your life. No one suspects a thing."

"But did you have to-" Shaking his head, Leo let it go. "The city will soon be swarmed with men searching for you. They've probably already begun."

"I know."

"They're looking for you," Leo repeated, kneeling beside her as he fished through his bag. "Luckily, I can do something about that." He pulled out an extra tunic and a knife.

"Are you sure about this, south lord? You can still walk away."

"Yes." Leo looked up. "I was given a task. To protect your people and Eckart's."

"And what is that?" She asked, touching the tunic.

"Johanna taught me how an evoker can make a convincing disguise with hardly a thing but their mind." He held up the knife. "And I'm a dab hand at trimming hair." He motioned for her cloak.

"I see." She pulled her cloak from her shoulders and tossed it to him. "Dyes and wool thread. These I can evoke."

"Perfect." Leo eyed her figure. Tall and muscled, but still womanly. "I have just the thing. A popular fashion with Athelstani ladies who ride."

Kiylla curiously watched as he knelt beside her, knife in hand. "Do you know how Truevan's swear bond?"

"No."

Asking for the knife, Kiylla flipped it around and cut a shallow gash in her palm. Flipping her hand upside down, she raked a thin layer of dirt away and squeezed a few drops into the hole before offering him the knife.

Following suit, Leo flinched as he cut his palm. "Don't think this means I've forgiven you." He warned.

"Why should you?" Kiylla said. "We are enemies."

Eyeing her closely, Leo flipped his hand over and let it bleed where hers had. Leaning forward, Kiylla covered the mound, sealing their mingled blood beneath the earth.

"No turning back now." She said, "So do your best work, south lord."

"I told you." Leo wiped the blood from his hand with a handkerchief. "If I know anything, it's good fashion." Gathering her tangled locks into his hands, he gently brushed them out before raking the knife through them. Strands of hair fell to the ground like rain, pooling in the blood of their sworn oath.

CHAPTER ELEVEN

EVOKER

FUGITIVE ON THE run: a title Eckart never expected to receive. Slowing to a stop, Eckart looked around, gaining his bearings. He had wandered into a wealthier district of the second tier. Each building rose two stories, guarded by thin iron gates and decorated with small yards of piled stones.

Pressing his back to a house's cold stone wall, Eckart caught his breath. Lavinia City was a maze. Neighborhoods, both rich and poor, filled the second tier, connected by winding, narrow streets. Numerous thin alleyways had provided Eckart refuge from wandering eyes and escape routes from oncoming guards. But how much longer could he keep up the chase?

Even if Chief Tamhas murdered Eckart in the end for stealing his prized jewel, Eckart still owed him thanks. Begrudgingly, the old man had taken Eckart under his wing and taught him what all Gaevral children learned: how to hunt, hide, and track.

The wind whipped at Eckart's hair, and water splashed across his cheek. The ordinarily clear skies had turned gray, consumed by clouds and light rain. A flash of lightning danced across the heavens, illuminating a crimson streak hidden behind the storm. An ashfall was brewing.

Eckart tightened his cloak and pulled his hood down. In Eglisfelde, the dungeons were carved beneath the castle. Surely, something similar was true here, yet he was reluctant to ascend to the third tier. Buildings in the entertainment district were large and spread out. Hiding would prove troublesome.

Shimmying to the corner of the house, Eckart peered into the street. Children played with a ball, wrapped like spheres in thick fur coats. The great wall of the third tier loomed behind them. The stairway must be near.

Ducking behind the wall to avoid the gaze of a passing couple, Eckart cursed himself. He was an evoker. Johanna had taught him the basics during their return journey, but the magic was far more challenging to control than his cefran talents. Memories surfaced quickly in Eckart's mind, and pulling them into being had proven simple enough. Keeping his concentration steady so the spell would last more than a fleeting second had been excruciating.

The cloudy skies made it difficult to tell, but it was probably evening. Eckart had been listening to the chimes of the church bells, hoping to keep track of the days. Two days had passed. Two days too many. The Dragosi men might have already killed Fionn, and every passing hour afforded them the opportunity.

Eckart had hoped a brilliant plan would come to him, but he had nothing. He was exhausted and deprived of sleep and food. Maybe it was time to stop lingering and thinking and do what Leo did best: just *go*. Taking a deep breath, Eckart forced his aching legs to move.

Shouldering his bag, Eckart walked down the street past the kids. They paid him no mind, and he passed behind the next house without trouble. The street widened ahead of him, reaching an intersection decorated with a large metal statue of a man working a forge. Throngs of people swarmed around it: the entrance to the stairwell.

Two knights stood at the stairwell's base, unwelcoming figures in black armor. Eckart presumed two more guards waited at the top. Down here, his cloak and leather vest were ordinary, but above, where Arsene had spoken of towering chapels and vast libraries, a man of wealth would draw fewer eyes.

114

Eckart could do this. Closing his eyes, he sifted through his memories for a solution. Coming up short, he checked for onlookers before pressing a finger to the crystal at his neck, searching for a clansman who had been to this city before. Images and voices flew past his eyes, like paintings viewed through hazy glass.

There. The blacksmiths for the Gaevral were a couple, both enthusiastic collectors. Years back, they had made a pilgrimage to this city, seeking a man whose weapons were famed throughout the Empire. Long retired, the elderly man they found had been dressed in a thick fur coat with a large wool hat.

Eckart hated the look, but he could imagine Arsene complimenting the outfit—proof the coat was high fashion. Honing in on the man within the memory, Eckart separated the clothing from its wearer, pushing the vision into reality. . .

A flash of brown light startled Eckart as his fingers pricked and glowed. The coat he'd envisioned wrapped his body, and the hat balanced delicately on his head. Spirits, he must have looked awful. But it worked. Now, he only needed to keep this spell alive until he passed the guards.

Raising his head and lowering the hat's brim, Eckart strode into the street, merging with the crowd, a tactic he had often used to escape notice in Clodia as a child. There was an art to blending in, becoming a speck amongst the many, slipping beneath the notice of the man beside you.

The church bell chimed, heralding the seventh hour of the evening. A steady stream of people ascended and descended the stairs, heading home as shops closed or catching evening entertainment. Though not much of an actor, Eckart attempted to mimic the tired, eager-to-get-home expressions the men and women wore.

The coat. The blacksmith. Eckart chanted the words in his head, holding fast to the man's memory. He stared straight ahead, vision obscured by his low-brimmed hat. Every muscle in his body tensed as he passed the guards and climbed the first step, and a wave of relief swept over him once he left them behind.

Holding fast to Fionn's bag, Eckart quickly ascended the steps, weaving past the sluggish climbers. Another pair of knights watched the crest of the stairs, facing outward to the streets. They gazed only upon Eckart's back and his ordinary brown hair as he passed.

Fanciful cobbled roads extended left and right, unlike the smoothed stone of the lower tiers. Two large establishments sat across the street, but their exteriors were the same: smoothed gray stone covered in pock marks from falling cinders, with nary a decoration to distinguish them from their neighbors.

Towering above on the highest tier, the black Dobrescu manor overlooked the city, perched like a bird of prey over its target. Now, all Eckart had to do was find its dungeons. Arsene had described the city to him, dubbing the mountain edges the 'hovels of the poor.'

Eckart turned left, carefully glancing up to study the signs. Not all made the purpose of their establishment clear. One appeared to be a library, another a meeting house. A third's risque sign painted it as a brothel, nearly as luxurious as the one in Clodia city. Eckart's spell was slipping. Here would have to do.

Turning off the road, Eckart climbed the building's steps, pausing to glance down the road. A group of soldiers approached, doubtless one of the many search parties seeking his head. Pressing his hat down, Eckart hurried inside.

Lavinian buildings harbored vivid worlds inside their barren walls. Crimson and gold merged on beautifully painted walls, and low lights made them glow like ore and fire. At this time of night, the common room was packed with scantily clad women and their eager guests. Ignoring the girls and their patrons, Eckart scanned the area, counting several doors leading to private rooms.

Only one was open. Ducking inside, Eckart closed the door behind him and felt his head pound as he released his spell. The expensive hat and coat faded away, revealing the disheveled man in the simple tunic and vest.

Turning around, Eckart pressed his back to the door as he scanned the room. A bed with messy sheets sat in the corner, accompanied only by a small wardrobe. Eckart had hoped to find a tangible disguise in the closet, but he was out of luck. Darting to the window, he pulled his hood over his eyes as the door flew open.

A young woman stood in the door frame, dark-haired with a mole beneath her eye. "You have to buy a room, sir." She said with a heavy Dragosi accent.

Reaching into Fionn's bag, Eckart searched for her coin purse and pulled it out. "I'm looking for something. Ask no questions, and I'll pay you well."

The girl's eyes shot up. She was young, perhaps twenty. Eyeing the bag, she looked up expectantly. "Looking for what?"

"The dungeons." Eckart breathed. Hardly subtle, but he was running out of time.

Eyebrows shooting up, the young woman carefully studied him, and Eckart turned his head away. "We can do that kind of thing here, too." She said teasingly.

"Give me the location."

"Hm." She pointed behind her. "Down the road, all the way at the end."

Eckart dropped the coin purse into her hand. "No questions. No words."

The courtesan nodded to the window. "Thanks for your business." Stepping out, she cracked the door behind her.

Hoping she'd spoken true, Eckart threw the window open and dropped into the courtyard, boots crunching on the yard of tiny rocks. Darkness shrouded the city, making it easier to hide. Inching along the wall, he watched the shadows on the road until he caught an opening to dart back onto the streets.

Following the courtesan's directions, Eckart followed the cobbled streets until the buildings shrunk in size and decorative statues disappeared. A sheer rock face blocked the horizon— Mount Bruthine. The view was breathtaking. From here, the city seemed like a waterfall cascading down the mountain's slope.

All too soon, another obstacle appeared. The buildings petered off, the road barren of travelers. Craning his neck, Eckart strained to see what awaited him at path's end and spotted a large door built into the mountain face, guarded by the silhouettes of soldiers. But he'd never reach it like this.

Backing up, Eckart watched the doors scrape open as a group of men departed the dungeon. Spinning around, Eckart ducked behind a small, vacant building to his right and waited for them to pass.

Four of the group were ordinary soldiers wearing simple armor, but two stood out. One was an evoking knight dressed in steel and covered in a dark blue cowl. The other appeared to be a woman, but a cloak shrouded her features.

Old wind chimes hanging from the edges of the building jangled beneath a light breeze, drawing the woman's attention. Eckart breathed in sharply, sliding away from the corner, hoping she had not spotted him. Though he'd seen her face for a fleeting moment, her searching green eyes were naggingly familiar.

No, it could not be. Eckart was imagining things. No footsteps approached, and he cautiously peered around the corner.

The group passed him by, heading into the city. Struck by an idea, Eckart crept after them, hardly breathing and softening his footsteps. The group paused, the woman striding away, while the evoker paused to talk to the men. He must have dismissed them or given them new orders as they quickly scattered, heading in separate directions.

Sticking with the evoker, Eckart followed him to a tavern, its sign clearly marked with a tankard. Chewing on his lip, Eckart watched the door slam behind the evoker as he entered. Slipping into the dungeons would prove simple if he could disarm the man and take his uniform.

Pulling the door open, Eckart stepped inside. A large cask of ale stood behind the counter, and men lounged in booths along the wall, playing cards or dice. The evoker sat at the bar and tapped the counter, ordering a drink, his voice familiar: Ciprian.

Ciprian would recognize Eckart and remember his voice. He could not risk speaking with him. But maybe there was a means to catch him off guard. Walking past Ciprian, Eckart sat in an empty booth and counted the number of patrons. Eight men, one couple, and a single owner behind the bar. He could manage this.

As a teenager, Eckart had curiously sampled the Gaevral brewer's famed recipe, a vile brew called Builscor. It had knocked him flat, sending him into darkness for an hour. A second try had yielded similar results. Only on his thirtieth birthday had Eckart weathered the brew and kept his footing.

The old brewer insisted humans could not handle the drink. Time to put his claims to the test. Scanning every glass in the room, Eckart focused on the crystal clear memory of the dark brown ale, of its pungent taste. Pain prickled through his head, and he saw his finger alight beneath the table. Spirits, evoking was difficult.

The bartender placed a glass before Ciprian, and he swallowed the shot in a single gulp. Setting the cup down, he shook his head, already disoriented. A few worrying moments passed as the evoker shifted uncomfortably in his seat. But the spell had worked. Pressing his hands to the bar, Ciprian tried to balance himself as his senses departed.

Thud. Eckart turned to see the man sitting in the booth behind him slam into the table face-first. His wife gasped, reaching forward to shake his shoulders. Rising, Eckart heard another man choke and gasp before falling backward out of his chair.

"My lord?" The bartender asked as Ciprian slid from his seat and crumpled on the floor. "Ash and cinder." He cursed, racing to the evoker's side.

Seizing his chance, Eckart stood, grabbing a bottle from the table. As the bartender knelt beside Ciprian to check his pulse, Eckart muttered an apology and brought the bottle down on his head.

The other patrons were occupied with their unconscious members or teetering on the edge of consciousness. Nobody glanced in Eckart's direction as the bartender slumped over. Working quickly, Eckart grabbed Ciprian and dragged him behind the counter.

A terrible pounding crashed in Eckart's head as he searched for the door leading into the storage room. Pausing to listen for commotion, he hid behind the bar as he dragged Ciprian through the door and kicked it shut behind him.

The man was already rousing, eyes fluttering. Yanking off his cowl, Eckart undid the straps of his armor and pulled them over his tunic. The helm covered all but his eyes, and the cowl hung low over his brow. They both sported but short stubble, the lower half of their faces similar enough in the dark. Fitting the gauntlets over the robe's loose sleeves, Eckart backed away from Ciprian and returned to the bar.

Ignoring the chaos of the passed-out patrons and their worried or laughing cohorts, Eckart exited the tavern, recalling Ciprian's stride and mimicking the stiff gait. Now, he hoped the guards at the dungeons would ask no questions.

Evokers were exceedingly rare. Nearly all hailed from noble families. That alone granted them rank, but to be one of the few trained officers? Surely, Ciprian could go where he pleased.

Two soldiers stood guard outside the dungeon's heavy stone doors, though Eckart doubted the sentries here saw much action. They glanced at him as he approached, one stepping aside to push open the doors. Nodding to him, Eckart passed into the dim cavern.

The first checkpoint cleared. Eckart stood in a barren hall lit with scant torches, paths peeling off in three directions. Open archways to his left and right led into offices, where a guard in a heavy cloak poured over a ledger on a wide desk. A guard emerged from the darkness of the passage ahead and looked at Eckart curiously.

"Back already?" He asked.

Nodding curtly, Eckart walked past him, trying to seem like he needed to be somewhere urgently. Shadow engulfed him as he descended a slope into the halls of cells. Cramped cages of stone lined the dungeon's labyrinthine corridors. Three men passed him, walking patrol routes. Sneaking out would not be easy.

Where was she? Cefra could see far better in the dark than humans; Eckart could trace the outlines of inmates, and none he'd passed so far matched the woman he sought. Another slope in the hall descended further into the mountains, leading to a different section.

The air was colder down here, quieter, free from the murmurs and yelling of the inmates above. Only five halls made up this portion of the dungeon, and Eckart peered down each, listening for signs of life. He noticed a man leaning against the wall down the second hall, but he was no ordinary guard.

Dressed in black armor adorned with a gold-trimmed surcoat, the man's fluted helm was embellished with drake's wings. A royal knight. This had to be the place. Steeling himself for a confrontation, Eckart approached the cell he guarded.

Larger than the others, this cell housed two prisoners: a woman huddled in the corner and a man sitting against the opposite wall. Both were familiar, but Eckart had not known Wulf was imprisoned as well.

"Sir Ciprian?" The knight's voice was muffled beneath his helm. "Why have you returned?"

If Eckart spoke, the knight would glean his identity. Eyeing the sword on the knight's belt, Eckart hesitated as he thought on his feet. Only one option presented itself, though it would throw them into danger.

Once before, Eckart had been imprisoned in the cramped cells beneath Femora city. Hours had wiled away in darkness and solitude while he contemplated his fate. No greater source could feed his

120

magic's catalyst. The loneliness from those days surged through him as he summoned the innate magic in his blood.

Rain fell from the ceiling, dousing the torch. The fire sputtered, and the knight jolted from the wall, drawing his sword. Lunging forward, Eckart wrapped his hand around the cascading water, sending frigid waves through the liquid as he reformed it into a spear and drove it through the knight's chest.

Choking, the man grabbed at his wound as his knees failed him. Grabbing his helm, Eckart jerked, snapping his neck to give him a clean death. Catching the falling body, Eckart quietly lowered it to the ground and searched his belt for the keys but found nothing.

Shit. Grabbing the bag hidden beneath his robes, Eckart dug for the twisted hairpin Fionn used as a lock pick. Finding it, he pushed it through the bars. "Quickly." He hissed.

Wulf's face changed when he heard Eckart's voice. Fionn lunged to her feet, eyes blazing with strange light, as she grabbed the hairpin and shoved it into the padlock.

"Eckart." Wulf breathed. "You brilliant bastard."

Returning to the corpse, Eckart drew his blade as Fionn clicked the door open. "Here." He said, offering the blade to Wulf, handle first. The man scowled at the weapon, preferring a spear, but accepted it nonetheless.

"Seoras says there's one entrance and a sewer grate," Wulf whispered. "You're waterborn. Can you sense that?"

Eckart blinked at him in confusion. Had this human just said Seoras? "Sense water?" Eckart repeated, focusing on the coherent words. "Maybe." He spun around. The buckets in the cells had to be dumped somewhere.

"This way." Fionn ran down the hall, and Eckart pushed Wulf ahead of him.

Guarding their backs, Eckart watched for any signs of movement. Once they were seen—and they would inevitably be seen—Lavinia city would descend upon their heads.

CHAPTER TWELVE

SETTING SUN

NOTHING. Not one sign of Eckart had turned up in the mountain city. Arsene wondered if the man had simply vanished. The unexpected man-hunt had sent Vasille into an impatient rage, leading him to suggest an early execution for the other prisoners.

One other prisoner, at least. Wulf's pyre had been canceled, and Vasille had ordered he be kept in the dungeons, alive.

Why, oh why, had Arsene picked a lunatic for a partner? Any sane man would have sealed their lips and ignored Fionn's plight. Wulf could have retired to the countryside with enough gold to live the rest of his days. Instead, he rotted in a cell awaiting whatever sick scheme Vasille had devised.

Leaning on the wall, Arsene peered down at the lower tiers of the city as he fiddled with Death Knell, cleaning out its barrel and taking its pieces apart so he could fit them together again. Pointless work, but it kept his hands busy.

An evoker's perfect memory was a curse as often as a blessing. No matter how Arsene strained to forget Fionn's song, the lyrics played over the silence of the night as though she sat behind him, strumming her lute to the tune.

> *Memories reach through the annals of time*
> *But none can recall those days we spent*
> *As kindling not yet caught ablaze*
> *When you were still you, And I was still me*

> *Recollections of eld, not yet locked in place*
> *Hazy and blurred, they slip through your grasp*
> *Reaching for the man who was always someone else*

The words must have been coincidence. How could she have known? How could a meandering cefran bard have peered into his heart and found truths not even Arsene had uncovered?

Phantoms had overcome him during their time in the Earth Father's realm. Memories of Marius distracting his thoughts had forced secrets from his lips. Secrets he'd told no one but her. Frowning, Arsene recalled another line from the song.

> *The mask slips from a hollowed face*
> *Cast aside, cracks appear on perfection*
> *The empty void you'd always concealed*

Wulf's recurring dream haunted him with images similar to these lines. Whatever entity lingered in Fionn's mind carried memories of a portal in a forest of glowing orange trees—identical imagery to the tapestry Marius had eagerly studied. But that was a relic from bygone days when the cefran city of Tiene had still stood.

A century had passed since the Tiene clan had been scoured and scattered. The archaeologist who had uncovered the tapestry dated it another two centuries back. How could someone living now recall those times? Who was this entity within Fionn?

Or rather, *what* were they?

More than Fionn's song haunted Arsene's memories. So did her face. *Why?* Women like her weren't his type. Elegant, sultry, alluring: words Arsene would use to describe those he'd pursued and bedded. Words that did *not* fit Fionn.

But no woman had matched his jabs with wit the way Fionn did. She wasn't eye-catchingly beautiful, but her voice. . . He could have listened to it all day.

Arsene nearly dropped Death Knell, remembering the night he'd taken her to the second tier for drinks. He hadn't planned to kiss her; the impulse had surprised him, too.

The moment she'd leaned in, he'd fled. Had he indulged, allowing her to disappear would have been impossible.

Agitated, Arsene snapped his flintlock back together and shoved it into its holster. Night had fallen once more, but the black firmament cracked with growing crimson light. An ashfall loomed on the horizon, likely to start before dawn arrived.

Chaos had overtaken Lavinia. Soldiers ran to and fro, seeking their lost prey, spreading outside the walls to the surrounding region. Arsene ducked out of the way of a passing patrol as he walked the road back to the manor. Darkness overtook the red, and Arsene saw clouds obscuring the firmament.

Heat crackled in the winter freeze. Soon, the frigid mountain city would be consumed by fire, as hot as summer in Athelstan. Removing his mantle and hanging it over his arm, Arsene nodded at the guards by the manor gates and passed beneath the drake statues' gaze as he entered his childhood home.

The manor was quiet, but Arsene could see a faint light from the hearth in the parlor. Wavering, he watched the fire's shadow dancing on the walls before deciding to approach. Dropping his cape on the back of an armchair, he stepped around the coffee table and stood before his mother.

Aurica's hair fell loose around her shoulders, pooling in the folds of her black nightgown. Creases framed her eyes, and deep lines traced her mouth, but she was still the picture of beauty and perfection. Unattainable and unreachable.

"Mother," Arsene said softly. "Can we talk?"

"You speak as if you are not my son." She said, inviting him to sit.

Lowering himself slowly into the chair opposite her, Arsene chose his words carefully. "You seemed angry last we spoke."

"I was. . . vexed. We did not intend for you to learn anything more than you already knew. Now that time has passed, I've relaxed and. . . and realized how you've changed."

"I have? How so?"

"You're quieter. You wait to be addressed. And your eyes. . ." She trailed off. "Perhaps hardships as a sellsword taught you a few things."

Quieter? Wulf would find that amusing and inaccurate. Trying not to think of his partner, Arsene changed topics. "This journey was my first real responsibility. Maybe you should have given me an Imperial imperative sooner."

"If only there had been one." Aurica agreed.

He cleared his throat, tugging at his cuff. "The appearance of the heir will shake the world. Eyes will be on Marius, on her. Questions will be asked, fingers will be pointed."

"We're well aware. But we've been preparing for years."

"Still, problems are bound to arise." He shifted in his seat. "What I'm trying to say is. . . What do you need from me?"

"Well," Aurica gazed out the back window. "Dragos will need a Duke. I intended to pass the mantle to your cousin, but perhaps I needn't."

"Hm? Is Marius planning to abdicate the throne?"

"Yes. Perhaps you would be a worthy successor after all."

Arsene rubbed the bridge of his nose. He was a fool. Marius' portrait hung beside Relia's because the Empire needed an Emperor.

"I'll pass," Arsene said. "Give it to Istvan. My place is at Marius' side."

Aurica smiled cheekily. "As the royal shield?"

"I'd prefer that to a Ducal office."

"I'm sure Marius would, too." Aurica picked up a wine glass from the end table. "I've heard you've mastered a new evoking technique. You used it to interrogate that Llaqtan witch."

"Mastered is perhaps a strong word," Arsene said.

"Nonsense. Do you know how long it took us to even grasp the concept? We searched for years." Aurica took a sip and set the glass aside. "Yet you find one little journal and crack the code."

"You're talking about Tettiena's experiments." Arsene presumed. "What did you intend to use it for?"

"For the girl. We needed her to forget the details of her past." Aurica paused. "The task will not be simple. Maybe you can help Tett."

Arsene rubbed his hands together. "We took a prisoner in Femora, and I searched his memories yet found nothing. Tettiena covers her tracks well. I'm impressed. Surely, she needs no aid." He leaned back. "Though, more than once, she aimed to kill. Did she realize it was me she nearly beheaded?"

"After a fashion. We cannot afford to err. And dead men tell no tales." Aurica explained. "Especially when we are so close."

"I can't say that makes me feel better, Mother."

"Apologies. Perhaps you should not have wandered where you did not belong." She tapped her glass. "But it did bring you to Yuri Llaqta. Fate weaved as the goddess willed. This must be her way of tying the threads together."

"Well, your sect is right about one thing. Marius. . ." Arsene trailed off. "Marius would make a fine Emperor. History suggests those with good intentions coupled with absolute power leave a prosperous kingdom in their wake. But, there's just one thing I don't understand."

"What's that?"

"Where do the jewels fit in?"

Aurica uncrossed her legs and leaned forward. "They're the doors. The cause of the planar overlaps. The world will heal without them, and all will be as one."

"They don't seem like ordinary jewels. Do you simply smash it with a hammer?"

"No." Aurica shook her head. "No, it's much more complicated. But with the cefra in captivity, Tettiena was able to draw the answer from her."

"She has? Where is she now?"

"Speaking with Relia," Aurica said softly. "She did raise the girl. She wanted to say goodbye."

"And Relia speaks fondly of her." Arsene agreed, standing. "Thank you, Mother. I feel like I owe Marius an apology. I was short last time we spoke." He bowed his head and picked up his mantle.

"Arsene," Aurica called after him. "I'm glad you're back. For Marius' sake."

For Marius' sake. Bittersweet pangs raced through his blood for hearing his mother speak the words, for hearing her say the joy was not for her.

Walking stiffly, Arsene slowly ascended the stairs. He wanted to fall in line, to make the right choice. But curiosity overcame him, and instead of heading east to Marius' chambers, he turned down the western hall, seeking the guest room.

Muffling his steps on the rug, Arsene leaned on the wall outside Relia's room and strained to hear what was being said within. Faint murmurs reached him, but no distinct words. When did Tettiena intend to erase Relia's memories? This very night?

Relia had not spoken of her mother often, but their relationship had seemed fair. When questioned, Relia insisted her mother had been kind and accommodating, if controlling and secretive. Such hovering had sent Relia into the capital, seeking freedom and answers.

But it was not abuse that had seen the girl flee. Maybe Tettiena wished only to say farewell, and the unfortunate deed would come later.

Straightening out, Arsene turned to leave but paused when the door creaked. Tettiena emerged, hood down, revealing the full breadth of her features. She clicked the door closed behind her.

"Forgive me," Arsene quickly said. "I wanted to check on Relia but realized she had company."

"She's fine." Tettiena approached Arsene. "You were elected to safeguard the jewels for now, yes?"

"I was," Arsene confirmed. He bit back his usual witty retorts. This woman had nearly severed his head.

"May I?" She held out a hand.

Removing the leather satchel beneath his cloak, Arsene dropped it into her palm. Tettiena turned her back, walking a few paces away as she pulled the sack open and examined its contents.

"Surprisingly light," she murmured. "The bag feels empty. I expected them to be heavier for their size."

"So did I." Arsene agreed, foot tapping nervously.

Satisfied, Tettiena sealed the bag and returned it to him. "Good work in Yuri Llaqta." She commended. "And in Sylfestra, I suppose," she said wryly, sauntering away.

"Thank you," Arsene responded, watching her shadow disappear down the hall. Shuddering, he attached the bag to his belt and stared at Relia's door. Better for him to stay out of their way.

Relia would forget him soon anyway.

Shoving his hands in his pockets, Arsene walked to the east wing. Marius' room sat at the end of the hall, overlooking the slope of the mountains. Light shone from the door crack; Arsene could hear his brother pacing before he knocked.

His knuckles tapped the door, and it flew open. Marius was dressed as though prepared for a meeting, enveloped in a thick fur-lined mantle. Lowering his hand, Arsene tucked it into his pocket. "You're going to be sweltering soon."

"Hm?" Marius' brow wrinkled. "Oh, the ashfall." He pulled Arsene inside and shut the door.

The royal suite looked brighter than Arsene recalled. Father had decorated with dark colors, but Marius had swapped most furniture out for softer shades, off-whites, and pale golds. A warm breeze drifted in from the open window, fluttering the curtains.

"I wanted to apologize." Arsene began as Marius grabbed a stack of papers from the corner table.

Marius nearly dropped the papers, whirling around with a shocked expression. "*You* want to apologize."

"Aaaand you're ruining it."

"Sorry. Go on."

"I was confrontational last we spoke. I apologize."

"It's alright," Marius assured him, dropping the pile onto the end table. "I'd be more surprised if you weren't angry. If anything, I owe you an apology."

"You don't." Arsene folded his arms and walked to the window. "It was the goddess herself who deemed me unworthy, right?"

"Right. . ."Marius confirmed. "You've opened your mind but don't entirely believe, do you?"

"Baby steps, brother." Arsene leaned out the window and studied the great red crack in the heavens. Heat emanated from it like a furnace, dampening when clouds covered it once more.

Marius shrugged off his mantle and rolled up his undershirt's sleeves. Joining Arsene by the window, he sat on the sill. "I've done a poor job."

Ducking his head back inside, Arsene looked at him quizzically. "Of what, exactly?"

"With you," Marius said somberly. "There's a tenseness to your shoulders in every room of the manor save mine. You were afraid of everyone. Mother, Father. Vasille. I should have protected you."

Arsene stood, frozen. Silent. He had no idea what to say.

"Maybe we can start over. Put Death Knell to its proper use."

"I thought you refused to use that name?" Arsene asked, a smile sneaking up on him.

"It's awful," Marius confirmed, grinning. "But, I'm proud of you. You've grown into a fine young man."

Coughing, Arsene waved a hand and walked away. "Don't be so quick to make assumptions. You'll be disappointed."

Chuckling, Marius shut the window. "In that case." He split his stack of scrolls and handed Arsene half. "Help me with this."

Wincing, Arsene flipped through the missives and sank onto the couch. "I shouldn't have said anything."

"No." Marius sat next to him. "You shouldn't have."

Arsene awoke, confused. Sitting up, a blanket slipped from his shoulders. Disoriented, he rubbed the sleep from his eyes and noticed Marius standing by the window.

Realizing he had fallen asleep, Arsene tossed the blanket off and stood. Hearing the rustling, Marius looked over. "You got through two letters." He said helpfully.

"What can I say? I'm not cut out for this," Arsene said sleepily. Falling asleep in Marius' room was familiar and comfortable; as a child, Arsene had often been afraid to return to his room alone.

Marius laughed but frowned when someone rapped on his door. Gesturing for Arsene to step back, Marius grabbed his mantle and threw it around his shoulders before pulling the door open.

From his spot in the corner, Arsene could see the shadow of a man bow to the duke. Out of breath, he spoke urgently. "My lord. There's been an attack in the dungeons. The cefra is missing from her cell."

"What?" Marius snapped.

"Their guard was found dead, and the cell opened. We've mobilized every man we can reach to find them."

"Ash and cinder." Marius cursed. "Give me a moment. I'll be with you shortly." He cracked the door and whirled around, grabbing a pair of boots and lacing them on.

Arsene raced to his side. "What, are you going after them yourself?"

130

"I'm going to help." Marius finished one boot and moved on to the next. "She cannot be allowed to escape."

"Then let me help-" Arsene began.

Finished, Marius rushed to the door and yanked it open. "No. It's too dangerous. Stay here." He ordered before sweeping outside.

Clenching his fists, Arsene stared at the door, watching the shadows retreat down the hall. Fionn had escaped? No, the messenger had said prisoners. Fionn would go nowhere without Wulf. They were free, but for how long? The entire Empire would hunt them.

Stay here. Arsene had just disarmed the world's most powerful evoker and returned home triumphant, but Marius sought to shield him like a small child?

Irritatingly perfect man. Always think of others before himself.

Bursting from his brother's room, Arsene bolted down the hall and into his room. Distracted, he left the door open as he yanked off his doublet and belt, sifting through his bag for his traveling clothes.

A voice shouted in his mind, demanding to know what he was doing, begging him to turn back. But Arsene had no answers, nor did he stop. Pulling on a soft tunic, he grabbed his old coat as something familiar clicked behind his head.

Death Knell. That was the sound of the hammer pulling back in preparation to fire. But his gun had been safely secured to his belt, which now lay on the floor behind him. . .

Holding up his hands, Arsene turned slowly to see his own flintlock leveled at his head. Johanna stared at him grimly. "I don't think I need to tell you what this does."

"Johanna?" Arsene's voice emerged in a higher pitch. "What are you doing?"

"You carry the jewels. Hand them over."

"Whatever you think, you're mistaken. I'm heading out to aid my brother-"

"Hand them over," Johanna repeated.

Pausing, Arsene stared at the woman he had known for years. She had not attacked him when Arminda ordered when he was outnumbered and easy prey. Johanna would not threaten him now over a mere suspicion of his betrayal.

"One question," Arsene asked, nervously staring down the barrel of his own gun. "Why?"

"They're going to destroy them," Johanna said. "The doors. The keys to the other side. I won't allow it."

Ah. Arsene's bewilderment drained away. The girl he attended college with had kept journals of her mother's notes, heretical writings on the connection between aiceils and planes. The mother's life's work, inherited by her daughter. No wonder Beau had decided to keep details from the girl and hand the jewel to Arminda for study instead.

"In that case," Arsene cautiously lowered his arms. "We're on the same side. Because Fionn has the last, and if they find her, they'll take it."

"But not if we get to her first." Johanna caught on quickly, and asked blissfully few questions. Shoving Death Knell into its holster, she offered him his belt. "You have them?"

Reaching into his pocket, Arsene pulled the sack out and held it up for her to see. "Right here. We need to go while they're distracted."

Checking the hall for onlookers, Johanna dashed out the door. Strapping his belt on, Arsene snatched up his bag and quickly stuffed a spare cloak and waterskin inside before chasing after Johanna.

She crept down the hall, listening to movement on the first floor. Hearing the front doors fly open and several pairs of boots run outside, she raced down the hall toward the stairs.

"Wait," Arsene whispered, touching Johanna's back as he jogged to Relia's room.

Finding the guest chambers, Arsene remembered the door unlocking and burst through. Recalling the way Relia had greeted him before, he back-stepped as a rapier touched his chest.

Relia clutched the blade in one hand while holding a balled-up cloak in the other. No longer the well-dressed princess, she had donned the gambeson and leather trousers from her time in Femora. Hair pulled tightly back, she flicked her ponytail over her shoulder as she sheathed the blade.

"What are you doing?" She demanded.

"Rescuing you?" Arsene suggested.

"I overheard the commotion." Relia grabbed her bag and tossed it over her shoulder. "I'm going to find them."

"Do you have a plan?"

"Not yet." She admitted sheepishly. "But now that you've unlocked the door. . ."

"Good." Pushing her out the door, Arsene glanced back at the noble gown thrown haphazardly on the floor. "Follow me. I've broken out of here unnoticed before."

Johanna loitered impatiently at the stairs. She yanked her hood over her braid as they arrived. "Hurry."

"This way." Arsene hissed, flying down the steps.

Once before, Arsene had been accused of blasphemy. Rather than face the charges, he'd fled through the hidden passage buried in the wine cellar floorboards. An old escape route, the underground tunnel led into the mountains.

Running had seemed the only option, back then. Arsene wondered if he should have stayed, if Marius would have protected him.

Not this time. The moment their treachery was realized, Arsene's chance at a future would be severed for good.

CHAPTER THIRTEEN

VICAR

LEO FASTENED HIS cravat over his coat, turning in the mirror to ensure every piece of fabric was aligned. Tying a sash around his belt, he sheathed his sword and stepped outside.

This morning, the Parnesius manor smelled of freshly baked bread, a pleasant scent that almost set Leo at ease. Tapping his boots together as he mustered his courage, Leo grabbed and steadied his trembling hand.

"Someone's nervous," Thurston observed.

Leo heard the other man approach but did not look at him. "I'd rather fight a melee than have dinner with the Chamber of Lords."

"Shadows, why?" Thurston disagreed, walking into view. The floral doublet he'd donned looked truly terrible on him.

"What *are* you wearing?"

"Noble fashion?" Thurston furrowed his brow and looked down at himself. "Just because you've only seen me in armor doesn't mean I don't know how to dress."

"Clearly you *don't* know how to dress." Leo exhaled. "Alright. Let's get this over with."

They entered the dining room together, an enormous room squashed under the even larger crystal chandelier hanging low from the ceiling. Consus sat at the table, reading a scroll. He wore a coat similar in style to Leo's, a pale jade to match his eyes.

"What's that?" Leo asked.

"A change of plans," Consus muttered, finishing reading. "The Archbishop has asked for one of us to brief him. I suppose I'll send you."

"What for?"

"I don't know." Consus set the letter aside. "Read it if you like."

Grabbing the parchment, Leo unfolded it and scanned its contents. The letter declared recent events significant to the church and requested a private meeting with one of the surviving officers of the First before the Emperor's meeting began.

"I'll go." Leo agreed.

A servant entered and set down a tray of freshly cooked breakfast. As a child, Leo had despised the smoked fish Clodian's ate, but it smelled delectable now. The hunger he should have felt rumbling in his stomach fled, and he found his appetite turning to nausea.

"I'm not hungry," Leo announced. "I'll meet with him now."

"The cathedral is closed." Consus uncrossed his legs and pulled a plate toward him. "Eat. You're injured."

"And delicate," Thurston added, sitting across from Consus. "By the way, Leofric. We have answers from our prisoner."

"The mercenary?" Leo looked up expectantly.

"Yes." Thurston drawled. "He was a pirate. They closed the case."

Outraged, Leo glanced at Consus, whose face tightened in anger. "I asked for another interrogation. I was denied."

"Pirate, my ass." Thurston muttered, grabbing a plate.

Grabbing a biscuit, Leo picked at it idly. Kiylla should be safe, but he worried nonetheless. Someone passed in the hall, a tall man in a flowing green cloak. Leo caught only a glimpse, but it must have been Lord Parnesius.

"Your father isn't much of a socialite," Leo observed.

"No." Consus agreed, layering smoked fish on his toast. "I inherited my talents from my mother. She could talk for hours."

"Did Eckart live here with her?"

"Here? Not quite. Father assigned him to the shed out back." Consus paused thoughtfully, remembering something he chose not to voice.

"It's late enough." Leo declared, wrapping his uneaten biscuit in a handkerchief. "I'm heading out."

"Walk slowly," Consus advised.

Leo caught a few words from Thurston before the voices faded away. ". . . seemed strange to you. . .?"

Grimacing, Leo wondered if Thurston was talking about him. Most likely. Surely Leo could conjure a reasonable excuse for being on edge the past few weeks. Perhaps the sinkhole. The gravity of the catastrophe sank in every time Leo looked at Kiylla, and pangs of guilt racked him, screaming he was betraying the dead.

Today felt warmer than the last. Sucking in the brisk air, Leo calmed his nerves as he retrieved Temple and mounted, directing her out the gates and onto the street. This time, he headed toward the city's heart rather than its outskirts.

Shadows, Clodia felt entirely different today. Many of its soldiers had marched for Yuri Llaqta, but every remaining man was stationed on the streets, assigned to search for the fugitive. Wanted posters already adorned many shops, quick sketches depicting the wild-eyed woman in brown robes.

Leo admired the accuracy of her likeness and felt relief flood his chest to know how different she appeared now.

Trying to lift his spirits, Leo recalled bringing Eckart to the grand cathedral and how the cefra had squirmed with boredom and discomfort every step of the way. How many times had Eckart snarled at Leo for cutting his hair and trimming his beard? The thought made Leo smile.

No place was more beautiful than the road to the palace. Flowering trees lined the white stone road, their branches threaded with golden ornaments. When the sun fell directly on the road, the path shone and blurred with heavenly gold, as though it were the entrance to Viridia's domain.

Leading Temple through the path, Leo dismounted when he reached the royal square. His eyes snapped to the palace and its stained-glass windows. Dragging his head away, he hitched Temple outside the church and stepped through the garden gate.

The fountain had frozen over in last night's chill, and the roses planted around its base had wilted. High hedges boxed the garden in, guiding those who entered to the cathedral's doors. High on the spire, the bell chimed the eighth hour of the morning.

Pushing the double doors open, Leo entered the church. Three Athelstani chapels could fit inside the main room; seas of pews on multiple levels stretched between him and the great statue of Viridia behind the altar.

Jogging down the steps, Leo flinched as his boots echoed in the empty space. A priest emerged from a door on the rightmost side of the building and hastily met him.

This man was positively ancient, wrinkles within wrinkles folding his bald head. His green robes did not bear the sigil of the laurel; he was a lower-ranking clergyman.

"May I help you, sir?" The old man asked politely.

"The Archbishop asked to see an officer of the First," Leo said.

"Ah." The man nodded. "This way."

Slowing his pace to match the old man's, Leo followed impatiently, wishing the ancient priest would hurry. Ascending the steps took a lifetime. The old man led him into the upstairs hall and bid him wait by the balcony.

Leaning on the banister, Leo observed the grand cathedral from above. Shadows, Eckart had been right. This palace was blindingly white. After a few minutes, Leo's eyes began to ache as he longed for the gentle night of his homeland.

But more than searing light pained him. He felt like Viridia herself gazed upon him in fury. Wriggling under the unseen glare, he backed away.

The old man returned, and Leo gratefully followed him down the corridor into an office. But no Archbishop awaited him. The Vicar stood behind the desk, encased in green robes stitched with golden laurels; he peered down at Leo from above his hooked nose.

"Lord Vicar," Leo said in surprise.

"The Archbishop is with the Emperor." The Vicar's deep, gentle voice said. "I will take your account."

Every hair on Leo's body stood on end, and a shiver raced down his spine. His instincts screamed at him to run. Instead, he approached the desk and stood opposite the tall clergyman.

"Tell me your account of the sinkhole and the events in Femora." The Vicar instructed. "Every detail." He nodded at a wiry scribe sitting in the corner, parchment and quill in hand.

Clearing his throat, Leo fulfilled the request, recounting the sinkhole from his point of view.

Strangely, The Vicar seemed eager for the account to end and hastened Leo past the details, save when Leo reached the night of Femora's great wave. Figuring Consus had pardoned him, Leo freely shared the tale of Eckart's rescue from the dungeon and the barrier the half-cefra had conjured.

Interrupting the final leg of the tale, the Vicar leaned forward. "You attacked your fellow soldiers."

"For good reason." Leo said hastily. "Eckart had been imprisoned wrongfully. I knew someone was framing him, but I-"

The Vicar motioned for him to stop. "That's enough." He peered at the scribe, ensuring the account had been recorded before beckoning Leo to follow him outside. "The Emperor's meeting is soon. Follow me."

Confused, Leo glanced at the scribe, who paused with a quill mid-air, surprised by the abrupt finale. Offering the wiry man a bow, Leo followed the Vicar outside.

Descending the stairs, The Vicar glanced back. "I heard your ship was attacked."

"Yes. We were lucky to escape."

"Hm." The man looked thoughtful. "Did you learn who was responsible?"

"No," Leo answered, omitting the prisoner from his answer.

"Must have been Forsaidh pirates. They've been known to stray that far west." The Vicar fell silent.

Touching his sword hilt, Leo's fingers danced on the pommel as he watched the Vicar closely. Perhaps the worry was needless. No one would be so brazen as to murder him in such a public place.

Whoever wanted the ship sunk desired their deaths to be hidden.

The silence remained until they reached the palace promenade. Halting, The Vicar turned around with a smile. "The weather is nice, is it not? You should wait here for your comrades."

"As you say." Leo nodded, watching the Vicar drift down the path.

Shaking the nerves from his shoulders, Leo bounced on his heels, admiring the statue of the first emperor erected in the garden. Roses had been sculpted around his collar to remind the viewer of his divine locks.

Biting his thumb, Leo turned to see Consus and Thurston approaching. "You're early," he called.

"What are you doing here?" Thurston called back. "You're supposed to be across the way."

"I'm already done," Leo said, quieting his voice and glancing up at the royal guard stationed by the doors. "Shall we wait together?"

"Who did you meet?" Consus asked.

"The Vicar."

"Really?" Consus' eyes narrowed. "Tell me about it. Leave no detail out."

Thurston cleared his throat. "Our dear general was worried about you."

"Can you blame me? Someone wants our heads." Consus gestured for Leo to speak.

Folding his arms, Leo considered sharing more than the encounter. But as much as he wished to trust his old friend, the hour was too soon.

LEO HAD NEVER sat with the Chamber of Lords. Six men from prestigious Sigillite families claimed the titles, most of whom Leo had never met. Despite the honored occasion, Leo had eyes for only one man, the lord he recognized.

Beau Rosa, the Lord of Commerce, smiled politely across the table from Leo. He reclined in his seat, hands folded on his black coat, silver cane leaned against his leg. Well-kept with a neatly trimmed mustache, nothing about him appeared sly or untoward.

Nor did he look much like his daughter. Johanna's light brown skin matched her Truevan countrymen, and her eyes were a gentle brown. Beau was dark as a trueborn Sigillite, his eyes nearly black.

140

Not wanting to draw his attention, Leo glanced around the round table. The Emperor had aged. Wan and wrinkled, he looked thin beneath his white mantle. The crown of golden laurels resting on his brow pressed down limp hair. Hawkish eyes darted about the room, searching every shadow for enemies.

Vicar Faunus, of course, headed the clerical branch, handling matters outside the church while the Archbishop controlled matters within. He sat between Beau and an elderly woman who greatly resembled Arminda, from her ebony skin to off-white robes. Lady Lucullus, Leo believed, the head of evocation.

Consus had attempted to tell Leo the names of the three men sitting on the left side of the table, but he had already forgotten. Glancing between the rugged man closest to him and the heavy-set man furthest away, Leo strained to recall the family from which they hailed. The lords of agriculture, military affairs, and law, though he did not know which was which.

Consus leaned forward in his seat, delivering his account of their travels. Leo had tuned most of it out, distracted by his unconscious glances at Beau. As his eyes drifted off the Emperor again, Leo saw Thurston glaring at him and felt the prick kick his shin. Sitting straight, he gave the conversation his full attention.

A stained-glass window depicting Viridia framed the Emperor's back; in her palms, she cupped the world, its edges pouring water into an empty void.

"Nonsense." The Emperor barked, interrupting Consus again. "You claim the ship was Clodian?"

"It's only a guess," Consus said patiently, though this was the fifth interruption. "They were no pirate ship, of that I can assure you. We must continue the interrogation."

The gruff man with short-cropped hair and rugged skin spoke up. "Surely someone at the docks would have seen the ship leave or made a record of its passage."

"Drusus is right," Beau added. "I can arrange for an investigation."

Drusus. Leo strained to remember the name this time.

"Forget the pirate." The Emperor seethed. "You let the Llaqtan witch run free. I should have you hanged and quartered for what you've done."

Consus took the threat well. "It was our responsibility, and we failed. We will bear whatever punishment you deem necessary."

The heavy-set man in the golden doublet raised a hand. "That won't be necessary. One of your evokers was a traitor; the other sent away. We should have provided you with another. The error is ours."

Ah. Leo remembered who this was. Lord Chaucius, the magistrate of judicial affairs. What a relief to hear him speak those words.

"Why did the witch wait?" The Emperor demanded. "Why flee now, when she's within reach of Clodia, if not because she seeks to destroy us as she did the First?"

Paranoia seeped from his words and restless eyes. Leo looked away, not wanting to meet the gaze.

"She cannot replicate that attack," Consus assured him. "The means by which she conjured such a spell have undoubtedly already reached Lavinia and are in their evoker's capable hands."

The Vicar cleared his throat. "Perhaps, in the meanwhile, the troops should be called home. She has no cause to attack should the war end."

Leo glanced at the Vicar in surprise. He protested the war?

"No!" The Emperor slammed a fist on his armrest. "You'd have us send a message of our weakness? You'd allow our men to go unavenged?"

Leaning back, Lord Drusus ran a hand down his scarred face. "The Vicar speaks sense. Yuri Llaqta is no ordinary land to be conquered. I already voiced my concerns for the new march, and my opinion has not changed."

"I agree." Lady Lucullus spoke with an elegant accent. "New evocation should be cause for concern, pause, and study. We cannot be outclassed."

The Emperor's teeth set. Maybe the rumors were true, and he saw this war as his only means of a legacy. Would the news of Relia's appearance change his mind?

If only Leo could say something. Arsene's suspicions of Relia's heritage were just that: suspicions. A chance remained the Dragosi Duke would find them unfounded, and the girl was nobody.

The Vicar backed down. "It was merely a suggestion, your radiance."

"You." The Emperor barked, staring at Leo. "Trenowyth's second son, yes? The reports say you freed the half-breed, yet the general pardoned you."

Consus spoke up. "The act was necessary to save the lives of the Third-"

The Emperor ignored him. "How can we know your sympathies for lesser beings do not extend to Llaqtans as well? Were you not watching the woman when she escaped?"

Stunned, Leo froze. Consus leaped in to save him. "Leofric was injured when Kiylla escaped. He did not inherit his family's bloodline. An evoker far outclasses even the finest knight."

Thurston spoke up for the first time. "We evaluated her for weeks. She did not speak; she showed signs of succumbing to phantoms. Her escape came as an immense shock."

Abated, the Emperor's interest faded. "Someone must answer for this." He declared, drumming his fingers on the armrest. "Yet we are short on men. You three will remain here and add to their efforts."

"You are most gracious." Consus bowed his head. "It will be done."

Beau stood, adjusting his coat sash. "Our witch slipped from the hull quite a ways from shore. We should search the bay for her body."

"She may be lost," Lucullus suggested. "A Llaqtan in poor condition could not hide for long in Clodia. But I will see if the evokers I have left can aid in the search."

"Good." The Emperor waved a hand. "Dismissed."

Rising, Leo slammed his boot into his chair leg, eager to escape. Gluing himself to Consus' backside, he breathed a quiet sigh of relief when they stepped out of the meeting chamber into the hall.

The palace was just as Leo remembered from his youth: a verdant indoor garden with soft green carpet, flower boxes, and plentiful windows artfully crafted to paint the shapes of flowers and trees when the sun flooded through.

Consus turned around, eyebrows raised. "Leofric?'

"Sorry." Leo stepped away from him and bumped into Thurston.

"Scael's maw, Leofric." Thurston cursed. "Why do I always run into trouble when you're around?"

"What did I do?"

Rolling his eyes, Thurston tucked his hand in his doublet's pockets. Leo grimaced. The flowery doublet looked worse on him now than it had this morning.

"How good to see you again." A charismatic voice emerged from the doorway behind Leofric, and he felt his muscles tense.

Beau's cane tapped softly on the rug as he walked around and offered a bow to the three knights. "After what you've been through, returning home must be blissful indeed."

"Indeed," Consus repeated dryly. "Yet our duty persists."

"So it does." Beau bounced on his heels. "I wish you the best of luck, of course." He tipped his hat and strode away.

No sooner had Beau turned the corner than Consus spoke. "I don't trust him."

"Neither do I." Thurston agreed.

"He's up to something." Leo declared, slipping past his friends. "I'm going to keep an eye on him."

"Don't get yourself into trouble," Thurston advised.

"Report to me if you learn anything unusual," Consus ordered. "We have search efforts to direct." Touching Thurston's arm, he directed the other knight to follow.

Walking with haste, Leo caught up to Beau and trailed several paces behind. Nodding polite greetings to anyone he passed, Beau hummed to himself as he exited the palace and waltzed down the promenade onto the royal square.

Pulling his hair loose from its bond, Leo raked it back and unfolded his cloak, wrapping it around his shoulders. Beau followed the golden passageway back to the heart of central Clodia. When the decorated trees parted, rows of packed shops and taverns housing hundreds of people appeared.

A woman leaning against a lamppost on the crowded street corner whispered to Leo as he passed. "Following Beau?"

Leo paused beside Kiylla, now unrecognizable to anyone who had seen the Llaqtan witch. Boyishly short hair fell neatly to her chin, the pale brown skin lightened by cream to resemble an Athelstani's complexion. Dark makeup traced her eyes, concealing her fierce countenance and painting an alluring gaze. Dressed in a pale green floral tunic, she appeared as a lesser lady from the country of night, one Leo could be acquainted with.

By imperial standards, she looked more fetching now than before. But Leo wasn't sure he preferred the new appearance. Something about her intense eyes had been captivating.

"Go around," Leo whispered back.

"Try to keep up, south lord." She strode down the road, running parallel to the one Beau walked.

Flipping his hood up, Leo watched her figure merge with the crowd before trailing Beau. The man hid something grave, and Leo was going to uncover it.

CHAPTER FOURTEEN
DESCENT

ECKART WATCHED THE dungeon guard pass the shadowed hall, holding his breath until the man turned down another corridor and disappeared. Motioning for Wulf and Fionn to follow, he darted around the corner and raced toward the door at the far end of the hall.

Throwing himself through a battered door, Eckart entered a cramped, foul-smelling chamber with a heavy grate set in the stone floor. Fionn fell to her knees beside it, grabbing the bars and dragging them off.

Ignoring the dried grime staining the metal, Wulf leaned down, helping her detach the grate and pull it loose. A thin shaft descended into the darkness, just wide enough for them to fit through. Leaning down, Eckart strained to see the bottom, where the chute exited into the city sewer system.

Shouts reverberated across the stone walls: Their escape had been discovered. No time to waste. Eckart's head ached from evoking, but he could afford another spell. Gritting his teeth, he stared at the hole in the floor and recalled the ladder leading to the Parnesius' shed loft.

Steel-colored light flashed as a metal ladder shimmered into being, clamped to the stone shaft. Fionn leaped into the hole, grabbing the handles and sliding down. Eckart pushed Wulf ahead of him, taking up the rear as they descended into the gloom.

The sound of lapping water and the foul stench of waste wafted up from below. Violet light crackled to life in Fionn's palm as she summoned a ball of lightning to guide their way. Eckart's evoked ladder ended just short of the chute, forcing them to drop a few paces to the floor.

Sharp pain throbbed in Eckart's knees as he landed on cold stone. Coughing, he released the spell, hoping the guards were not brave enough to jump after them. Squinting to see in Fionn's dim light, Eckart spun in a circle.

Two stone walkways framed a river of murky water flowing in either direction. Heading west would bring them outside the city while heading east would take them below the streets.

"This way," Fionn ordered, turning east.

"Wait." Eckart grabbed her arm. "We need to leave, not trap ourselves back in Lavinia's walls."

"Leave if you must." She barked. "I'm not going anywhere without what's mine."

That voice, the echoey tones—Eckart had heard it before, in Femora. Dropping Fionn's arm, he let her go.

"Arsene had the jewels. He'll be at the manor." Wulf called as he raced after her. He glanced back at Eckart. "Where did you get *those*?"

Grabbing the flowing sleeves of his stolen Evoker garb, Eckart rolled them back. "From Ciprian."

"How did you manage that?"

"Tell you later."

"Good." Fionn's emerald eyes gleamed like beacons. "We can make use of you."

"Do you know where you're going?" Eckart asked.

"The wind will show me," Fionn said cryptically, turning around and darting into the darkness.

Arsene climbed the ladder and pushed the trapdoor open, poking his head out to scan for guards. Blinking his eyes to adjust to the darkness, he remembered a trick Fionn had taught him and ducked back into the underground tunnel.

"What's wrong?" Johanna hissed.

"Nothing yet," Arsene murmured, holding up his palm and remembering the orange flowers blooming on the trees of the Dragosi aiceil. "Remember the underground aiceil we snuck into as kids? Follow my lead." The flower blossomed in his palm, and Arsene bit down on the bitter petals.

Fire raced through his face and eyes as red light outlined shapes in the darkness. Arsene could see the mountain face and thin path winding through its peak. Nobody was around. Waving the women up, he crept down the path, listening for activity.

"Incredible." Johanna breathed. "Where did you learn of this?"

"Fionn," Arsene whispered. Two quick flashes of orange burst behind him as they conjured flowers of their own.

"Ow," Relia said quietly as she climbed up. "Are my eyes *supposed* to burn?"

"It'll pass," Arsene promised, leading the way. "I know this place well. The only escape from the dungeon would be the sewers. There's an entrance nearby."

Though an ashfall brewed in the heavens, rain cascaded over the mountaintops, slicking the rock. Through the lens of fiery petals, rain droplets appeared as golden crystals descending from above. The trip might have been pleasant if not for the heat brewing within the icy wind.

Flipping his collar up to guard against the ash, Arsene followed the same treacherous path he'd taken once before. Rarely used, these passages had been carved centuries ago, intended as an escape route from the city should it fall under siege. The royal line proceeding the Dobrescu family had fled this path when their rivals bent the knee to the Empire. The bodies had never been found.

Reaching an intersection, the trail branched into three; two wound down and west while a more prominent path sloped upwards. Holding up a hand to signal the women to wait, Arsene turned west but froze when he heard the distinct sound of voices coming from the upward slope. Pressing his back to the mountain face, he listened.

Johanna crept to his side, pressing a hand to the rock. "Two voices. Sounds like men."

"What are they doing out here?" Arsene muttered. "Take that path." He pointed to the narrow gap to their left. "I'll follow in a moment."

Nodding, Johanna rose and jogged through the gap, and Relia reluctantly followed. "Will you be okay?"

"I'm one of them." He assured her.

Standing, Arsene hugged the cliff side as he walked up the slope. After a sharp rise, the trail leveled out, where it would curve around and connect to the highest tier. Did guards search these paths for the fugitives?

The men's voices became clear as Arsene reached the crest of the slope. ". . .can't be out here much longer. Ashfall's coming."

The voice was unfamiliar. But the one who responded had spoken to Arsene far too many times. "Then make haste!" Vasille hissed. "Every inch of the mountains must be watched."

Viridia's tits. So much for a quiet escape. They were about to have the worst kind of company.

Leo had teased Eckart over the years about his musk-ridden scent, one Eckart was proud of—the aroma of soil, pine, and wood. But the odor of this sewer would force even the blonde fop to admit Eckart smelled like perfume by comparison.

Pinching his nose, Eckart jogged after Fionn, following the glowing violet light crackling in her palm. Lavinia's sewers were as labyrinthine as their city, rising and falling multiple levels, with countless sluice gates directing water and sewage flow.

The nobles on the highest tier would be prioritized for flowing water. The sewers would lead them to the manor. But how they would survive once they reached it was another story.

"Here." Fionn stopped, panting. She held up the ball of lightning, illuminating a hatch above their heads and a rusted ladder against the stone walls.

Wulf darted ahead of her, climbing the ladder and pushing the heavy latch aside. With a horrendous scrape, he created a hole wide enough for them to crawl through and poked his head through, checking for guards. Waving his arm, he beckoned them to follow.

Scampering up the ladder, Eckart emerged in a cramped alley between two packed buildings and hurriedly pulled the hatch back into place. The mountain face was a few paces away, the streets clean and cobbled. Lanterns glowed ahead but not behind. Shimmying around the building, they hid in the mountains' shadow.

"This way." Fionn pointed west. "This road ends soon, though."

"Let me lead," Eckart suggested, peering around the building's corner. Their alley merged onto a singular road, well-lit by frequent lampposts. Two guards passed under the light, heading their way.

Wulf kicked a rock, and it skidded past Eckart's boots. Whirling around, he stared at the mercenary in disbelief, but Wulf shook his head and pressed a finger to his lips. Back to the wall, Eckart heard the soldiers heading their way.

Spear pointed forward, the first guard cautiously turned the corner and spotted them. He opened his mouth to yell but was cut off as Wulf dove forward and shoved the spear aside with his sword before tackling the soldier. The second guard rushed forward to help, but a sphere of water wrapped around his head, muffling his startled yelp.

The prick of pain Eckart felt from loss of blood was nothing compared to evoking headaches. Focusing on his spell, Eckart held the water around the guard's head as he flailed, trying to escape the watery prison as his breath ran out. Once the man's eyes closed and his limbs fell limp, Eckart released the water, drenching his body and the surrounding stone.

Wulf yanked his sword from the first guard's throat and stood. "Help me get his armor off."

Obliging, Eckart undressed the man he'd drowned so Wulf could don Dragosi ebony armor. Dragging the bloodied body behind the building, Eckart piled him with his partner.

Snapping the drake-winged helm over his head, Wulf nodded. "Let's go."

Shrouding herself in her cloak, Fionn hid in their shadow as they approached the manor. Few buildings filled the fourth tier; the cluster of smaller buildings they walked past, the royal barracks, and the manor.

Far more activity surrounded the barracks. Soldiers gathered in the yard, receiving orders from senior officers. Candles illuminated two windows on the front of the barracks, and the restless wind shook the black banners hanging from its friezes. Should they emerge from their cover, there would be nowhere to hide.

"Stay here." Fionn hissed.

"You're going alone?" Wulf whispered.

"Stealing is what Fionn does best," the girl insisted. "You'll only get in the way." She stared at the lanterns lining the street. "The storm will douse the lights. Make for the passage behind the barracks." She pointed. "A thin crack leads to an old mine. Slip through."

"*Wait*," Wulf pleaded, trying to pull her back, but she slipped his grasp.

"Be careful." Eckart murmured as a heavy gale swept over the mountainside, jarring loose rocks from the peaks and sending them tumbling to the streets. Flickering beneath the light rain, the lanterns snuffed out in unison as the gale swept the mountainside.

Sudden darkness overtook the street, and Fionn vanished. Fingers dancing on his bow, Eckart scanned the shadows for the passage she'd mentioned.

"Hold a moment." Wulf touched Eckart's arm. "I'm going to the barracks."

"Are you mad?"

"Yes," Wulf said plainly. "My spear, they probably confiscated it there."

"You'd risk everything for a spear?"

"I would."

Eckart recognized that tone of voice—he'd employed the same when returning to the Qoyllan camp for Dilsaeth. Nodding, Eckart lowered his arm. "I'm the evoker here. Stay with me."

Unable to see in the pall, Wulf stuck close to Eckart as he navigated around the barracks to its front doors. A patrol of six men dashed past them, and Wulf quickly grabbed the doors and ushered them in.

They were in luck. A lavish common room of dark tile greeted them, and a door to their right led into an impressive armory. "Go," Eckart whispered, sending Wulf inside while he stood guard.

Nearly all tables were empty, but the stairs thundered with activity as men raced down from their quarters. A booming voice echoed above, someone ordering the men who had been abed when the prisoners escaped.

Hoping to look important, Eckart stood straight and folded his arms, scanning the scene. The knights flew by without question, but an officer in a brilliant red cape descended the steps and gazed at Eckart.

Shit. Eyes darting to the door, Eckart tensed as the officer approached.

A hand grabbed Eckart's elbow. "Let's go," Wulf ordered, flying back out the door.

Whirling around, Eckart followed, hearing the officer call to him from across the room. "Where are you-"

Slipping outside before the man could finish the interrogation, Eckart slammed the door and dashed around the building into the training yard, climbing up and over the fence and dropping down on its other side.

Wulf landed beside him. "Spirits." He cursed. "I can't see anything. Where is this mine supposed to be?"

Fire erupted ahead as torches were struck to life. The brilliant red outlined the shapes of soldiers swarming the mountain passes, searching for the fugitives. "Cacmun." Eckart cursed. "What now?"

"You." A female voice demanded. "What are you doing?"

Eckart's heart plummeted. He knew that voice, its soft yet elegant Sigillite accent. The words streamed together like thick molasses, the familiar slur Mother had spoken with.

Turning, Eckart looked left to see a woman holding a torch approaching them, her dark cloak billowing around her boots. The torchlight illuminated the face beneath her cowl, one Eckart had adored in his youth, though now it was creased by age lines not present the last time they had seen one another.

But would Tettiena even remember him?

Drawing Death Knell from its holster, Arsene stepped around the cliff side to peer down the path. Where did this lead? A mine had once

sat in this area but had been decommissioned decades ago. Had a new tunnel been dug to connect it to the fourth tier?

In that case, the royal barracks should be dead ahead, yet darkness swallowed the city beyond the mountain path, visible to Arsene only by the orange light burning behind his eyes. Fire flared to life as soldiers lit torches to guide their way.

Rain fell in Arsene's eye as he scanned the figures. Most were Lavinian knights, but he spotted an evoker in steel armor and a blue cowl standing beside the balding worm himself. Vasille shouted orders, instructing the men to quickly relight the doused lanterns and resume the pursuit.

Arsene could not say he hated many people. Most received apathy or indifference. Vasille was a different story. Readying himself for a confrontation, Arsene stepped into the open and approached the Chancellor.

Two knights leveled their blades at Arsene but lowered their weapons when they recognized the prince. Vasille strode forward, wiping rain from his face. "You! What are you doing here?"

"Searching for the prisoners," Arsene answered calmly. "Though, I admit I'm following the crowd. Do we know they're here?"

"Not quite." The evoker answered in a deep voice. "They fled through the sewers. While they could emerge anywhere in the city, they'd likely try to use the mountains to slip out the back."

"Go," Vasille ordered. "Scour every inch of the pass and guard its exits."

The men around him jogged forward; the direction Johanna and Relia had departed in. Licking his lips, Arsene quickly mustered a distraction. "Wait." He commanded, holding up his palm.

The soldiers paused, awaiting his word.

"I knew them well," Arsene said. "One was attached to their steed. I'd bet my life they returned to their inn's stables."

"We already have men down there." Vasille retorted. He raised his hand to order the men forth, but something interrupted him. His eyes gleamed in the torchlight as he slowly lowered his arm. "You knew them." He repeated. "And here you are."

"Speak plainly, Vasille." Arsene snapped.

"You and the cefran girl were sent to Yuri Llaqta together, no? Perhaps the long, *lonely* months on the road grew a bond between the two of you."

"I don't like anyone, Vasille," Arsene said dryly. "Cease with the childish insinuations. We haven't the time." He addressed the men. "I'm an evoker. These paths are treacherous in the dark, but I can find my way. Let me handle this."

"She couldn't have gotten far," Vasille said. "After what the men did to her, she'll hardly be able to walk."

Arsene's eye twitched, and he bit back uncouth words. Was Vasille telling the truth or hoping to get a rise out of him?

"So she'll be easy prey. All the more reason not to risk the men's lives." Arsene gestured back toward the city. "The Flaming Lake. Check there." Hoping they'd listen, he turned to leave.

"Stop him!" Vasille barked.

The deep-voiced evoker heeded the command. Bright fire outlined metal bars as dungeon cell doors sprung before Arsene, sweeping across the pass and connecting with the mountainside. Path blocked, Arsene spun around.

"Marius is not going to be pleased with you," Arsene warned. "Antagonizing me while we're all in danger."

"I watched you." Vasille stepped closer. "You went out, alone, with the girl before her capture. You lavished her with gifts. You danced with her. My eyes saw."

Vasille had been spying on him? Arsene should have expected as much. Gritting his teeth, he tried to worm his way out of the accusation. "That was then. The situation has changed, and I've adapted."

"Are you hoping to find her yourself?" Vasille pressed, drawing closer. Orange flames danced along his outline and trailed the tail of his crimson mantle. "Shame. She won't know your face."

Touching his holster, Arsene scowled. "What did you do?"

"I smashed that little crystal of hers—a fitting punishment for her crime. Whatever foul magic fueled her has been lost alongside her mind." Vasille smiled, hoping to garner a reaction and prove Arsene's treachery. "You'll find naught but a hollow shell withering away."

He spoke of her maevruthan crystal—the shard containing her memories, the link to her people's pond. Without it, her mind would be as blank as a newborn's. She would cease to function, with no means to return home. . .

Drawing Death Knell, Arsene remembered the most straightforward yet essential memory: loading the barrel with gunpowder and a ball of lead.

"Not that you'd want her back. She's been defiled beyond use." Vasille taunted.

For years, Arsene had hated this man. Hated his slimy attitude, his irritating voice, and the way he kissed the sitting Duke's boots while antagonizing the youngest son every chance he received. Now, he'd gone too far.

And Arsene no longer had any excuse to refrain from killing him.

"You really shouldn't have said that," Arsene warned.

Bang. Smoke plumed around Arsene as the bullet flew into Vasille's cheek, tearing through his head. He screamed in pain but was quickly silenced as a second bullet tore through his mouth. Shocked, the evoker lost concentration on his spell, and the bars behind Arsene collapsed.

Two more bullets ripped through Vasille's chest and leg. Leaving him alive to die a slow death, Arsene's eyes shot to the knights surrounding the Chancellor. Stunned, they froze temporarily before registering Arsene's crime. Shouting, they charged him. The evoker's fingers glowed as he prepared a spell.

Beneath uneven light, shadows danced and distorted. Recalling every shade cast in the sunlight, Arsene covered the cliff faces with darting shadows running in every direction. With only torchlight to guide their eyes, the knights quickly lost sight of Arsene as the illusion confused them.

Tearing down the mountain path, Arsene slid down the sharp slope and tripped over himself as he searched for the women's blazing outlines. One came careening towards him, and Arsene dug his boots into the rocks, dragging a line through the gravel as he skidded to a stop.

Johanna's features became apparent as she ran into him, grabbing his arm. "What happened?"

"We need to go," Arsene shouted.

"This way." She commanded, turning on her heel.

The men would follow them. But hopefully, Arsene had bought them some time.

Eckart stared at his mother, overcome with emotion. Horror, sorrow, hatred, anger, and joy raged through him, nauseating. The dark shadows of Lavinia city were the last place he expected to meet her again.

Tettiena had yet to recognize Eckart. "What are you doing?" She demanded.

Stepping in front of Eckart, Wulf answered. "Awaiting orders, my lady. Where would you have us search?" The mercenary attempted an impression of Arsene's accent, speaking with choppy, heavy syllables.

Tettiena's eyes narrowed. She knew something was wrong. "Who is your commanding officer?"

Were she anyone else, Eckart would shoot and run. But they had not met back up with Fionn, and he could not bring himself to move. Wulf grabbed his spear, knowing full well they had no suitable answer.

Fingers flashing in the dark, Tettiena threw her hand forward. Something grabbed Eckart's cowl like a coat hook had caught the fabric. It yanked, forcing his head backward and tugging the hood loose.

Head snapping back up, Eckart's blood froze as he saw the woman preparing another spell. But the light gathered around her fingers died, and her eyes flew wide. Stunned, her mouth fell open as silence took her.

She recognized him. His Mother had not seen him since he was a child, yet she immediately knew him.

"Eckart." Tettiena stuttered.

Finding his voice, Eckart stood protectively in front of Wulf. "You already knew who you sought. Why are you surprised?"

"Because. . ." She trailed off. Perhaps seeing him in the flesh was different than hearing his name. Lunging forward, she extended her hand. "Give it to me. Give it to me and go free."

"I can't do that."

"Yes, you can," she pleaded. "I don't want to hurt you. *Please.*"

Grimacing, Eckart felt like time slowed. To whom did his allegiance lie? To the woman who had raised him, snuck him rides in her carriage, and pushed hot food through the shed window? Or to the girl he'd found broken in the wilderness, laughing at herself for falling, pitifully slumped over his shoulder as he hauled her back to Gaevral lands?

"You collect oddities." Leo had said one day while drunk, watching Eckart rescue an overturned turtle with a fractured shell. *"Useless little things that have no other home. I think I've figured out why."*

"I'm sorry." Eckart breathed.

Tettiena outclassed him. Within an instant, she launched another spell, so fast Eckart barely caught the light upon her fingertips. Something slammed into his chest, throwing him aside, and thick vines wrapped around his arms and neck, pinning him to the barrack's wall. A heavy thunk shook the wall as Wulf was thrown against the wall and similarly pinned.

Stepping over him, Tettiena knelt and grabbed Fionn's bag. Writhing against his bonds, Eckart cut his wrists on the vine's thorns as he strained to escape.

Bang. A crack snapped through the mountains. Tettiena's head shot up.

Someone screamed in agony far in the darkness, though Eckart could not tell where. Another crack followed. And another. He knew that sound: Arsene's strange weapon.

Gasping, Tettiena sat up, dropping the bag as soldiers nearby rushed toward the sounds. Snapping herself out of it, she looked behind her and threw herself away from Eckart as a gale mighty enough to be seen in the shadow slammed into them.

Terrifying force swept over Eckart, roaring, deafening winds. Squeezing his eyes shut, he felt the vines slip loose as Tettiena's spell failed. He grabbed the bag and tried to stand beneath the relentless tornado.

Another roar rose over the ripping winds, one belonging to a creature rather than nature. Snapping his eyes open, Eckart looked into the clouded sky to see crackling lightning illuminating the leviathan of wind—Seoras.

Plunging down, the leviathan slammed into the barracks, cracking the stone and throwing soldiers aside. Wulf stumbled into Eckart, grabbing onto his arm to keep from flying away. The eye of the storm centered on them as the leviathan's massive head whipped around them. Emerald eyes shone into theirs, granting them a moment's warning.

Not again! Eckart barely managed a curse before the creature swept them up in its winds. Tangible lightning protruded from the creature's back, handholds Eckart desperately grabbed as he tried to right himself and strained not to scream. Sparks shot through his fingers, burning his hands.

Wulf yelled in surprise and horror as they were dragged away. The peak of Mount Bruthine rose into view as the leviathan darted up and over it, then miles of crag lands and rolling hills drowned in complete shadow stretched before them. Bolts of lightning surged through the leviathan's body, and then it plunged.

They were free-falling. The leviathan had gone limp. Shrieking, Eckart saw the ground rising to greet them, with nothing to catch their fall. They would be dashed upon the rocks. But he was an evoker. He could save them, couldn't he?

Nothing came to mind. Do something. *Do something.* He shouted repeatedly in his mind.

Something gave. Something tore. And the ground was upon them.

Racing through the night, Arsene and Johanna careened to a stop as they reached a sheer cliff. Orange and red outlined the plunge, and the knights' fiery silhouettes gave chase a hundred paces behind them.

"This way!" Johanna pushed him toward a barely visible sloping path.

Losing his footing, Arsene slid down the mountain, sharp rocks digging into his boots. Mud rushed up underfoot, gathering around him and Johanna, her fingers glistening the color of Llaqtan soil. A river of mud pulled them down the slope, the same he'd seen in her homeland.

Relia waited at the bottom of the slope and helped Arsene to his feet. "Are you okay?"

"Not yet." He shouted, pushing her forward.

Thunder boomed overhead, shattering a piece of the mountain to the east. Staring up, Arsene watched as the leviathan shot overhead, moving so quickly it was visible for only a heartbeat. The creature darted over the mountain's peak and out of sight. Horrible roaring followed in its wake like a tornado pursuing them.

"Ash and cinder!" Arsene cursed. "Was that Fionn?"

"Go!" Relia hollered back.

Teetering on the narrow path, Arsene gazed down the sheer drop. A defined road ran along the cliff, curved and smooth, wrapping the mountain's edge. Johanna raced down its length, and Arsene followed.

Whipping around, Johanna launched another spell. Rock crashed down on the path behind them, falling from nowhere and covering the narrow path. Reverberating bangs trailed down the cliff as some boulders tumbled to the world below.

"That should keep them," She yelled, whirling around.

The winding path ducked into a cavern, plunging them into cold and shadow. Their footsteps echoed, their heavy breathing bounced off the walls. Anxiety heightening in his chest, Arsene felt it would burst.

Erupting from the short underground stretch, the path widened as the cliff shortened. Tripping on a boulder, Arsene caught himself and noticed something moving overhead. Glancing up, he saw the vibrant outline of a large bird tearing overhead and disappearing behind the mountain face.

No, not a bird. That was a drake, the red scaled wyverns only the finest knights in Dragos rode. Fleeing foot-locked soldiers would be far simpler than escaping the clutches of flying beasts native to these peaks.

Focusing ahead, Arsene scanned every possibility. This path would lead them out of the city, but what then? They had no mounts and no escape route. With every soldier in Lavinia chasing them, their prospects were grim.

The trail curved sharply right, bending around an outcropping. Arsene grabbed Johanna and pulled her to a stop as they rounded the bend.

The path ahead was blocked. Marius stood in their way, a drake snarling behind him.

"Marius!" Arsene blurted out.

The Duke answered with a spell. Fire erupted around Arsene's feet, shooting up above his head, shaping into a blazing wall barring his path forward. Skin burning from the heat, Arsene backed away but felt another surge of flame rise behind his back. Relia grabbed his arm and pressed herself to his side, escaping the fire behind them as Johanna backed into his chest.

"Stop," Marius instructed. "You have nowhere to go."

Hand trembling on his flintlock, Arsene gazed at the Duke. Behind the wall of fire, the vision outlined in flame, Marius' hair burned like flowing lava, and his burgundy mantle shone like a ruby stone cast under torchlight. The drake's rings spread behind him, making it appear as though they belonged to the man.

Mother's favored.

The goddess' chosen.

Irritatingly perfect.

"You want me alive?" Relia shouted. "If you so much as scratch them, I'll-"

"I would never hurt my brother," Marius shouted. "But I need him to stand down."

Metallic thuds sounded behind them, and Arsene turned to see black-clad knights approaching from behind. Boxed in. Trapped.

Kiylla's frightened face appeared clear as day in his memory. Her hand extended toward Fionn, desperate and terrified. Two words had emerged from her mouth: the Llaqtan name for the plane of moving earth, the domain where the Earth Father dwelled.

But Cerei Talav was more than the Llaqtan's name. It was cefran in origin. And Arsene knew what the Tiene had called the overlap of ash and cinder before their histories had been forgotten.

Hand tightening on his satchel as the knights closed in, Arsene spoke a single word, fingers brushing the gems hidden within the leather.

"Bruthine."

A tear sounded across the mountains as the fabric of reality rent. Beneath Arsene's feet erupted a portal, a gateway framed by a silver arch, the same Marius had eagerly pointed out in an ancient tapestry.

Arsene glimpsed Marius' panicked face before they plummeted into the unknown.

CHAPTER FIFTEEN

SCHISM

MARIUS THREW OPEN the royal barrack doors and sped up the stairs. The conference room was abuzz with activity. Several officers gathered around their commander, arguing—about the ashfall, about the leviathan they'd glimpsed, about the other's incompetency and dis-coordination.

Brushing past them, Marius stepped into the war room. Rasvan looked no worse for wear despite the wound he'd taken a few days prior. One arm bound in a sling, he ran the other across his mustache repeatedly as he scanned the city map laid across the table.

Marius stood opposite him. "Should you be up?"

"Can I afford not to be?" Rasvan's deep voice rumbled with pain.

"I suppose not." Marius agreed, scanning the map. "Have the men found anything?"

Wincing, Rasvan stood straight. "We don't know. I'm sending men to sweep regions north of the city the moment the ash clears." He looked up as an evoking knight stepped into the room.

Saluting, the cowled man delivered foul news. "Two knights have been found dead in the dungeon. We've brought them out for identification."

"And Ciprian?"

"He hasn't reported,"

"Find him," Rasvan barked. Saluting again, the evoker departed.

Viridia whispered at the back of Marius' mind. *I don't think Seoras is here any longer.*

What do you mean? Marius questioned.

He has a tempestuous presence. It's gone.

The leviathan had bolted through the sky unsteady and flashing violently. Its strength had been failing. Could they have struck the ground and died?

"Ash and cinder," Marius murmured under his breath. "The danger the fugitive poses cannot be understated. Send out warnings to every tier."

"Yes, my lord."

Turning on his heel, Marius flew down the stairs, mind racing. For everything to catastrophically implode after years of unabated progress. . . he hardly knew what to do.

Aurica awaited him at the bottom of the steps, gripping her voluminous dress tightly. "Did you hear the news of Vasille?"

"Oh, I heard."

Heat burst through the door as Marius held it open for his mother. Pulling her shawl around her mouth, Aurica lowered her voice. "He's dead. Murdered."

Marius walked past her. "Shame." He never liked the Chancellor. A boon had arisen from this night, after all.

Aurica reeled. "Arsene butchered him. In cold blood."

"It wasn't all that cold. Poke a drake and expect to be bitten." Marius retorted, marching down the street. He needed to find Tettiena.

"How can you say that?" Aurica darted in front of him, blocking his path.

"I heard he taunted Arsene before his demise. Boasted about raping the woman he loved." Marius said calmly. "Tell me, do you approve of that?"

"He was trying to prove the boy was a traitor."

Falling silent, Marius glared at her. Retreating as though struck, Aurica's face paled. She realized her error. The one to whom she spoke.

She questioned the judgment of the *goddess*. Stepping around her, Marius entered the shadows where lanterns had been doused.

Ash drifted from the heavens. Within an hour, the intensity would rise to burning embers and choking smoke. The manhunt would be postponed until its end, but Marius doubted the delay would matter.

Their quarry had already vanished.

Men scurried around the half-lit street, seeking shelter before the fiery rain began. Raising a hand, Marius felt for raindrops, but only hot ash grazed his fingers. The unusual rainfall had ceased suddenly after persisting for two full days.

"Marius." Tettiena emerged from the shadows of the mountain and approached, hood pulled over her eyes. One hand gripped her cowl, concealing her mouth. "We should get indoors."

Aurica trailed behind as they returned to the safety of the manor. The lights had been snuffed in here as well. Darkness greeted them, save for a flickering candle in the parlor, where the steward began his rush to relight the estate.

Seoras must have doused our lights. Viridia mused.

Did he take anything? Marius wondered.

I'm not sure. Nothing of value was here.

Waving a hand, Tettiena evoked a candlestick and guided them to the parlor. Setting the candle atop the mantle, she knelt to kindle a fire. Flames burst to life in the obsidian fireplace; rising, Tettiena reached into her cloak and unfurled her fingers, revealing something thought lost.

Relief swept over Marius like a drug when he saw the sapphire jewel resting in her grasp. Once held by the Creiv, gifted to the Gaevral, the Faerdain jewel was still theirs.

"I thought Arsene-" Marius began.

"I asked him for a glimpse." Tettiena clenched her hand. "He didn't seem to realize I'd removed this." She glanced away.

Marius titled his head. "Why did you take it? If you didn't trust him. . ."

"This one's. . . special." Tettiena said evasively. "I wanted to see it."

The Faerdain jewel was connected to her bastard son. Though she rarely mentioned him, Tettiena still harbored lingering remnants of motherly love for the boy she'd long lost. Marius could understand that.

"Good." He ran a hand over his face. "Arsene activated the Bruthine gem. Trapped in that place, they'll be in grave danger."

Bruthine will not welcome them. Viridia agreed. *We have little time.*

Aurica sank into the armchair behind Marius. "And he took the heir with him. You're the only one who can reach them now." She tapped her fingers on the armrest. "I can cover for your absence."

"With luck, I'll find them quickly. Arsene's reasonable. I can talk him out of this."

"Reasonable?" Aurica spluttered. "When you find him, kill him."

Jaw-setting, Marius glowered at her.

Aurica grimaced. "Your unreasonable attachment to him has already put us in jeopardy. You'd choose him over the goddess?"

"Maybe he would not have fled if *you* had not pushed him away."

"*I* pushed him away? You know your brother. He's ungodly. Selfish. Narrow-minded." Aurica spat. "He's exactly the kind of man we're hoping to oust."

Marius knew she was right. Arsene had been a foul-mouthed child who broke every rule set for him. Blaspheming in church, he'd rolled his eyes through sermons and disrespected the clergy when their back was turned. Hoping he'd grow out of it, Marius instead watched his brother discard altruism for self-service.

But he didn't care. Arsene was his little brother. And nothing could change that. With seven years between their births, Arsene would always be the little child who'd clung to his older brother's leg after a nightmare.

"The nascent seed of faith has bloomed in his heart." Marius said. "I will talk to Arsene. And if I find out you ordered his death, in my absence. . ."

Aurica lowered her head, realizing she had twice offended the goddess.

"What should I do?" Tettiena's voice roused him.

Composing himself, Marius stared at the gem in her palm and the rain cascading into an endless ocean beneath its surface. "Beau is in Clodia. You would be safer with him."

"You want me to safeguard it?" Tettiena asked. "Would it not be better to simply destroy it now?"

"No," Aurica said quickly. "It's not time. The people must be united against their common enemy before we can begin."

Relieved, Tettiena wrapped the jewel in a handkerchief and carefully stored it in her breast pocket before covering it with her cloak. "I'll aid Beau, then, see that Clodia is prepared for Relia's arrival. Assuming you bring her back in time."

"I will," Marius promised. "Mother, mobilize the Drake guard. Have them keep an aerial view of the countryside." He turned to leave.

Aurica rose. "You're leaving now?"

"Every moment could spell their deaths."

"Be careful." She pleaded. "And what of the cefran girl? She simply vanished, along with the men."

Marius paused, brow furrowed. *Where would Seoras fly when under duress?*

I can't say. Home, perhaps? Maybe they died. Maybe they simply hide. Viridia suggested. *They alone spell their doom. Fionn is giving out.*

"Spread the word across the Empire," Marius suggested. "Every wall shall display the faces of the enemy until they are found." He marched toward the wall.

Brown twigs blossomed from the black stone, weaving into an archway of blurred, red light. Viridia could traverse the planes as no other being could, yet their course was not so simple. Without knowledge of Bruthine, Arsene could have sent himself to any corner of its fiery depths.

However long it took, Marius would find him. There could be no more room for sympathy, for error. Unconscious, delirious, memories cleansed, whatever it took, Marius would drag Arsene home.

I understand your sympathy, Marius. Viridia whispered. *But you must let him go. He has chosen his course, and for men such as him, only death awaits.*

CHAPTER SIXTEEN
THE SPIDER'S WEB

FEW LIBRARIES EXISTED in Athelstan. Most common folk could not read, and lesser lords rarely kept personal collections. Stories were shared among friends by starlight and seldom committed to pen. Only the capital had a full-fledged collection of historical tomes and imported fables.

Leo had ordered countless books from that place to adorn his shelf. But even for how splendorous Leo found Eglisfelde's library, this Clodian athenaeum made Athelstan's finest collection seem a paltry pile of children's books.

Three stories of books towered above Leo's head, lined on spiral wooden shelves. Tapping the wood, he admired the artistic craftsmanship. Yet, for all its glory, there remained a solitary problem. Most books were fiction, tales of glory, or famous plays. The entire second story was dedicated to sheet music and ballad books.

On a typical day, Leo could spend hours among such tomes, but today, he sought factual accounts.

Oh, how Eckart would laugh.

Turning around, Leo examined the patrons. They did seem the artistic sort. One table housed what appeared to be an entire theatre troupe in garish garb gathered around a scattered pile of sheet music. Sigillus was not called the land of muses for nothing, Leo supposed.

Sighing, he danced up the spiral stairway, flinching as the sun poured through the windows into his eyes. Holding up an arm to shield against the rays, he searched the aisles until he finally located what he sought: historical chronologies.

A broad category. Examining the daunting rows of bookcases, Leo scoured the spines for something relevant. Three shelves down, he found a newer book on the topic he sought: Yuri Llaqta, The Failed Imperial Conversion Attempt of 637 SE.

Flipping the book open, Leo leafed through the pages. This account should detail the missionaries sent to Yuri Llaqta following the war and coup that ousted Imperial troops. Beau had been a significant part of this. If anything could glean insight into the man, perhaps this could.

Feeling around for a seat, Leo found a table hiding from the sun behind a pillar and sank into its chair. Heeled boots clicked on the floor as someone approached, but he recognized the green floral pattern on their long coat.

"This is impossible," a female voice with a thick Llaqtan accent said. "Your people's superstition prevents anything factual from being written."

Leo glanced up at Kiylla's heavily powdered face. "Your people don't even write anything down." He whispered.

"So? We keep records in our own way." She dropped her book onto the table and sat opposite him. "Find anything?"

"Beau proposed the peaceful conversion and led the missionaries," Leo muttered, turning a page. "He married the chief's daughter to prove coexistence was possible."

"He proposed the operation? He never said."

"Yes, but he taught the Qoyllans traditional Viridian, not whatever sect he truly follows."

"Wouldn't that be too bold, even for him?" Kiylla proposed. "I can't find anything on aiceils, let alone a different sect who lives within them. If they are as forbidden as you claim, I wonder how such a practice began."

170

"Don't ask me," Leo shrugged. Eckart had shared little about the aiceil cloister Fionn found. "We knew it would be hoping for too much." Leo paused, reading a page. After the operation's failure, Beau came under fire for the wasted expenditures and was accused of Llaqtan sympathy.

The Vicar was the one who calmed tensions and reminded the Chamber of Lords the purpose of Viridia's messengers: to spread the seeds of her divinity across all lands, no matter the hardships required.

So, they were allies. Beau had warned Consus of an alleged cefran threat then turned around and tried to drown thousands of men while sparing but one witness. One witness who could come home and blame the cefra. The Vicar must have been his ally, and perhaps, the man who ordered their ship sunk.

Strange. Why were they so fixated on a few tribal people who did not live within Imperial lands? Nothing within these pages spoke of cefra.

Snapping the book closed, Leo rose. "I need to learn more about our current Vicar."

"Surely an important figure's life is well-known."

"Not really." Leo returned the book to the shelf. "High-ranking clergymen come from noble families typically, but they forsake their name and lands when they take the oath. Faunus is his clerical name, not what his parents bestowed."

"Ah." Kiylla's brow wrinkled. "Troublesome."

"The problem is, I have no idea where to look." Leo leaned on the shelf, searching for anything written on cefra.

Kiylla rose, and leaned beside him. "I saw you loitering by the ballad shelves."

"It's not everyday I peruse Clodia's finest collection." Leo pulled out a book, shook his head, and returned it. "The greatest bards and playwrights live here."

"Why did you become a knight, then?"

"I didn't have a choice. Second son's lead their family's men." He glanced at her.

"Hm. We Llaqtans become what we choose." Kiylla said.

Leo tilted his head. "I never asked. What did you do? Besides being a radical hero?"

She pursed her lips, staring at him reluctantly. "I. . . trained our horses."

"You did?" Leo forgot the bookshelf and turned to face her. "Why didn't you say? You and Eckart would have been kin."

"I let him go, partially because. . . " She trailed off. "Because he came back for his steed."

Leo grinned. Annoyance shot across Kiylla's face, and her mouth tightened into a pout. She whipped around, listening to something before trotting to the banister and peering over its edge.

She muttered something in Llaqtan. "I need to go." She turned on her heel and disappeared into another aisle.

They had not agreed upon a meeting spot, but Leo supposed they would reconvene near the docks. Confused as to why she had departed so quickly, Leo returned to his search but found nothing about the other race.

Drumming each spine as he walked, Leo arrived at the end of the aisle. Tapping echoed on the floors behind him as though mimicking him. Turning, Leo swallowed heavily when he saw a well-dressed man in a long, dark coat walking with a silver cane.

Beau's dark eyes smiled as he approached. "Leofric. I did not take you for a history enthusiast."

"I love reading!" Leo blurted out. "What brings you here?"

"I was searching for you. Someone pointed me here." He beamed. "Are you done? I'd prefer to walk and talk. The weather's lovely."

"Yes, I'm done." Leo ran a hand down his sleeve nervously. "Is something the matter?"

"No, no. I just wished to talk." He gestured with his cane and swiveled on his heel. "Come."

Glancing behind him, Leo followed the lord down the steps and onto the street. Shadows, Clodia was bright today. Shading his eyes, Leo scanned the people walking the street. Some walked with indifference, but others checked over their shoulders and hurried on their way. Fear of the missing Llaqtan prisoner had permeated the people.

"It's been years," Beau said, leading Leo west. "You were just a tiny child the last time I saw you in Clodia."

A carriage raced past, kicking up water from a puddle. Flinching from the splash, Leo ran a hand through his hair. "Has it been that long?"

"Longer." Beau joked. He paused at a street corner, under a hanging basket of flowers, wilted as winter arrived. "I feel terrible for what your Legion went through. For the troubles you faced on the seas." Turning right, he continued strolling.

"There's no need," Leo assured him. "Such is a knight's duty."

"Perhaps," Beau mused. "But you'll not refuse a small gesture of goodwill. I'd like to extend a dinner invitation to you at my estate."

"You're too kind, but-"

"We have much to discuss and might as well accompany the dialogue with good wine." Beau paused again under an unlit lantern. "And bring your lady friend with you."

"I'm afraid I'm not courting anyone," Leo said.

"Is that so?" Beau turned, a sinister glint in his eye. "Then why were you and Kiylla following me the other night?"

A lump caught in Leo's throat as he stared at Beau. The street was quiet, for being so close to the city center. A couple passed across the road, but few others.

"What are you-" Leo tried.

Beau interrupted again. "Let's not waste time. You're a wretched liar. An evoker does not forget the face of a woman he's known since she was but a babe."

Biting his lip, Leo stepped back. "Are you threatening me?"

"Not yet." Beau folded his hands on his cane. "Bring Kiylla with you. Tomorrow evening at the seventh hour. Fail to show, and perhaps I will share your little secret with your commanding officer."

Consus would be struck by the betrayal but would not hesitate to turn Leo in. Left with no other choice, Leo reluctantly agreed. "Fine. Are you going to tell me why?"

"As I said." Beau snatched up his cane. "We have much to discuss. Tomorrow night." He reiterated. "Seventh hour. Dress in your best." Smiling, he sauntered away.

At a loss for words, Leo remained rooted to the spot. A horse trotted by, hooves kicking up a puddle. Droplets flew past Leo's eyes, rousing him from his stupor, and he hurried down the street. Skidding to a stop, he peered into a less traveled road tucked behind two shops with only two denizens: a man unloading a cart into his shop's backdoor and the short-haired woman Leo sought.

Laying low, Kiylla darted toward him, but Leo grabbed her and pulled her aside, checking to ensure the other man paid them no mind. "We have a problem."

"Why do you always start like that? Just say what your-" Kiylla began.

"Beau. He knows about you. He's invited us to dinner with him, threatening to tell all if we refuse."

Kiylla's eyebrows shot up, and she stepped back, scanning the street as she considered the information. After a long think, she returned to him.

"A strange request. He is planning something, but I don't know what." She smirked. "But if Beau wishes to dance with fire, then let us meet his threat with flame."

The Rosa family defied Clodian style. Rustic wood furniture on cozy woven rugs reminded Leo of home, not of the sterile, stately capital. Potted plants and hanging ivy covered the building, accents to wooden sculptures of trees.

Even the dining table housed a tiny potted sapling, its leaves barely beginning to bud. Leo forced a smile, accepting a glass of wine from Beau's tall and thin steward, and returned to staring at the unusual decor.

"Is that appreciation, I spy?" Beau asked, grabbing a glass of his own. "Or distaste?"

"It's. . . different," Leo commented, fussing with his cravat.

Kiylla brushed her hair behind her ear. "He decorates to honor the goddess, just as back home."

Nodding, Beau raised his glass. "Precisely." He tilted his head. "I must commend the disguise. You hardly look like the girl I recall."

Leaning forward, Kiylla pressed her hands to her knees. "We have humored your whims. What do you want?"

"Impatient as ever." He set his glass down. "What does a dinner together mean, if not an invitation to camaraderie, to friendship?"

"A chance to poison someone." Leo offered.

"There are far simpler ways to kill you, Leofric," Beau said darkly. Reclining, he crossed his legs. "You, an otherwise devout knight, have allied with the Empire's most hated enemy. I cannot help but wonder why."

The steward returned, plates of grilled fish in hands. The smell was heavenly, but Leo could not muster an appetite.

Thanking his steward with a smile, Beau watched Leo expectantly.

"Why must I answer first?" Leo questioned. "From what I've seen, your actions have far surpassed treason into outright war."

"A bold accusation. One without cause."

"Oh, I have that in spades." Leo sat forward. "Should I recount the Femoran wave? Should I remind you who detained Eckart, who led Consus from the town?"

"Coincidence." Beau deflected.

Undeterred by the threat of poison, Kiylla dug into the meal. She had not been given much to eat during her captivity. Such food must have been a luxury.

Pausing between bites, Kiylla cleared her throat. "Leofric has seen the Earth Father. He came to me with questions. He might have simply handed me over if not for the ship that attempted to sink us."

"But I realized I'm in over my head." Leo set his jaw. "And could trust no one within the city. Let alone you."

"Oh?" Beau raised an eyebrow. "You think I sent that ship?"

"Who else? You wanted us dead in Femora. Why not finish the job?"

"Ask yourself this, Leofric. What cause have I to kill you?"

Biting his lip, Leo glanced around the room. "Because Femora did not go as planned. Because Consus became suspicious about your intentions."

"Shallow presumptions." Beau plucked his fork from the table. "Enough. We are here because I see a potential ally within you. Not a man I seek to kill." Confident and in control, he chewed thoughtfully as he stared at Kiylla. "She has surely told you of our correspondence?"

"Yes." Leo stared at his fork, unwilling to touch it.

"Then you understand where my sympathies lie." Beau tapped the table with his fork. "The Emperor is an unpopular man. How deeply have you paid attention to him?"

"Passingly." Leo balled his fists in his lap, sitting stiffly. "He began the first Llaqtan war as an eager young man. He changed the balance of the Chamber, granting the clerical branch immunity from accusations from all but fellow Chamber Lords."

"And you saw what happened in Fairborough as a result." Beau pointed with his fork.

"Yes," Leo said rigidly.

"And then he begins another war to reclaim his lost legacy." Beau stabbed a sprout with his fork. "One many protested, remembering how bloodied Llaqtan soil became in the past."

The two countries had been skirmishing for centuries. To be the Emperor who finally tamed the pagan beast. . . Leo understood why the man had leaped at the chance.

"So we kill him," Kiylla concluded.

"No." Beau cut his hand through the air. "Two paths follow from death: Your execution leads to a great spectacle, a renewed vigor from the people to end your people. His death leads to patriotism and desire for revenge from the party responsible."

"And," She concluded. "Both lead to a drawn-out war."

"Yes, but," Beau grabbed the bottle of wine and slowly refilled his glass. "What if we turn the people against him instead? We spread rumors. We heighten the Chamber's concern. We remind the people of those who died and those who will."

"So? You cannot depose an Emperor." Leo said.

"You can." Beau set the bottle down. "Our country was so named for the Sigil engraved in the palace floors—the mark of the goddess, writ with elaborate text. Have you seen it?"

"Once. The letters around the laurel were too small to read."

"There, the founders inscribed a law that has never been invoked. Should all six Chamber lords agree the sitting Emperor has betrayed the goddess, he will be replaced with one more worthy."

"Never been invoked?" Leo uncurled his fingers. "How would we convince them to make an unprecedented move?"

"We could not do so alone," Beau agreed. "But General Parnesius of the First saw the atrocities, the death, the futility. Would his words mean something?"

"Maybe, but he wouldn't-"

"No, he wouldn't. Consus harbors deep loyalty to his country and his Empire. But not necessarily to the man sitting on its throne now."

"So, Leo convinces this general to speak." Kiylla leans her elbow on the armrest. "Say it even works. Who takes the throne?"

"Leofric has already met her." Beau picked up his glass and sat back.

Relaxing, Leo stared at his plate. "Relia."

More questions floated through Leo's mind, but he bit them back. Every word from Beau's mouth could be a lie, and anything Leo said could reveal something he would rather keep.

"Who?" Kiylla asked.

"The heir," Beau answered. "The rightful heir. His daughter."

"And I'm to trust this girl will honor my people?"

"She will," Beau promised.

"Relia's an empathetic soul." Leo looked up. "Beau's right. It's a half-decent plan if I thought it would work." He stared at Beau. "What good does Consus' word do?"

"His father is close friends with Lord Drusus; they served together in the first war." Beau swirled his wine. "Do you see?"

"I have sway with Consus." Leo could see the reason in Beau's idea, the path to the other Chamber members. "And if I refuse?"

"Must I repeat my earlier threat?"

"No." Leo ground his jaw. "Fine. I'll do what I can to convince Consus and his father."

"You've always been a reasonable lad."

"And in return, we'll keep our silence." Leo glowered. "Because we could each ruin the other."

"Indeed." Beau agreed. "Step carefully. Your disguise is good, but no disguise is good enough to last forever. Lord Drusus can command the men to end the march, but only if the Emperor gives the word."

"I know that well." Kiylla rose. She grabbed the half-empty bottle of wine. "Thank you for the hospitality."

That horrible smile stretched across Beau's face. "The pleasure was all mine."

Eager to leave, Leo shot to his feet and followed Kiylla outside. A cloudy pall hung over the city, and mist permeated the air. Chilled by the foul weather, Leo shivered as the gates swung close behind them.

Gripping the bottle like a weapon, Kiylla spun to face him. "He is using us."

"For what, exactly?"

"I don't know." Kiylla pursed her lips. "He is a Chamber Lord. Does he think he could not convince his peers alone?"

"Maybe not."

"No matter. We shall use him in return."

"How?"

"I haven't decided yet." She looked away. "He is powerful. He has sway. Gold. Soldiers. And he is right. I was shortsighted to think of assassination. The people would demand blood."

"Most likely. But to convince the entire Chamber?" Leo rubbed his arms, warding off the cold.

"Consus has an eloquent tongue," Kiylla remarked. "Draw him to your side, and become the man from those stories you love so much."

"Now you're making fun of me."

"I'm not. You told those stories of yours with such enthusiasm. You sounded like a different man." Kiylla poked Leo's chest. "Become him. And perhaps they will listen."

"And what about you?"

"I will uncover the truth of this Vicar." Kiylla toyed with the bottle's cork.

Leo glanced down. "Decide you needed payment?"

"Yes. I have been through enough. I have earned some wine."

Wind howled through the lonely street and shook the birch trees. Profound anger ripped through Leo, and he could not keep it from his face. A snarl ripped across his lips.

Kiylla noticed. Stepping closer, she lowered her voice. "I do not regret what I did. I would do it again in a heartbeat. And you cannot forgive me for that."

"No." Leo agreed. "I can't."

"Then leave the past where it is, and pray the phantoms take my mind so that I receive the punishment I am due." Breaking his gaze, she disappeared into the haze.

Though he had been seething with anger, Leo reached for her arm, futilely. Kiylla was gone.

Part of Leo wished such a punishment upon her. Part of him wanted anything but. And another wanted to call for her to return and wile the night away with him, sharing the last of the wine.

Life had been simple, once upon a time. Now, Leo needed to convince Consus to follow Beau's scheme or face the traitor's pyre.

CHAPTER SEVENTEEN

REQUIEM

WULF AWOKE FROM a deep sleep to feel biting wind tearing his skin and howling in his ears. Gritting his teeth, his hands dug into soft earth as he struggled to his knees and tore his misaligned helmet off so he could see.

He stood in the sky. Black storm clouds churned around him, flashing with lightning and rumbling with thunder. Relentless wind ripped through every crack in his armor, every tiny hole in the fabric of his doublet. A sea of yellow grass bucked under the breeze, yet the purple flowers blooming from their tips remained motionless.

Was this a dream?

Someone lay crumpled nearby. Crawling forward, Wulf noticed dark blue fabric billowing in the breeze, clamped down by steel armor. Gasping, he rushed to Eckart's side and rolled him onto his back. Bruises covered one half of Eckart's face and burns streaked scars across his hands. And though he did not awaken, his chest rose and fell. Alive.

Desperate, Wulf searched the area for Fionn. He could see no further than five paces in any direction; the storm clouds covered the world like a thick fog. Flinching as he staggered forward, he braced to enter their pall and be struck.

Static rushed around him; his hair stood on end. Through the black, he glimpsed silver, a pile of hair scattered around a woman lying on her side in a field of lavender blooms.

Kneeling beside Fionn, Wulf brushed the hair from her eyes. Her jerkin was tattered, the undershirt ripped and stained with blood. Her eyes cracked open. "Wulf?" she asked weakly.

That was her voice, not the entity who controlled her. Relieved yet taken aback, Wulf hesitated before answering. "You remember me?"

"He does," Fionn answered. Unfurling her clenched fingers, she revealed an emerald jewel.

Wulf recalled seeing this stitched into her scarf. In this place, it radiated with divine majesty. Lightning thrummed in the heavens around it, reflecting the storm within the stone. Like a beating heart, the storm clouds appeared to circle the gem, the wind dancing in mimicry to the tornadoes raging beneath the surface.

"Are we alive?" Fionn asked groggily.

"I think so," Wulf answered, helping her sit up. "What happened? Last I remembered. . ." He shook his head, dazed. Clinging to the leviathan's back, they'd fallen to their deaths.

"Eckart must have done something." Fionn guessed, shakily standing. Clutching her cloak, she limped to Eckart's side and collapsed to her knees. "Eckart?" She asked, shaking him awake.

After a few tries, Eckart's eyelids tightened before slowly opening. Taking a moment to gain his bearings, he looked between them, disoriented, before sitting bolt upright.

"It worked?" Eckart gasped. "Thank the ancestors; it worked." He winced, touching his back. "Not well, though."

Smiling faintly, Fionn tucked the emerald jewel into her scarf. "You remembered this place's name? I'm surprised. Seoras thought you were tuning me out."

"I'm an evoker, aren't I?" Eckart tested his legs and stood.

He must have activated the jewel. Wulf scrunched his nose, trying to recall if Fionn had ever mentioned the name of the plane to which the emerald jewel belonged. Seoras' Breath. That's what her people called the relic.

"What is this place?" He asked.

"Casaliede," Fionn answered. "We should get moving. The storm's quiet for now, but it's ever-changing." She trudged away.

"Wait." Wulf grabbed her wrist. "What happened? With your necklace shattered, I thought your memories were lost, that you'd be mindless."

Fionn's countenance cracked with sorrow. "They're still gone—her memories. But something remains—the way Seoras saw her life. It's. . . confusing." She looked mournfully at Eckart. "*He* thought you were tuning me out. What did *she* think?"

"She?" Wulf repeated, concerned. "Why are you referring to yourself like that?"

"She doesn't feel like me." Fionn touched her head. "Is she me? The one through whom he sees the world?"

"Wulf." Eckart said tensely.

Something moved in the clouds. A mere impression within the shadows, a snake-like entity slithered through the sky, eyes bright as emeralds. Draconic spines surged with lightning on its back as it passed them by, ten times taller than their height. And then it vanished.

Wulf would have assumed he merely imagined the beast if not for Eckart's gaping stare.

Fionn blinked. When her eyelids reopened, they shone with otherworldly light. A familiar echo entered her voice as another spoke through her. "We have a problem," Seoras announced.

"You don't say?" Wulf said bitterly.

Stepping into a cloud, Fionn waved her hand, and the lightning dispersed with a gust of wind, revealing a stretch of yellow field. "The leviathan was never meant to be wielded by another. Fionn has bled herself dry. She will soon give out."

Wulf marched in front of her. "Then do something about it."

Glowering at Wulf, Seoras stepped away. "I might be able to. There exists within this place a heart, of sorts. I might be able to use the concentrated magic there to restore her lost blood." She looked over her shoulder. "But it will be dangerous. I don't know if we'll make it in time."

"Then what are we waiting for?" Wulf gripped his spear. "Which way?"

"Here," Fionn mumbled, wandering into the storm.

Releasing his spear, Wulf tried to follow her. Boots skidding through the mud as relentless gales forced him back, Wulf unstrapped the heavy armor he'd stolen and tossed it away. Some pieces barely touched the grass before the storm swept them away.

Lighter on his feet, Wulf managed to press forward, glancing behind him to ensure Eckart was still with him. Breathing heavily, he raised a hand to shield his eyes.

"Watch your step," Fionn warned.

Pulling his foot back, Wulf grimaced as the toe of his boot retracted from the cliff side. Pebbles tumbled off the edge, disappearing into endless darkness.

They *were* in the sky. Storm clouds extended in every direction, above and below. Lightning streaked deep in the darkness, and thunder rumbled somewhere below their feet, shaking the ground and swaying the grass.

"Spirits." Eckart cursed, noticing the drop-off before a cloud swept in and obscured it.

"Stay close," Fionn called.

Hurrying to catch up, Wulf stared at the woman inquisitively. "So what are you? A bird, a dragon, or. . . incorporeal?"

"The bird is my familiar. A stalwart companion through the ages." Seoras answered, voice thrumming in time with the thunder. "The leviathan could be called my truest self."

"And the rest?"

"Gods do not walk the land as people do. Not your ancestors, not Viridia."

Static surged through the clouds. Lightning flashed, blinding Wulf. Ducking, he shielded his head as pain reverberated through his bones. Eckart stumbled to his side, touching his shoulder.

"You alright?"

"For now." Wulf's voice was strained. Rubbing his eyes, he focused on Fionn and trudged forward. Hanging behind her, he looked to Eckart. "Do you think it's who it says it is?"

Eckart tucked his hair behind his ears, but the wind yanked it free. "I don't know. Legends arise from somewhere. Every play was based on something. Even if the truth is forgotten along the way."

"You don't sound convinced."

"My people worship them. Now I know at least one exists." Eckart stumbled under a powerful breeze. "Who am I to say he's not what he claims?"

"Imperials' fervent worship doesn't make Viridia real," Wulf murmured. Arsene had said as much countless times.

Arsene. Wulf's mind fell quiet, thinking of his partner. A distant bang, a sharp crack, had sounded across the mountains during their struggle with Tettiena. Arsene's flintlock—Death Knell. Who had he been firing at?

"Eckart," Wulf shouted over the wind. "Tell me about Seoras."

"Our fables, you mean?" Eckart replied. "I'm not a storyteller, and-" He buckled as another lightning flash blinded them. "I'd have to shout."

"I'll tell you myself." Seoras hissed back at them. "Later."

"Lucky us." Eckart tried to lighten the mood. Eyes darting to the ground, he stopped in his tracks. "Wulf! Look at this."

Steadying himself, Wulf kneeled down. "What?"

"Here." Eckart pointed at upturned dirt. "Something raked up the earth here." He paused. "Talons, I think. You can see them there."

Not much of a tracker, Wulf could only faintly make out what might have been gouges. Much of the loose dirt had blown away in the storm. "How big do you think it was?"

"Massive." Eckart spread his arms. "Thirty. . . forty paces across."

"Bigger than a scade?"

"Is that one of those Athelstani horrors?" Eckart yelled. "Yes. Bigger than Leo's descriptions, anyhow."

"Here. This way." Seoras' voice cut through the storm with ease.

Squinting, eyes dried out by the wind, Wulf did not see what Seoras pointed out until something brushed his head. Surprised, he drew his spear but relaxed when he managed to glean the shape of branches and leaves above his head.

Wide canopies of violet leaves reached into the storm clouds and pushed them apart. Lightning crackled through them, tracing through the boughs into the trunk before being absorbed into the ground.

Gasping for breath, Fionn slid down the trunk to the ground. "We can rest here." Raising a hand, she commanded the wind. Swirling like a whirlpool, it gathered the black clouds and pushed them away, creating a small pocket of tranquility.

Lightning struck down toward their heads but slammed into the canopies and fizzled out as though warded off by a shield. Figuring they would be safer here than anywhere else, Wulf dropped to a knee, grateful for a chance to catch his breath.

"Can we afford to stop?" Eckart asked.

"No," Seoras said. "But we will die all the same if we do not rest."

Nodding, Eckart sat beside Wulf heavily. Wulf looked him up and down. "How are you holding up?"

"I'm fine," Eckart assured him, turning over his burnt hands. Tearing a chunk off his robes, he laid it across his knee and cupped his palm. Water pooled within his grasp, gently freezing into a shard of ice. Wrapping it in the cloth, he pressed it against the burns and sagged with relief.

Fionn pulled up her knees—not Fionn, Seoras. Her demeanor shifted when the supposed god took hold. Her eyes darkened, and a severe mien replaced the gentle yet coy smile she typically wore.

"How close are we to this heart?" Wulf asked.

"I'm not sure," Seoras admitted. "It's not far, and yet, not easy to reach. But I might have an idea."

"What's that?"

Seoras did not answer. Wulf waited for a response before trying a different query.

"What is this heart, exactly?"

"The eye of the storm," Seoras explained. "If this world is a tempest, that place beats with the power of every cloud that has ever brewed."

"Sounds dangerous." Eckart looked up. "Are you sure you can harness it?"

The asshole god did not deign to answer. Annoyed, Wulf waited impatiently for a response before speaking up again.

"Do you think being cryptic makes you seem more, I don't know, mystical?"

"Would it kill you to be silent?" Seoras asked.

"I just don't understand." Wulf leaned closer to Fionn. "If you're a god, just heal her."

"I cannot." Seoras' expression darkened further. Shadows appeared below Fionn's eyes. "An evoker cannot mend a wound simply because you ask it of them."

"What exactly is the purpose of you, then?" Wulf demanded. "You force her on this quest, drain her strength, and cannot even prevent her capture or slow death?"

"I had no choice but to use her." Seoras hissed. "To send her after our relics. Do you know what happens if they succeed? If they crush these jewels into dust?"

"What happens?" Eckart asked tepidly.

"Gaps exist in the veil, where the fire of Bruthine blows in, and the shifting earth of Cerei Talav nudges Llaqtan soil," Seoras said. "This, humans have known for centuries. But more has been forgotten. From these planes, cefran magic arises. From there, we draw our charged blood. Seal them off, and we die the same as if we'd been sliced with a knife and left to bleed out."

"Wait." Eckart shifted the ice to his other hand. "Beau, the Duke, my mother. . . They want to exterminate the cefra? Why?'

"Do you recall what your mother used to say?" Seoras said quietly. "People merely fear what is different, but one day that will not be so?"

Eckart looked down. "She did." His face tore with grief when he raised his head. "To say that to my face. . ."

"I don't understand," Wulf said. "They smash the jewels, kill the cefra, and what, that's all they want?"

"No. They don't seek cruelty." Seoras denied. "Think of Femora. Beau and Consus would have returned to Clodia to announce another massacre carried out by cefra. The first sinkhole, enabled by cefra."

"They blame us for the massacre. For the wave." Eckart murmured.

"Other disasters would follow." Seoras continued. "Suddenly, the cefra would attack the Altanese and Sylfestran neighbors they had lived peacefully with for ages. The Empire would peacefully suggest humanity unite against its greatest foe." Seoras paused. "Create an enemy to deliver salvation. Bound as one they wipe out their foe."

"But that unification would only last for a generation." Wulf surmised. "Maybe less."

"Who can say?" Seoras agreed. "I don't intend to let them have it at all." He paused, staring into the distance. "The Dragosi prince was not in the manor. He was in the mountains, but I had to make a choice —rescue his gems or mine."

"You mean Arsene." Wulf watched the violet lightning crackle through the leaves. "I don't know why he was out there." Wulf paused. "Arsene is no saint. He'd do what he judged best for his survival and gain."

"Then he'll be in Dragos still. Once we escape, we'll find him, and take the jewels where they can never again be found, nor used." Seoras decided. "Now let me rest. And think."

"Wait. Fionn said her memories are gone, but yours aren't. Is she okay?"

Seoras gazed up, and Wulf feared he would not answer. But, eventually, he looked down. "When Fionn joined her maevruthan, my memories remained in her mind alone. They do, still, for they were never joined to her crystal. She can see you through my gaze."

"Great," Eckart said jokingly, nudging Wulf. "She'll hate you."

"No." Wulf furrowed his brow. "You sent me those dreams. You picked me for a reason. What did they mean?"

"Look within them," Seoras said cryptically. "And find the answer."

"One more thing." Wulf leaned forward. "Tettiena wants me alive. Why?"

"I heard as much." Seoras murmured. "I don't know. You're unremarkable. Now, leave me alone." Ending the conversation, Fionn's eyes closed, and a songbird flew through the trees, disappearing into the storm.

"Spirits. You're useless." Wulf turned around and scooted closer to Eckart. Wrapping an arm around his knees, he laid his head in his hand.

Wincing, Eckart removed his chunk of ice and checked his hands. "What's the story with your spear? To go back for it like that?"

"It was my father's," Wulf answered. "All I have left of him."

"Ah." Eckart understood. "Ah." He repeated, struck by a realization. "Fairborough."

"Right."

"Do you think he envisioned his son stabbing the Dragosi general with it? Or deciphering cryptic dreams from a god?"

Wulf chuckled. His Father had taken everything in stride. Would his face even have cracked? "I wasn't allowed to fight with him, let alone champion a false god. He'd be proud of my progress."

"Don't test Seoras. Humor his divinity, at least."

"I've never been good at keeping my mouth shut."

"I've noticed," Eckart observed. He leaned forward. "You promised us a tale, oh god of bards."

Fionn's eyes peeled open, and Seoras' intense gaze met theirs. "I said I would share. I did not say when." The eyes snapped shut again.

Eckart shrugged. "It was worth a try."

Sighing, Wulf flopped onto his back and stared at the violet ceiling of intertwined leaves. By nothing short of a miracle, they still lived. Without magic, without power, any promise Wulf made would ring hollow. He was but a man with a spear, far out of his league.

"Oh." Eckart reached back and pulled a small sheath from Fionn's bag. "This is yours."

His dagger. Grabbing the hilt, Wulf drew it from its scabbard. Just a shitty knife meant for cutting meat and snapping cords. How had it blossomed into so much more?

Shoulders sinking, Wulf realized Fionn could not recall the day she stole it nor the reason she had held onto it. Returning it to its scabbard, he fastened it to his belt. Maybe one day she could swipe it again, with that cheeky smile on her face.

He wanted to rush to Fionn's side, tend to her wounds, hold her close and tell her everything would be alright. A barrier kept her from him. The god of freedom who had stolen hers.

This foreign world was one of misery. Biting wind ceaselessly pierced Wulf's doublet and tore his skin. Walking against the currents was draining, and the ground felt ready to give out with each rumble of thunder.

Food was scarce. A few rations remained in Fionn's bag, but only enough for a few days. Wulf had insisted Fionn take the bulk of it. Watching her toss and turn in her sleep, chest rising shallowly, skin sallow and pale, Wulf realized Seoras spoke true. She was dying, bleeding out from the inside from a wound that could not be healed.

She had not felt well on the boat ride home. Why had he not noticed sooner?

"Seoras," Eckart called. "Say we find this heart, and it works as you hope. What then?"

"Then. . ." Fionn's voice echoed through the wind, hardly sounding like the woman Wulf knew. "Then we return to the Aeourant. The girl's memories must be restored."

"That's a world away from Arsene."

"If he's even still alive," Wulf added. "Who knows what's happening in Lavinia now."

Eckart closed his eyes. "I hope Tefnut's alright."

Wulf mustered a chuckle. "You and that goat. Relia's still there. I'm sure she'll take care of it."

"Sh." Fionn held up a hand, ordering them to halt. "It's near."

"What is?" Wulf asked. Seoras had yet to share this so-called plan.

Eckart watched the storm clouds around them, ears perking up as his eyes darted around. "Do you hear that?" He whispered.

Concentrating, Wulf listened. Thunder rumbled quietly in the distance, different from before. Heavy cracks had whipped across the heavens at random intervals, sending quakes through the ground. This thunder beat like a rhythmic drum in this distance, steady and constant. And it was growing louder.

"Very near." Seoras' voice dripped with anticipation. Fionn broke into a jog.

Racing to keep up, Wulf's heart beat rapidly as the drumbeats approached. Something moved in the clouds, a great shadow growing closer. Lightning screeched past, charging the flowers beneath the tempest with crackling light.

Fionn halted at an abrupt drop-off. Naught but endless sky awaited them beyond and below. Joining her at the edge, Wulf saw something break through the storm.

The drum beats soared to ear-shattering highs as a beast flew past. Great wings flapped, their reverberations clapping with thunder, dispersing the clouds. With a heavy thud that shook the sky, it landed on a floating island several paces away.

An avian as tall as a two-story building perched across from them. Four wings settled on its back as the drumbeats ceased, its feathers blazing with violet, black, and green, patterned like a butterfly's wings.

Long trailing feathers streamed from its head, deep charcoal surging with electric light.

It stared at them with bottomless, black eyes. Intelligent eyes. Watching them. Waiting.

Fionn's face cracked with nostalgia. "There she is," Seoras muttered. Snapping out of whatever reverie had claimed him, Seoras turned to Wulf. "We'll never reach the heart on foot. But stormsingers can be tamed."

"Spirits." Eckart breathed. "She left those marks. Are we sure we want to disturb it?"

Wulf glanced at the stormsinger's sharp talons, black ebony the length of a spear. "How do you tame it?"

"Respect," Seoras enunciated. "You only need earn the respect of a stormsinger who has shown itself to you. Once, I. . . I sang for one." Fionn closed her eyes, remembering deep pain. But was it her or Seoras who flinched from the emotions?

The enormous creature tilted its head. The feathers on its crown flexed, extending outward. Its motions were quick, jerky, alien. Wulf could tell it understood them and was listening.

"We've drawn its interest." Fionn opened her eyes. "But it will not wait for long."

"Then sing for it again," Wulf demanded.

"She can't." Seoras insisted. "Without her memories, she would be as a child floundering with her first lyre."

"Not her. You." Wulf pressed. "You're the god of bards, aren't you?"

"I. . ." Seoras stuttered. "I have not sung for. . ." He trailed off.

With every breath, Seoras sounded more like a man and less like a god. But he was confined to Fionn, trapped within her, formless himself. The songbird might heed his call, the wind might answer to him, but he could not speak with her voice or walk amongst the living.

What was he, really?

"You can't do anything without her." Wulf accused. "You've stolen her life, her everything. Without the heart, she'll die. You said you've tamed one before. *Do it again.*"

Fionn's eyes blazed with anger, but only fleetingly. Her eyelids drooped as the one within her mind considered the suggestion.

Stepping away from Wulf, Fionn teetered on the cliff and laid a hand across her heart.

A song erupted in the storm. The wind whirled in harmony, and thunder crashed like drums—just like the day Wulf had first glimpsed Fionn and fallen in love with her.

The voice that emerged sounded not like Fionn, not like the underlying echo in her voice when Seoras spoke. It sounded distant. Youthful. And the words belonged to a language Wulf did not understand.

But he gleaned their meaning. Palpable emotion traced through the wind, weighing on him and dragging him down: pain, isolation, longing. Eckart buckled under the weight of the song, his face creased with agony and understanding.

Water sprung from the ground like a fountain, and rain joined the storm as Eckart's magic surged. Panicked, Eckart sank to a knee and looked around, bewildered. He had not cast this spell—it had been drawn forth by the emotions.

Deep loneliness permeated Wulf's being—from the music and Eckart's magic—two cefran catalysts intertwining into one.

Through the deluge of rain, Wulf understood. The song came from them both. Fionn's despair at watching her clan across an insurmountable gap through a liar's eyes and Seoras' anguish sprung from missing something terribly.

Across the clouds, the stormsinger moved, extending its wings and bowing its head, responding to their call.

The music ended abruptly. The wind blew wildly, and the rain ceased. Eckart gasped for breath, wiping tears from his cheeks. Wulf touched his cheek and retracted his hand to see two water droplets.

"What was that?" Eckart asked, wild-eyed.

"Did you understand the words?" Wulf asked quietly.

"Only. . . only a few." Standing, Eckart regained his composure. "Something about a tower. Something about home."

"Enough." Fionn barked. Whatever vulnerability Seoras had displayed was gone now. "Get on. We're running out of time."

The stormsinger took flight, landing behind them, its talons raking through the muck. Lowering itself to the ground, it beckoned them to mount and ride into the unknown.

LAND OF DRAGONS

TUMBLING FROM A barren mountain layered with hot ash into a field of gentle flowers should have been impossible. Yet the soft blooms caught Arsene's fall, preventing injury. Death Knell slipped from his grasp and fell at his side, steel gleaming with orange light. Rising to his knees, he looked around wildly.

Incredible. A meadow of yellow flowers clustered around a riverbank where rich red clay plunged into crystal clear water. Stunted trees a mere three paces tall dotted the field, their thin branches covered with luminescent orange blossoms.

Just as in the aiceil. Just as in Marius' tapestry. This was Bruthine, the unreachable plane responsible for the deluge of fiery rain that had long since melted life from the Dragosi mountains.

Arsene's breath caught as he looked up. Perfect blackness coated the heavens, save for a streak of red centered above. Extending as far as the eye could see, the red belt bent with the world, circumnavigating this entire world.

Scales glimmered on the red belt, reflecting light from below. Was that a giant serpent clinging to the sky?

Shooting to his feet, Arsene grabbed Death Knell and shoved it into his holster. An ashfall had begun back home, but this place remained still. Arsene held out a hand, feeling for falling debris lest it be invisible. Only humidity brushed his fingers as the searing heat of this place struck him. Strange. Fog gathered on the ground, as though rain had recently fallen.

Unfurling his fingers, Arsene stared at Diorbhail's Ember. The ruby looked nothing like it had before. Flames licked at his hand, though they did not burn. Bright light surged within the stone as though lava threatened to overflow at any moment.

Pain flared through his hand, and a flash caught his eye. Whirling around, he pointed Death Knell at what he thought had been a person. Fire lingered in the air, imitating the shape of a woman clad in a flowing gown, and a face appeared in the flickering heat.

But then it was gone.

Lowering his flintlock, Arsene paced around the river, searching for the two women who'd been with him before activating the jewel. He saw no sign of Relia, nor Johanna. But he and Fionn had landed in the Earth Father's domain together. Had Arsene done something wrong?

Gritting his teeth, he looked up at the serpentine belt in the sky. It was moving, ever so slightly, like a snake slithering through black mud. Hearing a soft crackle, he whirled around, expecting to see the flaming woman again, but nothing was behind him.

Kneeling beside the river, he splashed water over his face. He had to find Relia, and get back home. There was no time for nerves.

Grabbing a handful of glowing orange flowers from the trees, Arsene knelt and filled his waterskin before choosing a direction and walking. The women could be anywhere. Or back home, in Lavinia city.

Ash and cinder, where was he even going? Part of him screamed to simply use the gem and return home; but the other couldn't leave the women stranded here.

Jagged black shadows appeared on the horizon, ominous through the thick fog. Swiping at the annoying haze in a vain attempt to clear it, Arsene froze when he heard something moving nearby.

Raising Death Knell, he narrowed his eyes, focusing on the shape approaching from the west. A woman in a tattered cloak and gambeson approached, her red hair fallen loose from a ponytail.

Arsene breathed a sigh of relief. "Relia!" Rushing to her side, he checked her for injury. A few bruises, but she was otherwise unharmed.

"There you are." She exclaimed. "Where's Johanna?"

"I don't know."

"I-" Her face blanched and she shut her mouth.

A roar reverberated through the earth. Every hair on Arsene's body stood on end. He'd never hear such a deep, powerful noise before. It sounded not unlike Fionn's leviathan.

"We need to find her. Now." Relia decided, drawing her rapier and leading the way.

"Wait. We need to gain our bearings."

"Follow the serpent!" She gestured up. "He runs north to south."

Electing to trust her, Arsene held his flintlock close.

They marched on in silence. A tiny, niggling voice at the back of Arsene's mind pecked at him. *Apologize.* It insisted. *Say something to her.* But Arsene apologized only to Marius, and even then, quite rarely. He swirled his tongue in his mouth, considering the idea, but was unable to commit.

Relia hadn't needed to know of her heritage. It would have only complicated her life prematurely. Swallowing, Arsene looked at the red-haired girl walking ahead of him.

"Relia. . ." He tried, trailing off.

"Yes?"

Rubbing his shoulder, Arsene hesitated. "You're the heir. Have you decided how you feel about that?"

"I haven't thought much about it," Relia admitted. "I'm not a ruler." She laughed, spreading her arms. "Look at me. I'd be a disaster in every sense."

"You could marry a politically savvy man."

"Who?" She shook her head. "Look at where we are. It's a problem for another day."

"Yes, but-" Arsene yelped. His hand had been pressed to the jewel bag, and a horrid burning coursed through his fingers. Retracting his hand, he shook the pain away as red light flared within the bag and slowly faded. "What in Viridia's sweet bosom was that?"

"Did you see that?" Relia asked.

Fire flared to life behind them, though it had no source. The face appeared again within the raging inferno, with limbs and the impression of a flowing gown. Arsene had but a moment to register the woman's features before she vanished, and the jewel fell cold.

"I thought I was hallucinating." Arsene muttered. He gasped. "What?"

A thousand thoughts raced through Arsene's mind, but he managed to give voice to one. "The tapestry."

Relia looked at him as though he were on fire. "What tapestry?"

"Marius' tapestry. It depicted woods like these, and people walking through a silver portal. . ."

The girl caught on quickly. "You think she's, what, a Tiene ghost?"

"I don't know."

Relia walked closer to Arsene, glancing over her shoulder. "Whatever it is, it's connected to the ruby."

"Yes." Arsene agreed.

Diorbhail's Ember. . . If Seoras was connected to Fionn, and in fact, *real*, then perhaps the cefran goddess Arsene had been fascinated by existed somewhere, as well.

Silence resumed. Arsene fell into thought as he walked. This place was calmer than he expected. Heat baked the air like the Thuatian desert on a sunny day, but no fire appeared on the horizon. A land of volcanoes, of unlivable lava—Arsene had always imagined Bruthine to be flame itself.

Instead, it was beautiful, the trickle of the stream a soothing melody.

"Hey, Arsene?" Relia asked softly.

"Yes?"

"When you say 'Viridia's tits'. . ." She rolled her head. "Well, I disapprove of your foul mouth anyhow, but I was thinking. . . If Marius really does hear the goddess' voice, then. . . then aren't you kind of saying Marius' tits?"

Bile rose in Arsene's throat, and he gagged. "Relia. What is *wrong* with you?'

"It was just a thought-"

"Learn to keep such thoughts *in your head*."

"I just—Ah!" Relia gasped, pressing a hand to her mouth and backing up.

The distant mountains sharpened into clarity. Obsidian cliffs trailed into the distance, running perpendicular to the great serpentine form in the sky. Shapes moved atop their peaks.

Creatures of unfathomable size, blurred red by the distance, walked atop the towering obsidian cliffs. Jutting his head forward, Arsene tried to make them out, but Relia beat him to it.

"Those are dragons." Relia said softly.

"Dragons are only myths. . ." Arsene said.

Majestic creatures told of in bard song lounged atop the peaks. To see them in such detail from so far a distance. . . they must be of unimaginable size.

"Wow." Relia grinned. "That was what roared."

"I'm glad you're excited," Arsene said facetiously. "Should we take another route?"

Relia rotated slowly. "Maybe we should follow the mountains? If Johanna saw the dragons, she'd definitely get closer. Looks like a forest starts there. Maybe we can hide from them."

"Good idea." Arsene agreed, jogging toward the woods at the mountain's base.

Orange-blossomed trees grew thicker here, the grass at their trunks feathery and light. Wincing, Arsene tried to look away from the phosphorescent flowers, but they grew damn near everywhere around him. Hopefully, the glare would distract the predator's eyes. But to know something so deadly was nearby sent anxious quivers through his spine.

Something did not feel right, but Arsene could not place what. He glanced around like a nervous rat caught in a trap but caught sight of only more blinding flowers. Relia bumped into his back upon occasion, disoriented by the alien light.

Their hiding place diminished all too soon as the landscape changed. Rocks jutted up from the clay, some piled in mounds, others a singular boulder. Glancing up at the mountain peaks, Arsene wondered why Johanna had ended up so far away.

And if they were even heading the right direction.

He heard something rustle in the grass behind him but turned too late.

Thud. An arrow slammed into the tree beside him, and another grazed his leg before sticking in the ground.

"Do not move, human." A voice laced with a thick cefran accent warned.

Silent as ghosts, figures emerged from the trees, bows drawn. Cefra. Distinctive pupil-less eyes watched them from deeply tanned faces. Hardly any clothing covered their body; white loincloths guarded their dignity, and golden sandals rose to their knees. Red paint, traced in patterns unfamiliar to Arsene, rose up their legs and ran down their arms.

A woman with orange hair bound in tight braids approached them. A streak of white paint dashed between her burgundy-red eyes. Stabbing an elegant silver spear into the ground, she looked between the three of them. "Never before have humans stepped foot here. Who are you?"

"You speak Imperial common?" Arsene's eyebrows shot up. "I find that more surprising."

"Our ancestors did," the woman answered coldly. "We keep safe their memory. Now, answer me." None of the men with her displayed understanding. She alone spoke their tongue.

"We arrived accidentally. By means of a jewel," Arsene said quickly.

"Jewel." The woman repeated. Arsene could tell the word meant nothing to her.

Relia tentatively stepped forward. "Are you Tiene?"

"Humans recall the name? Surprising." The woman gestured to her comrades, shifting into the cefran tongue. She spoke too quickly for Arsene to understand.

Two men approached, both fireborn cefra judging from their flaming locks. One roughly grabbed Arsene, feeling him down for weapons. They lingered on his flintlock, unsure what it was, and eventually elected to take it. Relia winced as her sword was confiscated.

"Trespassers," the woman announced. "You do not belong here. You will be taken before the Lady. She will determine your fate."

"And who is that?" Arsene asked.

"And you will be silent, lest your tongue be cut out," she warned sharply, motioning for her men to surround them.

One of the men pushed Arsene forward as the hunting party flanked them, guiding them in the opposite direction they had been traveling. Drifting closer to the mountains, Arsene gritted his teeth and gazed up at the peaks.

A glint of fire caught his eyes in the distance. The woman of flame returned, hovering beneath the mountain's shadow. For three winks, her visage burned brightly before vanishing. But Arsene could feel her gaze. Whoever she was, her sights had been fixed on him.

The ruby jewel burned again. Why?

The flaming-haired hunter shoved Arsene, and he stumbled. Perhaps Arsene should have surrendered into Marius' custody. Whatever the Lavinians would have done to him would be preferable to what awaited them ahead.

And yet, he could not deny the flare of curiosity that demanded the answer.

Dragons, evidently, were docile creatures. Arsene's teeth dug into his bottom lip, drawing blood. By the goddess, the enormous scaled creatures lounged but a few stories above his head, their great horned heads peering down from the cliffs to watch the procession passing below.

Intelligent eyes oversaw the procession of cefra and their captured humans, claws raking thick gouges in the obsidian. Staring into the Leviathan's eyes had been quite enough; Arsene wrenched his head away, forcing his eyes forward.

A road took shape in the wilderness. Dark stone lay over packed red clay, weaving through the trees and crossing over a river. Obsidian burst from the clay, forming small cliffs clustered like knives around the mountain range's base.

Judging from their bows and spears, their captors were a cefran hunting pack. They whispered to themselves in the cefran tongue, occasionally pointing at Relia or Arsene. Though he understood a few words of cefran, they spoke too quickly for him to keep up.

The fog slowly cleared, revealing their destination. A city waited at the end of the road, an architectural marvel the likes of which Arsene had never seen.

Stone black as night rose in towering walls, guarding a city built against a mountainside, tiered not unlike Lavinia. But while Mount

Bruthine was dormant, this mountain spewed lava from its peak. Glowing crimson flowed down its slope and poured into the city, coursing through deep channels carved on every level, illuminating every street.

Ash and cinder, but this place was crowded. People swarmed the streets and walkways built along the lava channels.

Soldiers in red-scaled armor stood watch at the gates and quickly cranked them open for the hunters. Arsene glanced behind them as they entered the city, watching the heavy iron gate slam shut behind them.

Cefra paused to gape at the strange humans. To Arsene's eyes, they looked no different from Fionn or Eckart's people. Cefra of every element lived here, but a majority had hair in shades of flame and cinder, with eyes to match.

But their sense of fashion was impeccable. Thin white cloth wrapped their waists and bound their chests. Countless pieces of onyx jewelry adorned their bodies: hairpins, earrings, rings around their arms and legs, and heavy bangles.

Confiscate every piece of jewelry on this street alone, and a man could proclaim himself a lord. By comparison, the Gaevral and Creiv seemed downright destitute.

More fingers pointed at Relia as their escorts guided them through the streets. Did they think she was one of them?

Avoiding eye contact, Arsene stared at the road. The houses resembled Dragosi styles, bare and without embellishment. Orange flowers clustered in flowerpots in many windows, serving as a light source. Heat rushed over his face as they ascended a ramp, its edges channeled to allow the rushing lava to pour through.

Lava should harden and turn to rock. But this liquid flame flowed like water, endlessly burning.

Despite this city's similarities to Lavinia, the cefran castle rested on the middle tier rather than the topmost. A grand palace of black stone greeted them, its courtyard smoothed obsidian decorated with a steel statue of a phoenix in flight. Magma flowed through tiny channels, crisscrossing through the promenade, outlining a symbol Arsene did not recognize. Was it meant to be an abstract mountain?

The guard directed Arsene away from the palace onto a stairwell leading underground. Darkness engulfed them as they trod down an echoing hallway before reaching sconces filled with orange flowers, phosphorescent in the gloom.

Another guard in red-scaled armor opened a heavy iron door, revealing a tiny dungeon of but six cells. Arsene was shoved inside, the door locked behind him. Relia received her own quarters across the hall.

Their escort locked them in without another word and left them in utter darkness.

"Well," A familiar woman's voice arose from the shadows. "I see they found you, too."

"Johanna?" Arsene peered into the dim corner of the dungeon.

A woman with raven hair bound in a braid reclined against the bars, sweat dampening her brow. "I just about landed atop a group of hunters. Did you mean to scatter us like that?"

Exhaling, Arsene leaned against his sweltering dungeon. "I still have the gem. I'll take us back home. But be ready; I don't know where we'll end up."

Pulling the ruby from his satchel, Arsene ran a thumb over it and cleared his voice. "Bruthine." He commanded, just as he'd done before.

Nothing happened. The stone dimmed, refusing to answer his summons. Standing straight, Arsene nervously flipped the gem from one hand to the other before trying again.

And again.

Be it cursed luck or intervention from the gods themselves, the jewel refused to answer his call. They were trapped here.

CHAPTER NINETEEN

STARLIGHT

EVEN RAINY DAYS in Clodia were beautiful. An unnaturally bright sun pierced through dark clouds, and shafts of light descended through the rain. Watching the sunlight reflected in the droplets, Leo wondered what Clodia's overlapping plane looked like.

Officially, the sun descended from Viridia's holy body and spilled from the afterlife. But if that was not true, what sort of place might lie across the veil from the white city?

The wind tugged Consus' hood off, and he pulled it back over his head. "The men in the western quarter have seen nothing. Something tells me none of our stops will yield fruit."

Leo stepped aside as a carriage rolled by, wheels splashing through a puddle. "Has Lady Lucullus' people found anything?"

"Searching the depths of the sea is dangerous work," Consus said. "They've made little progress thus far."

"Do you think Kiylla drowned?"

"At this point, yes. She must have thought death on her own terms preferable to execution."

"I guess so," Leo murmured.

Clodians treated rain like poison falling from noxious clouds. Athelstanis hardly noticed showers; storms swept through so often. Rain or shine, farmers attended their fields, and merchants peddled their wares. These Sigillites sprinted, holding luggage above their head and grasping their hoods as though worried the water would damage them.

Dragging his eyes from the panicked crowds, Leo tried to initiate the conversation he'd been pushing off. "I've been thinking."

Consus glanced at Leo. "Thurston would say something smart in response to that."

"Thank you for refraining," Leo grumbled. "You heard the Emperor at the meeting. Half the council seems to ill like the war, yet he persists."

Consus sighed heavily. "If it were up to me, I would never have initiated this conquest. We've already proven Yuri Llaqta cannot be claimed."

"Does anyone approve?'

"Oh, plenty. Especially those living in northern Sigillus, near the border. Hatred for the Llaqtans runs deep."

Chewing on his inner lip, Leo carefully worded his next question. "Do you think it would be possible to convince the Emperor otherwise?"

Stopping mid-stride, Consus turned to Leo. "To pull back? No. Why?"

"I can't stop thinking about it. All those men who died. Most were so young. Gone in an instant." Leo shrugged his shoulders, adjusting his cloak. "We disabled Kiylla, but we didn't expect her assault to begin with. We cannot assume the Llaqtans are out of options."

"Thurston mentioned you saying as much. He also told you we haven't the status to sway anyone."

"Do we not? We survived the first massacre. Maybe people will heed us."

"Wishful thinking." Consus resumed his earlier pace. "The war will end, I presume, much as the first did. With tepid occupation and an ensuing insurgency. The campaign is foolishness."

Frowning, Leo followed Consus. Approach the subject too harshly, and Consus would realize something was wrong. "But that's pointless." Leo huffed in frustration. "Needless loss of life, for nothing."

"I agree with you. You're preaching to the choir."

"We might not have sway, but others do. Your father knows Drusus. Maybe he can reach the Emperor."

"He's tried."

Leo hesitated. This was not going well. "Well, maybe all he needs is backup from officers of the First. If we explained the dangers, the Emperor might see reason."

"Maybe. The Chamber lords govern smaller affairs, but decisions ultimately fall to the Emperor. He cannot be overruled."

"So you won't even try?"

Consus stopped again, face wrinkling in thought. "Leofric." He said shortly. "You have not been known to draft plans." He paused. "For anything."

"Well, I might have one now." Leo shifted from foot to foot. "You saw Relia. If the heir returns, order could be restored. The country would rejoice."

"Oh, absolutely." Consus agreed.

"Laws exist that allow the Chamber to overrule the Emperor. He could be replaced with his heir."

Consus gazed stoically at Leofric for an agonizing period. Finally, he responded. "He could. The war might be forgotten even without interference if the Duke arrives with the heir."

"Maybe," Leo agreed, watching Consus resume his stride. "But if not, we should talk with your Father." Jogging, he caught up. "Meet with Lord Chaucius, make our plea. And, and the Vicar. He opposed as well."

"You feel strongly about this. Fine, I'll speak with my father, see what I can do."

Relieved, Leo relaxed, trying to relish the beautiful, rainy day, even if he was the only man on the street who found the deluge enjoyable.

A woman gasped in indignation, and heavy footsteps splashed toward them. Rudely shoving through the crowd, a knight in an Athelstani blue surcoat with dark hair locked eyes with Leo.

"Thurston," Consus said. "News from the west?"

"That and more." Thurston grabbed Leo's arm and yanked. "You'll want to see this."

"See what?" Leo tried. Glancing at Consus for approval, Leo followed Thurston down the market's main street.

Throngs of people adorned Clodia's central square at any hour of the day, but Leo had never seen this many gathered before. Most directed their attention toward the main platform, a host for performances and executions alike. Noticing the two knights, the civilians stepped aside to allow them past, whispering amongst themselves.

A teen-aged boy with dark skin and a patchy hat shouted news from a scroll for all to hear. ". . . an unprecedented assault on Imperial lands. The Dragosi Duke and his inner circle have been attacked. . ."

"Dragos?" Leo blurted out.

"Look there." Thurston turned his head toward one of the pillars holding up the platform's roof.

A wanted poster hung from the marble depicting a face Leo knew all too well. A perfect likeness of Eckart stared into the crowd, ice-blue eyes painted vividly to declare his race. Beside him hung the image of the woman who had called him friend, the freckle-faced cefra with emerald eyes and skin pale as an Athelstani's.

". . cannot be known if the cefra work alone or for their kin. . ." The crier continued.

"This is ridiculous." Leo hissed.

"I figured you should know, "Thurston's eyes darted around. "But I don't have any further details."

Details. What crime had they been accused of? Leo needed to know. Reading the fine print of the posters, he found a sliver of hope: the cefra were wanted alive for questioning. Spinning around, he pushed through the crowd, roughly shoving past anyone who would not get out of his way.

A woman grabbed Leo's arm, startling him. Kiylla's disguise fooled him briefly, and he gazed at her stupidly until he recalled the dark makeup he had put on her.

"Where are you going?" She whispered harshly.

"I don't know," Leo admitted.

Dragging Leo down an alley, she checked for onlookers. "What's happening?"

"Eckart's been accused of attacking the Dragosi Duke." Leo blurted out. "But I don't know why. Or what. Or when."

"The duke?" She repeated. "And the accused is the cefra with the eyes of ice? Why?"

"He wouldn't have done anything like that. He's been framed. I'm sure of it." Leo stumbled over his words, grabbing her arms. "The vision. What the Earth Father warned of. It's coming true."

Kiylla stared at him gravely. "I don't understand. If what you say is true, then. . ." She trailed off, her intense brown eyes scanning the wall.

"Then what?"

"I have been following our Vicar. His past might as well not exist." Kiylla hissed. "But I have a lead. A strong lead. And it may have everything to do with this."

"Then keep at it." He stepped away from her. "I've held up Beau's end of the deal. Time to use him in return."

✦ ✦ ✦

The shouting from the Chamber meeting echoed in Leo's head as he descended the palace steps with Consus. Clouds parted from the sun, relieving the dreary day of rain. But the news from within had been anything but good.

With word of a cefran attack in Dragos, more lords had been willing to listen to Consus and Leo's pleas to reconsider the war in Yuri Llaqta. Yet many had answered their calls for peace with fervor for a new war.

Consus straightened his cloak. "Twice now, my brother has been framed. Why him?"

"Maybe he was conveniently in the right place," Leo suggested. He froze on the stairs. "You think he was framed, too?"

"Of course." Consus reached the bottom and paused. "You know him better than I. Need I explain?"

"No, I'm just glad to hear it." Leo cleared his throat. "Have you decided what to propose?"

"I think so. For now, I'll suggest we recall two legions from Yuri Llaqta to reinforce our borders. But we relent from further escalation until we capture the fugitives, or learn more."

"Think we can convince them?'

"Lord Drusus is on our side. Follow my lead and his in the days to come."

"Right. Easy enough."

A man awaited them beneath the boughs of the gold-ornamented trees. Beau Rosa smoothed down his vest and approached, silver cane clinking on the walkway. "Ah, Leofric. Just the man I'd hoped to see." He glanced at Consus. "You two were well-spoken in there."

"Satisfied?" Leo asked warily.

Consus' green eyes flashed, wondering what Leo meant.

"Not yet." Beau smiled. "I have news, though. Your father's just arrived in the city."

"My *father*?" Leo balked. "What for?"

"Negotiating marriage arrangements for your dear sister. You've been away from home a while. Why not drop by and catch up?"

Leo bit his tongue. Was Beau threatening his family?

"I'll see that he gets the chance," Consus said. "You seem in agreeance with Drusus. Can we consider our interests aligned?"

"Of course." Beau set his velvet hat back on his head. "I have ever sought what's best for our people." Nodding, he waltzed past them back into the palace.

Consus watched him with narrowed eyes. "I find the haste in which our ship's attack was forgotten. . . interesting."

"So do I." Leo agreed though he suspected who was responsible.

"You know more than you're letting on." Consus raised an eyebrow. "I find it curious. The Vicar asked to see you alone before our meeting. Our captive claimed the clergy were involved in our attack, yet the interrogators ignored this. I think I might pay the cathedral a visit. Seek the Archbishop's council."

"Do you think the order came from someone that high ranking?"

"I do." Consus leaned in. "Whoever sought our heads wanted us sunk where none would find us. We would have been missing without resolution, likely for years. But they have not struck again. They hide in the shadows, hoping not to draw eyes." He stepped away. "I intend to find them."

"Consus," Leo called as his friend turned to leave. "Be careful."

Nodding, Consus pulled his winged helm on and marched away. Fidgeting, Leo loitered in the promenade. He did not want to see his father, but perhaps a visit *was* in order.

Escaping the crowded promenade of the palace, Leo followed the path flanked by decorated trees. A shadow emerged from behind a trunk and fell into step with him. Jumping out of his skin, Leo sighed when he realized it was only Kiylla.

Her hair gathered in curls around her chin today, and she flashed him a smile.

"You're playing with fire," Leo warned. "Loitering around the palace so often."

"I am your shadow, south lord."

"Right. . ." Leo muttered. "I'm going to see my father. I don't imagine you should come."

"I will eavesdrop, then." She folded her hands at her waist, imitating a polite lady. "How did your meeting go?"

"Chaotically. We mostly argued."

"I presumed. Why is your father here?"

Leo halted at a crossroads. His father's suite was nearby, but Leo had yet to rehearse what he intended to say. Turning right instead, he made for a cliff side overlooking the sea.

"I don't know," Leo admitted. "Beau said he was here to find my sister a suitor. I suppose that could be true."

"Your sister?" Kiylla asked, tilting her head. "You never mentioned her."

"I have two, actually. Evelina and Rose." He nodded at a passing pair of knights. "And my brother, Gideon. He's the heir. Rose has two children already. I was always closest with Ev."

"Does she wish to be married?"

"Yes, but. . ." Leo chuckled wistfully. "Ev was in love with Eckart."

"I can understand that. The ice-eyed one had a pleasant skin tone and rugged features. Much more masculine than your ilk."

"I'm perfectly handsome!" Leo took a breath. "She'd always drag us out onto the lake by our city. Eckart loved it. He's waterborn, see. They're like ducks."

Kiylla's mouth twitched, hiding a laugh. "Did you approve?"

"Of course. Who better to marry my sister than a man I trusted?" Leo's smile faltered, remembering Eckart's plight. He needed to help his friend, but how?

"This is lovely." Kiylla broke away from him, approaching the cliff. Bright blue waves churned against the rock below, glowing beneath rays of glittering sunlight. "Is your father down there?"

"I wish," Leo murmured, joining her.

"You two don't get along, then."

"Not really. He's. . .my father. He's always supported me and done what's best for me, but. . . We're very different people."

"My father died when I was six." Kiylla stepped closer to him. "I hear he was a gentle soul."

"Nothing like you, then." Leo jabbed.

"No, nothing." She nodded, agreeing. "You care much for this cefra. You recklessly saved him when I captured him." She peered at him. "What brought you two together?"

"A failed hunt." Leo laughed awkwardly. "I, um, was a new squire. I wandered into Gaevral territory, and, well, they shoot trespassers. It's not my finest tale."

"And he saved your life?"

"Forcefully escorted me home, more like."

"Fate is funny." Sunlight streamed into Kiylla's brown eyes, highlighting tiny flecks of gold and green he hadn't noticed before. Her gaze met his. "Your eyes match the sea."

"Do they?" Leo cleared his throat and looked away, brushing his bangs from his eyes. A warm flush rose to his cheeks.

"And you look much whiter out here. But soon, you will be like roasted tarbe." She touched his arm. "We should get you inside."

"You're in a suspiciously good mood." Leo accused. "Why?"

Perhaps unaware of the answer herself, Kiylla glanced at the sea. "I made a gamble. It has a chance to pay off."

"You mean if we convince the Chamber?"

"Yes." She blinked slowly. "I don't think I'll get to go home. But at least I got to see these waters."

Sadness struck Leo with her words. "I'll get you home. You're a hero to your people."

She smirked. "And you to your people. For we each defeated the other."

Leo laughed. Fate was a funny thing.

"Now, let's go see your father." Kiylla took his arm and guided him away.

Nervous flutters danced through Leo's stomach as she leaned on his arm, but he couldn't place why. "Are you really going to eavesdrop on us?"

"Of course, south lord. I am your shadow, remember?"

Halting in his tracks, Leo regarded Kiylla. "Whoever sent that ship hasn't tried to kill us again. Why?"

Kiylla leaned closer. "Beau said something when I was a child. 'You could leap into the water and attract the attention of every fish in the sea, or you could reach in, so gently as to cause no ripples, and retrieve your lost item from the depths without disturbing a soul.'"

Searching for the true meaning behind the words, Leo glanced over his shoulder at the sea-side cliff. "Beau wants to take power without anyone realizing there was a coup."

"Pirates can lurk at sea, but only traitors would assassinate their own in the streets." Kiylla looked away. "Beau has chosen a new course for us. Only time will unveil our fate."

Father always stayed in the same suite, a stately building covered in sculpted pillars. Kiylla slipped away, and Leo approached the double doors reluctantly, straightening himself off before grabbing the knocker.

A few moments passed before a familiar attendant answered. A Trenowyth house steward, middle-aged with a bushy mustache, stepped aside. "Young Lord. Your Father is out, but you're welcome to stay until he returns."

"Thank you." Leo said, entering. He paused in the foyer, deciding what to do. It would be nice to lay back and close his eyes for a while.

Trotting up the stairs, he pushed open the door to one of the guest rooms. He and Ev had always shared this suite, as children. The gold quilted bed had more than enough space for two kids, but they had built a wall of pillows between them to keep the other away.

Laying down, Leo pulled off his sash and draped it over his eyes. Slowly but surely, his nerves melted away and he relaxed.

Something clicked, and Leo sat bolt upright as the window opened and a woman slid inside. Kiylla closed the window behind her and swept the curtains over the glass.

"*Kiylla?*" Leo harshly whispered.

"Nobody is here." She said. "I'm tired of sleeping on the dirt." Without asking permission, she dropped onto the bed.

"Do you *mind?*"

"Mind what?"

Shimmying closer to her, Leo leaned in, worried someone would overhead. "Are you trying to get yourself killed?"

Kiylla stared at him, unphased. "Your disguise is excellent. I have not received a second glance, save from lustful men. And. . ." She looked away.

"And what?"

"I feel safe with you." Kiylla chuckled. "Strange isn't it? You wouldn't be much help in a fight."

"Every time you compliment me, it feels like an insult." Leo rose and locked the door. Exhausted, he dropped onto the bed again and returned the sash to his eyes.

Kiylla stretched out beside him. "Marvelous." She murmured. "Perhaps houses have merit, after all."

Lowering the sash, Leo peered at her. She laid on her side, hips rising like mountains above the curve of her waist. His gaze traced up her body, landing on brown eyes watching him sharply.

Grabbing a pillow, Leo stuffed it between them. "Stay on your side." He ordered.

"I intended to." She said, humored. "Do you make these walls often?"

"This illustrious wall kept my brat sister away."

"Johanna and I used to do the same. Though, I can't say I ever did so with those I danced under starlight with."

"What does that mean?"

"It's a Llaqtan expression." Kiylla chuckled. "Go to sleep. I shall not breach your wall."

Smiling, Leo found his thoughts drifting to comforting memories. But when he thought of home, it was not the Trenowyth manor that came to mind.

CHAPTER TWENTY

COSMOS

ECKART HAD RIDDEN but two mounts in his life: his beloved stallion, Dilsaeth, and the carriage his mother had occasionally invited him inside. One remained in the dredges of his memories, while the other had been left behind in Lavinia.

Despite the mundanity of his life, he now rode on the back of an indescribable creature. Every color of the rainbow flashed in the beating of powerful wings; violet flashed through its body like lightning, painless to the touch. Soft down feathers supported their weight, vibrating with an eternal hum.

Drums beat around them, the sound of the creature's wings. And a world unlike anything he'd seen expanded above and below.

The sky of Casaliede had no end nor beginning. A world-consuming storm enveloped every inch of this place. Wind raged with green streams in its currents, violet flashing through the black clouds. Electric colors pulsed around them like a dance.

The stormsinger dived, avoiding a tiny chunk of floating rock. Eckart grabbed the beast's feathers, and Wulf lurched forward, arms wrapped around Fionn in a vice-grip. Heart beating out of his chest, Eckart caught his breath when he realized the stormsinger would not have dropped them. They remained balanced on its enormous back.

Maybe his waterborn nature had attuned him to the endless sea Chief Tamhas had cast him into, for this place seemed altogether more deadly.

Black clouds parted below to reveal an island adrift among the clouds. Dancing lights flit across the meadow of purple flowers, avoiding the shores of a silver lake, but Eckart could not make them out.

"What is that?" Eckart called, pointing down.

Fionn looked, but the voice that emerged belonged to the being inside her. Echoing, windy, elated. "Songs. Life."

Eckart stared at her, not understanding. ". . . what?"

"The chime of ornaments, the songs of birds," Seoras answered unhelpfully. "Look closer."

If only he could. To Eckart's eyes, they were but fleeting light.

"Look," Wulf called. "Water."

"I see it," Eckart said.

Wulf looked over his shoulder expectantly. "You're waterborn, right?"

"Yes."

Wulf gestured to the lake as though the rest were obvious.

"Do you think I sing merrily for every puddle I find?" Eckart chuckled. "You sound like Leo."

"Oh, don't say that." Wulf hastily turned around.

He bucked forward, grabbing Fionn as the stormsinger dove. Gracefully carving through the tumultuous storm, it glided above the lake and landed beside the shore. Kneeling to let them off, it touched its wings to the ground.

Legs shaky from a long ride, Eckart stumbled as he touched solid ground. Fionn dropped beside him. "We should rest." She announced.

Another violet-leafed tree stood guard over the lakeside, canopy catching lightning strikes and absorbing their energy. Crackling power traced through the boughs. A good enough place to rest. Dropping his bag beside its trunk, Eckart leaned on the tree and stared across the water.

Down here, the lights drifting by the shore had silhouettes. One almost appeared like a bird, but when Eckart thought he had a grasp on its wings, the shapes disappeared into an ethereal cloud of pale green light. With a wink, it vanished from sight.

Something itched at his ear, and Eckart swatted but found nothing. A hum or a whistle faintly dug into him, but he could not tell from where it came. Or if it was even real. The stormsinger's thrumming body pulsed like drums, accompanying the music as though an orchestra played just out of sight.

Part of it unsettled him. The other comforted. And the confusion made him desperate to leave this place.

Fionn sat beneath the tree and pressed her shaking hands to her thighs. Hand affixed to his spear, Wulf cautiously approached her. "How much further?"

"A day or two." Seoras' voice emerged from Fionn. "We're making good time."

"Do we have that long?" Wulf gestured to her. "You're shaking. You can barely stand."

"We have no other options."

"Fine. Then let me talk to Fionn."

The blazing light in Fionn's eyes dimmed, and the intense stare diminished to a confused haze. Blinking, she steadied her gaze and looked between the two men before gasping at the massive creature behind them.

Wulf knelt beside her. "How are you doing?"

"Bad," Fionn said honestly. "Is it true? That I'm dying?" She held out an arm. "Bleeding out inside?"

"Tell me what's wrong."

"My head hurts. Everything is blurry. The wind. . ." She flinched as a gale swept over them. "Isn't helping."

Wulf leaned over her, guarding her from the breeze. "That tree can't be comfortable. Here." Kneeling, he pressed her against his chest.

Figuring they could use some time alone, Eckart walked to a quiet spot by the lake. Ripples endlessly churned the water as a blusterous wind disturbed the surface. If a sun hid behind the cloud somewhere above, Eckart could not see it. No reflection gazed back up at him. Opaque, the lake could hide anything in its depths.

The phantom music surrounded him, distant humming, nagging, whistling, ever out of reach. Pangs of hunger racked through him; they had few rations and wanted Fionn to have the bulk of them. The sensation reminded Eckart of earlier days when he had misjudged the length of a journey from Clodia city to Altanbern.

Hungry and lost, he'd stumbled through the Argiris desert and passed far west of Piona. Not that he had money for food and water had he successfully navigated to the desert capital. By the kindness of a passing wagon, he'd secured supplies enough to drag himself barely alive to Gaevral lands.

But a different memory haunted him today. The carriage had rolled to a stop outside the palace, and Mother had bid farewell before stepping out. For seventeen long years, the sight of her smile had been the last he'd glimpsed of her face. As often as he dwelt on Tettiena Parnesius, so too did he wonder if her garden of golden roses still grew behind the manor.

Her favorite place. The spot where she had read him an epic ballad one summer when her husband was away.

Never again had Eckart expected to see her. Conflicted, he recalled the desperation in her voice when she begged him to take her deal and run. To survive. Even when he denied her, she had not harmed him.

To still be loved after so long should have sent waves of warmth through him. But Eckart felt only hollowness.

Holding out a hand, Eckart felt the wind. They would never start a fire under this relentless squall. If only he'd been fireborn. Fionn could use the warmth.

Beneath the tree, Wulf wrapped his coat around Fionn, tightly bundling her. She looked at him with an odd gaze, like someone who had been told much about a stranger yet had never met them.

Wulf's affections for her were plain to see. He gazed at her with a softness that did not appear on his stoic mien for anyone else. Eckart wanted to rejoin him, but he hesitated.

Mother had given birth to Eckart, her life's mistake. Lord Parnesius had cast the bastard from his house. The Gaevral had been hostile, a coldness slowly warming to accepting indifference. Eckart had belonged with neither.

Even Lord Trenowyth had watched from a distance, ensuring the cefra would not enter the Trenowyth home with Leo and sully its floorboards.

"Eckart!" Wulf called. "C'mere."

Brushing his bangs from his eyes, Eckart returned to the violet tree. "What?"

"Stand there." Wulf touched his elbow and directed him to Fionn's other side. "How's that?"

"Perfect." She murmured, eyes fluttering shut.

"Oh." Eckart sat beside her. "Are we the windshields?"

"For tonight." Wulf leaned back on his palms. Fionn nestled against him and quickly passed out. His brow furrowed, and mouth twitched. Wind drove against his back, fluttering his short hair.

"She'll be okay," Eckart assured him.

A hollow promise. Eckart had left Leo back at the war front, abandoned Dilsaeth and Tefnut in Lavinia, lost Relia in the confusion.

Wulf looked up. "I'm not going to sleep. Have any good stories?"

"There's the one where I met Leo."

"The tracking incident?" Wulf chuckled. "I think I heard his friend mention something about that."

"First of all, Thurston is not Leo's friend." Eckart echoed Leo's often-spoken words. "Well, I was hunting a deer that I'd tracked to the border. . . "

ECKART ROUSED FROM a light sleep to find nothing had changed. Wulf held Fionn protectively, eyes closed. Curled in a ball of black and violet, the stormsinger thrummed in its sleep beside them.

Rising slowly to avoid waking them, Eckart returned to the lake shore and tapped his waterskin, debating whether the strange water here was safe to drink. Their stores had run dry. Kneeling, he touched the water. Viscous and thick, it reminded him of the maevruthan.

Images flashed past his eyes, too quick to focus on. Sinking his hand deeper, he searched for them again but found only the touch of rock beneath the surface. Remembering the shadows hiding in Faerdain's fathomless sea, Eckart yanked his hand out and tentatively pulled his waterskin off his belt.

"Don't." Fionn's voice startled him.

The girl stood behind him, dwarfed in Wulf's coat. Eckart looked her up and down. "You shouldn't be up."

"No." She agreed shortly, sinking to her knees beside the water.

Reaching out, Eckart steadied her before returning his waterskin to his bag. "This water's not safe?"

She shook her head. Eyes growing in luminescence, a new voice overlapped hers. "Your catalyst. It's loneliness."

"Yes. Is that yours, too?"

"You speak as if I'm mortal." Fionn's head tilted playfully. "But, no. My catalyst was a creature from a story I wrote as a child."

"As a child? Then, you aren't. . ." Eckart trailed off.

Fionn's eyes flashed. "Are you a bastard? A fletcher unwanted by his kin? Or are you what life has made you?" Seoras' voice blustered with rage. It quickly quelled into sorrow. "What I am now is what you know."

"But you miss them. Someone." Eckart guessed.

Fionn dipped her hand into the lake. "I have not heard their voices. Maybe they are gone; maybe they no longer speak. I alone knew. I alone remain." The water trailed through her fingers, clinging to the skin as though reluctant to let go.

"Until the Earth Father intervened in the Shrine."

". . .yes."

"What are you?" Eckart asked, swiveling to face her. "Are you speaking through her, or. . ."

"I have no form of my own." Fionn raised her head, another voice emerging from her lips. "Through my bird, I see, through her alone, I touch this world."

Heavy footsteps approached. Eckart looked back to see Wulf marching toward them. "You admit it," Wulf said. "You're no god, merely a man masquerading as one. You have no right-"

Lightning crackled around Fionn as she scowled. "Do you hate the talented evoker who bloomed late in life? Do you slander the lord who was born a pauper?"

"They aren't *killing Fionn*." Wulf's voice dripped with hate.

The powerful wind whipped into a frenzy, slamming into Wulf and knocking him off his feet. Fionn's shoulders slumped as he hit the ground. She pressed a hand to her head, breathing deeply.

Startled, Wulf pulled himself up.

Eckart grabbed Fionn's wrist. When cefra overexerted, their blood waned, and hers already ran dangerously thin. Another spell like that could seal her fate.

"Don't push me." Fionn's voice was quiet. Eckart could not tell which of the minds within her spoke. With a shuddering breath, the echo returned. "Once there were four. They never saw what I did. I remained to watch."

"Watch what?"

Fionn sighed. "If something true can be known only to those who already know, how could anyone learn of it?"

Confused, Eckart glanced to Wulf for help. The mercenary blinked a few times before speaking. "The dreams. Is that what you're trying to tell me?"

Fionn gazed sadly at Wulf but did not answer.

Something only known to those who already know. The expression made Eckart's head hurt. Their hands were full enough with Dragosi soldiers chasing them and an empire seeking their heads.

What more could there be to fear?

"We should be off." Fionn tried to rise. "We're running out of time."

Eckart grabbed her hand and helped her up, gently guiding her to Wulf, who carried her to the stormsinger. Raising its head, the enormous beast watched them through intelligent black eyes and waited for them to mount. Rising slowly, it flexed its wings and raked its talons through the rock.

Sitting behind Wulf, Eckart paused to glance back at the lake. A strange sense of longing beckoned him back to its shores. Pushing the feeling aside, he grabbed a tuft of feathers and braced for take off.

"Wulf," Eckart said as the drumbeats of the powerful wings began anew. "Tell me about your dream again."

For a full day, they flew without end. Exhausted, starving, and parched, the storm had beaten Eckart down. And with each passing hour, Fionn's condition worsened.

Her skin was pallid, and her eyes barely opened. Seoras had promised the journey would take them only a day or two more, but it felt like she was slipping away. Eckart was not a man of medicine, but he could tell she would not last to see the morning.

The scenery never changed. What did the heart of a world look like? As hope faded, something in the air shifted, so gradually, he hardly noticed, and then, all at once.

The wind ceased, and thunder quelled. All sounds save the heavy beating of the stormsinger's wings departed, leaving them in a vacuum. Shifting to look around, Eckart saw clear skies devoid of light, of sun, moon, or clouds. Calm gray extended toward the horizon.

"What's going on?" Wulf sat straight, hairs standing on end.

"We're here," Fionn said weakly.

Something distorted the otherwise empty void, dead ahead. Leaning forward, Eckart stared at the anomaly, trying to make sense of it. Wulf gazed with him, equally uncertain.

A light shone behind the distortion. Around it, shapes moved yet remained still. A thousand leviathans swirled and raged, yet the next moment, they were but wisps of wind. Music, sharp flute, and whining violin played over the void and silenced.

The reverie shattered. Winds roared, tearing at Eckart's ears. Pained, he pressed hands to the sides of his head and strained to keep his gaze fixed on what lay ahead. Anchored to the nothing above and below like an ethereal tree, the distortion thrummed with thunder and flashed with lightning. The leviathans appeared again, infinite and vast. They vanished, and swirling hurricanes took their palace.

The music returned and faded. Overwhelmed, Eckart forced his head down. This thing was not meant for men to see.

The stormsinger landed with a heavy thud. Unaware any footholds existed in this void, Eckart was surprised to see solid rock beneath them. Lurching violently, the stormsinger knocked him off its back, and he tumbled. Landing on his side, he cursed and sat up.

Wulf landed beside him, but Fionn remained seated on the stormsinger's back. "Stay here." She called.

Clambering to his feet, Wulf held up an arm to shield his face from the erratic storm. "That's the heart?"

"Yes. You're not meant for it." She glanced at the strange anomaly. "I'm not sure I am, either."

"You're going in there?" Wulf balked.

"We must." Seoras' voice cut through Fionn's. "Cefra should mend naturally, as blood restores. But the leviathan was ever meant for one alone. It tore her apart from within."

"That . . ." Wulf struggled to describe the heart. "That *thing* is going to tear her apart!"

"It very well might." Seoras agreed. "But she is lost unless I can bestow upon her a piece of the storm itself."

The stormsinger's wings flapped as it prepared to take off. Wulf reached out but was knocked back as a powerful tailwind swept over them. Thrown to the ground, Eckart saw only the fluttering tail feathers as the bird swept away.

Gaining his bearings, Eckart studied the ground. They stood on a tiny island of floating rock, wobbling beneath the storm. Twenty paces composed the perch, and it seemed no more than ten paces thick. Kneeling, Eckart's stomach flopped as he imagined them being swept into the unknown.

"Shit." Wulf cursed, pressing an arm to the ground to keep his footing. "Shit." He repeated nervously,

The wind changed direction constantly, flowing in every direction. Music started and stopped; some instruments Eckart swore he recognized, others alien noises with haunting melodies. Gritting his teeth, he managed to raise his head but saw no sign of the stormsinger or its rider.

Something else captivated his attention. The leviathans swirling in the heart of this void did not appear as Fionn's did. They moved like undersea currents; their heads had no eyes. Only the vague impression of a draconic creature manifested in the distortion.

A gap appeared between them as though something were missing. A void, not gray like the skies nor black as night. But then, a bright flash of light blinded him, forcing his head down.

Something lingered here. Eckart could feel it. The wind stirred as though breathing; the thunder felt like a beating heart. He felt eyes upon his back from every direction, yet nothing surrounded them but gray.

The same feeling had come from the turquoise light beneath the sea of the endless ocean. Ancient, beckoning.

Maybe Seoras was no god. Not truly. Once, he had been mortal. Emotions familiar to Eckart had spilled through the echoing voice of the one within Fionn's mind. But this place made one thing utterly clear.

Seoras was beyond their knowing. Something more. Something linked to this ancient place. And whatever troubled him, whatever lay ciphered in Wulf's dreams, was something even older.

CHAPTER TWENTY ONE

PHOENIX

ARSENE IMAGINED WULF laughing at him, wherever the stubborn man was. Arsene had allowed his partner to be dragged away, and his reward had been a dungeon of his own.

Humidity permeated the dim cells. Rolling his sleeves up, Arsene wiped the sweat from his brow to no avail. Was this better or worse than getting caught by Marius? Arsene had no idea.

Relia tilted her head, staring at Arsene across the hall. "What do you think is happening back home?"

"Who can say? We kept you from my family's grasp. Without the keys to the Empire, their power is considerably lessened." Arsene looked her up and down. "Tettiena didn't get to you, did she?"

Frightened, Relia pulled up her knees. "She didn't touch my memories, no. But she's a far better evoker than any of us. If she gets her hands on me. . . if she finds us. . ."

"We need a plan," Johanna said from the darkness of her cell.

"Escaping here," Arsene announced. "We'll figure out the rest later." Shifting to better see Johanna, Arsene glared at her. "I'm still not sure I should trust you."

Johanna raised an amused eyebrow. "I worked for my father. But I was never privy to many details." She grabbed one of the bars. "Something became clear only recently. They wanted the jewels to shatter them. To seal away the other planes."

Arsene's brow furrowed in thought. Johanna's mother had studied the planes in far greater detail than any Imperial. Beau Rosa did nothing without intent; had he married her solely to unearth her studies?

"Johanna," Arsene asked. "What happened directly before your mother's death?"

Her grip on the bars tightened. "She had become fascinated by Olbhreis' Ore. She wondered if the Earth Father had crafted it for a purpose rather than mere ceremony."

"Well, she was right." Arsene leaned back, head clicking painfully on the stone

"Marius told me Fionn, or rather the thing that dwells within her, knew how the gems were created. And so, through his memories, so too could we evoke their destruction."

Relia's face wrinkled in confusion. "What did you mean when you said the thing that dwells within Fionn?"

"The leviathan. The creature she turned into. There's something more to it." Johanna explained. Her brown eyes flashed to Arsene. "My mother never found the Ore. She had an. . .accident."

"An accident?" Arsene pressed.

"She hit her head. Slipped and fell while on an expedition. " Johanna released the bars and slumped back.

Arsene chose his next words carefully. "Did your parents seem to be on good terms prior to her death?"

"Not really," Johanna answered, oblivious to his intent. "They'd been fighting often."

Nudging her towards his theory, Arsene cleared his throat. "And you and Beau got along?"

"Well, enough. He's my father. He's all I have left."

They fell into silence, listening to the drops of water sliding down the walls and the rush of lava somewhere in the distance.

224

"I don't get it," Relia said abruptly. "Why didn't the Emperor just have more kids?"

"Where did that come from?" Arsene muttered. He turned his head. "They tried. Conceiving you took them years. Seems one or both are infertile."

"So what happens to the throne?'

"Cousins and siblings fight over it. The Chamber approves one."

"But," Johanna added, "If another red-haired divinity appeared, the clergy would seek to overthrow the sitting ruler."

"I'm surprised you know that," Arsene said teasingly.

"I pay attention sometimes." Johanna huffed.

Relia drummed her fingers on her lap. "What if I go to the capital and claim the Duke attacked me?'

"He didn't. Multiple lords will back him up, insisting I kidnapped you." Arsene shrugged. "You're a woman. They'll claim hysteria and shove you in a tower."

Johanna sat in the corner of her cell. "My father's a chamber lord. My involvement could spell disaster for him."

"Or see you easily absolved." Arsene countered.

"Hm." Johanna's head clunked against the stone wall.

Shifting to try and get comfortable, Arsene flinched as pain raced through his dominant hand. Lifting his arm, he turned the palm over, but Marius had healed the wound. No bump, no scar. Just a phantom pain, he supposed.

Resting his head in his other hand, Arsene traced the outlines of every stone on the far wall, his mind racing, trying to find the path of thought most productive to their present predicament.

Fionn's cursed song hummed through the back of his mind.

Cast aside, cracks appear on perfection
The empty void you'd always concealed
Pretending to be the hero, burning so bright
A fire that leaves naught but embers in its wake

Marius, a blazing sun, and Arsene, the forgotten embers left in his wake. A fitting metaphor. Maybe Marius was right; he always was. Yet Arsene had turned his back on the man again.

Self-destructive. That's what Mother had called him. A boy born with the world in his palm who squandered it. Desperate to stand out, he'd walked the opposite path of his brother.

Was she right? No. All Arsene had wanted as a child was to follow in Marius' steps.

Hand quivering, Arsene grabbed his wrist. Poor Fionn. Had Vasille been speaking the truth? Had the Lavinian dungeons tortured her and worse? More importantly, why did he care? She was just a cefra bard with frightening eyes. . .

Arsene sighed. No sense fooling himself any longer. He only wished he could revive Vasille to shoot him all over again. How dare that worm harm one of the few things in this world that made Arsene

. . .

Happy. The thought came unbidden, and Arsene tried to shove it away to no avail. If he ever saw Wulf and Fionn again, the two could never be informed of the truth.

Arsene had glimpsed the leviathan flying over the mountains. With luck, they'd escaped and were safe.

Cracks appear on perfection. . . Wulf's dreams of the porcelain woman shattering to pieces. . . Had Fionn hoped to warn Arsene that Marius' intentions would lead to unintended catastrophe, or did the song hold deeper meaning?

Leaning back, Arsene closed his eyes. A world without the touch of the planes. The world Marius wanted to create. Where, in his idealistic mind, lasting peace could be achieved. Typical Marius. A self-sacrificing saint.

That world was impossible to imagine. But Arsene tried all the same.

The scrape of heavy iron doors could have woken the dead. Startled out of his doze, Arsene shot to his feet as orange light spilled into the dungeon. Two soldiers in red-scaled armor entered.

"The Lady will hear." One said in broken common. "One. Which will speak?"

Arsene hesitated, searching past the accent for the knight's intended meaning.

"I will." Relia blurted out.

Arsene winced, but he was too late. One of the guards unlocked Relia's cell and guided her out of the dungeon, slamming the door behind them. Johanna rushed to her bars and glanced across the gloom at Arsene.

"Better her than me, I suppose." She figured. "Do you imagine this Lady is their ruler?"

"Or priestess?" Arsene mused. "If these are the remnants of the Tiene. . . Well, we destroyed most of their recorded history."

"I know who they worshiped." Johanna slid back to the floor. "That's something at least."

"Don't sell yourself short. We vaguely understand their funeral rights, too."

Johanna chuckled but fell silent.

Cursing under his breath, Arsene paced his cramped cell. Why had Relia done that? She might have condemned them all. The girl spoke with the tact of a Sylfestran peasant and had no experience negotiating. If the world was kind, her sincerity would win her favor.

But the world was anything but kind.

Thirty minutes, perhaps an hour, passed. Time was difficult to measure in the dark. Eventually, the iron doors scraped back open, and the guards escorted Relia to her cell. She looked no worse for wear, perhaps agitated, her brow sinking low over her eyes.

"You." The guard pointed at Arsene, and his fellow opened the cell door.

Holding up his hands to imply cooperation, Arsene followed them outside, grateful to see light again. When they ascended the stairs to the courtyard, Arsene swore the scaled streak of red in the sky had changed position. The serpentine band appeared slimmer than before. Was it alive?

The guards waltzed casually past the lava channel, leading Arsene to the palace doors and pushing him through. Within, more resemblances to Lavinia appeared: black walls trimmed with gold, the floors tiled with a strange material the color of burgundy cloth. Twin braziers guarded the great entrance to the throne room.

With rigid discipline, the two soldiers drove Arsene inside, shut the doors, and stood at attention to either side of the room. Stabbing their glaives into the ground, they stared directly ahead at what Arsene could only assume was their Lady.

And she could put most human royalty to shame. Red hair bound in spiral braids sat atop an angular face of deeply tanned skin. Countless beads of gold and onyx decorated the loops of hair, and heavy earrings fell to her shoulders. Her legs were bare, her midriff exposed, but the white gown was heavily layered in the back, falling in cascades behind and around her golden sandals.

Pressing a hand to his chest, Arsene offered her a bow. One deep red eyebrow shot up, but the Lady otherwise did not react.

Her words emerged heavily accented, melodic, and quick. "A human," she observed. "Another vagabond?"

Frowning, Arsene looked over himself. His coat was charred and ripped, his shirt untucked and dampened with sweat. Running a hand through his hair, he tried to make himself more presentable.

"Vagabond?" Arsene repeated. "Is that how Relia introduced herself?"

Heels clicked on the echoing floor as the Lady approached, extending a hand lined with rings. "Let me see it. This jewel."

Obeying, Arsene pulled the Bruthine ruby from its bag and handed it to her. "Are you the Tiene's queen?" He asked.

"In a sense." She replied, pacing away and holding the faded gem to the hanging brazier. "This is the ancient archway. Crafted by Diorbhail's hand." She lowered her arm. "Where did you get this?"

"It's a long story," Arsene said. "Would you prefer the long or short of it?"

"Short. You humans are long-winded."

"Ahem." Clearing his throat, Arsene spoke quickly. "A remnant of your people sold it to the Sylfestran king for refuge. I helped one of your kin retrieve it."

"Sylfestran?" The Lady barked. "Some idiot sold it to that fae trickster?"

"Mhm," Arsene confirmed, a mite frightened. The Lady's hair caught aflame with her rageful words and slowly went out.

"Good." She decided. "It should not be in his hands."

"If you don't mind me asking." Arsene clasped his hands together. "Did your people flee here in the face of the Empire's wrath?"

"Yes." She confirmed.

"And you did not take the ruby with you?"

"Why would we? There was no coming back." Clutching the jewel, she returned to his side and studied him intently.

Perhaps Arsene had a means of appealing to these people. Making eye contact, he stood his ground. "I saw the remnants of your city. The temple you dedicated to Diorbhail. It was beautiful. At least, what remained of it."

"You are trying to win my favor."

"Ah. . ." Arsene snapped his mouth closed. "Well, yes."

An amused or perhaps triumphant smile ripped across her face. She toyed with the ruby, passing it between her hands. "Your vagabond friend claims to have been placed in captivity and fled. You helped her. But she would not give details."

"She speaks true." Arsene watched as the Lady circled him. "The Duke of Dragos seeks to use her status to advance his own. She refused. They held her against her will. The ruby was a last course of action, a desperate attempt to escape."

"I see Dragos has not changed."

"There's more. Let me ask you a question." Arsene blurted out.

The Lady paused at his side, eyebrow raised.

"Your people once sent couriers to the Aeourant, to the Creiv. Even the Gaevral." Arsene said. "Growing a vast wealth of knowledge, you exchanged experiences and truths. I offer the same. Your information, for mine."

The memory of Marius' tapestry returned to him, the faded cefran words scrawled across the bottom, the same as were carved in Diorbhail's statue in the dilapidated temple.

"Curiosity drives the fire and gives life to its kin," Arsene added. "May my passion kindle thee and warm my bones in return."

"You know her prayer. . ." The Lady trailed off. Snapping her fingers, she waltzed towards a side door. "Follow me, human."

Glancing at the guards, Arsene followed her through a dim hall into an enormous room. Shelves upon shelves of black stone rose to a vaulted ceiling, housing all manner of books, scrolls, and loose parchments bound together.

Great arched windows peered onto the volcano's edge, where flaming streams tumbled down the mountainside. Standing before the largest, the Lady turned to him. "Let us exchange. For once we spoke with our kin, and too long have we been isolated."

"Who should begin?"

"You. Ask your questions."

Marveling at the sheer quantity of writing stored in this room, Arsene chose his questions carefully. There was no telling how many he would get. "The huntress who ambushed us knew nothing of the jewel. But you do. What did you mean it was crafted by Diorbhail?"

"Our people have forgotten it. A purposeful choice." She trailed a hand along her braids. "We shall never return to Thruine. With each passing generation, fireborn become the dominant race. Eventually, we will need nothing but this home."

"Interesting. But you didn't answer my question."

"Diorbhail's Ember, one of four." The Lady answered. "The jewels threw open the doors, inviting the touch of other realms, allowing the cefra to breathe."

Arsene refrained from asking the question in his mind. If that jewel opened the doors, they were once closed. Marius sought to return the world to its natural state. A state not seen in so many millennia, the world had forgotten it ever existed.

And if these doors were closed. . . then the cefra would cease to breathe, as the Lady put it.

"Diorbhail made our world livable for her people," Arsene said. "Why?"

"Few remember the tale." The Lady said somberly. "We sought refuge. From where and why, no one remembers. But home was made there. For millennia, we lived alongside the humans, but never were we accepted."

Four jewels, one for each bloodline of cefra. Now, the picture was filling in. "I've no doubt you trust in Diorbhail. Doubtless, the other gods, as well. What of Viridia?"

"The Empire's deity?" The Lady inquired. "I thought nothing of her. Maybe she exists. Who can say?"

"I have no more questions," Arsene said. "Ask what you will, and I will share."

"Truly?" The Lady held the jewel up and sauntered to his side. "You would give more than you take?"

"So long as we go free."

"That is asking too much. You will remain here, but in more comfortable quarters." Waltzing to a stone chair, she sat and crossed her legs. "Tell me of my kin. Of their fortunes and history. What has become of them?"

"The Gaevral have the most tumultuous path. I'll begin there." Arsene leaned against the table beside her.

Fire caught his eyes, and he glanced up to see a blaze illuminating the library's center. A woman's face appeared in the dancing flame, the roiling blaze shaping her hair and gown. The briefest grin appeared on her face, matching the smirk in the Lady's blazing eyes.

Something had blessed Marius. Someone spoke to Fionn. Why could there not be more untold secrets hiding in places like this?

"Wait." Arsene's head snapped back to the seated woman. "Relia. What did you discuss?"

"She explained why you deserved freedom. And, I gave her a warning." The Lady said ominously. "That another of your kind has followed you here."

CHAPTER TWENTY TWO

TRUCE

OW LONG HAD it been since Leo attended a ball? Once upon a time, he'd loved the events—any excuse to dress in his finest, drink, and dance had been most welcome. He searched for the old enthusiasm but found only nerves instead.

Lord Barron Trenowyth had come to Clodia in search of a husband for his youngest, but Leo had not envisioned the social gathering taking place at Beau's estate nor for his father to insist Leo attend.

Father sat across the carriage, crowned by a new wig, his white finery betraying a slight gut. Arms folded, he stared daggers at Leo.

As the carriage jolted over a bump in the road, Father finally spoke. "I've heard what they're saying about you and Parnesius."

"They?" Leo feigned naivety. "Who, exactly?"

"You know what I speak of." Father chided. "What do you think you are doing?"

"What we think is best."

Father scowled, leaning forward. "The boy who would have been Emperor, advocating for his disposal—a feat that has never before been done. You don't think people will connect the dots?"

Leo grimaced, looking away. He had not considered that angle. "Why would they think that? I would not be next in line." He paused. "Or even *in* line. And what does Consus have to gain from aiding me? We're just trying to save what's left of our men."

"You've done enough," Father ordered. "Leave it alone." He looked away. "Bah. You might have earned an accolade had you not lost the prisoner."

"Hm." Leo avoided eye contact.

Leaning against the window, Leo observed the venue for the night: Lord Beau Rosa's estate. The place was more richly decorated than the last Leo had been here. Green banners hung from the old stone, and two stewards waited by the doors, bidding welcome to the guests pouring in.

Their carriage rolled to a stop, parking beside a dozen others lined along the manor's walkway. Opening the door, Leo allowed his father to exit first. A few nobles populated the courtyard, the ladies in green and brown wool and the men in thick suits of white or gold—women of the earth and men of the sky.

Frowning, Leo looked down at his royal blue overcoat. Athelstani colors. Would he stand out? A decade had passed since his last Sigillite party; he'd forgotten their etiquette.

Slowly closing the carriage door, Leo allowed his father to get ahead of him. A woman darted from behind the shadow of a nearby carriage, hiking up her skirt as she hurried towards the manor's gates. Slowing her pace, she fell into step with Leo, offering him a friendly smile.

Leo gaped at Kiylla before slamming his mouth shut. She had changed into a beautiful dress of layered jade silks and donned a heavy veil decorated with matching gems: attire she'd filched from Lady Parnesius' wardrobe.

Taking her arm, Leo pulled Kiylla aside. They ducked behind one of Beau's many trees. "Are you sure about this?" He whispered.

"Trust me. This is the best way in."

Nervous, Leo glanced up at the two-story manor. An ancient building riddled with countless rooms, Kiylla had insisted a break-in was better done when invited and when all attention was directed into a single room.

"Trust me." Kiylla squeezed his arm. "Though, I don't much like the name you gave me.

Mildred von Wardrieu: Thurston's cousin and a woman Leo had courted years ago. Mildred had a severe gaze and short hair, not the most fetching of women. Covered in so much makeup, Kiylla could easily pass for her.

Or so Leo had thought. Now that he stood beside Kiylla, she was far too pretty to pass for Mildred. High cheekbones, eyes flecked with gold beneath the light. . .

Forgetting his thoughts, Leo stared at her. Bravery, determination, loyalty. . . so much more than mere beauty colored her face.

"You look. . ." Kiylla tilted her head. "Blue."

Taking Kiylla's arm, Leo guided her inside. "And you look nice."

"Nice," Kiylla repeated the word as though it tasted sour. "I thought Imperial men said lovely. *Beautiful.*" She scrunched her nose up. "Never have I been more uncomfortable. I hope Beau intends to kill us on the dance floor."

Leo hesitantly chuckled. "Is that a joke?"

"I do not joke."

Nodding at the servant standing by the doors, Leo weaved past the gathering in the foyer and entered the ballroom. Nobody paid Kiylla a second glance, not that they could see much beneath the heavy fabrics and veil.

More people than he would have imagined attended this party. Even with a war on, plenty of men and women remained home, though most appeared either too old for war or too young. Several youths around his sister's age loitered near the refreshment stands, lanky in their oversized finery.

Wincing under the glare of the chandeliers brightening the white tile, Leo listened to the string quartet's lively waltz. Guiding Kiylla to where a few other young couples danced, he took her hand. "Just follow my lead."

Kiylla looked like she wanted to sarcastically retort, but she begrudgingly followed his lead. Her floundering steps reminded him of when he saw Eckart attempt a waltz. Uncivilized brutes, the two of them, with no understanding of art.

Leo wondered how the people of Yuri Llaqta danced. Maybe one day, Kiylla could show him.

"What do you think?" Leo whispered.

Kiylla's sharp eyes observed the dance floor. "I saw a pair of guards by the stairs. Are you sure it's uncouth to go up there?"

"It's considered impolite. That's the family's quarters."

"Hm. Why don't you distract Beau, talk to him? I'll find a way up there."

"Be careful. If we get caught-"

"I'll just kill them."

"You remind me of Wulf." Leo shook his head. "Never mind. What of the Vicar? Any news?"

Leaning her head closer to his, Kiylla lowered her voice, though he doubted anyone could hear them. "I managed to slip into the cathedral last night. I found something interesting."

"Do tell."

"He was visiting Fairborough, when it burned. The only clergy member who survived the massacre. Apparently, he outed his brethren and let the mercenaries in."

Leo stepped on Kiylla's foot, lost in thought, and she lightly kicked him in retaliation. Beau seemed a snake, scheming and wicked. The Vicar opposed corruption and opposed the war. By all accounts, he seemed a good man. Yet the two were allies.

They wanted to end the war, to kill the cefra. . . Leo's head spun, searching for a reason.

"That's all I found," Kiylla concluded. "Who was he before that? Who knows."

"Any information is better than none." Leo stopped, intending to ask her something, but he could not voice it.

She tilted her head, piercing eyes boring through him. "What?"

"Nothing."

Eyebrows furrowed, Kiylla watched the other women and imitated their steps. She knit her fingers through his, tapping on the back of his hand to the beat. Though Leo had brought her here to speak before splitting ways, he found nothing to say.

Neither did Kiylla. They danced in silence, eyes only for each other. Leo's hand tensed on her back, and his heart pounded against his chest.

Every time he met Kiylla's eyes, he glanced away only to immediately look back.

The intensity of her brown irises never wavered. She held his gaze, even when he flinched. A small smile played across her lips when she noticed his discomfort, and her hand upon his shoulder tightened.

Hearing the final note play, Leo dipped her and gracefully pulled her back up. He clutched her hand and held her waist even as the other couples stepped apart and the music ceased. The world around them blurred; Leo was entranced by the soft light shining on her lips.

"Leo?" Kiylla said softly. "Are we not supposed to stop?"

"Oh, right." He dropped her hand. "Be careful."

"You are always in more danger than me." Kiylla teased, picking up the hem of her gown and departing the dance floor. Fussing with his cuffs, Leo tried to parse what he was feeling.

A woman came to mind, a redhead of great beauty with an infectious simile. Relia was the Emperor's daughter, in all likelihood. And the Trenowyths had lost the right to marry her. Perhaps Leo would see her again, but not in that way.

Unsure why he'd thought of her, Leo scanned the floor for Beau. His gaze landed on a group of older men standing in a circle near the center, conversing with a younger man of about thirty.

A man with a sour face and short dark hair, whose sharp eyes landed on Leo instantly.

"Oh, no," Leo muttered. Straightening himself, he approached Thurston casually. "By the goddess' watchful gaze," He whistled. "I didn't think you went to balls. Do you even own finery?"

"What else am I supposed to do while we loiter here?" Thurston asked, rolling a shoulder. "Who was your date?"

"Hm?" Leo feigned confusion. "Oh, I don't know. She asked for a dance."

Thurston narrowed his eyes and searched for Kiylla, but she had vanished.

Glancing around the gathering, Leo recognized only one: Lady Lucullus, the older woman in the Chamber. She smiled at him politely, one hand on the stomach of her surprisingly plain brown gown.

The rest were older men in their fifties and above, though none Leo knew. They were all dark-skinned, likely Sigillite lords of some repute. A second Chamber Lord arrived, a pudgy-faced man in a gaudy white and gold doublet, his hair unusually long: Lord Hadrian.

Offering him a bow, Leo turned back to Thurston. "What were you talking about?"

"*I* wasn't," Thurston said unhelpfully.

"Ah." Lord Hadrian's gaze fell on Leo. "Sir Trenowyth. I didn't expect you tonight. Still hoping to sway my vote?"

Leo smiled politely. "I hear Consus paid you a personal visit the other day."

Hadrian chuckled, looking at his fellows. "Yes, young Parnesius has been rather insistent, begging me to think of the danger at home. Makes a man wonder what instilled such zeal."

"Peace, Hadrian," Lucullus commanded. "The survivors of the First know better than any how foolhardy the campaign was." She paused. "Is."

Disgruntled, Hadrian backed off. Remembering his deal with Beau, Leo pressed. "Why do you oppose the notion of withdrawing?"

"I'm opposed to enacting a law that none have before." Hadrian insisted. "It is outrageous to suggest we Chamber Lords defy the Goddess with his usurping. The Emperor will not withdraw. That is the end of the matter."

"Really?" Thurston said dryly. "You know, Leofric here moonlights as a court jester. Shall he recite you the tale of the First's fall? Or perhaps the Femoran attack that came from within?"

"I've skimmed the report. There's no need-" Hadrian's eyes darted behind them.

Before Leo heard Beau's voice, he knew who approached. And for once, he was glad for the man's appearance. "The report can hardly do it justice," Beau insisted, cane tapping on the tiles. "It poorly details the magnificent wave, nor outlines the depth of the tragedy."

Laying his hands on his cane, Beau smiled at Leo, dark eyes afire with mischief. Clearing his throat, Leo glanced at Thurston, hoping for support. "If you insist. Where should I start?"

Kiylla hated Athelstani fashion. There was so much cloth bundled in itchy, thick folds. Standing by a table lined with trays, Kiylla repressed the urge to scratch somewhere impolite while her eyes swept the dance floor.

Beau was clever; he might not keep anything incriminating in his home, but dismantling the Empire from within was a monumental undertaking. There had to be correspondence somewhere.

Grabbing a strange white cake from a tray, Kiylla held it to her mouth, watching Beau as he sauntered across the tiled floor to Leofric's side. Judging from the fluster on the south lord's face, Leofric had landed himself in another uncomfortable situation.

Leofric's friend, the cefra with startling icy eyes, had seemed clever. Why could he not have been the Imperial to whom Kiylla had sworn an alliance?

Though, the south lord had strengths of his own. Mainly in his pretty face, and the humor she drew from his flustered looks.

Beau egged Leofric on, encouraging him to speak, though Kiylla could not read their lips. It didn't matter. The lord of the house was occupied. Shoving the cake in her mouth, Kiylla waltzed to the archway and stepped into the grand hall. The guards remained on vigil beside the sweeping stairs, tucked behind two large potted trees. Two older couples stood on the carpet leading to the door, chatting.

Kiylla's memories of the shifting lands composed most of her spells. Practical back home but useless in a city like this. So, how best to distract these men?

Maybe there was a better way. Hurrying out the door, she trudged into the yard, pretending to fan herself beneath a great tree growing a few paces from the promenade. Glancing behind her, she waited until the steward by the door, and the knight at the gates turned away before bolting into the side yard.

As expected, another guard patrolled here, but he was alone. No sooner had the knight noticed Kiylla than a rock collided with his helm. A metallic thunk echoed through his armor before he dropped. Catching her evoked rock, Kiylla looked up.

Counting the windows, she picked the furthest from the ballroom. Remembering a set of thick stone stairs, they thudded into place against the worn stone of the manor, and she quickly ascended them.

The window was locked from the inside. Hefting her jagged stone, Kiylla smashed a small section of the glass and reached a hand through, carefully unlatching the padlock. Pushing the windows open, she dropped inside.

The dim space appeared to be a spare bedroom—sterile, dormant, and long unused. Pushing the door open, Kiylla peered into the hall—empty. Beau lived alone. None should be up here, save perhaps a maid.

Slipping down the hall, Kiylla cracked each door, searching for a study. Three doors down, she found the room she sought, a cozy office decorated with large vases now empty of flowers. Muffling her steps on the woven rug, her eyes swept over the stack of parchment on the desk.

Official matters, by the looks of them. Ledgers, letters, and accounts pertaining to banking and budgets. Not what Kiylla sought. Leaning down, she opened each drawer, searching for anything of worth.

The lowest shelf had an off-color back, lighter than the rest of the wood. Tapping it, Kiylla's ears perked up. A false back. Years ago, Beau was rarely separated from his bag, one Kiylla and Johanna had tried to find a false bottom in.

Locked with a small magnet, the bag's bottom could only be opened by pressing its opposing magnet against the right spot—a magnet the man had carried on his person. Clever Beau, but she and Johanna had proved just as savvy.

Searching his desk, she found an unassuming rock decorating the base of a flower vase. Grabbing it, she felt it along the hollow back until the magnet latched to the opposite magnet and pulled the hidden compartment loose, revealing a bundle of scrolls wrapped with twine and a small, old journal.

Quickly flipping through the pages, she found a load of gibberish; Imperial letters arranged in nonsensical orders painted the pages. Her back stiffened, recalling the tale of the ciphered journal Leo had spun. This must be more of their code language, designed to hide their treason should the documents be found.

Maybe she could decipher them later. Stuffing them under her dress, Kiylla froze as she heard footsteps walking past the door. Rising and slowly approaching, she leaned on the wall and peered through the crack in the door to see a woman with brunette hair tumbling down her back quickly dart into a room across the hall.

Who was this? A mistress? Kiylla watched as the woman reemerged and fled further down the hall, out of sight. Carefully pushing the office door open, Kiylla snuck down the hall and peered into the room the woman had briefly entered.

An austere sitting room waited within, filled only with a small mantle and a reading chair. Turning to exit, Kiylla found herself face to face with the brown-haired woman. Green eyes stared at her triumphantly.

"Kiylla," the woman said. "Beau said your curiosity would get the better of you."

Stepping back, Kiylla looked behind her: no windows adorned this room. She had no way out. "Speak."

"Let's make this quick. You're supposed to be working with Beau, yet clearly, you don't trust him. But we have the same goal—ridding your land of Imperial intruders."

"Why should I trust Imperials?"

"Our reasons don't matter." The woman's face sharpened. "Know this: if losses abroad will not rally the citizens into a fervor, then losses at home will. Especially if they spring from a different enemy."

Kiylla understood. "From the cefra?"

"Perhaps." The woman reached into her cloak, palming something. "I can help you. All I need in return is your aid."

Kiylla knew what this woman held. One of the cefran relics. Bereft of her own jewel, Kiylla was outmatched. "You're the woman who drowned Femora."

"And Leofric was among those who stopped me, yet you've chosen his aid," Tettiena said. "Well? Will you hear me out?"

". . . I have your word, your intentions are true?"

"Would I have attacked Femora, were they not?"

Kiylla studied the jewel-shaped impression beneath the woman's cloak. "You're going to destroy Clodia?"

"I'm going to force the Empire into another war," Tettiena said.

This felt like treason—the Earth Father stood for his cefran kin as well as the Llaqtans. But Kiylla needed time to decode these journals, time for Leofric's plan to unfold. Perhaps this Tettiena was worth heeding. Maybe Kiylla had no other choice.

"Whatever it takes to save my people, I will do," Kiylla said. "Tell me what you need."

CHAPTER TWENTY THREE

TWIN SOUL

ECKART STUMBLED FORWARD, grabbing a jagged chunk of the precarious rock the stormsinger had deposited them onto. The anomaly of storms, leviathans, wind, and light raged in the sea of colorless gray, growing in intensity. Should the winds intensify further, Eckart and Wulf would be tossed from the tiny island.

Wulf's knees buckled, and he dug his spear into the earth to keep purchase. Not wanting to look into this world's inhuman, unknowable heart, Eckart stared at the rock below him, ignoring the endless sky threatening to swallow them whole.

How long had it been since Fionn had disappeared into the heart? Time flew past at times, and in other moments, it stood still. Had she been gone half an hour or several days? Mind fraying, Eckart pressed a hand to his forehead and closed his eyes, straining to block out the howling gale.

Something burst. Light shot across the dark world, briefly illuminating them with electricity. Rushing and roaring followed like something approached. Something unfathomable.

Wulf shouted, distressed. "Eckart!"

Snapping his head up, Eckart looked up in time to see the Leviathan of storms shooting towards them, maw of swirling winds agape. It crashed into the tiny island, sundering the rock and sweeping the men up in its hurricane.

Not again! Captured by the Leviathan's gale, Eckart again tumbled to his death, as he had in Lavinia. But this time, the Leviathan was alive, in control, diving straight down of its own volition rather than falling limply.

And then it was over. Eckart's back slammed into something hard, and his breath caught. Vision falling dark, he felt around for something solid, something real. The ceaseless tornado fell quiet, and all he heard now was a calm breeze rustling through leaves.

Gasping for breath, Eckart sat up, vision returning. Wulf struggled to his feet a few paces away, fingers dug into verdant, thick grass. Fionn lay in a heap of curls and tattered scarves beside him.

Rushing to her side, Eckart rolled her over. Eyes fluttering open briefly, Fionn glanced between him and Wulf before her head lolled to the side. Color had returned to her skin and vibrancy to her eyes, yet Eckart could tell she was changed somehow. A glint appeared behind her eyes, gone too quick to glean.

Veins like pulsing lightning streaked across her skin, slowly fading. Wulf picked up her arm and checked her pulse. He exhaled in relief.

Had the Leviathan thrown them through a gateway back to Thruine? The noise had been so overwhelming Eckart had heard nothing but the wind. Standing, he looked around.

Rolling hills cascaded to their west, and tall, thin trees clustered on the rocky ridges to their east. It hardly seemed like winter here—the world in every direction glowed with vitality, a green so deep it sprung from a painting.

This must be Forsaidh. They'd fallen in Dragos and landed a world away.

"Forsaidh?" Wulf guessed, checking Fionn for injury.

"I think so." Eckart scanned the horizon, searching for signs of civilization. A noticeable path began to their south along the treeline, where frequent travel had worn down the grass.

Straightening his windblown robes, Eckart felt for his bow—useless; the arrows had all jarred loose. Drawing instead the sword

Ciprian had worn on his belt, Eckart strode forward, checking for travelers.

"Does she need a healer?" He called over his shoulder.

"She could use a proper dressing on her side," Wulf said, gathering her into his arms. "But otherwise, no."

"Might be able to find a town if we follow that." Eckart pointed to the dirt road. "What do you think?"

"Better than loitering around." Wulf decided, carrying her to the path.

Clutching the sword tightly, Eckart followed closely behind him. "What do you think happened back there?"

"I have no idea. But her eyes. . . " Wulf trailed off. "They were different."

"I noticed." Eckart agreed. How, though, he found difficult to put into words. "You look nice, at least."

Wulf glanced down at his torn doublet and fancy cloak. "Arsene said all Forsaidh natives dress like courtesans. Think they'll like my style?"

"My people say the same." Eckart chuckled. His face fell as exhaustion consumed him, and they both fell silent.

Tree branches surrounded them as they followed the worn path. The forest grew thicker with every step, guiding them up a path ravaged by cliffs. A misstep here could spell doom. Pushing Wulf aside, Eckart took the lead.

Something moved in the forest ahead. Halting, Eckart motioned for Wulf to be still and silent. Voices followed the movement. The shadow of a man peered from behind a tree, hand on his bow, but he quickly lowered it and strode forward to meet them.

Eckart sighed with relief. It was a fellow cefra—an Aeourant. Even had they not been in Forsaidh, Eckart could have gleaned as much from the absurd dress. The man wore no tunic, only leather bands around his biceps and trousers. Paint covered his skin, illustrating the dark wingspan of a falcon.

Spirits, but he resembled Fionn. Curly silver hair gathered in a bond at his neck, and freckles scattered in uneven patches across his pallid skin. Rich purple eyes regarded the men with confusion while concern appeared for the limp woman in Wulf's arms.

Recognition burst to life in those eyes. "Fionnuala?" He gasped, hand tightening on his bow.

"Peace." Eckart pleaded. "She's injured. Guide us to your territory."

The man studied Eckart. "You are not one of ours."

"No. I'm Gaevral."

"Law demands your safe entry," the man said, grimacing.

The Aeourant patrol joined their leader, similarly dressed in revealing armor. Weapons drawn, they barred the path.

"But I have no choice but to place her under arrest." The curly-haired man said grimly.

"What?" Wulf barked.

"This woman stole our most sacred relic." He gestured to her wound. "We will not hurt her. Nor you. But on this, I cannot budge."

Snarling protectively, Wulf took a step back.

The curly-haired man relaxed his stance. "Peace. She is my cousin."

That explained the resemblance. Eckart glanced at Wulf, nodding encouragingly.

Sighing, Wulf relented. "Damn thief. She was bound to get arrested sooner or later. She's just like Arsene. . ." He jerked his head up. "Lead on. But if you hurt her. . ."

"Relax, mountain-kin." The guard turned. "She is still one of ours."

Fionn felt like she awoke from a deep slumber. Reality sharpened, her vision cleared. As her eyes fluttered open, she could hardly recall where she'd been or how much time had passed.

Someone gripped her wrists, submerging her arm beneath a pond. Water pooled in her palm as it emerged. The silver liquid gradually hardened into crystal, leaving her palm dry. Then, the hands cupping hers threaded a cord through the crystal and strung it around Fionn's neck.

Memories. They flooded into Fionn like water from a broken dam. Memories of Father, his eyes like twinkling jades, his smile wide and inviting. Memories of the stream where she wrote her music, of the hut she had grown up in. But something was wrong.

Seoras. Seoras' memories were there like they'd always been, hidden and far away. Recollections of a man once mortal, who Fionn could never quite recall. But now, there was more. Memories of seeing through her eyes, yet not quite. . . her.

No, something more than memories felt out of place. A deep malaise permeated her being, radiating from within. Pulsing, jittering, forcing a tremble through her hands, but not like before. Not from weakness, from sickness. . . from something else. But what?

Disoriented and lost, Fionn cleared her vision and strained to see. She was. . . home.

The maevruthan's silver waters lapped under a heavy wind, the flowers growing between pebbles bucked under the breeze. Huts gathered in a messy cluster in the Forsaidh forest, lined with lanterns and colorful flags.

The woman holding Fionn's wrist hauled her to her feet. Red hair streaked with gray gathered loosely around the shoulders of a wrinkled woman with honey-colored eyes. Her free hand hung loose at her side. Mother.

"Back to your senses?" Mother asked somberly.

Everything crashed into place: the dungeon, Tettiena, the Chancellor, the horrible sound as her crystal shattered, and her mind fracturing. Seoras remembered all of it.

Their mission, their purpose. . . Fionn had failed.

Mother released her wrist and stepped back. A man grabbed Fionn's arms and gently forced them behind her while a second warrior stepped before her.

The man behind her had a familiar touch, and Fionn glanced behind her to see her cousin, Cormag. His visage was like that of a sibling, and the disapproving wrinkle on his mouth expressed much: 'I knew she would do something like this one day.'

"Take her away." Mother ordered.

Fionn was being arrested? Gasping, she lunged, but Cormag's grip was far stronger. "Arrested? What for?"

"For stealing Seoras' Breath." Mother said coldly.

"I didn't steal it," Fionn shouted, then bit her lip. Well, that was a lie, wasn't it?

Cormag steered her around, but Fionn didn't need his guidance. She knew where they headed. Overwhelmed, she looked at her mother, repressing the growing urge to call for her mom.

Cefran criminals were rare; most could not bear to steal or harm those they knew intimately, and those tempted knew they'd be caught. Still, every now and then, a rotten soul would trespass regardless and swiftly be condemned. His own memories would betray him, after all. Someone had seen Fionn flee and caught her in the act. Her guilt was certain.

The solitary pair of cells in the settlement rested beneath the barracks, buried in the earth. A creaky hatch in the building's floor entered into her gloomy prison. Her escort was gentle, at least. Cormag did not bind her wrists and allowed her to descend at her own rate. A waterskin and hunk of cheese were sent with her; Mother retained a soft spot for her daughter.

"We won't keep you here long," Cormag promised. "The Chief just wants to be fair."

"You don't sound all that angry," Fionn said.

"Saint's wind, Fionn." He shook his head. "You've always been touched in the head. Why not by the gods themselves?" He tilted his head, inquiring if she was ready. She nodded.

Fionn flinched as the hatch slammed above her head and locked. Dirt walls surrounded her, save for a barred window peering out at a mound of grass. Pressing her back to the window, she slumped to the floor.

Escape would be within reach if she truly wished, but Fionn felt wretched. She'd think over her problems later. The fluttering agony wrenched her heart from side to side, and it beat a thousand times faster than before. At least, so it felt.

Pressing a hand to her chest, Fionn tried to calm herself, to no avail. Closing her eyes, she tried to remember.

There was a man. Amber eyes, cold and hard. Fionn had decided to throw the world away for him. Why? He was cold, rude, an asshole. *Cacmun!* He hadn't even liked her!

There was more, too. A cefran half-breed, a young woman with bright red hair, and. . . and a gruff mercenary with beautiful blue eyes the color of the sea. They were strangers. Fionn had never met them before.

The day before stealing Seoras' gem, Fionn had pooled her memories. Every day since was gone from her mind. Seoras remembered, but. . .

Fionn furrowed her brow, squeezing her eyes tighter. She could remember them. Arsene had always flirted with her, and she never could tell if he meant it. Eckart had been a sweetheart, honest and straightforward. Relia had clung to Fionn, her lifeline in this strange new world until she'd found her feet.

And Wulf had held her while she cried, shielded her from the winds. . . She knew how Seoras felt about them. He and Wulf had clashed, screaming at one another, seething with hate. Arsene had not been worth the trust, Relia had been a pawn to leave behind. . .

Shouldn't Fionn see them that way if all that remained was Seoras' memories?

So why did their memories come with a breeze of warm fondness?

There you are. Seoras' voice rang clear over the confusion. *I wanted to give you a moment to orient yourself.*

Pain rattled in her mind. Usually, Seoras felt like a voice whispering in her ear, but now it felt like her thoughts roaring against her skull. Wincing, she felt her heart flutter faster, jittering wildly.

Did it not work? Fionn thought.

Ah. . . Seoras sounded uncertain. Fionn tilted her head against her will, grimacing. *I lied. When you transformed into the Leviathan, your fate was sealed. It tore you apart from the inside. Nothing,* nothing *could heal that. Not even the heart of Casaliede.*

Seoras had. . . hidden something from her? Yet it was true. She felt his thoughts as though her own.

I didn't know if my plan would work. Seoras admitted. *There was a hole at your core. A gaping wound. I sought to seal it, to stop the bleeding. Maybe it will last for only a day, maybe fifty years. I don't know.*

For once, Fionn did not need Seoras to speak to understand what he intended to say. From the heart of Casaliede, he'd plucked a piece of the plane itself and shoved it inside her. He'd lodged a piece of glass in her gash rather than bind it with gentle gauze.

Pawing at her chest panickedly, Fionn's breath came in short gasps. But what did that mean? The pulsing, fluttering inside her. . was it the shard of the plane about to give way to her delayed death?

Seoras pulled back, allowing her space. But they had no such separation anymore. She felt him withdraw, felt his presence in her mind, throughout her soul, pulsing in her blood. Uncertainty and worry plagued him and flowed into her.

What did this mean? She'd tried to separate the two of them for years, strained to extract Fionn from Seoras. Was she an empty shell hosting him? Would she drop dead if he left? What was he, really? An errant soul? A man hiding a world away, puppeting her like a marionette?

Burying her head in her knees, she rocked back and forth, wishing the world would stop spinning, wishing everything would just *stop* for a moment so she could breathe.

No rest for the wicked. Something clawed at her, a sensation of being elsewhere, of her two halves colliding. Shrieking, Fionn pressed her hands to her head, shivering.

No, it wasn't her other half. It was the songbird. Flitting over a branch and dipping beneath a roof sill, it dove for the bars behind her. Spinning around, Fionn knew it would appear before it arrived.

A little brown songbird shoved its way between the bars. Fionn reached out a hand, brushed its feathers, and felt it. . . disappear.

Staring at her palm in horror, Fionn's head snapped up. Someone approached.

The world outside was dark. When had night fallen? Boots moved in the gloom, stopping by her window. A man crouched, peering through the bars.

"Fionn?" Wulf asked.

Stunned, Fionn stared at him blankly. Myriad emotions washed through her. First and foremost, an intense desire to strangle him, to jolt him with a burst of lightning. This cur had antagonized Seoras ceaselessly, starting petty fights and disrespecting him—a god!

But fondness cut through the hate. Memories of longing, pining surfaced. Seoras had seen someone familiar in Wulf. Someone he desperately wanted to trust. After facing the darkness alone for so long, surely a man like him could help them?

And he'd been by her side ever since they'd met. More than a mere ally. As Seoras' memories welled up inside her, they didn't feel like someone else's. They felt like. . .

Fionn wanted to break the bars and throw herself into Wulf's arms. But she had decorum to maintain. Staring at his belt, she shoved an arm through the bars and grabbed the pommel of his dagger, yanking it loose and smuggling it into her jail cell.

Wulf looked down, patting his empty holster, before noticing the flash of steel in her grip. He choked, sounding like he might cry. "You remember?"

Not the way he wanted. Not the way she wanted, either. "I remember enough." She said. "Are you alright?"

"We're fine. Your people have been downright hospitable, all things considered."

"Then what are you doing here?"

"What do you think? Breaking you out." Wulf glanced over his shoulder. "You know this place better than us. Have any bright ideas?"

"No one's ever escaped the Aeourant's watchful eye."

"You have." Wulf shut his eyes and shook his head. "Your damn god stole the jewel. They can't arrest you!"

But Seoras did not want his people to know. He wanted them to remain in peace, blissfully unaware their lives hung by a thread. Fionn would vanish, saving their lives, and none would ever know.

And strangely, Fionn wanted that, too. No one would believe her, besides. If her tale was true, the memories would be in the maevruthan, but Seoras had kept them out.

"They won't believe me." Fionn glanced up at the hatch. "Mother will afford me a trial. I want to see her one last time. Say goodbye."

"But what if they-"

"I'll be exiled, not killed. There's no need to interfere."

"But if you're exiled-"

Fionn choked on a laugh. "I'd need a new clan. But that doesn't mean my life would be over. Seoras would remember, you see?"

Unwilling to leave, Wulf reached through the bars and took her hand. "I don't want Seoras to remember. I want *you* to remember. You've spent too long in his shadow."

An overwhelming rush of emotions surged through her chest. Anger. Annoyance. Indignance. A growing smile. Love.

"Go before someone catches you." Fionn hissed. "I'll be fine."

Wulf was stubborn. Irritatingly stubborn. But that quality had been one of the reasons Seoras had elected to trust him. Grimacing, he loitered at the bars before reaching through, caressing her neck.

"I'm not leaving you." He whispered. "Whatever happens, we'll be together."

Fionn smiled at him. "I know."

Reluctant to let go, Wulf rose and darted into the night.

Exhausted, Fionn sank to the cold floor. If she was exiled, her memories would deteriorate within a year, leaving her an empty shell even Seoras could not save her from. But that was alright.

A year was more than enough time. She'd ruined their plans, put them all in jeopardy. It was up to her to set it right.

Chapter Twenty four

ACCUSED

LEO ASCENDED THE palace stairs, hardly able to comprehend the gravity of the summons he'd received. After returning from patrol this evening, the last thing he'd expected was for Lady Parnesius to inform him of a summons from the Emperor.

What did the Emperor want with Leo? Straining to keep composure, Leo ran a hand through his hair as he arrived at the parlor door. A stained glass table reflected the sun's dying light, scattering images of roses across the Emperor's golden cape.

The weary man turned, beckoning Leo inside. The paladin following Leo shut the door behind them and remained on guard in the hall.

Clearing his throat, Leo bowed deeply. Pressing a gauntlet to his chest plate, he waited for the Emperor to speak first.

"Rumors have a way of traveling across nations, no matter how quietly whispered." The Emperor said, eyes wide. "As a member of the First, you must have heard."

Confused, Leo rose. "Rumors, your Majesty? What of?"

Eye bulging, the Emperor strode forward, like he intended to grab Leo's collar. "Of the red-haired maiden glimpsed behind the crowds of soldiers."

Leo stared blankly ahead. Only the elite of the church had the authority to declare royal lineage. Consus had forbidden him and Thurston from spreading rumors until the Duke made his declaration.

"Speak." The Emperor barked.

"A red-haired maiden?" Leo blurted out. "You mean-"

"My daughter." Desperation dripped from the Emperor's words. "She was there? Tell me, was she there?"

"I. . ." Leo swallowed. "I saw a woman that could match her description. She called herself by a different name and claimed to be a native of another land, but. . ."

"Why have I not been told?"

"The generals ordered her to return with the Dragosi party so the Duke might see if there was any validity to the claims."

Rage and hope flashed in the man's brown eyes. "She lives. . ." He breathed, wandering back to the window.

A pang of guilt flashed in Leo's heart. Taking a cautious step forward, he considered saying something more, but the door flew open, interrupting him.

Beau Rosa entered, absent his usual cane. "I have brought the other you requested, Your Majesty." Bowing, he walked past Leo.

Thurston, of all people, walked in, his countenance colored with confusion. His dark eyes met Leo's and conveyed a message: he had no inkling what this was about.

Unease churned in Leo's gut. The Emperor turned as the door fell closed behind Thurston. "You. I would hear your account."

"What of, your majesty?" Thurston asked.

"Of the the girl with red hair seen in your unit."

"Ah." Thurston strode forward, standing opposite the Emperor.

Launching into a brief but respectful tale, Thurston more eloquently repeated Leo's answers. Beau paced the room, hands clasped behind his white coat. White. Though white or gold were the colors donned by Sigillite noblemen, Leo had never seen Beau wear it before.

Beau's easy smile and quick charisma were absent. Intensity illuminated his nearly black irises as he oversaw Thurston and the

Emperor. As he moved behind Leo, he touched his arm, whispering so quietly Leo could hardly hear him.

"I am sorry, dear boy."

A flash of steel appeared in the glow of the window before a splash of scarlet stained the drapes and carpet. Leo gasped as a blade identical to his own pierced through the Emperor's heart before its twin cleaved across Thurston's chest and neck.

No man wielded the blades. They swept through the air. Conjured. An evoker's spell.

Darting forward, Leo reached for the sword at his belt, but his hand hardly brushed the pommel before something heavy slammed into his back and threw him to the floor. The world blurred as his head struck the tiles. Someone grabbed his wrists, forcing them behind his back.

Blood seeped across the floor onto his hair. Gurgles and gasps of pain filled the room as Beau shouted frantically for aid.

A knee pushed into Leo's back and Beau pressed a knife to his neck. A deathly whisper emerged from his lips. "How savage. The cefran sympathizer kills the Emperor and even his friend, who leaped to our liege's defense."

Horrified, Leo futilely strained against his captor as he watched the dying men hit the floor. The perfect mimicries of his blade struck the ground and vanished.

The parlor door banged open as two paladins charged in. They gaped at the bloody scene.

Rising, Beau drew Leo's sword from his belt and dragged it across Thurston's bloodied surcoat before jamming the blade through the Emperor's chest. Steel rang as the paladins drew their blades.

"I was too late," Beau said calmly. "I've subdued the assassin; quick, attend to his majesty."

What kind of sick joke was this? The paladins had seen Beau desecrate the Emperor's corpse. No longer restrained, Leo pulled himself up and glanced behind him.

The paladins stood in the doorway, slack-jawed, eyes glazed over. Leaving Leo's sword in the dead man, Beau sauntered back to Leo and slammed a boot into his back. Wincing, Leo could not muster the ability to struggle.

Whatever spell captured the paladins faded. One man rushed to the Emperor's side while the other kneeled beside Leo. A click of metal followed. Shackles. Leo tried and failed to pull his wrists apart, but they were bound by steel.

Leo's voice finally returned as Beau stood aside, and the paladin hoisted him up. "What are you doing? Beau was the one who murdered them. You *saw* him!"

A gauntlet slammed into Leo's head. "Silence, traitor." The paladin hissed.

The world spun as Leo was dragged from the room. More people arrived, footsteps thundering down the hall like drums. But all Leo could focus on was the smug smile on Beau's face.

For the first time in Leo's life, he had been inducted into the Chamber to join a meeting. But a few days later, here he stood again, this time clapped in irons.

Two knights restrained him as Lord Beau Rosa delivered his account of the Emperor's assassination to the Chamber of Lords. The room was crammed with every man and woman with a title to their name.

The Emperor was dead. Beau had murdered him. Murdered Thurston. He'd pinned the crime on Leo effortlessly, and the paladins heeded his commands despite the brutality they'd witnessed.

Surely the lords would not believe such a ridiculous tale?

Steadying his breathing, Leo skimmed the room, eyes landing on his father. Lord Barron Trenowyth would not look at his son. Disbelief colored his pale face as he stared at the man standing opposite him in shocked silence.

"This is ridiculous." Consus' cape fell over his shoulder as he slammed the table.

Beau started at Consus' interruption. "Lord Parnesius, I was there. I saw-"

"I have known Sir Trenowyth since we were children." Consus spat. "With all due respect, Lord Rosa, he is not a traitor and certainly no assassin."

"Hold a moment." Lady Lucullus held up a wrinkled hand. "First, Llaqtans wipe out our legion. Then, cefrans attack Dragos. Now, one of our own assassinates our Emperor?"

"Indeed." Lord Drusus' hard eyes flicked about the room. His grizzled face landed on Leofric. "It was a sloppy attack. One only a martyr hoping to be caught would attempt."

Leo bit his tongue. He had been told to speak only when the Archbishop or Vicar gave permission. Glancing at the two men at the head of the room, draped in their verdant green clerical robes, he saw two different expressions.

The Archbishop's old face paled with shock; the Vicar's eyes gazed down from above his hooked nose with an even expression.

A heavy-set man in a golden doublet joined those who stood from their seats. "Our Empire is falling to pieces, and we cannot even identify our foes?" He gestured urgently to the Archbishop. "Do you really believe one of our knights did this?"

"If not," Beau said calmly, "Then who did?"

Consus fingers curled into a fist. "I find it odd that you were the first upon the scene, Lord Rosa."

Beau's eye twitched, but his expression was not one of anger; he looked impressed. "Are you accusing me of something, Lord Parnesius?"

"I have yet to understand why you arrived at Femora, why you were there the night we nearly lost the Third."

"We had concerns over the state of our troops." Beau nodded to the Vicar. "Vicar Faunus sent me. He can confirm this."

The hooked-nose Vicar nodded slowly, his voice slow and drawling. "Following the tragedy of the First, we needed to ensure the remaining men had not lost heart. Lord Rosa is most familiar with the land. He seemed an obvious choice."

Satisfied by that answer, the heavy-set man turned his gaze to Leo. "What does the prisoner have to say for himself?"

Leo shot a pleading glance at the clergymen, and the Archbishop nodded his assent.

"I did not kill them." Leo insisted. "It was Beau. I saw him; he evoked my blade. He even desecrated the corpse right in front of the paladins."

Everyone stared in silence at Leofric. Their eyes glazed over, and their jaws slackened. The dumb expressions gaped at Leo for lingering seconds before their vision cleared, and they continued as if Leo had never spoken at all.

Lord Hadrian, the long-haired, pudgy-faced Lord of Agriculture, shot to his feet next. "We should be discussing matters of succession. The throne cannot be left empty at a time like this."

Consus interjected. "We have an heir. She was sent to Dragos to confirm her heritage."

Even Consus ignored Leo? Horror churned in Leo's heart. What was going on?

A few gasps sounded around the room. "Dragos?" Lucullus rocketed to her feet. "Then the cefra who attacked; they targeted the princess?"

Lord Drusus waved a hand though he remained sitting. "We're to believe the missing heir turned up, and no one knew?"

"She had not confirmed her heritage," Consus explained. "She was sent with the confiscated weaponry to the Duke. If we retrieve her-"

"If we retrieve her?" Lord Hadrian spat. "You had the heir in your care, and you lost her to cefra?"

"We have precious few details of what the attack entailed." Consus snarled. "Should you not be wondering why the Duke did not report this important fact?"

"We should." Drusus agreed.

"Leofric has nothing to do with cefra." Consus continued. "He's an Athelstani knight, and he was invaluable during our time in Yuri Llaqta."

Hope dared to join Leo's growing fear. Consus had his back. Judging from the expressions on Drusus and Lucullus' faces, they were inclined to believe Consus.

But his hope shattered the instance Beau spoke. "Leofric has everything to do with the cefra." He folded his hands on the table. "He's well-known to have been in close company with one. Suspiciously close company." Beau's black eyes stared pointedly at Lord Trenowyth. "Is that correct?"

Slowly, Lord Barron Trenowyth raised his head. "Yes, my Lord. My son was loyal to a certain cefra—the same who stands accused of attacking the Duke."

"Ah!" Lord Hadrian pointed accusingly at Leo. "So this is why you were advocating for our vote to overthrow the Emperor. When I abstained, you took matters into your own hands."

"That's a far-fetched accusation," Drusus spoke up. "Because he's acquainted with a cefra, he sought the bloody crown?"

The Vicar cleared his throat. "If I may?" He gestured to a wiry steward, who unrolled a scroll.

Reading in a calm, clear voice, the steward rattled off Leo's account of the Femoran wave, focusing on Leo's assault on the dungeons to rescue Eckart.

"As you can see," The Vicar drawled, "This one has betrayed his Empire for cefra before."

A heavy weight struck Leo in the chest as realization set in. This was why Beau had brought his father. Why Beau had asked Leo to help him sway the Lord's votes. Why the Vicar had wanted his written testimony. All for this.

Beau Rosa had caught Leo in his trap before he'd set foot on Clodian shores. Kiylla had been right; when Leo had not died at sea, Beau had chosen him another fate.

"Have you all gone mad?" Consus marched around the table toward Leo. "I interrogated Eckart when we imprisoned him. I watched Eckart aid us in the fight against Kiylla. I saw him head into Llaqtan territory, risking his neck to bring us information." His voice hardened. "You were the man who appeared the day before the wave and disappeared the day after. You were the man who wanted Eckart killed when he was the only one who could save us."

"Wrong, Consus." The Vicar interjected. "I sent Johanna Rosa to warn you of a Gaevral scout said to be carrying a weapon. You ignored her and allowed the cefra free reign. Allowed him to strike. And now you attempt to shield his allies."

Beau joined his chorus. "Cefra assault our troops. Cefra assaulted the Duke, and captured our missing princess. What for, if not to destabilize us? And now they've planted seeds of doubt by sending a human to kill our Emperor. We are vulnerable because you allowed it to be so. Their plan falls into place."

"Lord Trenowyth." The Archbishop's sharp voice sounded for the first time. "You know your son better than any. Would he stand by this cefra's side and forsake his own?"

Leo's father finally looked at his son. And before he spoke, Leo knew what those hollow eyes intended to say.

"Yes, your worship." Lord Barron Trenowyth said quietly. "He would. Of that, I am certain."

"Lord Trenowyth," Consus shouted. "Can you not see the treachery playing out before us?"

The Vicar nodded to a paladin guarding the door. "Seize him."

Consus stepped back when the man approached him and tried to wrest from his grip. "What is the meaning of this?"

"The mother's taint," Beau said quietly, "Infects the son. Your allegiance has been made clear."

The Vicar stood tall. "For the crimes of assassinating the Emperor, for failing to defend his legion, and for standing by traitors when holy blood stains their blade, I sentence Leofric von Trenowyth and Consus Parnesius. . ." The Vicar allowed a pause as a hush fell across the room. "To death."

CHAPTER TWENTY FIVE

THE PYRE

RAIN DRIZZLED FROM the bright heavens of Clodia. Leo stared into the sky, wondering what it felt like to join with the goddess.

The flower boxes in the square held dried, dead roses. Flocks of people gathered around the flowers' corpses, watching the great marble stage where two pyres awaited their criminals.

Jangling irons shook Leo from his reverie as Consus was dragged to stand beside him. From childhood to the present, Consus had always presented himself as a kempt, regal man. To see him now in a threadbare tunic and shackles. . .

Everything had happened so fast. Leo had hardly processed Thurston's death. Within an instant, Beau had convinced the nobility to execute their own for fear of cefran insurgents hiding amongst human cities.

Had Kiylla known? Had Beau asked her to aid Leo, knowing the Empire would turn from Yuri Llaqta to face its cefran enemies?

Leo's heart ached. Had she known?

"Leofric," Consus muttered. "Did you. . .?"

The question was unfinished, but Leo knew the rest. This was the first they'd spoken since the Emperor's death. "Of course not. You know who the culprit was."

The knight holding Leo knocked him upside the head, sending the world spinning. "Silence." The gruff voice behind the helm ordered.

Leo ignored him. "You shouldn't have stood by me."

Consus chuckled bitterly. "I never would have forgiven myself otherwise." His eyes swept the crowd. "Not even my father raised his voice. I alone dissented."

"About that. Something's not right-"

With a shove, the knights guided them onto the stage and toward their respective pyres. Cacophony rose from the crowd as the people whispered among themselves. Though Leo could make out no words in the rabble, he could glean their tone: disbelief. Many questioned if the knights had truly caught the correct foes.

Oil soaked into Leo's shirt as he was shoved against the pyre and bound to the logs. The Archbishop ascended the stage, dressed in white. His mantle flowed behind him as he took his position at the head of the stage.

With every ounce of his willpower, Leo strained to avoid looking into the crowd. Weakness took him for a moment, and he glanced over the blur of faces. Father's face sharpened amidst the horde, broken not by grief but by horror.

For good cause. The Trenowyth and Parnesius families would never recover from such a blight on their houses.

Spreading his arms, the Archbishop called for silence, and the chatters slowly hushed. "Good people of Clodia. I understand your confusion. How could our own, our finest, betray us in the most terrible manner?"

The drizzle ceased, and the sun brightened. Beneath its glare, a shadow intensified on a nearby roof. A woman's shadow.

"While our eyes were focused on the war, the cefra slipped their most precious weapons to the Llaqtans. They assaulted the holy city of Lavinia. And now, they've stolen away our blessed Emperor."

Murmurs in the crowd restarted, hushed only when the Archbishop's voice rang anew.

"They even hide allies among our own kind." He gestured to Leo and Consus, strung up on their pyres. "These men turned their blades against the goddess. They have forsaken their people. And we will not allow this transgression to go unanswered."

Two lesser clerics ascended the stage, lit torches in hand. Leo's throat tightened. This would not be a quick death.

As the clerics took their positions, the Archbishop recited the words granted to all accused of heresy. "From the Goddess, these lost souls have strayed. Should their accusations be false, may the goddess ward them from her wrathful flames and take them into her earthen embrace."

The clerics raised the torches, flames burning bright beneath the blinding sky. Glancing up, Leo saw the woman's shadow again, standing atop the tallest building, hand raised as though clutching something.

"Should their accusations be true, may the flames of hell burn this rot that taints her soil." The Archbishop boomed.

With a heavy bow, the clerics held the torches to the base of the pyre, catching the oiled logs alight. Heat licked at Leo's feet as a blaze burst to life, quickly spreading upward.

Panic raced through Leo as the pain intensified. A primal instinct kicked in, and he searched the crowd, finding his father. Guilt raged across Lord Trenowyth's face as he looked away. Every ounce of Leo wanted to scream, to beg for help, but he ground his teeth and squeezed his eyes as he braced for the agony.

Someone else screamed. Shrieks and yells broke from the crowd: men, women, and children. A horrible sound rang over their voices, a tear like the sky had been torn open by a god.

Choking on the growing smoke, Leo tried to see what was happening, but his eyes stung, refusing to open. Something slammed into the pyre behind him. His bonds loosened, and he tumbled to his knees, gasping, desperately trying to fan the flames traveling up his legs.

Icy cold snaked through him, piercing his veins like a knife. Wresting his eyes open, he saw Consus fall from his pyre onto a stone stage lined with ice.

Ice? Blinking, Leo stared into the crowd, stunned. Crystals of ice burst from the courtyard, rising toward the sky. A frigid chill seeped from them, visible to the eye. Frozen statues, their faces twisted in horror, stood rooted in place, clustered around the courtyard. A panicked crowd rushed from the area, pushing and shoving as they sought to escape.

As Leo watched, a young woman tripped. Ice from the crystals snaked through the ground, cracking the stone. The moment it touched her, it ripped across her skin, spreading like wildfire. Within an instant, she was frozen.

"Leofric!" A Llaqtan accented voice called.

What was going on? The flames doused on their own as the icy mist seeped toward the stage.

"South lord!" Kiylla grabbed Leo's collar and hauled him up. She looked like her old self. No makeup covered her face, revealing the light brown skin she had hidden for so long.

"Kiylla?" Leo stuttered, knees buckling.

"By the Earth Father," Kiylla seethed. "Get on your feet, Leofric von Trenowyth, and *move*."

She shoved him, and the gears in Leo's head finally turned. Finding his feet, he turned away from the courtyard to where a thin alley led from the execution stage to the dungeon. Consus slammed into him, pushing Leo ahead as he took up the rear.

Glancing over his shoulder, Leo searched for the woman whose shadow he had seen before the flames fell. She stood there still, a brilliant sapphire light shining within her palm.

The alley widened into a promenade leading to the dungeons. A guard drew his weapon and raced toward them but was swiftly knocked aside as a boulder jutted from the road and slammed into his flank, denting his mail.

"This way." Kiylla dragged them to the western road. A pair of guard horses, clad in green caparisons, danced anxiously, their owners crumpled by their hooves.

Limping, Consus grabbed the reins of the black horse, and Kiylla guided Leo to the brown mare. "What's going on?" Consus demanded, voice hoarse.

"Tettiena assaults your people," Kiylla said curtly, waiting for Leo to mount before pulling herself up behind him. "To make them believe the cefra have attacked."

"Tettiena?" Consus balked. "My mother?"

"Yes," Kiylla confirmed.

264

Cursing, Consus yanked the reins and directed the horse into a trot. They raced toward the eastern road. A chilling mist drifted through the air, and icy sheets tracked over the streets and marble walls. Tettiena's horrific spell was spreading.

Kiylla cursed in Llaqtan. "Turn around."

Behind them, the ice encroached from the south and east, leaving their only escape to the west. Grabbing onto Kiylla, Leo pressed his spinning head against her neck, watching as their horses weaved through the panicked crowd fleeing the touch of death.

"We have to stop this!" Consus shouted.

"With what?" Kiylla shouted back, barely audible above the pounding of hooves and screams. "Weaponless, magic-less, against an evoker like that?"

Gritting his teeth, Consus stared ahead, realizing she was right.

The smell of burnt flesh, flames, ice, and death filled the air— imagined or real, Leo couldn't tell. Screams rang in his ears. Cracks of ice, like whips against flesh, sounded where unlucky souls were caught in the wave of spreading frost. A great spire, like those in Yuri Llaqta, rose above the city, the brilliant sun reflected in its clear frost.

Leo felt like he would faint. Closing his eyes, he clung to Kiylla, trusting her with his and Consus' lives.

"Lay still." Kiylla barked.

Wincing, Leo clenched his fist, trying to keep from jerking. A nasty burn ran from his ankle to his knee, and every time Kiylla attempted to apply a salve to it, he ripped away from her.

Grabbing a chunk of his sleeve and biting down, Leo watched Consus pace their hidden camp in the woods. He rubbed his face, raked a hand through his disheveled hair, and stared through the oak trees into the night.

"By the heavens," Consus cursed, "What is my mother thinking?"

"I have only an idea," Kiylla admitted, roughly applying the salve before reaching for a roll of gauze. "To send the people into a fervor against an imagined enemy." Roughly wrapping Leo's wound, she spoke with a tightened jaw. "The cefra came to save their allies, confirming Beau's tale."

"I don't. . . I don't understand why she'd do this." Consus snarled. His fists tightened. "I'd love nothing more than to wring Beau's neck. No, *worse*." He whirled around. "And *you*."

Leo sucked in a breath as fiery pain raced through him. "I've told you, I can explain-"

"No, you cannot. To think all this time, you've been consorting with the one who murdered my men."

"I had good cause." Leo insisted. "I knew Beau could not be trusted. The Vicar tried to kill us all! I couldn't walk into the wolves den alone!"

"Then why did you not ask for my aid?"

"I didn't know if I could trust you, and. . ."

"You didn't think you could trust *me*. . . ?" He trailed off, staring daggers at Kiylla's back. "Yet her trust proved worthy. We are allies. For now. But don't think I've forgotten. Nor will I forgive."

"I would expect nothing less." Kiylla looked over her shoulder. "You have every right to hate. As do I."

Nodding curtly, Consus returned to his horse. "We need to move. We need supplies. Weapons. Armor."

"I'm sure I can find you some," Kiylla said. "But you two must rest first. The men are occupied with the city's disaster. Their search will be delayed." She paused. "You should know. Tettiena warned me of Beau's intentions. She wanted me to rescue you from the flames."

"What?" Leo asked, heart dropping.

"We made a deal," Kiylla said. "I did not think there was another way to save you."

Consus folded his arms. "Occupied with her spell, Mother needed someone else to spirit us away."

"Yes. To keep the hatred alive so that unrest would prevail until the day the daughter was crowned."

"Then the daughter must be found." Consus reluctantly released his horse's reins. "You're right. Tonight, we'll rest. But then there must be no delay."

"Where to?" Leo asked hoarsely.

"To Dragos. The place of the supposed attack, where the princess was last seen. We must find her."

Was there even a chance they could find Relia? Leo scanned the shadows of the trees, wondering where Eckart was.

Kiylla stood. "Rest, " she ordered. "You have been through much. I will keep watch." Flicking up her hood, she walked away.

Exhaling, Leo laid back, trying and failing to process all that had passed. He heard Consus lay somewhere nearby and the angry, if affable, grumble that followed.

"This is your fault, Trenowyth."

Despite himself, Leo breathed out a laugh.

"He was worried about you," Consus said suddenly.

"Who?"

"Thurston." Consus paused, staring at the sky. "I think he knew what you were up to." Anger flitted through his words. "I will not die before trying to take Beau's head."

"I'll be there with you," Leo said softly. "So save half his neck for me."

Rolling his head to the side, he stared at the dark forest. Exhaustion gripped him. Beau had murdered Thurston and the Emperor in one fell swoop. Goddess only knew what had befallen Eckart and Relia. Innocent people had been killed by Tettiena mere hours ago. And he and Consus had barely escaped the flames themselves.

Pain streaked through his heart. Kiylla had known. But she'd rescued him, nonetheless.

Tossing, turning, and flinching each time something rubbed his wound, Leo tried to sleep to no avail. Scanning the shadows for Kiylla, he sat up and wrapped his arms around himself, checking to ensure Consus was asleep.

A soft snore arose from the man. Out cold. Rising, Leo limped through the trees.

Kiylla sat a few paces away, watching the thin path leading to the road. Hearing his heavy steps, she turned. "Why are you up, south lord?'

"Couldn't sleep." Leo winced, sitting beside her. "You know, your touch was nothing like a proper maiden. You're supposed to tend the wounded gently."

Kiylla stared at him with intense, hard eyes. "Surely you have learned by now I do nothing gently."

"Nothing?" He asked, mind wandering.

"You are lucky to be alive." She folded her hands in her lap. "Which means you owe me again, south lord."

"I don't owe you anything. Not after what you did to the First."

"No, I suppose not."

Hand trembling, Leo ran his fingers through his ragged hair. "Why did you take Tettiena's deal?"

"Because I wanted you to live." She said simply, staring ahead.

Frowning, Leo stared at her profile. Kiylla slowly turned, noticing his lingering gaze. Shrugging off her cloak, she laid it around his shoulders, but her hands remained on his arms.

"Did I not tell you." She whispered. "That those who sought to kill you would succeed?"

"Right before suffocating me, yes."

"You have a good heart, south lord. But, you are not cut out for politics."

Leo laughed, wincing as his muscles protested. "On that, we can agree."

They both said nothing for a while. Kiylla reached over, wetting the tip of her fingers with her tongue. "You look wretched, south lord. And you normally preen yourself like a pretty bird." Dragging her fingers through his hair, she straightened him out.

When her hands departed his face, Leo grabbed them and yanked her back. He kissed her with a mix of emotions he'd never before felt: anger, hatred, despair, and longing. It felt horrible, but it sent shivers of relief through his spine.

To his surprise, Kiylla did not hesitate, nor did she pull away. She kissed him with ferocity, pressing her hands to his face. Grabbing her shoulders, Leo pushed her down.

The man he once was would have recoiled at the thought of his dirty face, of his tattered garb. He would have flinched at the idea of lying rolling in the dirt. With a savage Llaqtan, no less.

When he pulled back to breathe, Kiylla braced herself on an elbow. "I warned you, south lord." She said quietly. "I do nothing gently. With your wound, I'm afraid I'll hurt you."

"You've done worse."

A hand made of stone erupted from the soil behind Leo, grabbing his tunic and pulling him backward. It crumbled into dust as he thudded on his back. Kiylla straddled him, loosening her tunic with a deft pull of their strings. Pressing her hands to his chest, she leaned forward and kissed him again.

Guilt bloomed in his heart, yearning to be set free. This was the woman who had murdered the First, who would have killed more, given the chance. How the dead would wail to witness his betrayal.

But the guilt could not escape. In this moment, Leo saw only the woman who had risked her entire being to protect her people, who had stood alongside him in their futile battle against Beau.

And the woman who had saved his life, though she had no cause to. Running his hands down her back, he laced his fingers through her trousers strings and pulled them loose. Kiylla grabbed the bottom of his tunic, ripping it off and tossing it away. He hardly felt the chill from the winter air as they laid back on their discarded clothes.

Heat rushed between them as he grabbed her hips and she aggressively mounted him. She moaned softly. Needing her to be closer, Leo wrapped his arms around her tightly.

He felt like an idiot. How many days had the sight of her smile sent butterflies through his heart? He should have kissed her on the dance floor, when he'd realized he did not wish to let her go.

Laying her head against his neck, Kiylla giggled, the first innocent, carefree noise he'd heard her make.

"I only just gave you my cloak." She breathed, "You're going to freeze."

"I feel fine," Leo said, distracted by her hips grinding against him. "What do you take me for?"

"If I voiced every word," she leaned in to kiss him, "We would be here all night." Tightening her thighs around his waist, Kiylla pressed her lips against his, and the world around them might as well not have existed.

Death awaited them tomorrow. But they still had tonight.

Chapter Twenty Six

BROKEN VOW

ARSENE HAD THOUGHT living in Dragos would have prepared him for the fiery heat of Bruthine. The ash that fell over his home proved but a taste of the plane's fiery wrath. Wiping a bead of sweat from his brow, he jogged to catch up with Relia's hurried gait.

Heat plumed from the fires of forges, where magma from the city's channels streamed into obsidian bowls. Some kind of dead lizard, its skin translucent and body filled with glowing red liquid, hung from a hook as a man hacked off its red scales. Down the street, a fireborn woman entered a shop with a bag of shined scales.

For all intents and purposes, the Tiene had fashioned themselves an utterly normal city in the bowels of an otherworldly plane. Madness.

Two cefran children, with eyes the color of glittering gems, stared at Arsene as though he were covered in scales himself. Was this how Fionn felt in a human city?

"Relia!" Arsene called.

"Hm?" She asked, glancing over her shoulder.

"Oh, your ears are working again. Marvelous."

"Sorry. Were you talking to me?"

Arsene walked alongside her. "Yes. What has you so distracted?"

Relia halted abruptly in the middle of the market square. "I'm thinking about what's going to happen when we return. When I'm presented to my parents."

"I'm more worried about surviving that long."

"They won't kill me." Relia asserted, continuing her annoyingly fast pace. "I'm going to be Empress. I have to think about. . . about what I'm going to do. How I'm going to rule. I don't know how to be a mayor, let alone a queen."

"I could advise you," Arsene suggested.

"Aha!" Relia whirled around and pointed. "I knew it. You ran to my aid because *you* wanted to be Emperor."

Pursing his lips, Arsene watched a muscled smith hammer out a sword. He'd never thought about being Emperor.

No, the title was too grand. A balance between importance and workload was necessary.

"No thanks," Arsene said. "But I wouldn't mind royal adviser. Maybe court evoker?"

"Hm-hm." Relia chuckled. She must have been only teasing. "You'd rather be. . . rather. . ." Her eyes twitched in confusion. "Heir to the Aeourant cefra's chief?"

"What are you talking about?" Arsene glanced away.

Smirking knowingly, Relia clasped her hands behind her back. Her joy lasted momentarily before worried thinking wrinkled her brow again. "The Emperor rules by divine right. By Viridia's right. Marius claims to speak with her authority, but. . ." Her head snapped up, staring at the massive serpent stretching across the onyx sky. "But for them to follow me, to heed me, I must show that she stands with me. But how?"

"A divine display?" Arsene suggested. "But what could we do that Marius could not dwarf?" He frowned, staring intently at Relia.

"What?"

"Nothing. I've only just realized how much you remind me of him." He paused. "Who I thought he was, at any rate."

"Frustratingly perfect?"

"Not that part. Naive. Idealistic. You would have made a decent match in a different life."

"Hm."

The click of heels on the obsidian road heralded Johanna's arrival. "Maybe we can put that reminiscence to good use."

"What's that supposed to mean?" Arsene asked, turning to face her.

Johanna brushed back the sweat-dampened bangs of her braid. "You don't believe in gods any more than I do. Marius' power comes from somewhere. From something he's remembered. In theory, anyone could do the same."

"But we'd need to experience the same." Arsene glanced at her hands. "Any luck?"

"No." She unfurled her fingers to reveal the ruby gem. "I can't help but wonder. . . The Lady implied Marius was here. Is it he who traps us, or someone else?"

"Are we ready to go?" Relia asked.

"About. I've finished committing everything from her library to memory and gathered our supplies in the foyer."

"Then let's go." Arsene glanced back at the sprawling obsidian city lit by fire before turning and marching back toward the palace.

Johanna's mother had believed aiceil's held the key to entering other planes. With the ruby refusing to answer their calls, they had no choice but to test the theory.

"If our plan works," Relia said, "And the aiceil takes us home. . . where should we go?"

"Fairborough," Arsene answered. "That's where Fionn was headed next."

"You saw the leviathan, too, right? Do you think they escaped?"

"I think Wulf has more willpower than most countries' entire populations put together," Arsene said. "I'd bet on it."

The Lady of the Tiene had graciously allowed them to stay in a small guest room, but the gift had come with a clear warning: they were not to leave the city. Flaming eyes of watchful guards had pursued them with every step.

Johanna stopped by the courtyard's phoenix statue. "Wait here."

"Don't get caught." Arsene whispered.

Nodding, she walked through the doors.

"You." A man's heavily accented voice barked.

Arsene turned to see one of the red-scaled guards approaching. "Yes?"

"The Lady wished to see you." The guard jerked his head, bidding Arsene to follow.

"Both of us?" Relia asked.

"No." The guard shook his head and motioned to Arsene again.

Straightening his coat, Arsene followed the guard up the stairs and back into the queen's obsidian throne room. The flaming-haired cefran queen stood between blazing braziers, arms covered in golden jewelry.

"You are leaving." She said, watching him with ruby eyes the same hue as the jewel.

"You've made it clear we're not to go anywhere." Arsene denied. "Though I wonder for how long you intend to keep us and for what."

The Lady had yet to answer and did not deign to now. Her eyes traced from his feet to his head. "Have you learned why the jewel will not answer your call?"

Arsene opened his mouth to answer but snapped it close. Her eyebrows rose slightly, and the corner of her mouth twitched into a smirk. She knew.

"Dare I guess," Arsene said carefully, "that it has been your doing?"

The Lady answered with another riddle. "The Lady of Fire has watched you from the first. Followed your every step. When again the land is safe, your jewel will heed your call."

"When will the land be safe?"

"Soon." Her chin rose. "I rescind my order. You may depart."

The escape plan Arsene carefully crafted went up in smoke. Shame. It would have been a good one, too.

"Thank you," Arsene said warily, "My Lady."

She dipped her head, coyly smiling.

Bowing in turn, Arsene's brow wrinkled. Did. . . did he speak with a priestess or Diorbhail herself?

And what of Fionn? Had she been a mere woman, or. . .

"I wish you every fortune," Arsene said, "and for the prosperity of your people."

Smiling, the Lady waved a hand, dismissing him. Tapping his glaive on the ground, the red-scaled guard led Arsene back outside, where Relia and Johanna waited.

"What did she say?" Relia demanded.

"We're free to leave." Arsene glanced over his shoulder at the retreating guard. "We need to hurry. Something's not right."

Aiceils were horrible places. Dens of otherworldly flora and geography even those outside the Empire refused to enter. What, then, did an aiceil in an otherworldly plane look like?

"There." Johanna pointed across the plain to a strip of barren soil marring the rich red clay. "The only question is, which aiceil back home is this?"

"Hopefully, the one near Valeria," Arsene said.

"Tread carefully," Johanna warned, tapping her boot on the barren strip. "I'm not sure what awaits us beyond."

Leaning forward, Arsene peered into the distance. The barren border was far wider than the aiceils back home, but he could see the beginnings of a forest at its end. Brown bark and broad-leafed trees, found in southern Dragos, gathered in thick clusters.

Nowhere in Dragos did they grow in such numbers. Was this really the place?

Johanna laughed. "To think. Aiceils on the other side simply look. . . normal." She paused under the first tree and looked up.

Arsene stared at the sky with her. Johanna postulated the same theory her mother once had: the veil thinned when overlap effects occurred. When ashfalls began, when night fell in Athelstan, when the land moved in Yuri Llaqta. Should you enter an aiceil during these moments, the veil might thin enough to step through.

"So," Arsene said. "What causes ashfalls back home?"

"An ashfall here, I'd guess." Johanna leaned on a tree. "I suppose now, we wait."

Pacing away from the women, Arsene pulled out the ruby and turned it over in his palm. Still dull. Whispering under his breath, he tried to activate it, to no avail. The gem had heeded his command once, and only once, when he escaped from Lavinia's mountains and brought them here.

Returning the jewel to its satchel, Arsene turned as Relia gasped. Following her gaze, he looked up to see the red-scaled entity in the sky moving with a frightening quickness. Like a sun rising at dawn, the tip of a serpent's head appeared on the horizon and circled the firmament.

"Viridia's tits," Arsene muttered. Remembering Relia's comment about Marius, he bit his tongue, regretting the curse.

"So it does have a head." Relia marveled. "Do you think that's what we're looking for?"

"Maybe." Johanna dropped her bag, eyes glued upwards, entranced.

Every instinct in Arsene's body commanded him to flee. The sheer size of the serpent's head matched that of the sun. Did it cling to an unseen ceiling or circle in the heavens where the stars hung? Backing up, he gritted his teeth as the head slowly followed the tail, cresting the sky directly above.

Its mouth snapped open, and a terrible wail escaped—louder than a hurricane and somber as a cry. Wind blew down from the force of its scream, and fire followed in its wake. Not ash, but flame tumbled from the sky in orbs the size of hail.

"That's it!" Johanna shouted, grabbing her bag and dashing into the woods.

Pushing Relia ahead of him, Arsene chased after her. He expected a sense of unease as they penetrated the aiceil's border, but instead, a breath of familiarity greeted him. This was the overlap with home.

Flame tumbled onto the trees, but no wildfire began. As though a shield of moisture enveloped the forest, the flame doused and turned to fog and smoke, thickening until Arsene could hardly see.

As they ran through the woods, Arsene reflected on Marius' words. This forest was nothing like Dragos: barren and rocky, the land of volcanoes and crags had no forests. Trees like this were rare sightings and only in the south.

If the overlap disappeared, if the door to this plane of fire was slammed shut, would forests like these sprout across the land?

The trees parted enough to reveal the serpent's head in the sky. Blurred by the strange air of the aiceil, the heavenly serpent appeared almost transparent, clinging to a firmament of black and pale blue.

"What now?" Arsene shouted.

"In the Earth Father's land," Johanna asked. "What did the rift look like?"

"A cave," Arsene said, recalling the cavern filled with a raging storm Fionn had dragged them into.

"A cave. . ." Johanna repeated, spinning as she searched for something.

"Arsene!" Relia grabbed his arm, fingers sinking into his skin.

Whipping around, Arsene saw movement in the trees; someone had followed them. Grabbing Relia's arm, he pushed her. "You two go. I'll stall. Yell if you find your theorized exit."

Trusting him, Relia nodded. Grabbing Johanna, she dragged the other woman deeper into the woods.

Grabbing Death Knells' grip, Arsene pulled it loose from its holster as he waited. The treeline broke, revealing exactly who Arsene expected.

Though the gem had been out of reach, though he should have no means to reach them, Marius strode towards Arsene, flaming hair glowing beneath the serpent's red light. His mantle trailed behind him like a shadow.

"There you are," Marius said calmly. "It took me longer than expected to track you down."

"Considering you couldn't have known where we were, I'd say a few days is remarkably good time." Arsene retorted.

Marius glanced at the flintlock. "I don't understand, Arsene. Why did you run?"

"I shot Vasille, in case you forgot." Arsene backed up a step. "The men were ordered to attack me, and I've never been one to go quietly."

"You were leaving before the altercation." Marius shook his head, taking another step closer. "For what? I thought I knew you. But, clearly, I don't."

"Yeah, well, the feeling is mutual."

Marius' face fragmented. "I am the man you've always known, little brother. Whoever has misled you, whatever falsities you have been led to believe, allow me to set the story straight."

No sign had come from Johanna, though Arsene wished she'd hurry up and find whatever she sought. A gap that appeared only in the right conditions—what if they missed it?

"Alright." Arsene gestured with the barrel turned down. "What is it I've misunderstood?"

"Once upon a time," Marius took another step closer, "I knew a boy who promised to shield me when I became Duke. Maybe you don't remember, but I once asked if you would support me even if I became the Emperor himself."

Arsene did not remember. But if Marius said so, it must be true. "Of course, I would."

"I want to help people, Arsene." He took another step closer. "I knew I would not be popular with the nobility. The goddess would not let our people starve, would not let our children die in war. But even the most benevolent king has limited power."

"But you have the goddess herself," Arsene said, flinching as Marius stopped a mere pace away.

"You saw what I did to your hand. And that is but the smallest of the miracles She can produce."

Glancing down, Arsene studied the hand gripping his flintlock. Kiylla's spell had broken his bones. The medics did what they could, but the bone had not mended correctly. It should have pained him for the rest of his days, but instead, it was perfectly intact.

"You've never cared for morals," Marius smiled somberly. "No matter how I tried to make you care. And so, I don't understand. Why did you run?"

A fascinating question. A place by the Emperor's side. . . Arsene had thrown it away.

"You're right." Arsene looked up. "I don't care about the cefra. I've never cared for anyone's fortune but my own. I want what I want and don't want to lose what I wish to keep. That's all."

Marius' eyes flicked over Arsene. "This is about her. Vasille's spies followed you. Saw how you cared for her. Or is it about the partner who went to his death at her side?"

"Both," Arsene admitted. "But it doesn't matter. Had Wulf possessed an ounce of intelligence and not thrown that spear, he would have dragged me into this anyway."

Lips pursed, Marius glanced at the ruby clenched in Arsene's free hand. "You haven't left. It didn't work for you, did it?" Fire danced in his amber eyes. "The Lady cut its magic the way only its creator could. She wants me to succeed. To find you."

"That's ridiculous. Why would a cefra-"

"Because her people live *here*." Marius interrupted. "Where they belong. Separate from us. Closing the veil would keep our people apart. We could not harm them, nor they us."

Arsene wanted to protest but found no words. So the Lady had been Diorbhail, after all.

Marius sighed and touched the side of Arsene's face. "Do you know what Fionn wants? What her patron, her false god demands?"

"A guess, at best."

"Why do you think she hides it from you?" Marius questioned. "Because she knows you would turn against her."

"And you know?"

"Seoras seeks the end of his rivals," Marius explained. "The Empire's expansion has pushed the cefran people to the brink. He thinks we've overstepped. If the Empire has too much power, then freedom has been expunged. And so to restore it, the Empire must be shattered."

"Why help the Empire stop Kiylla, then?"

"To take her gem." Marius shook his head. "From another point of view, Seoras is doing what he thinks is best. Protecting the world. His people. But we cannot coexist, and I must protect mine. And it affords me an opportunity to seize power and set the Empire to rights."

Arsene bit his lip. That wasn't right. Was it? Fionn had never given him the impression she intended anything like this. She had meant to head for Fairborough with the jewels. Fairborough. A tiny village that had lost its meaning in the wake of a disastrous rebellion.

Arsene gazed into Marius' warm, amber eyes. His brother spoke true. A pleasant voice caressed his neck, telling him so. Seoras had deceived him. The supposed god intended to destroy the Empire.

"Y-you're right." Arsene stuttered. "How could I not have seen it?"

Fionn had been lying. She was a charlatan, a thief. She had ripped Arsene from his rightful destiny. He ought to kill her for the offense. The thought surged with confidence, with utter certainty.

He flinched. Something was wrong. This voice was. . . wrong. Fionn sang to him from the recesses of his mind, drowned out by the reassuring comfort of the caressing whisper.

The mask slips from a hollowed face. . .

Cracks appear in perfection.

Her face swam into view. *What does an evoker forget?* She asked. *What they never believed.*

What had she meant?

Marius spoke again, but he sounded different. An echo underlined his voice, a whisper so gentle it slipped through the wind without notice. "If the thought of them troubles you, let me relieve you of the pain."

Memories shot to mind as Marius cupped his chin. Fionn's freckled smiling face and Wulf's exaggerated eye-roll drifted past his eyes. Laughter cascaded over sunlit fields as Fionn giggled, watching Arsene and Relia spar. Wulf nudged him in a tavern, pointing out a pretty maid glancing in their direction.

'*We're broke.*' A memory of Arsene's own voice appeared as he dropped an empty coin purse on the table of a tiny Athelstani inn. Wulf had leaned forward, shaking the purse to check.

That unassuming day had been the inciting moment leading them into Fionn's unlucky company.

'*Have you ever wished a moment could last forever?*' Arsene heard himself say, hand laced with Fionn as they danced under the night sky, their balcony overlooking the whole of Lavinia. '*For an evoker, it can.*'

The memories faded, washing away—stolen away. The warm comfort dissolved as Arsene realized Marius. . .

No. The entity within Marius was erasing his memories.

Panicked, Arsene jerked backward, finger twitching on Death Knells' trigger. Smoke filled the air as a bullet flew from the barrel, striking Marius in the side. Gasping in surprise as blood rushed from the wound, Marius backed away from Arsene.

Horror gripped Arsene as he realized what he'd done. He'd shot Marius with Death Knell. The invention meant to keep his brother safe.

"Arsene!" Johanna shouted urgently.

Her voice came from behind. With one last look at his brother, Arsene whirled around and sprinted. Black tendrils raced through the forest, grasping hands following his steps. He dodged the first that lunged for him. The second wrapped around his ankle and yanked, throwing him to the ground.

Rolling over himself, Arsene landed on his back and crawled backward, trying to break free of the shadowy spell's grip. More dark hands surged around him, surrounding him, as Marius' hand flashed with light, healing the wound in his side.

Why wasn't he evoking? Arsene's mind whirled, unable to focus on anything as he flailed.

A plume of flame burst to life behind him, the intense light cast from its blaze erasing the shadow grasping his legs. The tendrils shrank from the light.

Relia dashed to Arsene's side. "Get up!" She shouted, grabbing his arm.

Forcing himself not to look back, Arsene followed her. Johanna waited not far away, gesturing for them to come to her. "Here. Hurry!"

Fire raged behind Johanna, the only spot in the aiceil where the flaming rain pierced the forest's strange veil. A thin crevasse revealed itself in the ground, cutting a gash through the soil. An unnatural shade veiled it as though the fire had burned away the barrier between the planes.

"Go." Arsene ordered, turning around, Death Knell pointed forward.

Johanna slipped through the crevasse, and Relia followed. The shadows in the forest surged towards him, filled with more than mere darkness. Staring into their shade was like staring into nothingness itself.

Arsene saw Relia disappear and spun around, reciting a prayer to Diorbhail before sliding into the gap.

CHAPTER TWENTY SEVEN

ECLIPSE

MARIUS PRESSED A hand to his side, where Arsene's flintlock had torn a hole minutes earlier. Light faded from his fingertips as he finished mending the wound, but the tear in his tunic remained.

Stunned, Marius stared at the foggy trees where Arsene had disappeared. Every soul who had heard Viridia's reassuring voice had realized the truth of her words. Every soul. No matter how skeptical.

Arsene had understood. Had *heard*. What had wrenched him away in the final moments?

Seoras. Viridia breathed.

Gritting his teeth, Marius stepped back. He would not pursue Arsene. Misled by Seoras, his brother was running scared and would not listen. Marius refused to let harm befall either him or Relia.

There remained but a single option. Seoras must be drawn out of hiding to free those tainted by his curse.

Raising a hand, Marius focused. A tear ripped through the aiceil, creating a jagged gap between realms. Stepping through, he departed the humid forest and entered a city beset by the chill of early winter. A frigid breeze brushed his face, flecked with tiny snowflakes.

He stood atop a marble building overlooking the glorious capital of Clodia. A capital in utter disarray.

Towering pillars of ice rose into the air, cracking and falling apart as they slowly warmed. A layer of ice coated the central district. Statues dotted the streets, frozen mid-stride, their faces contorted in horror.

Tettiena had already struck? Marius had spent only a few days in the plane of ash and fire. Perhaps time moved differently there.

There. Viridia whispered, turning his head toward the docks.

Remembering a set of Lavinia's stone stairs, Marius evoked a passage from the rooftop to the road. Guards cordoned off the frozen sections of the city and patrolled every corner of the streets. Many hardly had any armor save a padded jacket, their faces indicating their youth.

How irritating. There would be no need to conscript children had the Emperor not started his ridiculous war.

Frigid seawater lapped against Clodia's white stone docks. Tettiena and Beau stood together on a quiet, unoccupied corner where a decommissioned trade vessel floated unused.

Tettiena's hood was down, her hair pulled into a taut bun. Her green eyes flashed in his direction as she approached. Both she and Beau quickly fell into a deep bow.

"What happened?" Tettiena asked, noticing the bloodied hole on his mantle.

"I'm fine," Marius said quickly. "Give me your report."

Beau folded his hands on his cane. "When our ship failed to sink, I thought of a new plan. Leofric played right into my hands, acting the part of a cefran sympathizer perfectly."

"And the Emperor?"

"Dead. Murdered by that same cefran agent."

"Good." Marius held out a hand. "May I see it, Tettiena?"

"Of course." Pulling the sapphire jewel from her bag, Tettiena handed it to him.

Turning the jewel over in his hands, Marius paced away from them. Under the relentless light of Sigillus' bright sun, the interiors of the jewel swam beneath the surface in perfect clarity. A churning sea beset by endless rain, turquoise light shining beneath the depths, and great cliffs rising into the sky.

"Ice," Marius murmured. "I expected another wave."

"I saw something in there I thought would serve our purposes better," Tettiena explained, nodding toward one of the ice pillars. "It worked. They're running scared. What few cefra were in the city have been attacked or arrested."

Sighing, Marius returned the jewel to her. "Change of plans. Destroy it."

Tettiena paled. "What? But I thought. . ."

Originally, Marius had intended to keep the jewels close for some time after ascending the throne. Killing the cefra before they united the Empire—nay, the entire continent—would have no purpose.

But with Seoras missing, and no means to draw him from where he hid. . .

Perhaps watching his kin die would drive Seoras out into the open. With Seoras' demise, the snag in their plans would be removed, and Marius could get Arsene back. The plan could proceed. War could begin, and with Viridia's divine might, the remaining cefra would perish at once.

"Seoras could be anywhere," Marius said. "I need him to make a reckless decision."

Viridia had met Seoras, long ago. She knew the pattern of his thoughts. Emotions controlled the Leviathan. And more than once, it had flown to its demise on an errant worry.

"I. . . understand." Tettiena took the jewel and turned around. She had seen Fionn's memories—no, Seoras' memories of the gem's creation—when Floraidh herself breathed life into the door between this world and the endless sea.

And if she had seen its creation, so could Tettiena undo its existence.

"What of the princess?" Beau asked.

"She's with Arsene," Marius said, teeth clenched.

Beau's eyebrows flew up. "Your brother aided her escape? I never would have guessed. . ." He laughed. "I never would have guessed she would flee to begin with." He touched Marius' arm. "What would you have of me?"

"I think I know what Seoras will do," Marius said quietly. "If I'm right, all I'll need is for you to stay by me."

"Of course, my lord." Beau dipped his head, turning to watch Tettiena.

The woman's hands trembled. She hesitated. Who could blame her?

That jewel was a door. The sole reason the veil thinned enough for the endless sea to brush against their world. Every waterborn cefra drew their magic from that realm. Should the door slam close, the magic in their blood would thin until it disappeared.

And a cefra could not live without the element that charged their very being. To shatter this gem meant more than condemning every waterborn cefra to death; so too would it kill Tettiena's firstborn son.

Wrapping her hands around the sapphire, Tettiena pressed it to her chest and closed her eyes. Her mouth warbled and her eyes glistened. Fingertips glowing with faint blue light, she cast the spell she had been most dreading.

The thin crystalline exterior of the jewel peeled away, releasing the tide of oceans and rain. Clouds gathered in the heavens, obscuring the sun and drenching the city in a sudden downpour. Ice grew like plants from the ocean, glittering with turquoise light.

Beads of water flew from Tettiena's hands, cascading past Marius' eyes as though in slow motion. And then they vanished.

The sea quieted. The rain stopped as quickly as it had begun. And every crystal in the city shattered, collapsing into a pile of shards.

Marius felt it. A thread snapping, a window closing. And life around the world halted in its tracks.

Tettiena's shoulders slumped. Nothing remained of Floraidh's Ice. Not even the moisture from its destruction.

Looking up, Marius watched the sun re-emerge and douse the city in golden light. Only a fool believed the world could be saved with pretty words and kind actions. Men were rotten to their core, and drastic actions were required to budge even the slightest change.

In the end, the world would be better for this. Peace would reign over humanity, guided by Viridia's firm but loving hand.

Marius closed his eyes. Mother had told him countless times the voice of Viridia was a blessing. He was chosen, she said, but. . .

He wished someone else had been given the charge.

CHAPTER TWENTY EIGHT

SHATTERED

AEOURANT TRIALS NEVER lasted long. There was always a witness with incriminating memories. One sift through the maevruthan's waters, and the accused's guilt or innocence was determined.

Fionn watched the rippling surface of the pond, battered beneath relentless gales. She had pooled her memories the day before stealing Seoras' gem and fleeing the village. Her memory of the crime had been smashed with her crystal.

But someone had seen her. Seoras recalled them. A hunter had glimpsed her, fleeing through the trees.

Hardly any red colored Mother's hair these days. Gray locks swayed in the wind as she knelt, hand submerged in the silver pool. The guild leaders stood solemnly around the maevruthan's shores, awaiting the chief's word.

Mother rose quickly, taking a deep breath. She had already seen the witness' memory. Reviewing it was but a formality. Turning to Fionn, she held her chin high.

"What does the accused say in their defense?" Mother asked.

Seoras' voice no longer whispered across the wind; it sounded in Fionn's mind, a twin echo to her thoughts, differentiated only by a male's tone.

Let them not think they've been abandoned. Seoras thought. *Let them think they are safe.*

"You saw the memory. What else is there to say?" Fionn said.

Emotions tore across Mother's face: annoyance, anger, and grief. "A quiet girl in the cook's guild does not steal our most ancient relic on a whim."

"It was not on a whim," Fionn said. "But that does not erase the crime."

Mother's face twitched. She didn't understand. Shoulders tensing, she turned to the guild leaders. "Well?"

The warrior's guild leaders spoke first. He gestured with his spear at Fionn. "Her human companions say concerning things about the Empire. We should interrogate her if she means to keep mum."

"Nonsense." The smith's leader, a rugged earthborn man, spat. "She offers no defense. She's a thief. Exile."

"I disagree." The cook's leader, a younger woman with a flaming braid, stared daggers at Fionn. "I know this one. She swiped anything from the pantries she could get her hands on, aye, but she's no blasphemer."

Smiling, Fionn looked down, listening to them bicker. What had Wulf told her people about the Empire? Chancing a glance at the crowd gathered behind the maevruthan, Fionn glimpsed Wulf and Eckart, watching anxiously.

Eckart gripped Wulf's arm, holding the human back. They muttered to one another. Fionn could read Wulf's lips. 'I'm not going to attack, Eckart. Calm down.'

Focusing on the leader's deliberation again, Fionn noticed the herbalist's leader, a waterborn with ocean-blue eyes, staring rigidly into the distance, a pallor creeping up her face.

"Well, Saorise?" Mother asked, addressing the herbalist. "Saorise?" She asked again.

Clutching her throat, the herbalist fell forward onto her knees. A shriek came from the streets, and Fionn whirled around. A young child collapsed, grabbing his head, writhing on the ground in pain as his

Mother raced to his side. A mother with bright blue eyes who fainted before she reached him.

All three were waterborn. Panic surged through Fionn's heart. "Mother!" She shouted.

Mother grabbed the herbalist's shoulders as the woman slumped to the ground. Gently laying Saorise down, Mother stood, listening to the cries echoing from deeper in the settlement.

The meeting broke without words. The warrior's leader raced away, shouting for his men, while the others scrambled in confusion. Hearing Wulf's voice, Fionn searched for him again.

Eckart staggered but remained conscious. Racing toward them, Fionn reached his side as he collapsed onto his hands and knees. Laying a hand on his back, she studied him for injury.

"What's wrong?" She asked, voice trembling.

Eckart didn't answer. It was as if he didn't hear her. Hand on his spear, Wulf's eyes darted around the village, counting the bodies crumpled on the ground. "What is this? An attack? A spell?"

The songbird flitted through the trees, soaring over huts. It peered down on the ailing, noticing a concerning similarity.

"They're all waterborn." Fionn breathed.

"What does that mean?"

"It means. . ." Fionn bit her lip. "It means Floraidh's Ice has been destroyed."

Fionn wrung her wrists together, glancing around her childhood home.

Father's little animal figurines still littered the house; the albatross he'd made rested on her bedside beside a white lyre. A warm fire crackled in the hearth, and tapestries flushed the wood with color.

Wandering to her bedside, Fionn picked up the lyre. She plucked a few strings and flinched when they twanged out of tune. Strange memories flooded her mind.

Seoras' mother had been cold. She'd not hated him; she'd been indifferent. A second woman had filled the role.

Fionn's mother was very much like that woman. Stern but caring. Buried beneath a pile of work, with little time for affection.

The door creaked open, and Mother entered, scarf loose and dress disheveled. "We've come to a vote." She announced. "To delay your trial in light of recent events.

"How are they?" Fionn asked, laying the lyre down.

"Walk with me and see."

Hesitating, Fionn picked up the white albatross her father had made her. She remembered the grin he'd worn while explaining its symbolism.

'Albatrosses herald a coming storm and the advent of long-awaited reunions.'

Tucking it into her bag, she followed her mother outside. Pausing by the maevruthan, Fionn looked around. She had never seen the Aeourant like this. Guards raced in a frenzy, spreading out to watch the borders. Every herbalist and healer had been called home to tend the collapsed waterborn, and several huts had been turned into makeshift clinics.

A quarter of their people had become deathly ill overnight. Hundreds.

As Fionn's gaze followed an herbalist rushing into a hut crammed with cots, her eyes landed on her mother. "You have a knowing look," Mother said. "What curse has befallen us?"

"One of the gods has perished," Fionn said quietly.

Alarm flashed in Mother's honey-colored eyes. Her head darted between every hut and every soul. "Gods. . ."

"I might have an idea," Fionn said, "but there's only a slim chance it will work."

Calming her breathing, Mother stared at her, countenance laced with sorrow and understanding. "Why did it have to be you?"

Fionn had always wondered if her parents had suspected the truth about their daughter. Hearing her mother speak now, she found her answer. Though the details eluded them, Mother had always known.

Swallowing, Fionn took her mother's arms. "I have to go, Mother. Let me leave."

"Those awaiting trial cannot leave the bounds of our land." Mother said sternly.

"At least let me see Eckart, then."

Guiding Fionn back inside their hut, Mother spoke with unusual theatrics. "Stay in your room." She ordered, slamming the door. "You're lucky I've allowed this rather than a cell."

Tilting her head in confusion, Fionn studied her mother. Water welled in the corner of her eyes, and she pulled Fionn into a hug. Tight, enveloping, the kind you gave someone upon your last meeting.

Releasing her daughter, Mother pressed her hands to the sides of Fionn's face before finally backing away. "I have much to do. Stay put." She swallowed and swept back outside.

Mischief ran in the family. Mother was up to something. Trusting her, Fionn sank onto her bed, content to rest. She felt Seoras' thoughts humming, felt his memories stirring to life.

He was nervous.

The door slammed open, and Fionn sat up with a start. A man most mistook for her brother crept in like a thief and hastily shut the door with his foot.

Cormag deposited a burlap sack on the table and approached her, hands awkwardly placed on his hips. He cleared his throat but said nothing.

"You're the captain of the guard." Fionn pointed out. "Shouldn't you be patrolling?"

"Oh, aye." He confirmed. "I needed to drop something off first." He loitered awkwardly before clapping her shoulder. "Best of luck, cousin."

Turning stiffly, he hurried out the door and locked it behind him. Narrowing her eyes, Fionn rose and opened the little sack. Several neatly packed rations and waterskins were stored within.

Realizing her mother's plan, Fionn grinned, sliding the ration pack into her satchel and returning to bed. A few hours remained before the sun fell. Time enough for a nap.

A tap on the window roused Fionn from her slumber. Night had fallen, and the moon illuminated shadowed men behind the glass. One raised a spear. A heavy thud broke the lock, and the window swung open.

Wulf vaulted the window and landed beside Fionn's cot. Bathed, beard trimmed, he wore fine black leather armor that fell to his knees.

"You look dashing," Fionn said.

"Quick." Wulf grabbed her elbow and pulled her up. "There are no patrols at the eastern gate." He spun around, taking her by the waist. "Are you alright?"

"Fine."

Nodding, Wulf released her.

Grabbing her bag, Fionn glanced at her home one last time before jumping out the window. She landed in the soft grass bordering the forest and met with Eckart, his brunette locks tied in a ribbon and fur cloak billowing in the breeze.

"Eckart!" She exclaimed. "You shouldn't be up-"

"I'm fine," he assured her. "We need to hurry. This way." Gently pushing her, he guided her into the trees.

Wulf walked closely behind her. "You weren't lying about your people. They were too kind."

"Did my Mother pay you in more than fashion?" Fionn asked.

"She paid us with the most valuable thing she owns." Wulf smiled at her.

Eckart whistled. "Leo would be proud, Wulf."

"I take it back, then." Wulf joked. "Ah." He reached under his jerkin. "One more thing."

Wulf pressed a warm stone in Fionn's palm. The emerald jewel. Seoras' Breath.

Wonderful. Seoras thought. *Now we don't have to steal it.*

Eckart guided them through the woods, at home in dark forests. His steps were less sure, his gait slower. His half-blood nature had shielded him from the worst of the suffering, but the cefran half was still dying.

"It's unusually quiet," Fionn murmured. "Cormag must have shifted the patrol."

Eckart turned to answer but was interrupted by Wulf snorting. "What?" He snapped.

"Nothing." Wulf grinned knowingly. "I'm just sad Fionn didn't get to see your face when-"

"Shut up." Eckart hissed.

Wondering what they were talking about, Fionn looked up at Wulf. He leaned down, happily answering. "Eckart will need a new clan, right? The Gaevral will want his head." He nudged her. "Is your cousin single?"

"Yes." Fionn smiled. "Ah."

"Wulf's blowing it out of proportion." Eckart insisted. "Be quiet, or we'll be caught."

Winding and weaving, Eckart led them to the eastern gate, a tiny dirt road with a rickety wooden fence. Two horses, patterned with several colors, awaited them, saddled and fitted with supplies.

Without warning, Wulf grabbed her waist and hoisted her onto the lighter horse. After ensuring Eckart had managed to mount his, Wulf seated himself behind Fionn and took the reins. Checking to ensure they had not been seen, Wulf ordered the horse into a trot.

"I don't understand," Wulf whispered. "I thought Arsene had the jewels."

"I did, too," Fionn admitted. "Maybe, he. . . " She swallowed. Had he betrayed them or fallen?

"So, it's been shattered." Eckart guessed. "That's it, then, isn't it? All the waterborn; we're going to die."

"I. . ." Fionn trailed off. Only Floraidh had the power to mend the jewel, and she had fallen silent ages ago. Seoras had an idea, but it had never been tested. "I need to find Arsene."

"An evoker!" Wulf exclaimed. "Could they evoke a new jewel?"

"No." Fionn denied. "Didn't Arsene teach you the rules of evoking? You cannot evoke a living thing. And the jewels are a piece of the planes."

"And they're alive." Eckart said quietly.

Pulling out the emerald jewel, Fionn stared at the blue sky. She tapped her fingers on its surface. Arsene had been in the Lavinian mountains the night of their escape. But had he been fleeing his family or aiding the search for the fugitives?

Smashing the sapphire jewel went against Marius' plans, surely. Which meant. . .

"He's drawing us out." Fionn guessed. "Marius. Holding the other jewels hostage with a clear threat."

"Return, or he'll murder us all." Eckart presumed. "Then we go to Dragos."

"Once we get closer, I might be able to locate Arsene and Relia." Palming the jewel, Fionn focused on the fiery country.

"Wait." Wulf jerked the reins, pulling the horse aside. "We need to talk."

"Is now really the time?"

"Yes. What happened back there? In the world of storms?"

How did Fionn explain? A thousand lightning bolts had raced through her, agonizing, burning. Something not meant to flow through her veins had surged to life, and Seoras' once-distant thoughts had become clear as crystal.

Strange. These men were so familiar, though Fionn should not recognize them. But Seoras did. Once, his memories had belonged only to him, hazy recollections Fionn could hardly grasp. Now, they flowed through her mind, intertwined with hers.

Seoras saw Wulf through her eyes—an irritatingly stubborn man with a handsome face and attractive figure. His blue eyes twinkled when he grinned, and his laugh encouraged her to join. Concern raced through his face when he looked at her. Never had he left her side.

Were these Seoras' thoughts or Fionn's? A question that had plagued her for years. Now, it seemed trite.

They were *theirs*.

Unsure what this meant, Fionn shivered, taking a breath. She felt different.

"Fionn." Wulf prodded gently.

"I'm fine now. Physically, at least." She answered. "But, Seoras and I. . ." She trailed off. "Whatever he used to heal me is not ordinary magic. I'm not used to it yet."

"You're doing better than expected," Eckart said. "I thought you'd have no clue who we were."

"Seoras remembers you, so I do, too. He was there every moment I was."

Wulf grunted, frowning. "I saw his statue in your little wind chime garden. The prick looks exactly how I imagined."

"A fop?" Eckart raised an eyebrow.

Fionn's jaw set, and she swiveled in the saddle. "Handsome? Majestic? And it is called a Faedrail, not a garden." Crossing her arms, she looked away. "To stand in the presence of a god is an honor. You should be kneeling."

Wulf gaped at her. Words belonging to Seoras had flown from her lips but not in his voice. Fionn had said those words. And she felt the bristling annoyance as deeply as Seoras.

"Luckily for you," Fionn continued. "We don't have time to discipline you. Let's go."

Wulf grabbed her arm and spun her around. "She's healed. You promised you'd let her go."

"We did heal me," Fionn said. "But I told you, I'm. . . different now." She looked away hastily. Would he still care for her like this?

Of course, he wouldn't. Wulf hated Seoras. Even if Seoras felt anything but.

A truth she'd never known revealed itself. Seoras had been fond of Wulf in precisely the same way Fionn had. Seoras' presence shrunk, embarrassed, and Fionn's cheeks reddened as she shared his emotions.

"You mentioned a place," Eckart said. "Where the jewels could be hidden."

Swallowing, Fionn glanced at Wulf before answering. "Fairborough."

Wulf did not react the way Fionn expected. His eyebrows shot up in surprise, but he did not pale nor protest. Determination washed over his countenance, and he nodded.

Holding up the gem, Fionn whispered, "Casaliede." The emerald answered. An unseen knife ripped the fabric of the world, opening an archway into another place.

Wind and storm roiled beyond. A place that beckoned with an intensity Fionn could not ignore.

"Casaliede is no place for horses." Fionn said. "We'll need to be quick."

Steadying her fluttering heart, she rode through the silver archway into the world whose fragment gave life to her heart.

CHAPTER TWENTY NINE

CHALLENGE

LEO WRAPPED THE leather bracer around his arm, eyes glued to the mountains. Crimson streaks cracked the heaves, heralding an ashfall. Finding shelter from the coming storm would be all too easy; hundreds of tunnels and caverns riddled these hills.

"You're sure they'll live?" Consus' voice echoed in the cavern behind Leo.

"Yes." Kiylla hissed. "You care greatly for a people who have betrayed you."

Fitting a knife into the sheath under his wrist, Leo turned as Consus emerged from the cave, testing the weight of the glaive he'd lifted from the now unconscious Dragosi patrolman.

"It'll do." He decided, returning it to his sheath. Wrapping a cowl around his chain mail, he joined Leo by the cliff side.

Their journey from Clodia had been fraught with danger. Imperial patrols had ridden out, searching for the escaped assassins. Yesterday, they'd passed the border, only to be met with a heavy presence of Dragosi soldiers.

Consus had decided to march for Lavinia and follow the patrols. With more information on Relia's whereabouts, the Dragosi knights could lead them to their quarry. The men would gather where they suspected the cefran fugitives hid.

"Noticed anything?" Consus asked.

Leo shook his head. "No patterns. They're searching the entire mountain range."

"Then our girl is not here." Kiylla decided.

"If they have come this far south." Consus mused, pulling his cowl around his mouth to block out the ash. "She must have headed in this direction. Stay here. I'm going to get a better look."

"Be careful," Leo whispered. Consus slipped from their hidden crevasse into the ash-ridden valley.

Kiylla joined Leo, arms folded tightly, eyes glued to the sky. "And they say our home is strange."

"I've not spent much time in Dragos." Leo tightened his cloak. "I'm not looking forward to spending hours in this weather."

"Neither am I." She looked him up and down, lightly punching him on the shoulder. "You look noble again."

Leo looked down at the chain mail he'd stolen from the Dragosi patrolmen. "This is hardly fine steel."

"Better than rags." She said, "Though I prefer you in nothing at all."

Taken aback by her forwardness, Leo choked on his words. "I thought you said I wasn't masculine?"

"You're not." She said earnestly. "You are very pretty."

"Is that supposed to be a compliment?"

"Yes? I said you were not masculine. I never said I preferred my men to be."

Leaning on the cliff, Leo stared at her nervously. "We haven't really gotten a chance to talk. . ."

"Because you are trying to hide us from Consus." She finished his thought. "But he knows. What is there to say?"

"A lot," Leo said, but he could not think of what.

"You Imperials make everything so complicated." She gently squeezed his hand. "But, fine. We will talk when a chance arrives."

Relieved, Leo leaned forward to peer around the cliff. A cloaked figure rushed toward them as Consus darted back into their hiding space. Before Leo could speak, Consus grabbed them both and pulled them down.

And not a moment too soon. Bright red creatures with broad, dark wings darted over the mountains. Drakes. Men in elegant suits of armor rode upon their backs, glaives in hand.

Dragosi Drake Riders. Leo had never seen them in person before. He flinched and looked down as they soared overhead.

Consus quietly watched the drakes as they fanned out, flying over the southern mountains. "To have deployed them. . . Relia is here, somewhere." He pulled Leo up. "We're on patrol. Don't do anything suspicious."

"I'm the actor of us, Consus." Leo shielded his mouth with his cowl. "I'm more worried about you."

"I can pretend to be a soldier." Consus paused. "If nothing else."

Mounting his horse, Leo waited for Kiylla to grab one of the fallen men's glaives and grab the horse's saddle before directing the steed into a slow trot. Consus took the lead, watching the heavens.

A drake to their east doubled back and disappeared behind the rise of a mountain face. It must have landed; Leo heard a heavy thud in the distance and the sound of scattering rocks.

Jerking his reins, Leo turned east, following the slope of the mountain. Another sound carried across the valley, a crack.

"I know that sound." Kiylla gasped. Climbing onto the saddle, she grabbed the reins and ordered the horse to run.

Shadows clung to the cliff sides, lit by crimson fire. Leo yanked the reins as they reached a crossroads of thin trails, ordering his horse to stop.

A drake lay motionless in the center of the pass, a man still hooked to its saddle. Dismounting, Leo drew his sword and cautiously approached to see if the rider still lived.

A shadow emerged from the cliff behind him, and metal touched the back of Leo's head. "You'll drop your weapon." A Dragosi-accented voice said. "If you enjoy living."

It took Leo a moment to place it, but he recognized that voice. Arsene.

A flash of steel swung past Leo's eyes as Kiylla leveled her glaive at Arsene's throat. "Back off." She ordered.

Arsene lowered his strange flintlock. "Ash and cinder. Leofric? And you're-"

Whirling around, Leo backed away from the flintlock. A woman's voice emerged from the shadowed crevice behind Arsene, followed by a stream of red hair.

"Leo?" Relia gasped. She grabbed her sword when she saw Kiylla.

They looked dreadful. Arsene's pants were torn from the knees to the ankles, sweat dampened their skin and clothes, and their hair hung limp and wet. Johanna emerged next from the crevasse, black braid swinging around her shoulders as she raised her hand, fingers lit with a spell.

"It's alright." Leo pushed Kiylla's arm down.

"Kiylla?" Johanna breathed.

Consus appeared, their other horse in tow. "By the. . ." He trailed off.

Eyebrows knit in confusion, Arsene glanced between them all. "We don't have time to gape. Are you friend or foe?"

"Depends," Kiylla growled.

"Friend," Leo interjected. "We're here to help." He glanced around. "Where's Eckart?"

"Isn't that the question of the hour?" Arsene muttered. "Follow me. We can use an old mine shaft to evade their notice."

"I know it too," Johanna said, striding south. Her gaze met Kiylla's as they passed one another. "Hurry."

"Wait," Relia called. "We'll not get far without mounts. And. . ."

Arsene's eyes darkened. "We could ambush a patrol."

"How intelligent are drakes?"

Johanna answered. "Brighter than a well-trained dog, I'd say."

"Lady Rosa," Consus said sternly. "Do not encourage whatever foolhardy plan the princess is conjuring."

"Think about it." Relia insisted. "If one of us posed as a drake rider, we could survey the entire pass." She spun to Arsene. "You're the prince. Would one heed you?"

"Maybe," Arsene answered.

Kiylla yanked Leo's arm. "One's coming. He must have seen his kin land."

Leaping off his horse, Consus drove them all into the crevasse the others had been hiding in. Heavy flapping rang over the mountains as a second drake descended, landing near its fallen brethren. Its nostrils flared as it surveyed the valley, sniffing.

Relia bolted from their hiding spot. Tensing, Leo lunged after her, accomplishing nothing but revealing himself as well.

Seeing a red-haired girl, the black-clad rider grabbed a horn from his belt. Before it could touch his lips, the bone horn shattered like a heavy hammer had struck it. Startled, Leo noticed a flare of light diminish on Relia's fingertips.

"I want to negotiate, " Relia called. "And unless you want to end up like your friend, you'll listen."

The rider grabbed his weapon but faltered when he noticed Arsene and Johanna behind her, fingers gently glowing to showcase their magic.

Glancing around, the rider tested his options. "What do you want?" he asked tentatively.

"Your drake." Relia smiled.

KIYLLA LOWERED HERSELF to the ground, as though bowing. The drake watched her curiously, sniffing around her before slowly dipping its head. Cautiously, she reached out, touching the tip of its snout.

The drake's rider looked on from the crevasse, hands bound behind his back. Consus had been exceedingly gentle with the man to avoid angering his draconic partner. Kneeling, he quietly asked a few questions. Trusting Kiylla could handle the beast, Leo joined him.

"How many of you are there?" Consus questioned.

"The bulk of the company is a mile west," the man tilted his head. "We lost their trail a few miles north and fanned out."

"How does the search for the cefra fare?" Leo asked.

The drake rider shook his head. "They vanished. We've seen no trace of them."

Standing, Leo stared at the cliff face. What did that mean? Johanna approached Leo, gently tapping his elbow and pulling him aside. "Tell me the full of what happened in Clodia."

"We don't have time for that," Leo whispered back. "Beau accused us of murdering the Emperor. Tettiena attacked the city center. We fled."

Her eyes drooped. "As for us, we emerged from an aiceil near Valeria. They found us and have been pursuing." Blinking a few times, she gazed at him intently. "My father accused you. But who did the deed?"

"Beau," Leo said.

Johanna released his arm and looked away. Wind rushed over Leo's back as the drake shook its wings. Rising, Kiylla marched over to them.

A hint of joy illumined Johanna's brown eyes. "So you have talent with more than just horses."

"A drake is not unlike a horse," Kiylla retorted. "As a token to prove we are allies." She pulled a bundle of parchment from her cloak and handed it to Johanna. "I stole these from Beau."

"Arsene." Johanna held out the letters.

Snatching them, Arsene quickly leafed through the documents, handing half to Relia.

"Anything?" Leo asked.

"Mm." Arsene's eyes swept back and forth over one letter in particular. "'Fairborough is ideal if my wife is to be believed. They experience more shadow storms than any other region.'"

"My wife. . .?" Johanna repeated. "If these are Beau's letters, he speaks of my mother."

"I think so," Arsene confirmed. "I don't have the context to understand much else, but. . ."

"We can mull over it later," Kiylla said. "Who will ride?"

"One moment." Consus requested, turning back to their prisoner. "Is there anything else we should know? News from Lavinia?"

"Lady Aurica rides with the main host." The drake rider said. "She intends to request the legions return to aid the search."

Arsene strode forward, offering a hand to the drake. Its head cocked as it sniffed him; perhaps they had met once before. "I will ride." He announced.

Nodding, Consus rose. "You're a good man, " he told their prisoner. "I hope you survive when your traitorous masters see their due." Sheathing his glaive, Consus grabbed his horse and passed the other to Leo.

Ride for the mine," Arsene said. "I will join you shortly, and when I do, we'll need to flee with either haste or ingenuity."

Relia shifted from foot to foot nervously. "What are you planning?"

"My mother is there." He grimaced. "I want to draw her attention."

"Shadows." Leo cursed. "What for?"

"Think about it," Arsene gestured vaguely. "We cannot run forever. At some point, we must turn the tide. Relia and I have already discussed this; we must make the Empire realize its princess has been betrayed."

Consus ran a hand across his beard. "Make them remember who the goddess stands with. You want an audience."

"Precisely. Where better than Fairborough? Fionn intended to go there; so did Beau." Arsene mounted the drake, and it rose, wings spreading. "You're clever, Johanna. When you see a great host descending upon your heads, do something about it."

"I'll come up with something. We've no shortage of evokers." Johanna promised.

"Good," Arsene said. "Hurry." Taking the reins, he ordered the drake to fly. Wind swept over the valley as it took off, mighty wings carrying it into the sky.

"Take the lead, Johanna," Consus ordered, passing one of their four horses to Relia.

Kiylla climbed up behind Leo, and he drove their horse into a trot, following the black mare Johanna rode upon. Leaning against his back, Kiylla whispered.

"Stop doing that."

"Stop doing what?" Leo whispered back.

"Scaring me, south lord." She said. "Twice now, I've thought you were dead. Stop putting yourself in danger."

"I'll try," Leo promised, watching the blood-streaked sky and the long drake cutting west across the heavens.

ARSENE HAD RIDDEN a drake once in his youth. All Dragosi princes did. Back then, the ride through the sky had terrified him. After his horrific journey on the leviathan's back, the drake soared the air smoothly, no more fearsome than a quiet carriage ride.

Ash tumbled from the heavens and obscured his vision. Pulling his collar up to shield his mouth, he searched the mountainous paths for the main host. With an ashfall beginning, they would have stopped to take shelter.

Red cut through the sky to his right as a drake sharply descended. Guiding his to follow suit, they burst through an ashen cloud where a heavy cliff side spread outward as it rose, providing shelter below.

There they were. A few drakes, and several patrols. A horn sounded, calling any errant soldiers back. Arsene hung back, watching flying and foot patrols return to the camp.

Now to find his mother.

Gently nudging the drake, Arsene gritted his teeth as it plunged toward the ground. He found his mother quickly. Surrounded by armored me, the lone woman in an extravagant black traveling coat stood out.

The drake landed with a heavy thud just outside the camp's perimeter. Lady Aurica's head snapped in his direction, blonde locks piled atop her head in an intricate, braided bun. Recognition and fury raged in her eyes as Arsene slid off the creature's back.

Steel rang through the mountains as weapons were drawn. Raising a hand, Arsene shouted across the night to his mother. "Hold. If you want the princess alive, you best not kill the only man who knows where she is."

Waving the soldiers down, Mother marched toward him. "Where is she?"

"Why would I hand her over that easy?" Arsene smirked at her. "Who's taking care of the city, Mother? I know Marius is away, and will likely be. . . occupied, for some time."

Worry replaced the hate in Mother's gaze. "Rasvan has it handled. What did you do?"

"What could I have done?" Arsene took a step closer, feigning confidence. There was no room for error to pull off what he wanted. "He's the Goddess' chosen, blessed by power and light mere mortals cannot fathom. Even the princess is a mere speck in comparison. A paltry commoner."

"You're stalling." Mother seethed. "Tell me where Renata is, or face death."

Shaking his head, Arsene motioned behind his back for the drake to come. "You always had eyes only for Marius. Your beloved. But you made a mistake, in never noticing your other son. For while the oldest became the goddess' chosen, you missed when your youngest became her destroyer."

That caught her attention. Her eyes widened.

"If you want the princess," Arsene grabbed the drake's neck. "Then you'll have no choice but to chase me down. And reclaim her." Mounting the drake, he yanked its reins, ordering it to take flight.

"Kill him!" Mother shrieked.

The drake pounded across the ashen rock, wings spreading to take flight. An arrow whizzed past Arsene's head, and another crashed into the drake's back leg as it soared into the air.

Swiveling in the saddle, Arsene watched as a horde of red wings took flight and horses charged from safety, risking an ashfall to pursue their enemy.

Perfect. Now they had but keep the hunters at arms length until they arrived in Fairborough; the unassuming little town that had been the center of everything.

Chapter Thirty

WHOLE

FIONN STARED AT the luminescent moon, pondering her error. She had meant to tear open the veil and bring them to the fiery city of Lavinia. Unfamiliar with Dragos, she had erred, instead ferrying them to northern Athelstan.

Wind flowed through the porch, creaking the old wood. The inn's sign swung back and forth. Quiet chatter and soft candlelight spilled from the windows.

Leaning forward in the rocking chair, Fionn pressed her hands to her eyes. A songbird flitted through the air, tracing the patterns of the wind. She had never felt it so intimately before. Every breath of the wind was hers, her fingers brushing the world and mapping its roads.

Now, she had but find Arsene, and pray he remained an ally.

The creaky inn door flew open and slammed closed as Wulf joined her. He'd removed his armor and wore a thin white undershirt, its buttons loose to reveal the top half of his chest. Rolling up his sleeves, he ran a hand through his hair and leaned on the wall beside her.

"Any luck?" Fionn asked.

"They have one room." Wulf crossed his ankles. "Eckart's elected to sleep with the horses."

"Of course he has." Fionn chuckled.

"What about you?"

"Still looking. I'm tired, though. It might need to wait until the morning." She reclined in the rocking chair, content to take a breather.

Wulf watched her quietly. "Can we talk?"

"Always."

"I wanted to ask you about him. About Seoras." Wulf's eyes narrowed. "What is he, really?"

"I somewhat recall an argument you two had." Fionn knit her fingers together. "He was mortal, once. But that was a long time ago."

"How long?"

Fionn hesitated before giving the answer. "Thousands of years."

"That's ridiculous."

"Believe what you wish," Fionn said. "That's what faith is, after all." She paused. "His story is not mine to tell. But he was never merely ordinary."

"Fine." Wulf pushed off the wall and stood before her. "I had a feeling nothing would get him to talk. He prefers being mysterious." Wulf knelt, placing a hand on her knee. "I care more about you, anyway."

"You want to know about what's going on?" She looked away, mouth tightened into a thin line. "When I was growing up, I thought I was hollow. Our shamans say we each have a soul, but I didn't think so. Everything I knew, everything I felt came from him."

"I can understand why," Wulf said softly. "When we found you outside of Femora, you weren't in control. You're like a puppet he can pick up when he wants."

"Yes. . ." Fionn agreed. Athelstan's moon shone brightly, spilling white light over the porch. "I worried endlessly about the truth. Who I was, buried beneath him. I thought everything I felt was a sham, an imitation."

"You're you, Fionn." Wulf tightened his grip on her knee. "I've seen the difference. Trust me."

"Ha." Brightening, Fionn turned to face him. "It's funny. I don't think so at all. Seoras is part of Casaliede. And now, a part of Casaliede beats within me. Our thoughts are in sync. And I have no memories of my time with you. Only he does." She leaned forward, taking his hands. "But when I look at you, I don't feel any different. My thoughts aren't any different. I didn't lose anything. Not really."

The answer came to her so suddenly she couldn't believe she'd never realized it before.

"I've spent my life trying to be rid of him, longing for a life without him. Wondering, if only I'd been me if I'd be happy." She bit her lip, and tears brewed in her eyes. "I can't heal what's wrong with me. It's been a part of me from the very beginning. There is no Fionn without Seoras. There never has been."

Wulf didn't like her answer. He shook his head. "Fionn-"

She cut him off. "It's the truth. Or do you know a Fionn free of the Leviathan's call?"

Wulf's eyes darted away. He wanted to protest; Fionn could see it in his eyes. Stubborn ferocity surged on his face as he gritted his teeth, refusing to relent. Her grin widened with every second he strained to deny the truth.

Finally, he gave in. "I don't." he exhaled exasperatedly. "That doesn't mean I approve of what he's done to you."

"Well, it's not ideal," Fionn admitted, twirling a strand of her hair. "I would have preferred to be normal."

"Pah." Wulf snorted. "There is no Fionn who would have been normal." His gaze dropped to her hips.

Fionn followed his eyes to the dagger resting on her belt. "Oh, Seoras was no thief. That's all me."

"I know." Wulf stood. "I can tell the difference." He folded his arms. "Can I see it?"

"What, your dagger? No."

"Harpy." Wulf jabbed, pulling her to her feet. "C'mon. We have a long road ahead. Let's get some rest."

"Gladly." Fionn followed him to the door as Eckart emerged from the inn. "You doing alright?"

"Well enough." Eckart rubbed an arm, glancing between them. "How long will it take? My death."

"I don't know. The planes have never been sealed before. You're still here, so it will take at least a few days, maybe weeks."

"I'll help you as long as I'm able, but if it gets bad. . ."

"We're not leaving you," Wulf said firmly.

Eckart smirked. "You're more like Leo than either of you would admit." He dipped his head and trotted down the steps before Wulf could protest.

Lost in thought, Fionn followed Wulf through the inn, bumping into his back a few times as he led her to their tiny, cramped room. A single bed with a solitary sheet sat beside a small table; the moonlight spilled over the pillow.

Pushing the curtains aside, Fionn leaned on the window as Wulf closed the door. His footsteps echoed on the floorboards as he came up behind her and laid his hands on her shoulders. Fingers slid down her arms before his hands dropped from her elbows onto her waist. Wrapping his arms tightly around her, he rested his chin on her head.

Fionn's voice warbled. "I don't deserve everything you've done for me."

"No." Wulf agreed. "You probably don't."

Half-smiling, half crying, she bit her lip and whirled around. He stared at her intensely before pushing her against the window and pressing his lips against hers. One hand rose from her hip and ran through her hair.

The old part of her that hesitated, held back by guilt, believing herself unworthy of trust, fell silent. Instead, a single word screamed from within.

Finally.

Grabbing her thighs, Wulf picked her up and carried her to the bed. Dropping her onto the sheets, he yanked her scarf off and tossed it aside before climbing on top of her, mouth locked with hers as he unlaced her jerkin.

Pressing her hands to his chest, Fionn stopped him. "You don't mind it? That everyone will see you?"

Wulf's eyes darted to the new crystal hanging around her neck. "This is nothing compared to what Eckart said the Gaevral leather workers do."

"Well, that's disappointing."

He looked down, laughing as he tossed her shirt aside. Giggling, she laced her fingers through his hair, sighing in bliss as his mouth dropped to her neck and breasts.

How she'd ached for the touch of another all these years. Tracing a finger down his chest, she undid each button one by one. Growing impatient, she reached for his trousers and loosened their clasp.

"Fionn," Wulf protested. "There's an art to building tension."

Indulging him, she laid back, heart skipping out of her chest as he pulled her trousers off and grabbed her waist, mouth pressed between her legs. Ecstasy raced through her, but for only a moment. The impatience returned as a desire she'd never felt burst to life.

"Enough tension." She said, pushing him aside so she could rip his belt off.

No sooner had his trousers hit the floor than Wulf grabbed her, pushing her onto the pillow. His hands caressed the sides of her face, and he gazed into her eyes, hesitating.

"What?" She whispered.

"Whatever happens. Wherever the road takes us. I promise to protect you."

"Softie." She teased, brushing his cheek. "Now, fuck me."

"Happily." Wulf murmured into her lips as he spread her legs with his. His fingers laced through her hair as they made love, holding tightly as though worried she would disappear if he let go.

FIONN STARED AT the wall, unable to sleep. True night in Athelstan was darker than shadow. The twilight hours of the world were lit by the moon and stars elsewhere, but here, a pure, unbreakable abyss consumed the world.

Unable to sleep, Fionn ran her fingers along Wulf's arm as the warmth of his chest rose and fell against her back. Her mind raced. Worrying about Eckart, fretting over Arsene. Wondering if Relia was all right.

"You're supposed to be sleeping," Wulf murmured into her hair.

Startled, Fionn sat up. "How could you tell?"

Sleepy, Wulf leaned on an elbow. "You snore."

"I do?" Fionn touched her throat, embarrassed.

His brow furrowed, and he sat up, looking around for the bedside table candle. A tiny flame faintly illuminated the room, and Wulf turned back to Fionn, grunting in satisfaction.

"What?" She asked.

"Now I can see your breasts."

Glancing down at her bare chest, Fionn rolled her eyes. "I had a thought."

"That's dangerous." Wulf smiled dumbly in contentment.

"I told you the first part of Aeourant courting but never the second."

Interested, Wulf sat up and met her gaze. "I thought the second part was getting married?"

"For cefran pairs, yes." Fionn undid the clasp around her necklace. "But when you marry a human. . ." She pulled her crystal off and motioned for him to turn around.

"Is that a good idea?" He asked. "I mean-"

"If you're worthy, you'll take good care of it." Fionn reached around his shoulders and gently set the necklace between his collarbones.

Accepting the grave responsibility, Wulf touched the crystal gently. "I will."

Relieved, Fionn laid back. "Maybe now I can sleep."

"Wait." Wulf laid a hand on her stomach. "The dreams; I need to know what they mean."

"Arsene lies a lot." Fionn blurted out. "Do you see through them often?"

"Most of the time." Wulf tapped his nose. "He makes the faintest expression when he lies, like he smells something off."

"Oh, I hadn't noticed that." Fionn paused, committing the hint to memory. "So say you did see through Arsene's lie, but then a voice whispered in your mind. A voice that said the opposite, and you believed it with all your heart."

"Why would I?"

"Because it sounds like your own thoughts. Like your mother's voice heard as a child. Like a god calling to his children. You do not know why, but it's absolute." She hesitated. "Do you remember the night we slept on the river shore with Relia?"

"Yes."

"I told you something, then. But you stared at me blankly, like you'd forgotten. Someone had whispered that what I said was a meaningless lie better left forgotten."

Wulf's blue eyes flicked between the candle and her face. "I think I'm starting to understand, but. . ."

"I'm trying to tell you something as best I can," Fionn whispered. "When something else stamps out my every word."

"Try it," Wulf said suddenly. "Tell me what you did that day."

Sitting up, Fionn stared at him curiously. It was worth a shot. "Some. . . entity hides within Marius. A fae. It calls itself Viridia. Seoras is the only one who can see her. A being of wrongness, whose perfect skin barely conceals the terrifying void within."

Though Wulf had been listening intently, his eyes glazed over. When they snapped into clarity again, he waited, anticipating her words. "You. . ." He trailed off. "Did you say something?"

"Yes." Fionn sighed. "I told you. Whatever it tells you, whatever it shows you. . . you'll believe."

Unsettled, Wulf tensed. Reaching over, he doused the candle and wrapped her in his arms, pressing her to his chest. "I don't know how Seoras influences my dreams. . . but tell him to give me another."

Once upon a time, Seoras' actions had been foreign to her. His magic had sprung to life without her knowing or understanding. She felt a hum in her mind as Seoras reached through the thin veil between worlds and dove into the eternal storm from which the Leviathan hailed.

Was she doing this, or him? Maybe both. Gently, the clouds parted, reshaping into familiar images Wulf had seen before. One more chance to share the truth before the darkness drowned out her song.

CHAPTER THIRTY ONE

ONE LAST SONG

SHEBOROUGH. A tiny peasant village of dying grass and muddy roads, the white-wood houses stained from years of use. Sprawling farmlands grew vibrant crops under the enormous, looming moon.

Arsene's journey had begun here, the day he and Wulf had set their course for Sylfestra. And now he returned, feeling like an entirely different man.

Nobody in Asheborough had paid them much mind. Most villagers wore heavy cloaks to keep out the cold, so their group's concealing garb did not attract much notice. Johanna had offered a few coins to a farmer to let them rent his barn for the night.

Arsene had released his borrowed drake at the border. Shame. He'd begun to grow fond of it.

Leo dropped his horse's reins and nodded at Arsene. "I'll keep first watch."

"I'll join you." Kiylla offered.

Consus frowned, glancing between the two, but kept silent. Arsene had noticed an unusual tension between them, the unmistakable glances and touches of two people sleeping together.

A controversial affair, to be sure. As a man fluent in the topic, Arsene knew better than to bring it up.

"I'll take second," Arsene suggested. He watched as Kiylla tucked a loose strand of hair behind her ear. Her frighteningly intense eyes betrayed her ailment: she had succumbed to permanent phantoms. Her eyes darted about at times, watching memories that interrupted her present.

Yet she retained enough senses to function. And though she had cast Arsene into the Earth Father's domain and permanently injured his hand, they now stood as allies.

"Do you want company?" Relia asked.

"Of course not." Arsene smoothed back his hair. "You're the princess, soon to be Empress. You will sleep through the night. Allow your vassals the duty."

She chuckled. "I'd feel bad."

"Best get used to that feeling," Arsene advised.

Tapping wood caught his ear and he glanced up to see a bird on the roof sill. Brown with beady green eyes, it cocked its head and peered at him. Arsene backed up. He knew that bird.

"Viridia's tits." He murmured, whirling around, eyes darting over the fields. The bird took off, soaring down the southern path.

Chasing after it, Arsene heard someone call after him but ignored their voice. Diving into a thin path between the colorful fields, the bird flew to a woman and vanished into her outstretched hand.

A cloak and cowl billowed in the wind around her. Throwing back her hood, she revealed a pile of silver curls and pupil-less emerald eyes. Fionn smirked at him.

The gall. To cheekily summon him and then *smirk*, after all they'd been through. . .

A brunette man draped in a white fur cloak emerged from the fields, guiding a horse. "Ancestor's sake, Fionn." Eckart muttered, "Stop running off. . ." He trailed off, noticing Arsene.

Wulf was a step behind him, whole and unharmed. Finely crafted black leather armor fluttered around his knees, and his hair was neatly combed. And here, Arsene stood, tattered and dirty.

This was the part where he would say something witty. Arsene had rehearsed their reunion in his head. But when the moment arrived, words failed him. Jogging forward, he wrapped his arms around Fionn and pulled her into a tight embrace.

A mirthful sound met his ears as Fionn flung her arms around him in return. She laughed.

Pounding footsteps heralded the arrival of someone new. "Eckart?" Leo shouted. "Scael's maw!" He cursed, running forward and tackling the half-cefran man. A blur of bodies hit the ground.

Arsene caught a glimpse of Wulf's amused expression. "Good to see you too, partner."

Releasing Fionn, Arsene looked her up and down. She appeared no worse for wear, though something was different about her eyes. They shone brighter than before. But more than that, they. . .

Arsene couldn't quite place it. They had more depth. Like how a corpse's eyes betrayed its demise, her eyes spoke of someone else.

"Are you alright?" Arsene asked. "Vasille said—"

"I'm okay." She assured him.

"How did you find us?"

"Fionn did," Wulf answered, watching Eckart peel Leo off him.

"You look nice." Arsene nodded at Wulf. "And like a proper mercenary again, if a well-paid one."

Chuckling, Wulf clapped Arsene on the shoulder and nodded at Leo.

Leo's grin vanished. "What's wrong?" He peered into Eckart's eyes. "You don't look well."

The half-cefra did appear pallid, his eyes deeply shadowed. Eckart glanced at Fionn, wanting her to answer. She stared intently at Arsene. "The jewel. Tell me you still have them."

"Right here." Arsene patted his satchel. "Save one. Tettiena-"

"I know." She said somberly. "We. . . have a lot to discuss."

✦ ✦ ✦

"I insist you sit," Consus ordered, shoving Eckart onto the barn's floor. "If Fionn speaks true, you need to conserve your strength."

"I'm fine," Eckart grumbled.

Relia sidled closer to him, hands wrapped around her knees. "If you don't keep watch either, I don't have to feel so bad."

Laying a firm hand on Eckart's shoulder, Consus silently ordered him to stay put. Johanna paced behind them, fingers fluttering nervously.

"What have they done?" She said harshly. "The world could be thrown off balance. No one could guess the long-term effects of sealing off a plane."

"They think it'll create a utopia," Arsene said. "A world where every land is the same: safe, habitable."

Kiylla sat beside Leo. "Then, we are safe for a time. If what you say is true, they will want to keep the remaining jewels until they've begun their crusade on cefran kind. They cannot start a war with no one to kill."

"True." Arsene tapped a foot on the floor. "One thing bothers me, though." He stared at Leo, who sat bolt upright. "You say Beau turned the Chamber against you and Consus. But how? It seems a far-fetched tale at best."

"I know." Leo agreed. "It's like. . ." He paused, lips pursed. "Beau set me up, led me into traps that would make me seem guilty. But even then, it was like everyone at the council was immediately willing to accept his words as the unequivocal truth."

Arsene grimaced, and Kiylla noticed. "You think you know why?"

"Not quite." Arsene nervously tucked a stubborn lock of hair behind his hair. "Marius tried to convince me I had been misled, that I'd misunderstood him. I. . . believed him. Instantly. *Me*."

Relia tilted her head. "The world's worst skeptic." She threw up her hands. "Then it's foolproof. What are we supposed to do?"

"Not quite foolproof." Consus said. "Think. If Beau could instantly convince the world we were traitors, why did he wait to carefully sow the seeds of doubt?"

Arsene considered the suggestion. "You're right. What Marius tried to convince me of, I'd always believed. It was true that Fionn lied to me; she admitted as much herself."

"And the wave." Eckart said, voice gravely and weak. "They still wanted to set me up to take the fall."

"If seeds of doubt exist," Arsene theorized, "The magic struggles to take hold. But if the idea has begun to flourish," His head snapped up. "An evoker forgets what they never believed."

Fionn smiled at him. "Then there's only one thing to do," She said. "I'm headed for Scael."

"Scael?" Leo echoed. "Why, and how?"

"The jewels will be safe there." Fionn insisted. "There's a place where. . . where no one can reach but me." She looked at Johanna. "It sounds like you figured out when gaps in the veil appear."

"To enter Scael. . ." Johanna murmured thoughtfully. "You'd need to be in an aiceil during a shadow storm."

Leo stared at her wide-eyed. "Are you mad? You want to run around during a shadow storm?"

"It's more complicated than that." Fionn shook her head. "You have to be in the aiceil as the eye of the storm passes over."

"That's even worse," Leo protested. "Shadow storm eyes are lethal. No one has ever been touched by one and survived." He spluttered. "They're lucky if their remains are even found."

"It's risky." Fionn agreed. "But it's the only way in. And I can protect us." She looked at Arsene. "Have you decided your plan?"

Arsene stood. He needed to pace. "If what I think is correct, some deeper power gives Marius and his, let's call them 'lieutenants,' unnatural charisma. So we'll give the common man a choice: believe Beau and his ilk or the princess herself. Naturally, we'll provide encouragement to choose the latter. Something to overcome their unnaturally potent lies."

Wulf narrowed his eyes. "Go on."

"We're going to lie, of course," Arsene said. "Relia doesn't actually have divine powers. But without doing something drastic, we cannot overturn the tale Beau has spun."

Johanna paused by the fire. "But what can we evoke that couldn't be seen through?"

"Something from Bruthine, perhaps," Arsene suggested, running a thumb under his nose. "The speech priests read before pyre executions; it speaks of the goddess' holy fire and her earthen embrace saving the innocent."

Leo flinched, and Consus looked sharply up. "I know that more personally than I'd like. We could work with that; Leo and I already survived."

"I'm still working on the details." Arsene sighed. "But we have enough evokers here who've seen the other planes to create spells the common man would gape in awe at."

Consus nodded. "We have several days left of travel. Time enough to come to a solution. For now, we should rest."

Wulf stood, grabbing his spear. "I'll take first watch."

"I thought-" Leo started.

"You're nobility, Leofric." Wulf reminded him playfully. "The peasants ought to take first watch."

"I recently escaped execution, if you've forgotten."

"So did I."

"If you insist," Leo waved him off. "Peasant." He added, forcing himself to smile.

"I'll join you." Arsene offered, following Wulf outside.

Finding an overturned barrel, Wulf sat where he could view the entirety of the farm's dirt paths. Arsene leaned on the wall beside him, and Fionn sat on the floor between them.

"Messana," Arsene said abruptly. "We're close now, just a quick boat ride across the Athelstani sea."

Wulf stared at Arsene like his hair was afire. "What?"

"Sylfestra didn't work out." Arsene continued. "We need a new country to find work in."

Snorting, Wulf shook his head. "It never stops raining there. Your coat will get wet. It won't work."

"It won't rain anymore," Fionn said listlessly. "The endless sea has been sealed away."

"Then, there's no problem." Arsene said. "I hear they have a different sense of fashion there. Might be fun to try something new."

Wulf leaned forward, hands clasped. "I'm surprised you're here."

Arsene swallowed, looking down. "So am I."

"I'm sorry," Wulf said. "Whatever happened to bring you here. . . I'm sorry."

His partner knew him all too well, though his thoughts went unspoken. 'Marius must have betrayed you for you to have come here.'

"Wulf." Arsene looked up. "Can I borrow Fionn a moment?"

"Only a moment." Wulf agreed, leaning back and sharpening his spear.

Rising, Fionn followed Arsene behind the farmhouse into an empty yard. The subtle limp that marred her steps in the days before her capture was gone. Her eyes had brightened considerably, and the pallor had left her skin.

She was still pale as a ghost, but no longer in a deathly sense.

"What's on your mind?" She asked, almost cheerily.

Tucking his hands into his pockets, Arsene stared at the sea of vibrant crops. Now that he was here, he hadn't any idea what to say. He looked into her horrifying eyes, noticing something new in the shimmering emerald.

Before they'd parted, Arsene had seen the same inferiority, the same sorrow mirrored in her gaze. Now, he saw timelessness, a depth he couldn't hope to reach, a wailing that traveled forth from the distant past.

Like she had hurt for so long, she no longer felt the pain. Only numbness.

Was she silently communicating it somehow to him, or. . . or was he imagining things?

"I admit," Fionn said, glancing away. "I thought you would betray us in a heartbeat."

"Did I not promise to let you rob me?" Arsene retorted.

"Yes. But things changed when I got captured. It wouldn't be worth the risk anymore."

"It wasn't." Arsene agreed, gaze flicking down. Wulf had lobbed a spear at the man restraining Fionn without a second thought. It had taken days for Arsene to consider rescuing her.

"So. . ." Fionn asked. "What changed?"

Staring up at the fading moon, Arsene took a breath. "Marius is like the sun. Bright, shining, larger than anything else in the world, and a driving force behind life itself. A symbol of the goddess, something nobody fears but loves."

"To you, especially."

"Yes, well. . ." Arsene smirked. "Answer me a riddle."

Opening her mouth, Fionn snapped it close when she realized he had echoed the words she'd said to him on the boat ride home. "Alright."

"What is the only thing that can eclipse the sun?"

Fionn's eyelids fluttered as she considered the question. "The moon?"

"Oh, come now, you're more poetic than that."

"I was only joking." The corners of her mouth wobbled as she tried to smile. "I would say, then, something intangible. Something more important than warmth, than life." She paused. "Love."

"And it makes you end up in bloody Athelstan."

Laughing, Fionn flew forward and hugged him tightly. Jaw clenched, Arsene smoothed her hair and trailed his fingers through her curls. "We never would have worked." He said softly.

"No, of course not."

"You're too emotional."

"And you're too much of an ass."

"Cacmun was the cefran word, wasn't it?"

"Mhm." She mumbled. "But, I suppose it would have been a fun couple of nights."

Arsene chuckled. "Give yourself some credit. A fun couple of weeks, at least."

"Who said it was I who needed the credit?" Grinning, she pulled away. "I'm glad you're here." Cupping his face, she kissed him on the cheek. Smiling, she knit her hands behind her back and danced away, returning to Wulf.

Pulling Death Knell from its holster, Arsene turned it over in his hand. A brief pain flickered through his previously broken hand, and he held it up, examining it for a wound. But it was mended. Marius had healed it.

Sighing, he took apart the flintlock and put it back together again. Some people only wished to live without regrets. But such a thing was impossible. Arsene only wanted people to remember him, not those who swallowed him in their shadows.

He would put on the greatest show the world had seen, fool those swayed by enchanted lies. Leave a mark on this world it could never forget.

As he snapped the final piece of Death Knell back into place, he heard the strum of a lute and the beginnings of a song.

Quietly returning to where Wulf kept watch, Arsene leaned on the barn wall, watching. Fionn stood a few paces away from Wulf, gaze cast over the fields like she was singing to nobody but herself.

When the sun sets, the world is bathed in red
Colors stream through bitter leaves
A flower blooms under winter's thumb
Plucked in the morning and dead by dusk

You paint the sky, hoping night will never come
Clutching stolen grace you don't wanna return
And memories just don't seem like they're enough
To keep the flower from turning to dust

Was it enough to hold it in your arms?
Will it be forgotten when morning comes?
If some moments last a lifetime

Then let the flower bloom forever in twilight
By your side
Where it always belonged

CHAPTER THIRTY TWO

FAREWELL

ARSENE HELD UP a lantern, its soft glow piercing the fog drenching Fairborough's early morning streets. The sun would rise in two hours, yet no sign of dawn appeared in the black sky.

Wulf walked stiffly, muscles tensed. Most of the town was still asleep, locked in their humble wooden houses. A defined cobbled road overtook the dirt paths as they drew closer to the chapel. Nobody was up yet, save a lone horse and his rider.

Eyeing the passing messenger warily, Arsene glanced at Relia, ensuring her hood shrouded her red locks. Her head craned up, taking in the sight of the famous chapel.

"That's it?" Relia asked.

"Yep," Wulf said curtly.

The courtyard surrounding the chapel outshone the building; unlike most small villages, the spacious area was decorated with hedges and flower boxes, though winter had killed most of them. An ancient chapel rested behind an old iron gate, stone walls covered in creeping ivy spiraling toward the bell tower.

Set on a high hill, the chapel overlooked the aiceil behind it, though Arsene could hardly see it in this pall. Black bark trees swayed under the breeze, growing from silver grass dotted with luminescent flowers.

So that was Scael. Aiceils were a preview of what waited in the world beyond the veil, never quite showing the whole truth of the other realm.

Fionn wandered away, flicking her hood up as she approached an overlook. Scanning the courtyard, Arsene turned in a circle as he mapped out their plan in his head.

"Perfect." He muttered. "A stage before a respected chapel."

"Are you sure about this?" Relia pressed.

"So long as you are."

Sighing, Relia stared at the chapel. "I don't feel I have what it takes to be a leader. Will anyone really listen to me?"

"You do," Arsene assured her. "Remember how you demanded you be the one to speak with the Lady? Or when you ordered the drake rider to give up his mount?"

"I didn't really order him. . ." her shoulders slumped. "I can only do that when I'm being impulsive."

"Be impulsive, then."

Wulf stared at the ground, perhaps the spot where he'd last seen his father alive. "If what Kiylla says is true. . . If a shadow storm strikes before our pursuers arrive, you'll evoke without the aid of the jewel."

Arsene pulled out Diorbhail's Ember and turned it over in his hands. Kiylla said evoking what lies in the other planes was unbearably painful without its corresponding jewel; its door. Would his planned spell fracture his mind?

"Nothing exists in this world like the fire in Bruthine." Arsene returned the jewel to his pocket. "It's our best bet."

"We'll wait here for them." Relia decided. "I'll propose a trial of faith." Worry fractured her face. "What if Marius is there? We don't know what he can do."

"Who do you think will show?" Wulf asked.

"My mother." Arsene tapped his palm, thinking. "The heir to the Empire is in jeopardy, and with the Emperor dead, I wouldn't be surprised if several names of import appear."

"One of the traitors will assuredly be there." Relia guessed. "I'll target them."

"Mm." Wulf's brow knit. "And what if their enchanted lies undo our efforts?"

"Then we lose," Arsene said, surprisingly unworried. "And we can share a pyre, Wulf."

"You sound awfully calm about this."

"We're dealing with the unknown." Arsene shook his head. "I don't know what to expect. It makes me more curious than frightened."

Wulf finally smiled. "Curiosity is going to be the death of you."

"I think it's already claimed me," Arsene murmured, watching Fionn lean over the hedge wall to observe the aiceil below.

LEO BRUSHED HIS horse's coat, studying the fields. Who would have thought fate would bring both he and Wulf back to Fairborough more than ten years later?

Eckart leaned on the cobbled wall behind him. With each passing day, the shadows under his eyes deepened, and he'd begun to shiver. Eckart, the man who dove into lakes in the middle of winter, *shivering*. Leo grimaced, worried.

Stepping back, Leo laid a hand on his sword hilt and turned to Eckart. "Feeling alright?"

Wrapping his fur cloak around his shoulder, Eckart looked up slowly. "I'm sorry." He said, ignoring the question.

"What for?"

"I keep thinking about it. How you almost died."

"So did you." Leo pointed out.

"I'm dying as we speak." Eckart joked dryly. "Do you think Dilsaeth's okay?"

"He's back in Lavinia with Tefnut, no?"

"You remember her name?"

"Of course I remember the blasted goat's name." Leo rolled his eyes. "I hope so. If we manage to come out of this alive, we'll have to retrieve them. At least I can trust Lady Parnesius to take care of Temple."

"That's good." Eckart's icy eyes narrowed, and he grabbed the horse's reins. "So, you and Kiylla."

Placing his hands on his hips, Leo looked away. "Mhm?"

"Do you think I haven't noticed? Whenever everyone's quiet, you stare at her like you're remembering something altogether more pleasant."

Flustered, Leo opened his mouth to deny the claim, but it was true. "She's. . .ah. . ."

"Good in bed, I take it." Eckart chuckled. "I never imagined you fancying her. I figured you would hate her for the rest of your days."

"Believe me when I say that would have been simpler." Leo grabbed the reins, standing closer to Eckart. "It's never going to work out. And every day I keep entertaining this, the parting will only be worse."

"It's more than a tryst, isn't it? You fell for her somewhere along the way."

Leo had. He glanced away, trying to remember when the murderer he loathed had changed into the relentless, brave woman he admired.

"I'm hopeless, aren't I?"

Eckart grinned. "I've been saying that from the first."

"Are you talking about me?"

Leo jumped out of his skin and spun around. Kiylla strode towards them, wrapped in a tattered brown cloak. She laid a hand on Leo's chest and smiled at Eckart.

"The half-breed and the knight who took sympathy on their Empire's oldest enemy." She glanced between them. "Leo said you tell the story better."

Leaning on the horse's flank, Eckart folded his arms. "I do. But I'm surprised Leo would allow me to embarrass him in front of *you*."

"Please." Kiylla teased. "The south lord embarrasses himself enough as it is."

"I do not." Leo spat.

Kiylla's fingers danced on his chest, parting the collar of his tunic. Stiffening and turning bright red, Leo glanced at Eckart, who snorted loudly.

"So I was out hunting," He began, "When I heard a bloodcurdling scream. The mists had arrived, you see. And a certain Athelstani squire had never seen them before."

"You've skipped over several important details." Leo interrupted. "Nevermind. I'll tell it."

"Leo, it takes you days to finish one simple story." Eckart's head slowly rolled to the side, and he stood upright. Following his gaze, Leo noticed Consus exiting Fairborough's gate and turning in their direction.

Stepping away from Kiylla, Leo put some distance between them.

Eckart held up a hand. "I'll intercept," he offered, walking away. "You do know he knows, right?" he called over his shoulder.

"I know. . ." Leo murmured.

Meeting Consus across the field, Eckart tapped his arm and turned him away. Kiylla's eyebrows shot up, and she stared thoughtfully into Leo's eyes. "Ah!" She exclaimed. "A lifetime ago, you asked to talk. We have not been alone until now."

They hadn't. Spare minutes had been found along the road to slip into the woods, but not for a serious conversation. Swallowing, Leo turned his back to Consus. "With the duress we've been under. . . I mean, you and I. . ."

"Llaqtans mate young." Kiylla interrupted. "Paired off by our parents, we stitch our own tent and move out."

"You never mentioned if you were married or not."

"No. I cannot say I have ever been in love. And we do not force people to mate if they do not wish." She ran a hand down his chest and balled her hand into a fist. "My mother would. . .accept you, I think."

"Can you truly imagine me living as a herding nomad?"

"Yes." She smiled. "You could bring him. Your home." She nodded toward Eckart. "Does he not need somewhere new to dwell?"

Kiylla had a point. Leo watched Eckart and Consus return to Fairborough, mind drifting to the future. It was a pleasant idea, if not the one he'd imagined for himself.

"I've always wanted kids." Leo blurted out. "Eckart loves kids, but I don't think he intends to have any of his own. He'd make a wonderful godfather."

Kiylla's eyebrows shot up. "Are you asking me for children right now?"

"N-no, I mean. . ."

Chuckling, Kiylla leaned her head against his chest. "To be honest, south lord, I do not expect to return home. I never have. I don't think you expect it of yourself, either."

Leo lowered his head. She was right about that. "Be careful. Are you sure the Imperials won't find your hiding spot?"

"They will be oblivious. My spells will join Arsene's only once they believe their goddess has arrived." She looked up at him. "As always, it is you I worry for."

"Me? I have sentry duty. Once I spot the Imperials, I get to ride to safety."

"Good. Then join me so I can protect you," Kiylla hesitated. "I am glad you came to speak with me in Femora that night," she smiled sadly. "I like you, south lord. Perhaps in another life. . ."

Taking her hand, Leo forgot about everything around them, everything he'd been through. He leaned in to kiss her, brushing the hair from her face. "In another life." He agreed, pressing his forehead against hers.

THE AEOURANT SETTLEMENT was loud and raucous. Doors meant nothing; a closed one kept out weather and bugs, not people. Cefra shared everything. Knew everything about one another.

When Fionn and Wulf retired to their tiny inn room, the others backed off, allowing them privacy. A wonderful concept, if strange and lonely.

Wulf pulled off his gambeson and hung it over the wardrobe. Watching him undress, Fionn fidgeted with her scarf nervously. She had not grown accustomed to Seoras' thoughts humming in harmony with hers.

We'll be in Scael soon. A one-way trip.

Wulf wanted to go with her, but Fionn could not let him. She'd slip away in the night, hoping tendrils of darkness appeared in the sky while the others slept.

What of you? Fionn wondered.

I . . . Seoras trailed off, but Fionn knew what he would say. *There is someone I'd like to see. It's been. . . a very long time.*

For how long Seoras had obscured the man's face and memory from Fionn, she could see him in perfect clarity now; they had matching eyes. Fate had wrested them apart for all eternity.

Something Seoras had said in the Earth Father's domain surfaced in her memory. '*I wonder if he still lingers there. If he remembers.*'

He does. Fionn assured him.

Seoras did not answer, but Fionn felt comfort flow through them both.

Deeply mired in her thoughts, Fionn did not notice Wulf sit on the bed beside her until he pulled her into his arms.

"What's wrong?" He asked.

"Everything," Fionn answered.

Wulf chuckled into her hair. "That's fair." He brushed a lock behind her ear. "I could take your mind off it."

"I'm not sure anything could."

"Is that right?" He growled, flipping her onto her back.

A thrum of excitement raced through Fionn's chest as he climbed on top of her and kissed her. Evidently, it didn't take much to seduce her. But the worry would not subside. It gnawed at the back of her mind as he tugged her shirt off and ran his hands down her breasts.

Grabbing a fistful of his hair, Fionn kissed him with hunger. This would be the last night spent with him. She wanted to live in this moment for as long as it would last.

Tears burned hot in her eyes, threatening to spill forth. Not wanting Wulf to know what she was thinking, Fionn flipped herself over, burying her face in the pillow.

The emotions quelled as Wulf undressed her and traced his mouth up her spine, landing at the base of her neck. He grabbed her hand, lacing his fingers through hers and pulling her arm above her head. Through the brewing emotions, Fionn released a shuddering sigh as she felt him push inside her.

Wulf nuzzled her head, and a harsh whisper met her ears. "I love you."

Gasping to hide the escaping tears, Fionn squeezed her eyes shut, desperately trying to bask in the moment she'd yearned for all her life.

To know someone fully. To trust in them at your most vulnerable moment. To know they would always be by your side, no matter what came to pass.

And to drown in sorrow, knowing you had to leave them behind.

CHAPTER THIRTY THREE

DEATH

FIONN WAITED FOR the deepest night to fall over the town of Fairborough before she rose. Carefully extracting herself from Wulf's tight embrace, she slipped from the bed and quietly pulled her clothes on.

Wrapping her scarf around her neck, she stepped outside and glanced down the hall. Everyone was sharing a room. Arsene and Johanna had bunked together across the hall. Pulling a hairpin loose, Fionn fit it into their lock and jimmied the door open.

Soft moonlight spilled across the lone bed in the room. Ever a spoiled prince, Arsene had claimed the bed while Johanna slept on a bedroll near the door. Tiptoeing past her, Fionn studied the bedside table, where Arsene's belt lay beside Death Knell.

Unclipping the leather bag from his belt, Fionn checked its contents before stowing it in her trouser pocket. Both jewels were inside. She hesitated, staring at Arsene's face. Should she wake him and bid farewell? He would not stop her the way Wulf would.

No, maybe she was wrong. The Arsene she had first met would not have stopped her, but the man he'd become would.

Leaving them be, Fionn crept back outside and locked the door behind her. Steeling herself, she walked through the common room and pushed open the inn door. A cold breeze met her face, throwing her scarf wild.

Most thought shadow storms appeared without warning. But Seoras could sense them, feel the wind stirring in the heavens, circling far above what man could see. One would arrive by dawn.

Shouldering her bag, Fionn strode down the dirt road, heading for the outskirts of town. Fairborough slept around her, quiet and still. Grabbing a paint horse from the stables, she mounted the steed her mother had gifted her, wondering what had become of Tipple, her once stalwart companion.

Scael awaited. There, she would store the jewels. Seoras would shatter the passage between realms behind her, sealing both Fionn and the keystones inside. Forever.

Long ago, Fionn had not feared this part of the journey. The end.

Now. . . she wanted to stay.

Wiping away a tear, she focused on her goal, trying to forget what she left behind. A low-hanging tree branch brushed her face, snapping her back to attention. Clicking her heels into the horse's flank, she rode faster, dead leaves crunching under-hoof.

Seoras sensed the danger a moment before it arrived: the forest itself rising to kill her.

Vines burst from the soil, entangling the horse's legs and yanking it off its feet. Fionn tumbled from the saddle as a tree branch whipped across her face, drawing blood. She hit the ground, thorny vines wrapping around her, tearing into her skin as they constricted.

The horse screamed, flailing as it tried to escape its bonds. Struggling to her knees, Fionn scowled at the man approaching her through the boughs.

Auburn hair trailed behind him, curling in waves down his white cloak. Amber eyes stared at Fionn with both sorrow and determination.

"You like to play the part, don't you?" Fionn gasped.

Marius' eye twitched, unsure what she accused him of.

"Using nature. Pretending to be her."

Grimacing, Marius knelt beside her, cloak fanning out like a pool of holy light against the night. "I didn't want to hurt you."

"Didn't you? I would die anyway when Seoras' Breath shattered." Glancing around, Fionn stiffened. She would break from her bonds, but not yet.

"An unfortunate necessity." Marius looked away. "There is no clear path to a better tomorrow."

"Right. Easy for you to say, *Emperor*." She snarled. "So, are you going to make someone else do it? Or are you going to kill Arsene yourself?"

Anger flashed over Marius' face. "You are the one who dragged him away, who fed him false lies."

"Was I? Do you even know why he left that night? Why he dreaded returning to you?"

The anger faltered. Marius withdrew slightly. "He did?"

Through Marius' guise, Fionn could feel the entity within. A wrongness pervaded him, and his eyes shone with light that belonged to something else. Wind stirred his hair, unable to outline the void hiding within—just as it had so many years ago when Seoras alone could see through it.

"Yes, he did." Fionn spat. "I think he knew, deep down, that you and your mother were traitors."

"I'm only doing what's necessary for my people, just as Seoras is." He leaned closer. "I know my brother. Arsene would sell his mother for a copper coin. He couldn't care less if he were a loyal citizen or a heretic so long as it benefited him. So why did he choose the hard road?"

Fionn didn't think there was just one reason. Arsene was a complicated man who held his cards close to his heart. Within Marius' soft gaze, she saw dread building—reluctance and self-hatred.

"He's your brother. You tell me." Fionn said, watching as Marius rose. "Do you really believe in her?" Fionn asked. "Viridia?"

"How can you ask that?" Marius retorted. "Do you doubt His voice?"

"I doubt he's a god." Fionn smiled slightly. "I know him for what he really is. Can you say the same of yours?"

Marius' face faltered ever so slightly. The soothing breeze of Viridia's voice whispered in Fionn's mind, but she ignored it. The lie had no effect when Seoras had seen through her so long ago.

Brushing Fionn's words off, Marius pushed her cloak aside, searching her for the jewels.

"Did you find your answer?" Fionn asked as he ripped off her satchel.

"I know!" Marius growled. "I saw you two. I know what he felt. Never in his life has my brother been happy save for when he returned to Lavinia with you and that man."

"So Tettiena kills her son, and you murder the woman your brother came to love," Fionn murmured. "Viridia asks much of you. And, inevitably, you'll have to watch him burn. Will it be worth it, then? Knowing Relia will always hate you?"

Marius' hand trembled on the pouch strings. Eager to be away from her, he turned his back, opening the bag to check its contents.

"He thought the world of you," Fionn called after him. "It broke his heart to learn he was wrong."

Marius whirled around, "You know nothing-"

He blurted the words out in anger. Just what Fionn was waiting for. The wind whipped into a frenzy as she whistled, shrill and high. Thunder clouds brewed above the forest, gathering into an electric charge that burst from the heavens and slammed into Marius.

A golden barrier of pure light shielded Marius with only a second to spare. The force of the lightning threw him backward. Losing concentration on his spell, the vines fell from her body, and Fionn shot to her feet.

Shadowy thorns lined with blood roses whipped toward her. Stepping back, footsteps in beat with the thunder, lightning flared to life on her fingertips, shooting across the tendrils and setting them aflame. Bright red mingled with the flashing light of the storm, outlining the Duke in white.

The shard Seoras had used to plug the wound in her soul surged painfully. Wind ripped from her being, coalescing into a leviathan. It whirled around her before lunging forward, grabbing Marius in its jaws and throwing him to the ground, head hovering above his neck.

Twirling her hand, Fionn captured a bolt of lightning that shaped itself into a spear of crackling energy. Standing beside Marius, she pressed its tip to his throat.

Seoras could outmatch the fae entity in battle with ease. But the danger had never come from its martial prowess.

"I feel sorry for you," Fionn admitted. "I don't think Arsene misjudged you. I think it has you fooled, too."

A glimmer of doubt appeared on Marius' face and vanished instantly. Whatever voice spoke within his mind wiped away her words.

Dropping to a knee, Fionn hesitated. She didn't want to hurt Marius. But how could she convince him of anything when the void within could whisper perfect lies, undoing any truths Fionn spoke?

Sparks crackled around her fingers. What if killing Marius spared the void within? What if the entity escaped and possessed another? Seoras had never planned to kill it, never known how. He'd only sought to hide the jewels out of its reach.

How did one kill a fae? One who lacked a form, one who hid from all the world's eyes? Seoras had been told, long ago, that a fae died only when an unremarkable mortal became the opposite of that which they embody.

But could the words of the fae king be trusted?

Grabbing Marius' hand, she stared into his eyes. "Read my memories. See the truth."

Grimacing, Marius tried to yank his hand away. Blood poured from his neck where her spear pierced and was summarily burned by the lightning. Pained, he hesitated, and in that fleeting moment, curiosity appeared in his eyes, a perfect mirror for the light Fionn had glimpsed so often in Arsene's.

The moment was all it took. Fionn felt him crash through the barriers of her mind, boring into her thoughts. Her memories whirled around her, a cacophony of words and sounds she could hardly register as Marius drank her entire life in.

Unsteady and chaotic, memories belonging to Marius flowed into her. Nights where he'd sobbed, horrified by what must be done. Nights where he'd hovered over his baby brother, the prince who never belonged.

Something flickered around Marius, a barely tangible shadow. It shot behind Fionn. Rising, she spun around and found herself face to face with a man who should not be here.

Wulf was dressed for battle in his black gambeson, spear clutched in hand. Rain from the storm dripped down his face, outlining his sharp jaw. Seeing him, Fionn hesitated.

Lunging forward, Wulf drove his spear into Fionn's chest. Gasping, she clutched at the shaft, hands grabbing air as he yanked the weapon free. Blood surged from the wound, soaking her jerkin as unbearable pain burst through her.

This wound was fatal. Even as Fionn's hands grasped at her heart, straining to staunch the blood, she knew it was futile.

Falling to her knees, a whirlwind flew to life in her head. Her. Seoras. The fragment of the storm's heart.

Cracks snaked through Wulf's face, revealing an inky void beneath his skin. Grabbing her scarf, he yanked it off and pulled the emerald jewel from its cloth. As Wulf held Seoras' Breath up, Fionn could feel the god she harbored trying to stitch her back together, mending the wound threatening her life. Lightning crackled down her chest, searing the wound shut.

Wulf tossed the jewel to Marius. "Shatter it," he instructed. Wulf's mien faltered, and his voice changed pitch. The darkness wavered, and the cracks reshaped until a woman with brilliant rose-colored locks stood in his place.

The white gown trailing around Viridia glowed beneath the lightning. Marius grabbed the jewel, face contorted in pain and confusion, and did as she ordered. Clenching the emerald in his hands, he focused on it. His fingers glowed.

Fionn felt the jewel shatter. The exterior broke into a thousand pieces, releasing the storm harbored within. Lightning and thunder intensified, trapping them in a dome of violent tempests.

Take it! Seoras hissed.

Time slowed. Fionn could see every strand of the jewel's essence escaping its cage—the tiny piece of the plane—the same that thrummed within her—the magic Seoras had pulled into this world to force open the door.

Reaching out a hand, Fionn grabbed for it. She remembered the heart of Casaliede, the swirling leviathans, the beating heart of a place not meant for the living. Agony flared on her fingertips and traced down her being as a final flash of lightning illuminated the sky before every ounce of magic faded.

Fionn collapsed. Through blurred vision, she could faintly see someone approach and kneel beside her, feel them touch her side, and pull something off her belt. A dagger flashed beneath the glare of fire—Wulf's dagger.

Straining to see, Fionn tried to focus on Viridia. But as the woman with red hair stood and turned away, Fionn saw the black cracks marring her beauty writhe as the woman's guise shifted anew.

Silver curls bounced on a lithe woman's back, and a lavender scarf fluttered around her neck. Tucking Wulf's dagger into her belt, the freckled cefran woman held up the pouch containing the surviving jewels before turning away.

Taking one last look at Marius and Fionn, the fae turned away, striding into the forest as Fionn's world fell to darkness.

She felt Seoras' presence one last time, comforting and soft, before death claimed her.

You're okay, little bird.

CHAPTER THIRTY FOUR

FINAL MEMORY

Some time in the ancient past. . .

SEORAS MISSED THE sea. The color of its waves, the glint of the moonlight. He missed the sight of flowers in bloom, of smiling faces, and bright eyes.

For years, he had assured the others he'd grown used to blindness, but the words had never been true.

Wind danced around the sea, tracing the lapping waves and caressing the grass. It bounced off the walls of the tower, slipping between the cracks of windows, and plunging off the rocky shore into the depths.

The world, outlined in touch.

Trudging to the cliff, he mumbled, "An heir would like to depart, thanks."

It was an abridged version of the formal incantation, but the magic binding the tower didn't mind. Water surged up from the sea, hardening into a bridge of ice. Shouldering his lyre case, Seoras marched across it and slid down the slope onto the gentle beach of black sand.

Reaching down, Seoras felt around for the rock he sensed and picked it up. Trying to remember how this was done, he stepped back and lobbed the rock.

A heavy plunk told of its demise. It hadn't skipped once.

Despondent, Seoras grabbed his lyre and plucked a few strings. All of them rang discordant and out of tune. Flinching, he pulled the lyre away from his face.

The wind traced a man, warning Seoras of his arrival. His wavy hair was bound at the nape of his neck, ornate armor was strapped over a flowing surcoat, and a heavy shoulder cape concealed his right arm.

The Lord Paragon approached.

"Throwing rocks in a fit of rage, now?" A warm, charismatic voice asked.

Seoras sighed, lowering his lyre. The wind swept past them, nearly tearing his scarf off. "I was trying to skip it." He corrected, plucking another string.

"Want me to teach you how it's done?" The paragon knelt, finding another stone.

As he palmed it, Seoras recalled the face he could no longer see. Auburn hair like fire, golden eyes filled with kindness. His mien had always comforted Seoras in dark times.

"I know how it's done." Seoras said. "In theory."

Chuckling, the paragon tossed the rock and caught it. "It's all in the shape of the rock and the flick of the wrist." He threw the stone, and Seoras heard it skip seven, eight times.

"Is there anything you aren't good at?" Seoras asked.

"Have you seen my love life? Or heard my speeches? I've had practice with this, is all. It's good for bonding. And relaxing."

Relaxing. What right did Seoras have to relax? Hugging his lyre to his chest, he stared at the ground, feeling the wind rustle his curls.

The paragon picked up another stone. "Your birthday is coming up. I presume you've forgotten?"

Seoras looked up. "Oops."

"Twenty-five. By all accounts, you'll finally be an adult." The paragon ruffled Seoras' hair. "Maybe it's the freckles, but you still look sixteen to me."

"I feel sixteen." Seoras agreed, not minding the old display of affection. Leaning down, he patted the grass, finding a stone. Running a finger over it, he traced its shape.

Hints of joy had appeared in the years since, but time felt like it had stopped, back then.

The paragon sighed. "It's been years. How long will it take for you to forgive yourself?"

"My life was never worth anything. He should have lived, and I should have died." Seoras said. "Nothing will change that."

"Do you think that's what he wanted?"

No, of course not. But Seoras did not say the words. He clutched the stone, tracing circles on its smooth surface. Guilt hung heavy on his soul, like a weight tied around his ankles, dragging behind every step.

Placing a hand on Seoras' shoulder, the paragon took his wrist, tilting Seoras' hand. "You want to throw like that. Flick the wrist before releasing."

Following his instruction, Seoras raised the stone to throw but lowered his arm. He sighed heavily.

"Love's a funny thing." The paragon wandered around Seoras, searching for another rock. "We cling to life until faced with losing another. Then, suddenly, we're willing to throw everything away." Joining Seoras by the cliffs, the paragon palmed the stone and threw. "I miss him, too. But he wouldn't change a thing."

Five, six. The stone fell into the water and sank.

"You'd do the same for any of us. It's why I think you'll be a good father." The paragon paused. "Besides, I like to think he's still out there, somewhere. It helps."

Seoras wanted to believe that, too. He hoped it was true. "He would be horrified by the news."

"Oh, absolutely. Did I not just say we still think of you as being a child? And you're the first of us to have your own?"

Seoras chuckled softly. He lifted the stone again and tossed it across the water. Two, three. It sank.

For months, Seoras had warbled back and forth on a decision. What if his child was a boy? Should he name the baby after the one he'd lost?

No. Names made in tribute were for the dead. So long as hope remained that a reunion awaited on the horizon, the name would stay his alone.

"I think I finally have it," Seoras announced.

"Mhm. Maybe next time you can make it skip four times."

"Not the damn rock." Seoras huffed. "A name."

The paragon bounced on his heels eagerly. "Finally? You're cutting it close, you know."

"I know." Seoras picked up another stone. "Make a guess. Do you think it will be a boy or a girl?"

"Mm." The paragon paused, thinking. "I think it'll be a boy."

"Then, it's settled." Seoras lobbed the stone, listening to it skip. Five, six. . . "I'm going to name him Fionn."

CHAPTER THIRTY FIVE

SHADOWS

ULF AWOKE WITH his arms empty. Feeling the bed for Fionn, he sat upright when he realized she was missing. Her bag and clothes were gone. Panicked, Wulf fumbled for his dropped shirt and pulled it on.

The door creaked open, and Fionn entered. "Oh." She said sheepishly. "I was hoping to return before you woke."

The tension in Wulf's chest evaporated. "There you are." He grumbled, buttoning his shirt. "Where did you go?"

"I stepped outside because-" She shook her head. "Hurry. A shadow storm's coming."

"How can you tell?"

"Seoras can sense them before they arrive," Fionn said, slipping out the door.

"Wait!" Wulf called. The door slammed.

Sighing, Wulf scrambled out of bed and hastily dressed, strapping his spear to his gambeson. Straightening his hair, he flew out the door and down the steps. Leo and Kiylla waited by the door.

"Wulf." Leo greeted him. "I think a storm's coming."

Striding to the window, Wulf peered out. The oaks surrounding Fairborough swayed under a growing wind. Kiylla stood on her tiptoes, watching the squall with interest.

Footsteps hammered down the stairs as Arsene joined them, still buttoning his vest. "Shit." He cursed. "I was hoping this would come *after* the Imperials arrived." He grimaced, glancing out the window. "We don't have time to wait for another. It could take weeks."

"You're sure you'll be alright?" Wulf asked.

"I'll be fine." Arsene raised his chin. "I escaped unscathed, remember? You were the one who ended up in a dungeon."

"Think you can use that against me?" Wulf jabbed him in the chest. "I remember the incident with the Viscount's daughter vividly, so don't test me."

"Fine. We'll call a truce." Arsene suggested, smiling.

"Truce." Wulf agreed.

Johanna trotted down the steps, binding her raven locks into a braid. "Wulf. Do you have the jewels?"

"Fionn does."

"We should leave. We don't want to miss it."

Nodding, Wulf noticed motion out of the corner of his eye and felt something slam into his chest before he registered Relia's approach. The red-haired girl wrapped him in a tight hug.

"Be careful." She pleaded.

"I have the easy job," Wulf assured her. "You're the one I don't envy."

"I've got this," Relia promised. "I have to."

Turning from Wulf, she ran to Fionn as the bard joined them. The two women hugged tightly, Fionn whispering something into Relia's ear. Smiling warmly, Fionn ran a motherly hand down Relia's hair and stepped away.

"Ready?" Fionn asked.

Wulf glanced around. "What about Eckart?"

"I don't want to wake him. He needs his rest." She glanced at Leo. "Tell him and Consus we've left, would you?"

"He won't like that," Leo warned.

"I know," Fionn said softly.

"Don't fuck this up," Arsene said, grabbing Fionn's arms. "And don't fret. This world is in our skillful and suitably theatrical hands."

Kiylla snorted. Acting aloof, Arsene gently hugged Fionn, but Wulf could see a nervous tremble in his fingers. They lingered on her, unwilling to let go. Eventually, he pushed her away, feigning confidence and disinterest.

"Go already." Kiylla pushed open the door. She grabbed Johanna's wrist as the other woman passed, squeezing gently.

The two Llaqtans shared a look filled with nostalgia from a time when they had been friends. Johanna clutched Kiylla's hand and squeezed back before walking away.

Fionn dashed after her, but Wulf loitered by the door. "Leo," He said, "tell Eckart to take it easy. I'll find a cure for him, yet."

"Can you promise that?" Leo asked somberly.

"I wish I could," Wulf said, dipping his head as he strode out the door.

Wind rustled Wulf's cloak as he made for the stables and pulled open the creaky wooden doors. He froze.

One of their horses was missing. The painted mare Fionn's mother had given them.

Johanna's face wrinkled when she noticed the discrepancy, and she tilted her head, concerned.

"What's wrong?" Fionn asked, grabbing a black horse.

"A horse is missing," Wulf said. "Did someone take it out?"

"Maybe? She was my mother's steed. And trust me," Fionn chuckled as she handed Wulf the black horse's reins. "The old girl ran away a lot."

Something didn't seem right. An annoying prick of pain tugged at Wulf's heart and mind. But, Fionn spoke the truth. Wulf had no reason to disbelieve her. Why would he?

She spoke true. Of course she did. Why was he worrying?

Forgetting all about the painted mare, Wulf mounted the stallion while Johanna borrowed a steed Kiylla had stolen from Clodia. Wulf offered Fionn a hand and seated her behind him. She wrapped an arm around his waist and pointed north with the other.

"Quickest route to the aiceil skirts the forest, there." She looked up as the clouds thickened and turned dark. "Hurry."

Driving the stallion into a trot, Wulf watched the road nervously for approaching soldiers. This reminded him of his first visit to Fairborough: flames lit the night, blood soaked the soil, and screams flashed in the back of his mind.

Shaking aside the growing dread, he focused on Johanna as she rode ahead. The cold deepened, and the wind intensified. Wisps of shadow appeared like streams of ribbon flowing along the breeze.

Swiveling in the saddle, Wulf glanced behind them. A funnel of purest black swirled in the heavens south of the village. Within minutes, it would be upon them.

Hooves pounding on dead leaves, they rode through the forest, down to the aiceil at the base of the chapel hill. Barren land greeted them, where grass disappeared, soil blanched, and trees died. Twenty paces across the desolate strip, black bark trees with silver leaves bucked under the storm.

Silence greeted them as they passed the border of the barren world. Breath stilled. Wind halted.

Noise and chaos returned instantly as their horses flew through the trees of the aiceil. A night sky loomed overhead, illuminated by two brilliant moons. White light spilled over them, beckoning them forward.

"Here!" Fionn shouted suddenly, yanking the reins.

The stallion reared in fear. Bellowing winds pounded Wulf's ears as Fionn pulled him off the saddle and dragged him down. Johanna leaped off her horse and crouched, hands held above her head, one curious eye peeled open to watch the coming eye.

Terrified, the horses bolted. Gritting his teeth, Wulf let curiosity get the better of him. He stared at the sky as the black funnel approached, cleaving through the dead land into the world of the aiceil.

Darkness itself arrived. Shadow. Whirling and churning, carrying chunks of rock and broken branches along its path. Closer and closer. Wulf's heart pounded out of his chest.

Then, it was upon them. The roar intensified until Wulf was sure his eardrums would burst. A powerful force slammed into his chest, dragging him up and throwing him aside.

Wulf landed on his back, greeted by a world so silent it startled him. Pressing a hand to his chest, he regained his lungs and dragged himself into a sitting position. Fionn lay sprawled nearby, and Johanna was curled in a ball, hands pressed to her head.

Standing, Wulf stumbled over to Fionn and helped her up. "Are you okay?"

"I'm fine." She panted. "Maybe a little bruised."

Relieved, Wulf finally took stock of his surroundings. They stood on a hill illuminated by brilliant moonlight and glittering stars. A canvas of beauty the likes of which he had never seen painted the heavens.

Unnatural dark clung to the silver grass and dead flowers. Light snow fell over the world, blanketing them in white. Like fog gathered after a rain, shadows plagued the land.

And it felt. . . wrong here. Nausea brewed in Wulf's gut, but it was not from rotten food or sea sickness. He could not place it. Pressing a hand to his mouth, he studied the sky again and noticed something he had not before.

A gash tore open the firmament. A sickly light spilled from behind the night, like blood pouring through an open wound.

"The hard part is done," Fionn said, offering Johanna a hand. "Now we only have to walk."

ARSENE LEANED ON the inn window, watching the shadow storm, flinching each time debris crashed into the building, or a tendril of shadow slammed into the window, reaching for the denizens inside.

Teeth gritted, hands clenched in a vice grip, Eckart was glued to the spot beside Arsene, a palpable fury emanating from him. Leo had been correct. Eckart had not taken the news of the other's departure well.

Consus paced the inn's empty common room. "There goes the eye. Any moment now."

Kiylla tapped her table, counting the seconds. Agitated by her countdown, Leo grew more nervous by the moment. "Quit it." He hissed.

She retracted her hand in a hurry. "Sorry." She whispered back.

The funnel passed over the hill, cresting the chapel. Arsene could not see the aiceil from here, but the storm's eye would have struck the other's by now.

Stepping away from the window, Arsene tried to calm himself. They had their own troubles to focus on now.

Turning to face Kiylla, Arsene's words escaped him as burning agony tore through him. Taken off guard, he yelped and dropped to his knees, grabbing at his hand.

Glancing down, he saw a jagged scar tear across his palm, knuckle bones bending out of place. His fingers trembled as a wound thought healed returned to haunt him.

Leo rushed to his side. "Are you alright?"

At a loss for words, Arsene stared at his hand—the hand Kiylla had marred and the wound Marius had healed.

"Let me see," Relia demanded, kneeling beside him and gently taking his wrist. Her brows furrowed in confusion before shooting up in alarm. "This was. . . But, I thought. . ."

Everything struck Arsene in an instant.

The mask slips.

Pretending to be a hero.

The man who was always someone else.

Words from Fionn's song. Its meaning finally became clear.

Beau spoke woven lies. Lies so deep and thick they concealed the truth Fionn had attempted to convey to Arsene. To Wulf. Lies that made even Beau's most outlandish accusations seem believable.

Lies so powerful, Arsene had instantly believed Marius when he'd tried to turn him against Fionn.

This had never been a healing spell. It was a sham. An illusion. No wonder it had occasionally pained him; it had never been healed! Marius had told Arsene the wound had mended, and Arsene had believed him.

Gasping, Arsene shot to his feet. They were all in danger. In far graver danger than he had ever believed.

No evoker had this power. Not even Marius. Something beyond knowing, like Seoras and the Lady, gave Marius this strength. But if this entity cursed the land with a silver tongue. . .

Did even Marius know the truth?

SOMETHING FELT. . . wrong. Wulf had not felt like this since the day he and Leo had broken Eckart from the dungeons of Femora, and seen the wave come crashing down on the fractured city.

Shaking off the foreboding aura, Wulf stared at Fionn's back as she walked. She seemed distant. Aloof. Occasionally, she would flash a smile over her shoulder, but. . .

Johanna's attention lingered on everything except her companions. Awed by their surroundings, she took notes of every plant and unusual sight. Wulf turned his head, watching the glittering waters of the silver lake.

A silver lake, like his dream. But where was the tower?

"Fionn," Wulf asked. "Is there a specific place you want to store the jewels?"

"Yes." She answered. "A secure location. You'll see."

"You could always just tell me." Wulf huffed. "Hey, Seoras. When we get where we're going. When the jewels are safe. Will you let Fionn go?"

Fionn froze in her tracks. "Fionn has never lived without Seoras. What if she dies upon his departure?"

"You're the god," Wulf said bitterly. "Shouldn't you know?"

"Not all gods know everything."

Teeth clenching, Wulf swallowed his anger. Why did he have to fall in love with a woman shackled to something he could not save her from? Supposedly, she and Seoras saw eye-to-eye for the first time in years, but Wulf still worried about her.

Fionn deserved a life of her own. A life Wulf wanted to share with her.

Tightening his grip on Father's spear, he jogged to catch up with her and grabbed her hand. She glanced up at him and smiled. "Not much further now," she promised.

"Hm." Wulf swallowed, watching the moonlight dance on the rippling lake. "It's going to be strange when all this is over. I mean, you managed to win Arsene's heart. I thought he only loved himself."

"What do you mean?"

"Piles of men are going to throw themselves at you," Wulf said. "Flirtatious as you are, I'll have to fight them off."

"Ha." Fionn laughed. "I never considered myself charismatic. I used to think everyone in my tribe hated me."

Wulf ran a hand down her back. "Well, you *are* infuriating."

"Only sometimes."

Eye twitching, Wulf's fingers tensed on her lower back. Something about her voice. . . seemed off.

Surely, he was only imagining things.

They marched on in silence, following the curve of the lake shore. An ache grew in Wulf's legs from the hours of hiking. The air here felt thick and sickly, difficult to breathe.

Johanna stopped in her tracks. Following her gaze, Wulf nearly tripped over himself in shock. A black tower rose from the lake, ancient stone carved with elegant spires and buttresses. It rested alone on a rocky island not far from shore, where silver grass gave way to black sand.

This was the place—the shore from Wulf's dream—the shore he had stood upon countless times, overcome with dread, faced with the porcelain woman with red hair, her skin fragmented, revealing an empty void.

An empty void that preceded what felt like the world's very end.

Heart bursting, Wulf spun around, expecting to see the dreaded woman. But he saw only Fionn, a small smile playing on her face.

TUR ISAVLAIR

ECKART SAT ON the edge of the stable roof, running a finger along his bowstring. He and Leo had been deemed the most useless, according to Arsene, and had the illustrious honor of guard duty.

Leo fidgeted, pulling out a whetstone to sharpen his sword. He might have looked a commoner in his simple chain mail and trousers if not for the delicate blonde locks. Smiling, Eckart watched the road winding away from Fairborough.

Leofric von Trenowyth, once betrothed to the Empress, now an outcast beloved by a Llaqtan woman.

Head snapping up, Leo stared at Eckart. "Did you ever decipher my poem?"

"It seemed simple enough," Eckart said. "A farewell, right?"

"No!" Leo rolled his eyes. "Well, I suppose it doesn't matter now."

Chuckling, Eckart slung his bow over his back. "Fionn said it was from a famous play. She told me its context."

An Athelstani favorite, the words were spoken between a dying man and his twin brother. A promise that, even in death, they would be reunited.

"Ah." Leo raked his whetstone across his sword a final time. "Good."

"You gave it to me because of what you saw in the shrine." Eckart guessed. "You could have told me."

"I. . . don't know why I didn't," Leo admitted. "I knew in my heart you were in danger. Or maybe that I would do something rash to protect you."

"I'm sorry I dragged you into all this."

"You dragged *me* into this?" Leo laughed. "Doesn't feel that way. I was the one who consorted with the woman slated for execution." His face fell. "I should have. . . Tettiena was right there. I saw her shadow on the roof. I could have stopped her."

"No, you couldn't have," Eckart said. "You were tied to a pyre. I'm. . . coming to peace with it. What's troubling me is knowing how many others will die with me. All the people in the Gaevral, whose lives I've watched from beginning to end. . ."

Leo sat forward. "Fionn said there might be a way."

"Fionn is trying to give me hope." Eckart curtly denied. He chewed his bottom lip. Curse the girl for leaving without him. For not bidding farewell. What if he died before she returned?

A warm hand fell on Eckart's shoulder. "Whatever happens, I'll be here with you," Leo promised.

In the years they'd known one another, Eckart had always felt like the older sibling protecting Leofric. For the first time in their friendship, Eckart leaned on Leo's shoulder, grateful for his support.

How long would it take for their pursuers to arrive? Assuming Lady Aurica had taken the bait. . .

Something moved in the forest. Sitting up, Eckart watched the road, noticing a shadow flit across a trunk and pass behind obscuring boughs.

"What?" Leo asked.

"I thought I saw something. . . " Eckart muttered. Maybe it had only been a deer.

"Eckart!" Leo shouted, pointing down the road.

The barest smudge of color appeared on the horizon, growing closer. Narrowing his eyes, Eckart leaned forward. Carriages rolled down the dirt path, green banners waving from their sides. Men in steel armor marched alongside them.

"That's them." Eckart flinched, looking toward the forest. "I'm going to make sure others aren't hiding in the woods. Warn the others."

"Not a chance I'm letting you go out alone." Leo grabbed his arm.

"I'll be safe in the woods," Eckart insisted. "Especially if it is just a deer." He pulled his arm from Leo's slackening hold. "Go. I'll stay out of harm's way."

Growling in annoyance, Leo assented, sliding off the roof and grabbing a horse. Jumping off, Eckart landed in the dirt, wincing and nearly losing balance. Catching himself, he called his paint horse and pulled himself onto its back.

"Come back safe," Leo called, guiding his horse around. "Or I'll kill you myself."

"Same to you." Eckart smiled, yanking the horse's reins and riding for the forest.

Maybe he was overreacting. It was probably just an animal, but a gnawing curiosity and fear demanded he be certain. Throwing his horse into a gallop, he skirted the town and followed the edge of the forest, hoping to escape the encroaching caravan's gaze.

Diving into the oaks, Eckart knocked an arrow to his bow, eyes flicking around every branch and knotted root. His horse slowed to a trot, snorting, head held high.

So far, nothing. Eckart's hand trembled on his bow as he lowered the arrow.

"You have sharp eyes." A female voice called.

Whirling around, Eckart pointed his bow at a cloaked woman. She leaned against a trunk, arms folded over her deep green cloak. He recognized her bearing; it was permanently etched in his memory.

Tettiena pulled back her hood. Brown hair tumbled around her shoulders, brushing against her green eyes. Worn by wrinkles and lines, yet still the mother who had gazed at him with loving eyes.

"What are you doing here?" Eckart demanded.

"You drew us here, did you not?" Tettiena tilted her head. "Don't think I didn't see Trenowyth scurry away the moment you saw us."

Eckart's eye twitched. "Where are the others?"

She ignored the question, stepping closer. "You know you haven't much time left. Lay down your arms. There's no need for you to suffer anymore."

She took another step closer, and Eckart released the arrow, planting it at her feet. Unphased, Tettiena's fingers flashed. Vines, the same kind Relia favored, sprung from the earth and grabbed him, throwing him off his horse.

The usually gentle paint horse reared, turning to kick at the aggressor. Tettiena raised her hand again.

Panicked, Eckart threw an arm forward, unthinking. A thousand memories flew past his eyes. He unconsciously chose one.

Whatever spell Tettiena had been preparing vanished as she dove backward. Obelisks erupted from the forest floor, their stone a mismatch for Athelstani soil. One nearly impaled his mother before pain flicked through Eckart's head, and he lost the spell.

Rearing in fear, the horse danced backward, refusing to leave his master's side as he nervously stepped behind Eckart.

Catching her breath, Tettiena stood. "You and your horses. Some things never change." Her mouth twisted in pain. "Let me help you. I can make this quick." Drawing a blade from its scabbard, she knelt beside him.

Maybe Eckart ought to let her. He was useless to the others and doomed to death regardless. The quick end was preferable to slow torment. Squeezing his eyes shut, he tried to speak, but nothing came.

There was nothing more to say between them.

ARSENE PACED THE chapel courtyard, patience growing thin. Laying a hand on Death Knell's holster, he scanned the area.

Pallid commoners dressed in frumpy sacks went about their day, glancing occasionally at the strange trio outside the chapel. A few clerics in green robes peered out to stare at them, but none had spoken to them yet.

Relia had dressed down to make herself appear as innocent as possible. Parted from her beloved gambeson, she wore her hair down around a simple white dress and thick cloak. Consus guarded her like a hawk, hand resting on his sword hilt, green eyes flashing around attentively.

Out of sight, Kiylla waited for a signal. Her duty was a relatively simple spell, but cast out of sight at the advent of Relia's speech, it held the power to change everything.

Shrieks drew Arsene's attention to the cobbled road curving down the chapel hill. A horse thundered toward them, bearing a blonde nobleman on its back. Yanking the reins, Leo stopped in front of Arsene.

"They're here." He panted.

Nodding, Arsene signaled to Relia and Consus before turning back to Leo. But the man was already dragging his horse away to leave. "Where are you going?" Arsene called.

"Eckart," Leo answered. "He saw something moving in the woods."

"Leofric!" Consus barked. "You're to join Kiylla."

Dazed in his distress, Leo refused to follow the order. "Once I've found Eckart." Grimacing, Arsene watched him go. Eckart had the keen eyes of a hunter. If he had glimpsed a shadow, someone did lurk in the woods.

"You ready?" Arsene asked, turning to Relia as Leo's horse galloped away.

"As I'll ever be." She nodded nervously.

Squeezing her shoulder encouragingly, Arsene jogged to his designated hiding spot. An alley passed between two shops, angled away from the chapel, covered in boxes and wagons filled with wares. They'd tested it multiple times: from the courtyard, it was impossible to see anyone standing in the alley.

Sliding into the alley, Arsene pressed his back to the wall and waited. Nerves evaded him, and a strange confidence surged in his chest. He was a talented evoker. He could do this.

The minutes passed by in agony. A royal procession would not hurry, but the soldiers would search the town for the princess. Tapping his wrist, Arsene peered around the corner.

Something scuffed behind him. Whipping around, he drew Death Knell and pointed down the alley. Another sound followed, like a boot dragging across stone. A feminine cry of pain followed.

Confusion mingled with panic in Arsene's heart. Rushing down the alley, he emerged on its other side: a quiet, narrow street running between the backside of stores. A bloody woman leaned against a wooden door, face twisted in a pained grimace as she tried to walk.

"Fionn!" Arsene ran to her side and grabbed her as she fell.

She tried to say something, but Arsene ignored her, ripping open her blood-soaked shirt. A horrifying wound trailed from her upper breast to her sternum, heavily burnt.

An identical gash tore the back of her jerkin. She'd been pierced through. How was she still alive?

With the wound fully cauterized, there was nothing more he could do for her. But this didn't make sense. She had left with Wulf hours ago. Why. . . How. . .?

Grabbing Arsene's arm, Fionn focused on him. Her eyes raged with light, swirling winds and striking lightning pulsed beneath her pupilless irises. "They're here, aren't they?"

"Yes, but-"

"We don't have time. Let me help you." She gasped, trying to rise.

"What happened to Wulf?" Arsene demanded, pulling her back down.

"Is he not with you?" She asked, fear creeping into her voice.

"What does that mean? *You* left with him." Arsene hissed. "You should both be in Scael!"

Fionn stared at him in horror, but further conversation was cut short as an unmistakable sound echoed from the courtyard.

Armored boots, marching on stone.

"It's too late. I can't help him now." She gasped.

If Fionn had not departed with Wulf and Johanna, who had? Fionn slipped his grasp as he faltered in alarm.

"I have the power of a god," Fionn said. "What better for your show?" Steadying herself on him, she found her feet. "Do you remember Bruthine? Did you see the dragons?"

"Yes." Arsene believed he understood where she was going with this.

"Let's make one," Fionn said. "To rain hell fire upon them."

✦✦✦

SOMETHING IN SCAEL was broken. Wulf could feel it in the breeze, smell it on the air. The sickly gash pouring radiant light through the dark had corrupted the very fabric of this realm.

Not a living soul crossed their path. Not birds, not wildlife, not bugs. Silence followed them across the land.

Standing on the black beach, Wulf watched the silver waves lap against the shore. Did no fish swim in the waters? Did nothing here live at all?

Fionn ascended a rocky cliff, eyes glued to the black tower. Johanna trailed after her. "What happened to this place?"

Fionn didn't seem to hear her. She stared distractedly at the gap between the beach and the tower's island. "Wulf!" She called. "Come here."

Jogging to catch up, Wulf peered over the cliff, tracing the distance to the island. No gentle shore touched the waters; waves broke against sheer black cliffs. "That's a dangerous swim."

"A lethal swim." Fionn corrected. "The tower opens itself only to the gods and their chosen," She smiled. "Luckily, we have one of those. Do you want to say the words?" She stood on her tiptoes and whispered in his ear.

Staring at the tower, Wulf repeated her incantation. "Cimnich de ar vaile."

Nothing happened at first. Slowly but surely, the silver water rose like rain falling in reverse, coalescing into a bridge of flowing water that hardened into ice. Relieved, Fionn exhaled, testing the bridge before crossing.

Unsettled, Wulf tapped the ice with his boot and jogged to catch up. "What is this place?"

"A. . ." Fionn trailed off. "Stronghold."

"Helpful", Wulf muttered. "Something important to Seoras? There had to be a reason he kept showing this in my dreams."

Fionn paled and whipped to face him. Shaking off whatever had alarmed her, she continued walking the bridge. "Step carefully. This is a bad place to fall."

Johanna regarded Wulf with interest. "I noticed we did not arrive in an aiceil. How do we return?"

"There's another gem," Fionn said. "One that opened the door between this place and Thruine long ago."

"Are you sure they'll be safe here? Marius entered Bruthine without its jewel."

"This place is. . . different. The way we entered is the only way in. The jewel merely allows one to leave."

"Why?" Johanna asked.

"Because. . . " Fionn trailed off again. "It was never meant to open passageways, to inundate Thruine with elemental life. It was an escape route. Scael flows into Thruine, but not the other way around."

"An escape route? From what?" Johanna stared up at the radiant gash and nearly slipped. Grabbing her arm, Wulf steadied her.

"Questions for later," Wulf said. "I want to get back to the others as soon as possible."

"Mm," Fionn murmured, pausing at the island's edge. The tower loomed before them, a great black edifice shrouded in mist. Its spire reached for the stars, several stories overhead.

Wulf's heart raced. Seoras had hammered this image into his head. Though he was not an evoker, the memory had etched itself into his mind, clear as day.

He revisited every detail. The woman. The feeling she'd imbibed. The meaning behind her shattering skin, behind the collapsing earth and consuming flames.

"Finally," Fionn said, barely a whisper. "We've come to the end."

CHAPTER THIRTY SEVEN

GAMBIT

ARSENE DIDN'T WANT to let Fionn go. Soaked in blood, her clothes in tatters, he wanted to order her to stay put behind him. But Fionn wasn't the kind of woman who marched to anyone's tune but her own.

Winking, Fionn slipped from his arms. Heart aching, he watched her go before backing up and returning to his vantage point.

Slamming his back against the wall, Arsene peered around the corner. Relia stood tall before the Fairborough chapel, Consus by her side. Overlapping shouting came from the street, but Arsene could neither make out the words nor see who was yelling.

Suddenly, the voices hushed, and a figure came into view. Arsene had expected his Mother to arrive, maybe Beau. Instead, a high-ranking clergy member swathed in rich green robes strode across the courtyard, a golden laurel blazed upon his back. Narrowing his eyes, Arsene strained to make out who he was.

A thin circlet crested the older man's brow; this was the Vicar. What was he doing here?

A host of soldiers marched in an orderly fashion behind him, composed of both Clodian paladins and Dragosi soldiers. They'd doubtless not expected to find the princess unharmed, free of bonds, and alone.

A drake rider soared overhead, and Arsene shrank against the wall. Shit. He hoped Fionn knew what she was doing.

"Princess." The Vicar spread his arms. "How the goddess rejoices to see you unharmed." He glanced around the otherwise empty square. "Though I must admit, none of us expected-"

"For me to be here of my own volition?" Relia finished.

"Nor with this traitor." The Vicar's deep voice drawled. "What has become of your cefran captors?"

"There never were any," Relia said.

Arsene craned his head to count how many men gathered behind the Vicar. A few dozen, maybe? He shrunk as Paladins drew their swords and the Dragosi men brandished their glaives.

"They must be here, somewhere." The Vicar concluded. "Fan out and find them. Rictus, keep your men with me."

A dozen knights remained with the Vicar while the others splintered into groups of six. One unit of paladins was headed this way. Eyes darting around, Arsene searched for a hiding spot.

"Stop!" Relia's voice rang across the town. The soldiers halted, turning to their princess. "The Goddess stands with *me*, not you, *heretic*." She spat at the Vicar. "You are to heed my orders." She shouted to the men.

When had the girl learned to speak like that? Perhaps Consus's short lessons had paid off—the men turned to face the heir.

Now. They had to strike now. Glancing up, Arsene sought both Kiylla and Fionn's signals and saw them both at once. A breeze colored with strands of emerald brushed the spire as a beam of light descended from the clouds.

Raising his hand, Arsene prepared the most elaborate spell perhaps ever conceived. He had not planned for it, not until Fionn arrived a few minutes ago.

For their arduous journey to end on a whim. . . it suited them both.

✦✦✦

THE GREAT STONE doors of the black tower swung open, cutting a line through a thick layer of dust. Wulf raised a torch as he stepped inside, sweeping it across the vast chamber.

How old was this place? Furniture had collapsed into debris and ruin, and the iron stairwell in the room's center looked ready to disintegrate. The vaguest shape of a mantle, tall as two men, sat cold and empty against the far wall.

The crash of waves echoed in the dead, empty tower. It felt like stepping into a tomb.

"What is this place?" Johanna asked, awed.

"Does it matter?" Fionn asked, scouring every corner of the room. "Come, let's find what we're looking for."

A twinge of discomfort pricked at Wulf's heart. Every time Fionn spoke, something felt off. Maybe she was simply on edge.

Imprinting footsteps in the dust, Wulf approached the mantle and swept his hand across the ancient stone. Letters were carved into the surface. Sets of initials? They looked cefran. Pacing to the back window, he peered across the silver lake.

Perhaps it wasn't a lake but a sea. Waves rolled as far as his eye could see, where the orbs of the twin moons met with the water's surface on the horizon.

A creak of iron snapped him out of his reverie, and he turned to see Fionn testing the stairs. Rushing to her side, he pushed her back. "Let me go first."

"Always the gentleman." She teased.

Taking the first step, Wulf ascended, gritting his teeth. But it held. He reached the next story and found a hall lined with several rooms. Fionn brushed past him. "Search every room."

"What are we looking for?"

"A little. . . stone. A black stone." Fionn said distractedly, walking away.

Pursing his lips, Wulf turned to ensure Johanna had heard. Nodding, the Llaqtan woman chose a room and entered. Picking a door at random, Wulf stepped inside.

This tower could have been anything. Only dust, long-rotted wood, and crumbled stone remained. Checking the corners, Wulf turned as he heard Johanna call him.

"Wulf! Come see this."

Following her voice across the hall, Wulf joined her in another chamber. He froze in the doorway.

Five sigils were engraved across the room, two on the back wall and one on the floor. On the left wall, a serpentine dragon twisted inside an intricate circle, its maw open and eyes gazing ahead.

"Seoras," Wulf said, walking to the sigil and brushing his hand against the old carving. A pulsing emerald light traced through the carved lines, illuminating the room in green.

But it only lasted a moment. As though rejecting Wulf, the lights faded.

"Amazing." Johanna breathed, touching another. It glowed briefly topaz before fading.

Waving the torch around the room, he illuminated the others but didn't recognize their symbols. There was a bird of some kind, a wolf, and two others that seemed humanoid, but he couldn't tell what they were meant to be.

Fionn's voice whispered, startling him. "Ah." She said. "One room is intact."

"Quit sneaking up on me." Wulf rubbed the back of his neck.

"Hm," Fionn smirked, approaching the Leviathan's sigil. She brushed her fingers across it, and emerald light pulsed again through the carving. But as before, the light faded as though rejecting her. "Oh." She sounded disappointed. "I suppose the magic has faded with time."

Johanna's eyes glazed over briefly, and she sighed. "I suppose so. We should move on."

As the women left the room, Wulf examined the sigil. This was Seoras' carving. The others represented the remaining gods.

Seoras would never have walked away. He would have beamed at Wulf and proudly touched the Sigil, showing off how it glowed, danced, or whatever it was meant to do.

'*See? Do you still doubt me now?*' He would have asked.

Shaking his head, Wulf clenched his jaw. Something was wrong.

Fionn bypassed the third floor, ascending the rickety stairs to the fourth. Johanna watched the silver-haired cefra pass before turning to Wulf.

"I'll look around here," she said.

Nodding, Wulf chased after Fionn, disappearing into the gloom enveloping the tower.

RAISING HER TORCH, Johanna swept it over the dilapidated hall. A sickly sensation permeated Scael, seeping through the windows. Heels clicking on the old stone floors, Johanna tried to shake the sense she'd forgotten something.

For hours now, she'd worried someone had followed them. But she'd glance over her shoulder, and the feeling would vanish.

Stopping outside a heavy, crumbling stone door, Johanna hesitated before turning around, torch held high. The fire illuminated the shadow of a man as he stepped from the darkness.

Father. Johanna gasped quietly. Beau Rosa's twinkling dark eyes looked at her fondly. He smiled, resting his hands on his silver cane, a stark contrast to his simple black coat.

"When did you. . .?" Johanna took a step back.

"I've been here the whole time," Beau said. "Or did I slip your notice?"

He'd been here the whole time? Impossible. Wulf and Fionn had not seen him either, made no mention of another's presence. Shaking her head, Johanna's mind whirled in confusion.

"Why are you here?" She demanded.

"We always meant to visit Scael," he explained. "Why do you think Wulf's execution was called off?"

"You need to close off all the planes. Scael included." She realized. "But why Wulf? What do you mean?"

Beau's mouth curled into a sweet smile, the kind he gave when he had no intention of answering.

WULF SIGHED WITH relief when they reached the tower's highest level and released Fionn's arm. The stairwell had seemed ready to give at any moment, but it held until the end.

"There it is." Fionn breathed.

Holding up his torch, Wulf scanned the surprisingly small chamber at the top of the tower. Black glass windows protected the walls, allowing only faint strands of moonlight through. Dust coated every inch of the chamber save for an elaborate pedestal beneath the furthest window.

Dark stone curled upwards, holding aloft a display case, its glass frosted black.

"I suppose I can tell you the whole truth now," Fionn said. "About Seoras' dreams."

"I'm listening," Wulf said warily.

"That's our handiwork." She gestured to the pedestal. "We put an elaborate fail safe on it before leaving it here. Not even we can open it."

"We?" Wulf repeated. "You mean Seoras."

"Yes. In case one betrayed the others."

Wulf raised an eyebrow. "So, it's an enchanted box meant only to repel its keepers?"

Fionn huffed. "It is not a box." She gestured to the case. "Go ahead."

She wasn't telling the whole truth. Cautious, Wulf approached the strange pedestal and studied it again. "Why did you want to protect this one?"

"This one, it's. . ." She hesitated. "It's the keystone we used to reach your home."

"Scael is the cefran homeworld." Wulf guessed, trying to peer out the black windows. "What happened to it?"

". . . it's a long story."

Magic emanated from the pedestal, Wulf could feel it. He glanced back, noticing Fionn hovering by the stairs as though afraid to come any closer. Narrowing his eyes, he turned back to the strange case.

Shadows swirled beneath the dark glass, escaping its bounds and obscuring the very air. Waving aside the miasma, Wulf searched for the latch. The darkness cleared to reveal a simple lock bolted onto stone embedded with a mask.

Wulf retracted his hand. This mask looked exactly like the horrifying face the fae king of Sylfestra had worn, save in black instead of red. Sized to fit a full face, the material appeared like stone and yet, at the same time, like soft skin. Even unmoving, Wulf could feel something behind the mask, see shadows dancing when the expressions changed.

A memory struck Wulf full force, sending him reeling. Fionn's odd lyrics rang in his ears.

The mask slips from a hollowed face.

Nothing human had hidden beneath the fae king's mask. Blackness peered out. A void better left forgotten. The woman from the dream poured the same ichor from between the cracks of her shattered skin. She was a fae, like him.

Fionn had said the gems could be hidden in a place only she could reach, that there was something she could not tell Wulf, no matter how dearly she wanted to, *needed* to. But now she hung back as though afraid to approach?

Had it been fate that brought them all to Sylfestra, face-to-face with the fae king, who had happily made a deal with Tettiena? Happily gifted her the gem and attempted to capture them all?

It must have been. Wulf felt certain; this lock was enchanted, but not in the way Fionn claimed. It was meant to expel fae. The porcelain woman extended a hand on the shores of the tower because she needed Wulf's help. And should he give it, the world would fall into ruin.

This is what the dream was about.

CHAPTER THIRTY EIGHT

UNREMARKABLE

RIGIDLY TENSE AIR permeated the chapel courtyard. Every paladin and Dragosi knight froze, eyes darting between the red-haired princess and the Vicar. Face impassable, the Vicar paused before answering Relia.

"Heed your orders?" His deep voice drawled. "Of course, princess. The goddess flows through you. What would you have of us?"

Arsene's shoulders slumped in relief. Perfect. Kiylla and Fionn were in place, ready to move at his command. Now Relia had but speak the words.

Stepping forward, Relia raised her chin confidently, but Arsene could see her lower lip trembling. "You have accused this man behind me of heresy, accused Sir Trenowyth of murder. You have accused the cefra of plotting against our great Empire. You have framed others for the crimes you and your underlings have committed."

A glaring accusation. A few paladins turned to face the Vicar.

His face remained unchanged. "This is the heresy you accuse me of?"

"I know of the lies you've spun." She addressed the paladins. "Tell me, do they know Lord Rosa attempted to drown the Third Legion? Do they know I was attacked in Lavinia by the Dobrescu family?"

Her words did not have the effect they should. For a moment, it seemed the paladins reeled in surprise, but their eyes glazed over shortly thereafter.

Relia gestured to Consus, who strode forward to meet the Vicar in the center of the courtyard. "We all know the goddess' decree. Those who are guilty shall succumb to the flames as she burns away their rot. Those who are innocent shall be shielded by her earthen embrace. As her heir and vessel, I call upon Viridia to test you both."

Confident, the Vicar walked forward, deep green robes trailing across the cobbled stone. "Very well, princess. It shall be a quick trial, and it shall assuage your fears."

Grimacing, Arsene glanced around their audience. The knights stepped back, allowing the two men space, but no doubt colored their expressions. Several villagers emerged from their homes and shops to nervously watch the proceedings; they peered out windows and hid in door frames.

There it was: glazed eyes watched the proposed trial from all corners of the town. The expression Leofric claimed appeared on the Chamber Lord's countenances before condemning him to death.

The Vicar emanated such conviction. His gaze was strong, and his mouth turned in a slight smile. Was he bluffing, or would their show fail in the wake of the accursed enchantment that laced their tongues?

The knights already believed Consus was a traitor, assumed Leofric had killed the king, and knew the cefra plotted against them. The idea had flourished into faith. This spell had to eradicate every lie whispered by the traitor's lips.

Closing his eyes, Arsene breathed deeply. Looking up, he remembered a dash of crimson across the sky before an ashfall began. Heeding his order, Fionn sprung into action.

A roar erupted from behind the chapel, carrying the unearthly tones of a monster and the sweeping gales of a hurricane. The Leviathan burst from a hidden alley, rising into the air. The moment it appeared, Arsene cast a spell on it.

The fires of Bruthine had burned hotter and brighter than any others. He recalled the dragons lounging atop the obsidian cliffs, their

370

majestic presence, and their deep claws. Fire sprung to life around the Leviathan as the memories intertwined.

Flames caught on the Leviathan's wind, streaking past its body into the shapes of forelegs and back legs. An eruption of lava illuminated the air, where wings of magma grew from its sides. The Leviathan whipped through the air, coloring Fairborough in red before landing on the chapel, evoked claws of obsidian digging deep into the spire's rock.

An ethereal dragon of burning flame peered down on the world with blazing eyes, wings dripping lava down the sides of the chapel. The Leviathan was gone, a mere casing to shape Arsene's spell.

It took its toll instantly. A pounding headache threatened to break Arsene's concentration as his mind split in multiple directions, trying to tie the myriad memories into one.

Kiylla's spell followed. Blinding light divided the sky, casting rays across the courtyard, intensifying where Consus and the Vicar stood.

Gasps and shouts of fear erupted from the crowd as they gaped at the dragon. Some fled. The knights drew their weapons and backed up.

The Vicar was impressed; Arsene could read the old man's face. But the confidence he radiated never wavered.

Relia and Consus had not expected the dragon; the princess stood tall, shock fading from her eyes as she nodded encouragingly at Consus.

Something moved behind Arsene. Unwilling to break the spell, he ignored it.

Sharp pain tore through his midsection, and he buckled forward, gritting his teeth as he refused to lose concentration. The flames engulfing the Leviathan flickered but raged steadily again as Arsene leaned on the wall and whirled around.

Lady Aurica stood behind him at the alley's other end. Mother. A spear fell from Arsene's back and clattered to the ground, disappearing. Evoked. And light glowed at her fingertips. That had been her spell. Blood pooled on Arsene's shirt where the spear had pierced.

A laugh, of all noises, escaped Arsene. He fell to a knee as Aurica approached. His mother was going to kill him. How poetic and ironic.

But he would not break the spell—not until the moment he died. So he grinned at her as she raised her hand again, awaiting Relia's final command and the finale of their show.

✦✦✦

ECKART FELT HIS life ebbing away as he stared at the blade in his mother's hand. She could have killed him with any spell, yet she chose simple steel. Tettiena's eyes held grief and resolve as she knelt beside him.

"How long?" Eckart gasped. "How long had you planned this?"

Lowering her sword, Tettiena rested her free hand on her knee. "We knew of Viridia's chosen when he turned eight. Aurica informed those she could trust. Me, Beau, Vicar Faunus. Slowly, we drew others into our web. Men who'd lost a sister to the clergy of Fairborough. Those who opposed the Llaqtan wars. People who'd been wronged all over the Empire."

"Decades, then," Eckart concluded. "But, after my father."

"You thought I'd bear you, knowing your fate?" She shook her head. "I am not so cruel. You know this."

Reaching for his bow, Eckart pulled it toward him. "Then what changed your mind? You always seemed like you loved my father. Now. . ."

Chuckling, Tettiena looked away. "I often told Relia I admired the cefra—their trust, their ability to know one another completely. But they weren't always like that." Her eyes lowered somberly. "Once, they warred as we did. Killed one another. Destroyed their homeland."

"How?" Eckart's fingers tensed around the bow. "If we were all connected. . ."

"But the cefra weren't, back then. Coming here altered them, and disrupted their memories. Maevruthans became necessities only after arriving in Thruine." Tettiena shifted forward. "You see? If cefra could overcome their nature and achieve peace, so can we. We only need to alter our home to something more fitting."

Was she telling the truth? Eckart blinked, trying to imagine cefran cities, cefran kings, and wars between their people.

"It was never hate, Eckart," Tettiena whispered. "I am sorry it came to this. Let me grant you a painless release." She rose.

Eckart glanced at his bow. He had no hope of fending her off. Even had he been at full strength, her talents far outstripped his. Closing his eyes, he waited for the end.

The horrible sound of a blade piercing flesh met his ears. A woman gasped in pain and surprise. But Eckart felt nothing.

Opening his eyes, he saw a blade protruding from Tettiena's chest, steel drenched in blood. Leo stood behind her, hands gripping the pommel, face torn in a grimace as he twisted the blade and yanked it loose.

Fingers alighting, Tettiena lashed out, spinning to face her attacker. Darkness surrounded them, shadows clinging to the wind as it whirled into a storm. A shadow storm burst to life around them before she dropped to her knees.

The shadow tempest slammed into Eckart, throwing him backward. Blood seeped from shallow gashes on his upper arms and chest, and broken branches dug into his back as he slammed into a tree. Arms shaking, he pulled himself up, a surge of strength returning to his dwindling blood as adrenaline hit.

Flowers sprung from the forest floor around Mother, golden roses from her garden stained red by her blood. She turned to look at Eckart as her eyes dimmed, and she slumped forward.

Throat catching, Eckart searched for Leo, noticing a body lying not far from his mother's. It wasn't moving.

Rushing towards him, Eckart sidestepped the wilting flowers as he collapsed by Leo's side. His friend coughed, blood seeping from the corners of his mouth.

A horrible wound ripped through his stomach, pouring blood onto the leaves and staining his chain mail. Desperate, Eckart ripped off his cloak and pressed it to the wound, trying to stop the bleeding.

Leo laughed. "Kiylla will never. . . believe I got an evoker."

"Shut up." Eckart hissed. "You idiot. What were you thinking?"

"I was thinking. . . that you. . ." He choked. "Do you remember. . .the poem?"

"Of course, I remember your stupid poem!"

"Make sure. . ." Leo winced, mouth twisting in pain. "Kiylla hears it, too."

"Leo?" Eckart yelled in horror as Leo's eyelids fluttered close over his dimming blue eyes. "Spirits. No, no, *no*." He muttered, desperately, futilely trying to plug the wound.

When midnight calls, stars brush the land, and heavens fade to night. Pain and dreams dull to sleep, and flowers bloom where warmth has fled. And in that place of silent reprieve, I'll see again the one I seek.

A famous play. A famous line. A promise to meet again, in another life.

Leo had always expected to die. Why had Eckart not heeded the poem earlier? Why had he not cared about his friend's distracted gaze?

A smile remained fixed on Leo's face when he stopped breathing. Emotions caught in Eckart's chest, and he leaned forward, a sob escaping.

All he wanted was to protect the people he cared for, and when the time finally came, he failed utterly.

How dare Leo be the one to die in the place of a man already lost?

Teeth clenched, Eckart looked up through the canopy of leaves towards the chapel on the hill. Memories surged through him, chaotic and out of control.

The sparkling lake outside Trenowyth castle, the shouts of spectators gathered around the jousting arena, the streaks of color as a herd of horses galloped past, the golden roses growing in his mother's garden.

The youthful face of a naive squire, his blonde hair messy and scattered with twigs. He managed a proud expression as he stood straight, brushing off his royal blue surcoat, stamped with the heraldry of a rearing deer.

Fear replaced dignity so quickly. He ducked in horror, his black-haired friend shivering beside him as the squires experienced their first proper glimpse of Altanbern's bordering realm.

Mist had seeped through the ground, rising into the air, clinging to the pine trees, ascending the mountain peaks. Ghostly forms, the spirits of the ancestors, marched through the otherworld's haze.

But the Athelstani squires had thought them evil shades and screamed in terror. Eckart had grabbed them both and pulled them to the ground, instructing them to be silent and allow the ancestors to pass in peace.

He could still recall the innocent, dumb gaze of young Leofric von Trenowyth, looking up in awe at the cefra he believed had saved their lives, who crouched over them, protecting them from the ghosts.

Those soft blue eyes had drilled into Eckart's soul. How often Leo said Eckart liked collecting oddities, lost items and animals. He never knew he had been the first.

Mist rose around Eckart's ankles, shrouding the forest, roiling through the streets of Fairborough, clinging to the hill, and swirling around the chapel's spire. Shades moved through the mist, barely perceptible as he wailed in grief and longed to join them.

"How many people have died because of you?" Johanna questioned, taking another step back. "How many men in Yuri Llaqta? How many innocent civilians in Clodia?"

Beau followed her, face unreadable. "Small sacrifices, in the long run. But you nor your mother could ever see the bigger picture." He shook his head somberly. "Had only you listened, you would still be by my side."

"How could I be?" Johanna snapped, clutching her hand. "You wanted me to follow orders that would have destroyed everything my mother worked for! How could you? She was your wife!"

"Johanna, dear. I sought your mother for her knowledge. To bring us to this point. Her labors were part of our greater good. To defy me now is to spit on her grave."

All the anger dissipated from Johanna. Her gaze drifted from her father to the dark windows, to the silver sea and twin moons shining on a tower of purest black.

Arsene had asked about her mother, back in the dungeons of Bruthine. He'd worn a careful expression, prodding her, but she'd been too blind to understand his point.

Arsene had implied Beau had been the one to silence her mother. Because once Mother learned of his intentions to seal away the planes she so loved, she'd turned on him.

In her reverie, Beau reached her side and cupped her face. "You were always so bright. I was always so proud of you. But nothing, not even my personal feelings, can get in the way of us now, not when we are so close. I cannot sway your mind. You cling to your mother, and she blocks the goddess' blessing."

A seed of doubt need be planted for the enchanted lies to take hold. Mother, though she would never know, protected Johanna from them.

"I am sorry." Beau brushed her bangs back. "I will make it quick."

His fingers flashed copper, and Johanna barely registered his attack. A sharpened piece of metal arced through the air, intending to pierce through her skull, but she managed to evoke a shield to protect herself just before it struck.

Metal clashed against steel. Head ringing, Johanna collapsed, and the world spun. Pulling herself up, she tried to focus on the blurry form of her father.

She crawled away, trying to think of a plan, trying to live. She had to protect her mother. Protect what remained of her. She had to.

WULF STARED AT the fae mask embedded in the pedestal. Who did this belong to? For how long had Seoras known the threat to his people?

Thousands of years. That was what the asshole god had claimed.

But Seoras wasn't with him now.

"What's wrong?" Fionn called.

Tapping the pedestal, Wulf brushed a finger across the elaborate mechanism. There was only a simple lock. Should he wish it, he could simply break the display case open, unleashing the roiling shadow below the dark glass.

"Good news," Wulf said, turning around. "I can open it. But it's locked, and we don't have the key." He returned to Fionn, his heart thumping.

"No, we don't," she admitted, tilting her head. "I think it's only a regular lock, though."

"Right." Wulf steeled himself, steadied his breathing. "Should be simple enough to break it open." He extended his hand. "Can I see my dagger?"

"Of course," Fionn said, unsheathing the blade she'd worn at her belt for months. Flipping it to hold the blade, she offered it to him.

The world slowed. Time stopped. Wulf's heart sank when he saw the dagger readily offered to him.

376

His Fionn never would have done that. Even knowing its necessity, she would have refused, drawn the argument out, and smiled at him impishly. Had he asked for anything else, she might have obliged—but not the dagger.

The dagger meant something to her, something it had taken Wulf ages to truly grasp. It was more than a mere flirtatious item, more than a symbol of courtship.

Fionn believed they would not have to say goodbye so long as she held his dagger. Because she feared, above all else, a final farewell.

Grabbing the dagger's pommel, Wulf immediately drove the blade into Fionn's heart. Blood rushed over her jerkin as the blade pierced through her, emerging from the other side, glistening with blood.

Surprise widened Fionn's eyes as she stared at the blade protruding from her chest.

A memory bloomed in Wulf's mind, one long shrouded. Fionn had stared at him on the banks of the Illian river, trying to tell him something, something he had forgotten, something he could not hear.

"The dreams are meant to show you the truth." She said. "For a fae can only be killed when an unremarkable mortal becomes the opposite of what it embodies."

Cracks appeared on Fionn's freckled face as she shattered apart, her hands desperately trying to find purchase on the dagger. Wulf drove it deeper as the entity broke apart, the cracks on it seeping black ichor.

Nothingness peered back from the ichor, a world within worlds, an eternal space with no end. Wulf was frozen in horror as he gazed into the void hidden behind the pretty eyes.

Gritting his teeth, he yanked the dagger out and staggered back, arm aching where he'd wielded it. The bloodied blade clattered to the ground as the entity lost the shape of Fionn. Its face turned porcelain, its hair darkened to red. A white gown pooled around its feet as it burst apart, a horrible screech shaking through the tower, slamming into Wulf and throwing him into shadow.

✦✦✦

BEAU RAISED HIS hand as tremors raked through the tower. Vision clearing, Johanna looked up at the ceiling, its stone shaking, dust pouring over them. Stepping back, Beau snapped his head up, concerned.

A wave of force threw them both off balance, and a horrible, inhuman shriek echoed from above. Johanna heard a rock shatter as the scream fell silent. Memories struck her, overwhelming. Forgotten.

Beau had walked behind them as they traveled through Scael, watching them, trading glances with a porcelain woman with red hair. She'd stood on the rocky beach, whispering a command to Wulf.

"Cimnich de ar vaile." He'd said. Simple cefran, but Johanna had not understood the words, then. "An heir has returned home."

This tower did indeed hold ancient magic, but it had never been for the entity wearing Fionn's guise. It had opened its doors for Wulf. For the man Seoras had chosen to trust, to whom he'd entrusted the encrypted dreams.

So this was why Tettiena had wanted Wulf to live, why Beau had not simply knifed them both from the shadows.

Beau realized the entity's spell had faded. He hesitated, staring up in horror and confusion, foot twisted as he prepared to race upstairs.

Reaching out, Johanna allowed her memories to choose themselves. First, the great serpent from the sky of Bruthine came to mind. Then, the memory of her mother, black braid tied with a tiny blue flower, laughing as she tried to juggle rocks she'd found in an aiceil.

A serpent composed of stone burst from the floor, jaws wide. It lunged at Beau, jaws snapping close, stone washing with blood. A horrible crunch rang through the halls. Hand trembling, Johanna yanked her arm back, and the rocks lost their shape, clattering to the ground.

There was no time for this. Standing, she steadied herself on the wall, stumbling as the tower quaked again.

She had to get upstairs. This tower held the key to both their salvation and doom. They could not let it fall. Not yet.

THE FLAMING DRAGON peered down on those in the courtyard, fiery maw trembling as it growled. Every face turned white with awe and fear as they looked up at the divine creation.

Sunlight like Athelstan had never seen poured over the church, and mist rolled across the floor. Had Arsene not known better, he, too, would have thought he'd crossed the threshold into the space between their world and the goddess' domain.

"From the Goddess, these lost souls have strayed." Relia's voice carried across Fairborough. "Should their accusations be false, may the goddess ward them from her wrathful flames and take them into her earthen embrace."

The dragon roared, and lava coated the chapel's roof. Arsene flinched, his hand trembling as he held the spell. His wounded arm hung limply by his side, twitching in pain.

Pain raged through Arsene's shoulder as a dagger embedded itself under his collarbone, narrowly missing his neck. It faded as soon as it pierced him. Another of Mother's spells. Knees wobbling, he pressed his back to the alley wall, one eye on his dragon, the other on his mother.

Lady Aurica had never been a murderer. Spells meant to kill had never been her forte. Arsene remembered a softer lady who had delighted in entertaining her youngest son with displays of dancing fire and sparkling lights.

Those memories were so distant. So faint.

Drawing a real blade from her belt, Aurica strode toward him, ever majestic, stray hairs escaping her bun to fall across her face. Black cloth blurred around her as her traveling coat bucked beneath the Leviathan's wind.

Three paces. Two. One. Aurica was upon him. The spell had to end now, though Relia had not spoken the final words.

Another shadow appeared behind Aurica, and she turned in surprise as a hooded figure slammed into her, their blade clashing with hers. Stunned, Arsene turned back to the courtyard as blood seeped down his chest.

Relia raised her chin. "Should their accusations be true," She paused, "May the heavenly fires burn away the rot of those corrupted."

Now. The Leviathan pulled its head back, maw widening. Nothing would emerge. But the people needn't know that.

The final piece of the spell fell into place. The memory of fire flickering around the Lady herself, the bright blaze falling from the sky as the serpent in the heavens screamed, raining fire upon the land.

Brilliant flames poured from the Leviathan's mouth. The Vicar stepped back in horror as the fire washed over him and Consus, consuming them in a terrifying conflagration. Vision wavering, Arsene held the spell until he felt his head would split.

Saving Consus was up to Kiylla. Arsene had done his part. Once the two men had been soaked in righteous fire, Arsene's hand dropped, his memory slipped, and he sank to his knees.

The sharp pain as his knees struck the cobbled road returned him to consciousness. Pained, he looked left, where the hooded figure clashed with Aurica. Their swords pushed one another back, and they broke apart.

Terrified screams rang from the courtyard. Arsene raised his head to see blurred forms running, fire raging, and a man caught aflame, flailing in agony. Dragging his gaze back to Aurica, he saw her mouth twist in anger as she dropped her blade and raised her hand.

A perfect replica of Death Knell, the flintlock Arsene had painstakingly created with his brother, appeared in her hands. Arsene hadn't realized she'd ever paid it any mind, let alone learned its inner workings.

The hammer slid into place, and her finger pulled the trigger. A puff of smoke erupted from the barrel as a bullet soared across the alley and struck the hooded figure. He crumpled, the force of the impact and his fall throwing back his hood.

Maybe, in his heart, Arsene already knew who the man was. Maybe that was why he felt no surprise to see Marius's stream of auburn waves tumble from the cowl. Every ounce of pain disappeared from Arsene's wounds. He shot to his feet and ran to Marius's side.

A scream of absolute horror, of grief, erupted from their Mother. Crimson stained the white mantle beneath the ragged cloak Marius had concealed himself in.

Marius dared to chuckle as Arsene tore the bloodstained mantle and pressed a hand to the wound. "That was an impressive display, little brother. I'm. . . proud of you."

Arsene could hardly comprehend what his brother was saying or what he was doing here.

Why had he wielded a sword instead of magic? Why had Marius not put up a better defense against their Mother? *Why had he jumped between them?*

"I saw, for a moment, through that girl's eyes," Marius continued, "I don't entirely understand . . ."

"Marius, what are you saying?" Blood coated Arsene's hand as he tried to pack the wound.

"I still don't," Marius continued, his eyes hazy and far away. "But then I saw you, and I knew. . ."

Arsene's fingers trembled, and his vision darkened. He bit his bottom lip, trying to force through unconsciousness with pain. It didn't work. Voices screamed around him, darkness closed in, and the world swayed. His hands slipped from their work as his own blood raced down his arms.

He heard someone running towards them. Was Mother going to finish the job? Falling backward, he felt someone catch him and managed to peel an eye open to see who.

A disaster of a woman leaned over him, stained red with blood, light burns coating her arms and face. Tangled silver hair hung around a pale, freckled face. Her mouth moved, but Arsene couldn't hear the words.

But her eyes. . . pools of emerald, free of a black pupil, a wellspring of emotion both painful and bright.

They were beautiful.

CHAPTER THIRTY NINE

BROKEN SHORE

WULF AWOKE, NURSING the worst headache he'd ever endured. Sitting up, his hand struck the obsidian pedestal. He must have slammed into it.

Grasping for a handhold, he hoisted himself up. Nothing remained of the entity that had pretended to be Fionn. Not even dust.

Fionn. Wulf had walked away with an impostor. The woman he'd fallen asleep with had been his love; he was sure of it. What had become of her in the night?

His heart thudded out of his chest, and his head spun, sick with worry. He had to find her.

"Wulf!" Johanna called, racing up the stairs, hair frayed from its braid.

"Johanna," Wulf said, relieved he wasn't alone. "We need to get back."

"I don't know how, only Fionn. . ." She trailed off, eyes widening. "*Fionn* was never with us." She stalked past Wulf, brushing the dust from the pedestal.

"Here." Wulf brushed her aside and raised his spear, breaking the lock with the haft. Flipping back the black glass lid, he opened the display case.

Shadowed whirled around a jewel of pure darkness. Gloom lurked beneath its almost purple surface, a haze no man could see through. Johanna lifted it gingerly, deep in thought.

"They needed to destroy this, too." Johanna turned to Wulf. "This is our way home. But if we take it with us, anyone could use it to return. Anyone could learn when the veil thins in aiceils, and travel here."

Wulf swallowed. "Fionn never meant to come back. She meant to shatter this. To trap herself here with the remaining jewels."

Johanna's eyes darted around the chamber. "I can't allow that." She slowly reached into her satchel and pulled out the leather bag holding Olbhreis' Ore and Diorbhail's Ember. Palming them, she smiled at Wulf. "I'll send you home. Someone should remain to watch over these."

"Remain. . .?" Wulf repeated. "This world is. . . is *wrong*. Are you sure?"

"I'm sure." She picked up the fifth gem, the shadowy stone of Scael. "I can stay here and finish my mother's work. Protect her legacy." She took a deep breath. "Wulf, make sure the world forgets this particular legend, lest someone come looking."

"You want the world to go back to thinking the planes are unreachable?"

"I do."

"I can't believe it."

She chuckled. "Some lies are worth telling." Clutching her hand around the Scael stone, her eyes frayed with sorrow. "Now, go. Find the others." She ran a thumb over the black jewel. "Scael." She whispered.

An archway sprung to life on one of the black glass windows, like it had been meant to be carved there. A tear sounded as the fabric of reality tore open, and the once-opaque window peered out onto a perfectly ordinary plain of swaying grass and trees.

Giving Johanna one final nod, Wulf placed a hand on her shoulder before brandishing his spear and stepping through the doorway to home.

✦ ✦ ✦

BLOOD RUSHED THROUGH Fionn's fingers. It streamed through the cobbled alley, slipping between the grooves.

Arsene had smiled at her just before his eyes had closed. A genuine smile. The kind he never would have shown unless he thought. . .

Everything hurt. Fionn could hardly feel her hands as she tried to staunch the flow of blood. Wiping her eyes, she smeared crimson across her cheek as she snapped herself out of her panic and ripped off her cloak, quickly wrapping the wounds.

Looking up, Fionn glanced around the alley, at Marius lying nearby, at the spot where Aurica had been standing. She was gone.

Smoke drifted from the fire in the courtyard. A charred corpse lay in the center, little more than a blackened husk. Consus was unharmed. Fionn could see his rich green cape fluttering behind him as he stood vigil by Relia's side.

Through the throngs of paladins and Dragosi knights, the crowds of villagers, and the smoke left behind by the blaze, Fionn met Relia's gaze. Had the princess succeeded? Fionn had missed the finale. She had darted away once Arsene's spell had faded.

Pushing through the crowd, Relia ran toward Fionn, brilliant red locks flying behind her. She looked over the bloody scene in horror.

"Help." Fionn pleaded.

Relia dropped to her knees beside Arsene. "Go." She ordered, glancing back at the soldiers rushing to protect their princess.

Nodding, Fionn rose and dashed away, weaving through alleys to avoid the crowds. Countless voices rose as a single din, shouting, praying, screaming.

Embers fell from the sky like rain, lingering radiance bathed the town, and mist swept over their feet. Several villagers dropped to their knees in prostration as Fionn flew past them.

Though Fionn should have been dead, a strength born from desperation carried her to the stables. A couple horses remained inside, and Fionn grabbed an off-white mare and mounted her, driving her into a gallop outside the gate into the woods.

Arsene said Wulf had entered Scael. Any moment now, the whole world could come crashing down.

The wind churned around her, tracing the outline of every twig, stone, and tree. As the horse thundered along the forest road, her windsense found the shape of a man and brushed crumpled bodies hidden in the forest. Yanking the reins, Fionn turned towards what her newfound powers felt.

A horse appeared to her north, racing towards her. Seeing a man mounted on its back, spear drawn, her horse reared in fear, throwing her from the saddle. She landed on the dirt road and rolled to her side, grimacing in pain.

The black horse halted a few paces away, and its rider threw himself from the saddle. Fionn knew who it was before he reached her. The wind remembered his shape.

Wulf grabbed Fionn and pulled her up. "You're alive?" His voice warbled. "Spirits." He cursed, noticing the horrific scar on her chest, the blood-soaked tunic, and the burns crisscrossing her arms.

"Wulf?" Fionn gasped, equally surprised to see he was alive. "I-I'm fine, I have to-"

Ignoring her, Wulf pulled her into his arms and clutched her tightly. "What happened?" He growled.

Pressing a hand to his face, she turned his head, checking for injuries. A gash ran along his jaw. "What. . .?"

"We're fine. It's fine," he assured her. "I saw through it."

Fionn blinked at him, stunned. She hadn't been imagining things; the fae *had* stolen her face.

"I told you I know you." Wulf said. "I can tell the difference." He tucked a hand under her knees, intending to carry her to safety.

"No!" She pulled back. "Eckart. . ." Her head jerked toward the bodies she sensed nearby.

Hearing the plea in her voice, Wulf helped her to her feet and gently lifted her onto his horse. Following her directions, he drove the horse into a gallop.

Tree branches whipped past their faces as they darted through the woods. Yanking the reins, Fionn ordered the horse to stop and threw herself off its back.

Eckart knelt over a bloodied man. He raised his head upon hearing them but hardly moved. Rushing to his side, Fionn froze when she saw the bodies.

One was Tettiena, laid across a field of withered roses, a hole through her chest. The other was a handsome blonde knight, a smile etched on his face. Dropping to her knees, Fionn sat beside Eckart, at a loss for words.

"Idiot." Eckart spat. "I haven't any time left. Why. . .?"

Wulf knelt on Eckart's opposite eyes, teeth gritted. He cast his eyes away.

Throwing herself forward, Fionn wrapped her arms around Eckart and held him tightly. He'd always stiffened when she touched him before, but for the first time, he melted into her arms, face spun with shock and sorrow.

Seoras hadn't wanted anyone to know. Hadn't wanted anyone to be harmed or lost. The face of a boy who'd sacrificed himself for Seoras haunted his memories to this day. . .

Memories that were hers now. Three pieces of Casaliede pulsed inside her. The fragment Seoras had healed her with: whipping winds and striking lighting. The emerald keystone: the very essence of Casaliede and its open door.

And Seoras, the god who had once been mortal, who'd used every ounce of himself to heal her. Whose consciousness had intertwined with Fionn's, becoming one.

FIONN SAT ON the edge of her cot, staring at her palms. Wulf sat beside her, spear lying across his lap, and Consus paced before her bed. Across the infirmary, Eckart watched them from his cot, face blank.

"The Vicar burned, and I was spared." Consus finished his tale. "Whatever enchantment held them vanished. The proof of the goddess was laid bare before their eyes." He looked up. "One of my cousins, Lord Cassius, was among the paladins. He's been a godsend in organizing this mess."

"Good to hear," Wulf said, eyes fixed on Fionn.

He'd shared the tale of Scael with her. Her eyes drifted to his dagger, safely tucked in his belt. A smile tilted her lips. The dreams had worked. It had been a far-fetched idea, but in the end. . .

If only Fionn could thank Johanna for staying behind. For guarding that which kept the cefra alive.

"I wish I could stay." Fionn stood. "But there's something I must attend to."

"Yes." Consus agreed, turning to Eckart. "You must try. Too many lives are on the line."

Despondent, Eckart rose and pulled a cloak over his shoulders. He nodded wearily. "Look after them, Wulf."

Wulf's teeth clenched. He wanted to go with them, but he relented. "I will." He promised.

Extending an arm, Fionn sighed, whispering a single word. "Casaliede."

Power coursed through her as the plane answered its fragment's call. A silver archway sprung to life on the infirmary's back wall, peering into the world of storm.

Before she could depart, Wulf grabbed her and pulled her close, pressing his lips against hers. He deepened the kiss as he caressed her face before finally releasing her.

Smiling at Wulf, she took Eckart's arm and stepped through the portal.

ECKART HAD HEARD stories of Messana, the rainy city of wine, drunkards, and thieves. Relia's favorite book was set in the town he could see in the distance, a collage of colored buildings erected on stilts.

Taking a dragging breath, Eckart felt the beach beneath his feet and stared over the calm ocean. How many waterborn cefra had died already? He was only a half-breed, and already he felt like tomorrow could be the end. His breathing had slowed, everything ached, and remaining conscious was difficult.

"Are you sure?" Eckart asked.

Fionn looked down. "No. But it's all I have."

Eckart was a half-cefran. An evoker. Waterborn. One who'd seen the door to the endless sea and immersed himself in its waters. Only he could claim a deep connection to the severed plane and have the memory required to reach it.

Raising a hand as though attempting to grasp the horizon, Eckart closed his eyes. Evokers had perfect memories. No wonder he'd always been able to recall his childhood with perfect clarity. Even now, he

388

could see the day he'd stood on the ridges overlooking the Gaevral settlement with Chief Tamhas, wiping rain from his eyes.

A quiet hum. A horrible tear. And a silver gateway. Someone had pushed Eckart, and he tumbled through the door into the world of the endless sea.

Breathing deeply, Eckart opened his eyes, remembering it: the gateway to that realm of destruction and beauty.

Brilliant sapphire light danced on his fingers as agony raked through his head. Lights appeared above the ocean waves, painting silver across the blue. An archway tore open. Rain poured through the newfound gap between realms.

It was tiny. Insignificant. The thinnest of gaps, only a piece of paper could slip through. But it was enough.

Overwhelmed, Eckart dropped to his knees. He could see reality distort, warp where the paper-thin crack peered unto the endless sea. The sun disappeared. Darkness rolled in. Rain cascaded over the beach, pounding into the once-calm waves and whipping them into a frenzy.

Life flooded into Eckart's lungs, like the first breath taken after holding it for too long.

Laughing, Fionn dropped beside him. "It worked!" She gasped, holding out a hand to catch one of the raindrops.

It was a beautiful sight, the rain. They'd won. Though he should have been happy, Eckart felt only. . .

Silence lingered between them as rain drenched their clothes. Pulling her knees up, Fionn laid her head atop them and gazed at Eckart.

"It's annoying isn't it? When you're the one who should've been left behind."

A strange, echoing timbre laced her voice, but not like before. Eckart regarded her otherworldly eyes. "Seoras lost someone, too?"

"In the same way." Fionn confirmed. "Tis not always by blood, nor built in stone. To one another, the paths of life form. Feel the earth beneath your feet and follow it home."

Olbhreis' prayer. Eckart looked down.

"Leo found his. He protected it, the way you would." Fionn smiled sadly. "He would never take that from you, so don't take it from him."

Throat burning, Eckart wiped a tear away. Stupid bard. Why did she have to be right?

Fionn laid a hand on his chest and scooted closer. "Long ago, the cefra shared memories. But, instead of the maevruthan, it was through touch. We didn't have to; it was the deepest sign of trust."

Eckart raised his head to watch her. "We did?"

Taking his hand, Fionn laced their fingers together. "Share with me everything Leo was. That your mother was. Let me know it all so I can write a hundred ballads. So the world will never forget."

Tears welled in Eckart's eyes when he realized what she was offering. Tightening his fingers around hers, he touched her forehead with his, leaning into the comforting embrace as he shared all that he knew, all that he was, and all that was no longer.

CHAPTER FORTY

ANOTHER LIFE

MARIUS LEANED OVER Arsene's bed, his countenance a war between amusement and annoyance. Arsene sat bolt upright, vision blurry.

"Am I late?" He blurted out.

"You always are." Marius brushed an auburn lock behind his ear. "We only have an hour before we're expected to arrive."

Sighing, Arsene pushed his sheets off. Everything hurt, but he wasn't sure why. Maybe the dread had seeped into his bones.

"Relax, Arsene." Marius chuckled. "It's just a sermon. You'll survive."

"I think I'd rather die than go, actually." Arsene tried to roll over.

"No, you don't." Marius grabbed him and pulled him to his feet, dropping a mantle into his arms. "Get dressed." He turned away, then whirled around. "Oh! Maybe I can cheer you up."

"With what?"

"Your prototype." Marius grinned, grabbing a box from the nightstand and flipping it open.

Dropping the mantle, Arsene stared into the box with glee. The blacksmith had done a phenomenal job: the metal cylinder perfectly matched his designs for the flintlock.

"She's beautiful." Arsene marveled. "I think I'll name her. . . Death Knell."

Marius snapped the box closed. "I'm keeping this until you come up with a better name."

"What's wrong with it?"

"Everything. Now hurry," Marius said, shoving the mantle back into Arsene's arms. "Listening to the Vicar speak will do you good."

"Why? I thought we already decided I was a good for nothing."

"You are now, yes," Marius said. "But I still have hopes," he extended his hand with a warm smile. "That you'll be a good man, one day."

Taking Marius's hand, Arsene stumbled forward, passing through the image of his brother as it faded away. The black walls of his bedroom crumbled into stained wooden slats. Pain flared through him, and he tumbled forward, catching himself on a knee.

Where was he? Pain flared through his head as he looked around. Was this someone's house? He'd been lying on an uncomfortable bed of white sheets; his bag was strewn on a slanted shelf across the room. A tiny fire crackled in a small hearth.

Turning his head, Arsene sucked in a breath and stumbled to the other bed in the room. A body lay beneath the sheets, their head covered. Knowing what he would find underneath, Arsene pulled the blankets back.

Even in death, Marius looked composed and regal. Memories raced through Arsene, rattling against his skull painfully. Marius had jumped in front of Arsene, shielding him from their mother. And she'd had the audacity to. . .

Sitting on the edge of the bed, Arsene grabbed his brother's still hand. Cold, with but a fleeting streak of warmth clinging to the skin.

He didn't understand. Why had Marius come back? Why had he thrown his life away? The Duke's life had been in service to. . .

Viridia. Did that mean she was gone?

Gasping, Arsene recalled a memory he had never been able to before. The dangerous smile on Fionn's lips as she leaned toward him in the crumbled threshold of Diorbhail's temple.

"Viridia's not real." Arsene insisted.

"No." Fionn agreed. *"But your brother thinks so. That's what the fae in his mind claims to be."*

Jaw clenching, Arsene searched the empty room for an enemy. For someone to shoot. How dare that creature prey on his brother's goodwill, chasing him into lies that ended his life. . .

Irritatingly perfect man. Even after Arsene's final betrayal, Marius still loved him. Dazed and confused, his first thought had been to protect Arsene.

The door flew open, and a woman strode in. A torn black coat trailed around her boots, and stray blonde locks escaped her messy bun. Mother's eyes looked haggard as the door fell close behind her.

"It happened an hour ago," Aurica said. "Relia had hopes he would survive." Her head dipped, "but it's like he didn't want to."

"Relia," Arsene repeated, surprised by how hoarse his voice was. "Then she won them over. Does she know you're here?"

"No." She said shortly, moving to stand at the foot of the bed. "What have I done? I thought he was far away, that he was. . . I never imagined. . ."

Marius would risk his life to save me. Arsene thought. "Listen, Mother. Surely by now, you've realized-"

"Realized what?" Her amber eyes flared with anger. "That I should have been rid of you earlier? That you were so much worse than a failure?"

For once, Arsene had nothing to say. As a child, he'd long to hear glowing words of affection, of pride. He'd suppressed the desire as a teenager, though he still felt it.

For the first time, he realized nothing would have made Aurica change her opinion of her lesser son. It had never been his fault. Not really.

"Everything's in ruins." Aurica continued. Her hand tightened around something under her coat. "Are you pleased?"

"Pleased?" Arsene snapped. "Do you know nothing about me at all?"

"No." Lady Aurica said hauntingly.

Raising her hand, she pressed a dagger to her throat. Gasping, Arsene tried to grab her arm. The knife slid across her throat, cutting a deep gash and spilling the crimson of her blood over her black coat.

Her body went limp in his arms, and they hit the floor. Untangling himself from the corpse, Arsene stared at the fresh blood coating his bandages. But it was not his.

Wrapping his arms around himself, he gazed in horror at the bloody body of his mother, lying at the foot of his dead brother's bead.

The goddess wasn't real. No divine spirit to whom Marius had devoted his life would have allowed this to happen. His throat burned though no tears fell.

Standing, he backed away slowly, eyes flicking between the bodies of his family. His back slammed into the door, and he threw it open, fleeing into the night. Blackest night swallowed the village, and he stumbled in the middle of the cobbled road.

Pain flared in his chest as he sank to his knees, and new blood mingled with the stained gauze, this time from his wounds. Frozen and cold, he looked up at the sky. Starless, moonless, eternal.

For the sun had died.

ECKART WATCHED KIYLLA, trying to read her face. Intensity colored her eyes at all hours, and she always held her head high. Today was no different. A brown cloak billowed around her, and short brown hair brushed her cheeks as she stood by the ledge overlooking the aiceil of black trees.

Pulling his fur cloak around his shoulders, Eckart glanced away, wondering if he should say something. But finally, she spoke.

"I cannot stay here," Kiylla said.

"No." Eckart agreed. "You've lingered far too long already."

"I could not bring myself to leave." She turned to Eckart. "Did you know Consus asked me to oversee arrangements? He didn't want Leo sent to his family's manor."

Eckart hadn't heard that. He tilted his head. "Where did you suggest?"

"I told him to ask you." She said. "To wherever you will go, in whichever way you wish. You were his home." Sorrow finally broke the unflappable gaze. "And one should always be buried at home."

Home. . . Where did Eckart want to dig the grave? Somewhere close, so he could visit often and recite the tales Fionn would pen.

"I am ready." Kiylla turned back to the aiceil. She leaned on the overlook. "Read me this poem."

Reaching into his memory, Eckart retrieved the words. "When midnight calls, stars brush the land, and heavens fade to night. Pain and dreams dull to sleep, and flowers bloom where warmth has fled. And in that place of silent reprieve, I'll see again the one I seek."

"Ah." Kiylla's voice shook with a sob. "Our promise." Swallowing, she turned to Eckart. "Not in this life, but the next."

"Kiylla," Eckart said. "I'm glad you get to go home. Tell your people they're safe. That's what he wanted. And it's what I wanted."

"I know. That's why you let me go." She smiled. "Write to me-" She snapped her mouth closed and chuckled. "Have someone write to me. I will visit, too. I have many things to say to the south lord. He was supposed to come to me, so I could protect him. . ."

"Fionn can write the letters." Eckart promised. "I'll make sure you get them."

Nodding, Kiylla stared over Eckart's shoulder. "You should go. And so will I." Pulling up her hood, she walked away.

Eckart reached for her but lowered his arm. She would write. They could talk again when the tears had dried.

Footsteps startled Eckart. Consus approached. Relia had fitted him with proper paladin attire, polished steel, and a winged helm. He saluted by pressing a fist to his chest. Eckart snorted. "Honors? For me?"

"Why, of course, dear brother." Consus sounded cheerful at first, but his rigid stance slipped. "Kiylla is leaving, then? That's for the best. Did she tell you what I requested?"

"Yes. Give me some time to think it over." Eckart folded his arms and looked down the hill leading into Fairborough. "I can't go back to the Gaevral. At best, they'll retrieve my memories so I can pool them somewhere else."

"The Aeourant, then?"

"No. Fionn is exiled from her home. And I mean to stay with her."

Consus shifted from foot to foot, clearing his throat. "I bring an offer. A royal offer."

Raising an eyebrow, Eckart waited for his brother to continue.

"Her Highness extends an offer to Eckart of the Gaevral, once of the Parnesius household, to return to Clodia in the pursuit of restoring his family's honor by serving on the Empress' holy guard."

Drinking in Consus's formal invitation, Eckart stared at him blankly. "Relia wants me to be a holy paladin?"

"Yes." Consus nodded. "Both of us."

Home . . . Where better than with his long-lost half-brother and the young woman who had so desperately wanted to believe they were siblings?

"Take me to her." Eckart gestured.

Consus turned, leading Eckart down the hill to the chapel. Relia had been stuck here for the past few days, confined to the chapel while paladins fretted over her, the traitors were accounted for, and accounts were written down.

But they would leave tomorrow. A procession had been prepared to bring the princess home.

Three priests and a Dragosi knight surrounded Relia in the Chapel garden. She twirled a strand of hair, not listening to whatever the old cleric said. Noticing Eckart, she bolted to her feet and ran to his side.

Smoothing down her dress, she curtsied. "Eckart! Did you accept?"

Clearing his throat, Eckart side-eyed Consus before mimicking a royal salute, pressing his hand to his chest. "What would you have of me, your highness?"

Joy bloomed on her face. She must have expected him to say no. "Really?"

"Really."

Though it was uncouth for the next Empress, Relia hugged him tightly. A half-breed. In front of the nobility, no less.

It would take a long time for Eckart to forgive himself. Years would pass before he stopped blaming himself for Leo's death, for failing his vow. Years he could spend ensuring no one ever laid a finger on the Empire's hope.

✦ ✦ ✦

A pleasant breeze drifted across Fairborough. Stars twinkled in the black sky, the first signs of morning in Athelstan. Fionn could feel the wind brushing against every building, person, and bloom.

It was unbearable. How could Seoras stand it?

Fairborough was a mess. Scorched roads, burnt buildings. Soldiers littered the town, and messengers rode in and out daily. The lost heir had been recovered the day a deadly coup was revealed. The Empire was reeling, and so soon after the loss of their Emperor.

They had much work left ahead of them. But Fionn's part in this tale was finally done.

Wulf sighed, laying his head on hers. Trees, buckled and bent from the recent shadow storm, swayed over the town's gate, mere whispers in the gloom.

"I can't believe the prick's finally gone," Wulf muttered.

Offended, Fionn wrenched out of his arms and whirled around. "Seoras is not gone. He's. . . We're. . ."

Brow furrowed, Wulf looked her up and down. "To you, maybe. Even though I don't entirely understand, it seems like you're finally free."

Free.

Fionn turned away, staring at the night sky. She didn't understand what had become of her, either. Everything Seoras had been, the Leviathan, the Storm Rider, a man who became, to others, a god. . . now belonged to her.

No one remained who would mourn Seoras, save Fionn. She would hold his memory close. It was a part of her, after all.

A songbird flitted down from the clouds and landed atop Fairborough's gate. Fionn smiled at it.

Nothing had changed, and everything had changed. Days would come when she felt thoughts borne of Seoras, when a hollow ache bore a hole in her chest, when living seemed hopeless and bleak.

Pain and sorrow belonged to her as surely as the storm. They would trouble her for the rest of her days. But for once, Fionn felt she had the strength to face it. For once, not knowing who she was seemed a blessing.

"I don't understand either," Fionn said. "What am I. Who am I." She grinned at Wulf. "But I'm excited to find out. I've never had the chance before. Never had a future to look forward to."

Wulf stared at her silently before chuckling. "I think I already know the answer." He brushed his hand across her cheek. "But I'll humor you."

Taking his hand, Fionn closed her eyes and leaned against him. "Ah!" She dropped his hand. "I never said it back."

"Said what back?"

Wrapping her arms around his neck, she whispered in his ear. "I love you, too."

Wulf laughed, pulling her into an embrace. Quite the man she'd fallen for; slayer of gods and savior of the world. Fionn had quite a few ballads to write for him.

The songbird chirped erratically and flew away. The wind swirled violently around a street to the north, and terror pulsed in Fionn's heart. Ripping away from Wulf, she turned and ran in its direction.

"Fionn?" He called, chasing after her.

Cloak flapping wildly behind her, Fionn darted through the rousing villagers and slipped between a patrol of Dragosi knights. Vaulting an overturned crate, she rounded a corner and found what she sought.

Arsene looked down from the sky, a mess of blood and tears. His face changed when he noticed her, and he shakily rose. They had not seen one another since they'd parted in the alley.

Stumbling, she tried to find the source of the blood to check if he was bleeding. Arsene grabbed her hand and yanked her, pulling her into an embrace so tight it felt like he would never let go.

Wulf's heavy steps thundered down the road as Arsene lost his balance and collapsed, dragging Fionn down with him. The mercenary knelt beside them, cursing. "Idiot. You should be in bed."

Biting his lip, Arsene only shook his head in response. Rising, Wulf glanced at the door.

"Don't." Arsene snapped. "I need away from here. Now."

Wulf helped him up, gesturing for Fionn to follow. Hurrying through the dark, Wulf rounded a bend and leaned Arsene against a wall beside a slowly turning windmill.

Voice steadying, Arsene glared at Fionn. "I need to be filled in. Because evidently, Fionn disappeared, doubled, and died."

"Where do I start?" Wulf mumbled.

"Not here. Or now." Arsene interrupted. "Tell me what happens. After this.'"

"Well, Relia-"

"Not Relia." Arsene's voice trembled. "What happens. For. . ."

He didn't finish the thought, but Fionn could tell Wulf understood what his partner wanted. "We take a break," Wulf said. "I'm going to hire a luxury vessel to take us to Messana. Relia's giving me a hell of a payment, and I plan to use it."

Relieved, Arsene's head dropped. "That's. . . good. It's just a shame the entire Dobrescu line died here."

Wulf raised his chin in surprise, then nodded. "It is." He said gravely.

Swallowing, Fionn stepped closer to him. "It's not like a prince could be seen traveling with filth like us, anyway."

That's what Arsene wanted to hear. His head rose, and a faint smile appeared. For the first time since they'd met, his amber eyes softened, if only a hair.

"Come here," Wulf grumbled, grabbing Arsene's collar in one hand and Fionn's in the other. Gathering them into his arms, he held them close, warming them in his embrace.

The emotions Arsene must have been holding back all his life finally erupted. Leaning her head against his, Fionn wept with him.

A puddle of blood, ash, and misery pooled at their feet. But there would be time yet to heal.

Together.

CHAPTER FORTY ONE

THE SONG & THE EMBER

Three years later. . .

FIONN CLAMPED THE hairpin between her teeth as she gathered her curls into a bun. Pinning them back, she spun in the mirror, watching her black skirt swirl around her knees. Painted dragons flew across her exposed midriff and circled her arms.

She leaned in, running a hand across her cheek, watching the pulsing green light reflected in her eyes.

Satisfied with her appearance, she trotted down the stairs into her cozy home of rustic wooden furniture covered in fur throws. She whistled cheerfully to herself, heading to the mantle to retrieve her kettle, but froze when she noticed the songbird sitting atop the counter.

Turning, Fionn's good mood vanished. A man had his feet kicked up on her table, his face obscured by a scroll of parchment.

"You look nice." Arsene lowered the scroll. "Mm." He frowned in distaste and flicked a hand at her. A faint silver glow touched his hand, and a loose string on her skirt knitted itself back into place.

"Ugh." Fionn threw her arms up. "I *just* changed the locks."

"And I'm surprised you haven't given up trying to keep me out," he scoffed. "Honestly, take better care of your things. Do you have any idea how much that dress cost me?"

"If I know you, very little. You probably bargained until it cost only coppers." Grabbing her kettle, Fionn spun, trying to remember where she'd put her mug. "Wulf's going to break *your* lock off at this rate. How are you going to evoke your way out of this one?"

"My house is watertight. Wulf will never get in." Arsene frowned. Rising, he gestured at her with his scroll. "Have you seen Relia?"

"Not recently, why?"

"Good. I'll lay low here, then." Rolling up his sleeves, he stuffed the parchment in his trouser pocket and grabbed the cup she'd set out for herself. "Do you mind?" he asked, taking the kettle from her.

"No," Fionn said dryly, crossing the room. Hiding a smile, she wondered what new gambit Wulf would conjure to try and outwit Arsene's evoking. If there existed a lock an evoker could not crack, Wulf would find it.

A tiny stone basin the size of a bird bath rested in the corner, filled with viscous silver liquid. Dipping her fingers into the water, she pooled yesterday's memories into the tiny maevruthan she and Eckart shared.

Perhaps the tiny pool would flourish into a basin one day, but it was just the two of them for now.

A heavy knock broke her from the memories. Arsene glanced at her, shrinking against the wall and silently gesturing for her to answer it.

Wiping her hands off, Fionn opened the door and stepped back when she found an entire unit of royal paladins standing in her tiny garden. Staring up at the much taller helmed man, she waited for him to speak.

Instead, he bowed and stepped aside, allowing the Empress through.

Renata was draped in a golden dress of thin silk, her red hair bound back by hairpins and shrouded in a thin veil. "Sorry to bother you," she said earnestly. "Have you seen Arsene?"

Tilting her chin, Fionn resisted the urge to glance behind. "Why?"

"*Oh.*" Renata turned her head. "I know that tone. Where is he?"

Blocking the doorway, Fionn counted the paladins. Twelve. "Does he have an arrest warrant again?"

"Not this time." Renata cocked her head. "By the goddess. Did he not tell you?"

"Tell me what?"

Laughing, Renata flicked a hand. A moving wall appeared in the doorway, pushing Fionn aside. Shrieking, Fionn scrambled out of its way. Striding through the door, Renata waved her hand again, and the wall vanished.

But the house was empty. "Rat." Renata cursed, glancing around. "If you're hiding somewhere, know that I'll find you." She turned to Fionn, who still held her hands above her head. "I'm trying to offer him a position at court, and he's fleeing like I'm having him carted off to the dungeons!"

Lowering her arms, Fionn's eyes darted around her home, impressed with how quickly Arsene had vanished. "What position?"

"Court evoker. If you hadn't heard, Lady Lucullus retired."

"Do you want me to ask him?"

"If you would," Renata rolled her eyes. "Honestly, if he wants to decline, he just needs to give me a formal answer. But do try to convince him. There's no better man for the job."

"You have my word, your highness." Fionn bowed.

Renata pulled her up. "Thanks." Squeezing Fionn's arms, she smiled sweetly, and for a moment, she looked like Relia again. "Sorry for the intrusion." She turned but quickly spun around. "Oh! Eckart's leaving soon. Better hurry if you want to catch him." Bowing her head, she swept out the door and was quickly surrounded by her guards.

Hanging in the doorway, Fionn watched the procession depart before stepping outside and turning in the opposite direction. It was a fine morning. The sun warmed the city, brightening the white marble buildings. Flowers unfurled under its embrace. The first golden roses had begun to bloom.

As Fionn turned a corner, Arsene fell into step with her. "Is she gone?"

"You're getting good at that. Learning from me?" Fionn asked.

"Here and there."

"She's gone," Fionn promised. "Just decline her."

"Yes, but," Arsene sighed. "Part of me wants to accept. I'm forcing myself to say no by avoiding the matter entirely."

Fionn stopped, brow furrowed.

"Don't look at me like that. I know I'm being. . . complicated." He leaned in. "I'm right where I want to be, and I don't want my ego to ruin that."

Chuckling, Fionn kept walking. Now, his actions made perfect sense. To accept would be to reclaim the title he had thrown away years ago.

"Don't worry," Fionn teased, "I'll protect you from yourself."

"You're the only one who can." Arsene tucked his hands in his pockets, smiling.

With the sun shining on Arsene's hair, the red strands glowed like fire. The softness of youth had departed his features. Fionn often wanted to tell him he looked like Marius but could never find the courage.

"You know," Arsene said chipperly. "I have an idea for a song. Interested?"

"You do?" Fionn grinned. "Walk a little slower, then. I want to hear it."

The sun burned against Eckart's back as he read the letter again. When Relia had taught him to read, he thought the skill would be useful for reviewing reports, reading patrol schedules, and sneaking a peek at Fionn's rough drafts.

But nothing could have prepared him for what this letter described.

> *Dear Eckart,*
>
> *I hear you are serving the Empress. Some kind of special knight. I'll admit, the news made me wary of writing. I wanted to trust the girl like you did, but I knew better than to follow blind faith.*
>
> *Your Empress has made strides to bring peace. While I doubt tensions will be mended in our lifetime, or indeed even our children's, I feel safe enough to finally reach out.*

Eckart rolled up the letter and stuffed it into his pocket. Smoothing out his leather vest, he pulled his old fur cloak around his shoulders and tied his hair back with a leather cord.

Dilsaeth neighed impatiently, wide, feathered hooves stamping on the ground. Eckart quickly counted the bags tied to his saddle, ensuring everything was packed.

"Heading out?" Relia's voice startled Eckart.

The Empress leaned against the pasture fence, veil pushed up to reveal her soft brown eyes. She'd slipped away from her guards again.

"How many times does Consus need to remind you the dangers of traveling alone?" Eckart chided.

"I was just thinking about him," Relia interrupted. "He said not to worry; he'll cover in your absence. Take what time you need."

"I won't be gone long," Eckart promised.

Relia glanced away, reaching out a hand to Dilsaeth. "The kid has a good name. I take it you know where it comes from?"

The Ballad of Burgundy Rose: Leo's favorite. The main character was named Cynric. Eckart had heard enough about the tale from Leo to fill several tomes.

"I didn't realize Kiylla had a soft spot," Eckart said. "Or even knew about that one."

"She has good taste." Relia smiled sadly. "Be careful." She pet Dilsaeth and squeezed Eckart's arm before turning and vanishing.

Wretched spell. Consus would gray long before his years if Relia kept using it to slip away.

Taking Dilsaeth's reins, Eckart guided his stallion toward the northern gate, rehearsing what he would say. Maybe he would improvise. Talking with children had always been easier than speaking with people.

"Eckart!" Fionn raced toward him, skirt fluttering around her knees. She doubled over and caught her breath. "I can't believe I almost missed you."

"Did you forget it was today?"

"I thought it was tomorrow." She stood straight. "Are you sure you don't want company?"

Eckart peered over her shoulder. Arsene followed her, sauntering at a leisurely pace. Shaking his head, Eckart smiled. "I'd rather go alone. Besides, if everything goes to plan, I'll return with her."

"She did promise to visit." Fionn agreed. Frowning, she touched Eckart's arm.

Where once words had been necessary, a mere glance now sufficed. Sharing a maevruthan bonded them together. And with only their memories swirling in the silver waters, each other's lives radiated with crystal clarity.

"Do be careful," Arsene advised, finally joining them. "Tensions at the border haven't quite abated."

Nodding, Eckart mounted Dilsaeth. "Keep Wulf out of trouble."

"Heavens knows I try." Arsene held up his dominant hand in farewell, the sun outlining his jagged scar.

Taking a deep breath, Eckart calmed his nerves and rode for the gate. The news was bittersweet. Initially, Eckart's heart swelled with joy, but in the following moment, horrible sorrow pulled him into its drowning depths.

Staring ahead, he focused on the sweet. Life was not kind enough to ignore the good blooming in the dark.

FIONN WATCHED ECKART depart, hands nervously balled into fists on her chest. Had they known about the baby, they never would have let Kiylla travel home, alone.

Wulf had been asking Fionn about children recently, and she never felt ready. With Eckart becoming a godfather, his thoughts would doubtless linger on their own.

The future remained uncertain. The edges that once defined Fionn and Seoras had blended together. Twin shards beat within her heart, fragments of another realm.

Seoras had been capable of living beyond his years. But Fionn's life should have been cut short. What would become of her? Though she had grown used to her fluttering heart and newfound strength, she had yet to discern the full truth. She could die tomorrow.

Maybe it was time to release her fears. They had stopped her from living once, and she'd promised herself they never would again.

"Shall we?" Arsene asked, brushing past her.

A two-story building loomed behind the pasture. A metal plaque displayed the establishment's name: The Blackheart Mercenary Guild.

A cacophony spilled from these doors whenever Fionn opened them. Men as young as fourteen and as old as fifty gathered in the main hall. Most skirted away from her and fled her path. One too many displays of fuming anger had hammered an invaluable lesson into the men: don't touch or leer at the commander's wife.

Suspecting where she'd find her husband, Fionn slid out the side door into the training yard. Sure enough, Wulf stood with his back to them, dressed in a long black coat with a silver cape. Several new recruits were doubled over, breathing heavily. One lay on the floor, curled in a pitiful ball.

Noticing his company, Wulf paused the drill. "Take a break," he ordered. Sheathing his spear, he rushed to Fionn's side. "You look lovely. Is today special?"

"It is, in fact." Arsene grabbed Wulf's arm and dragged him inside. "That and you forgot Eckart was leaving for Yuri Llaqta today."

Wulf grimaced when he realized his mistake. "Did he already-"

"Mhm." Arsene shooed them into the meeting room, slamming the door behind them. "Look at this." He handed Wulf the scroll he'd been reading earlier.

Unrolling the parchment, Wulf paced around the table, eyebrows rising and falling. "What does it say?" Fionn asked.

"The king of Forsaidh just passed." Wulf read. "His brother is leading a coup on the throne, declaring the princess inept. Fionn." Wulf asked. "What do you know of the royal family?"

"The reigning king was beloved, I think. My mother had nothing but good things to say about him."

"Sounds like an easy decision, then." Wulf decided.

"Oh, but there's more." Arsene folded his arms. "Read the second page. Strings of mysterious disappearances are plaguing every major city."

Fionn nudged Arsene. "Is that our side of the job? I thought you'd struck Forsaidh from our list of viable countries."

"What makes you think that? Warm climate? Beautiful women?" Arsene grinned. "Beautiful women, who hardly wear any clothes? Sounds like our next job to me. Besides, I'm curious."

"Pen a letter to the princess. Ask if she requires aid." Wulf ordered. Noticing Fionn's uncertain gaze, he repeated his mantra. "It's the right thing to do."

"As you wish, oh captain mine." Arsene grabbed the scrolls back and nudged Fionn. "Excited to go home?"

"Honestly," Fionn closed her eyes. "Yes," she opened them. "We'll have time to wait for Eckart's return, right? I want to meet Leo's son."

"I'm sure. There's still plenty to be done."

"Then get to it." Wulf clapped Arsene on the shoulder and pulled him away from Fionn. Gently cupping her face, he kissed her. "Keep the goat outside, yeah?"

"But Eckart said to take good care of her." Fionn giggled. "Oh, and don't stay late today."

"Why?"

Pressing a hand to his chest, Fionn stood on her tiptoes to whisper in his ear. "I think I'm ready to start trying."

Genuine joy flashed across Wulf's face, followed by lust. "I'll take a half-day." He promised, winking. Reluctant to leave her, he backed through the door, returning to work.

When Fionn turned back to Arsene, he was staring into the corner, eyes flicking around as though following something.

Fionn had long suspected he was afflicted with phantoms. But Arsene never spoke of his troubles. His countenance displayed hints of mirth but also sorrow. What memory did he see?

Snapping out his daze, Arsene smiled at her. "I have a letter to write and a budget to manage. Have you seen the coin Wulf's been flinging around lately?" He threw up his arms. "Honestly. Where would he be without me?"

"In an early grave," Fionn said.

"I'm glad someone understands that." He paused, hand on the doorknob, looking like he wanted to say something.

How many times had Arsene worn that expression, hesitating? Whatever he wished to voice, he never did. Nodding, he opened the door.

"Arsene?" Fionn called.

"Hm?" He paused in the doorway.

"Can I dress *you* this time? You'll stand out in Forsaidh wearing that, and not in a good way."

Crossing his ankles, Arsene studied her attire. "Alright, thief. I accept. But I have high standards." He tilted his head. "Go get your goat, already."

Sighing, Fionn brushed a loose strand of hair behind her ear and walked to the window, swinging it open and slipping outside. She landed in the pasture and waded through the tall grass, calling for Tefnut.

The spotted goat Eckart had stolen in Yuri Llaqta trotted over, bell collar ringing. Relia had sent a royal decree to the Lavinian stablemaster demanding the return of several steeds and one small goat.

Tying a rope to Tefnut's collar, she led the goat back to their house. Emotions hung heavy on her today, and she wanted nothing more than to sit in her garden and finish her song.

A lantern flickered as she passed, the flame sputtering and dying as a breeze rushed through it. Embers flared, scattering over the street. Catching one in the wind, Fionn let it dance between her fingers before she finally released it, returning it to the sky.

But while the rest of its kind fell to the road and died, this ember grew into a spark and caught alight. And for the briefest moment, it shone as brightly as the sun.

STARSCOURGE

JOHANNA SAT ON the steps of the black tower, double-checking her bag. Her evoking powers had dimmed with time. Once, she could have been certain she had packed everything she needed. Now, she doubted herself.

Satisfied, she snapped the bag close. Surviving in this dying world had been arduous, but she'd made do. Berries still grew in the silver hills around the lake, and some fish survived in the waters. It wasn't pleasant, but it was enough.

Slinging her bag over her shoulder, she tightened her braid and danced down the steps. Reaching the rocky edge of the island, she leaned forward and whispered, "Cimnich de imine."

Ice surged from the lake like rain falling upwards as it coalesced into a bridge. Taking a deep breath, Johanna glanced up at the twin moons casting the tower in soft, white light.

When Wulf had stepped through the portal to Thruine three years ago, Johanna had realized her mistake. He was Seoras' chosen, the one allowing them entry to the ancient tower. Once Wulf departed its walls, the tower should have cast her out or crumbled beneath her feet.

But it hadn't. The moment Johanna had vowed to stay behind, the moment she'd touched the black stone, a connection had formed.

All three jewels rested safely in a satchel at her belt. Pulling the black stone out, Johanna ran a thumb over it. Diorbhail's Ember looked like a dull ruby, and Olbhreis' Ore appeared but a paltry rock. Shadows surged beneath the black stone, seeping shades that caressed her touch.

This one's owner had claimed Johanna as its heir. And so the tower had become hers.

And that meant the stone's creator still dwelt here. Somewhere. The last of the ancient cefra.

Johanna had miles and miles to explore of this world of endless night, countless secrets to uncover, and a patron to meet.

Smiling, she returned the bag to her belt and strode across the bridge. Time enough remained before this world died. Time enough to find her answers.

MORE STORIES WILL BE TOLD IN THE WORLD OF THRUINE

In

Death of the Glass Angel

Coming 2025

and

The Starscourge Chronicles

Coming 2026

GLOSSARY

Aiceil: A strange landmark, usually a forest, marked by a border of barren, dead land. The Empire declares them holy sites, forbidding entry. As a result, few know what lies in the woods beyond the dead soil.

Altanbern: A mountainous, frigid region to the south of the Empire. Home to scant peoples in scattered villages, as well as the Gaevral cefran tribe.

Bruthine: The name for both the dormant volcano in northern Dragos, and also its overlapping realm of fire and ash.

Cefra: A race of people known for their elemental magic and pupil-less eyes. Nearly all live in isolated tribes outside of Imperial Territory.

Catalyst: The means by which cefra utilize their inborn elemental powers. One cefra might conjure spells through music, while another must be enraged to cast. Each catalyst is unique, ranging from physical items to moods.

Casaliede: The realm overlapping the island nation of Forsaidh, said to be a world of endless storms.

Clodian Empire: The largest human empire. Consists of four smaller nations: Dragos, Athelstan, Thuatia and the seat of the capital, Sigilus. A theocracy, it is ruled by a holy Emperor.

Evoker: Human mages. The talent is rare, normally inherited by noble families. Wielders can conjure items, events, and senses from their own memories. Beyond magic, evokers possess perfect memories, able to recall the smallest details in perfect clarity.

Faerdain Eigain: The realm overlapping Messana. Endless rain pours over a fathomless sea, hiding a turquoise world within its depths.

Forsaidh: An island nation across the ocean east of the Empire. The people there live vastly different lives from those on the mainland, worshiping a large pantheon and intermingling cefra and human. Home to the cefran Aeourant Tribe.

Maevruthan: The silver pond in each cefran tribe's settlement. Within the strangely viscous waters lies the tribe's memories: here they can see each other's pasts in perfect clarity. Cefra cannot retain their own memories, and must deposit their minds into the pond. A crystal necklace forged from the silver waters serves as their link to the pool when they leave home.

Messana: The nation west of the Empire, a coalition of merchant's guilds known for wine, rain and thieves.

Planes: Theorized worlds that lie out of reach. Some scholars think they overlap the lands, causing strange effects such as fiery rain and endless night, but they have never been proven to be real. Each country overlaps with a different plane, and suffers different effects.

Reitath: A cefran celebration in which a young man or woman comes of age, and joins their memories to the tribe's maevruthan.

Scael: The realm overlapping Athelstan. Not much is known about it, save it causes a near-eternal night to curse the land of pastures and knights.

Sylfestra: A nation of humans and fae said to be ruled by the fae god himself. Lies in the woodlands to the west of the Empire. Home to the cefran Creiv tribe.

Tiene: Once the fourth cefran tribe, their people lived in a grand city. After warring with Dragos and its Imperial allies, many were slaughtered, and the rest scattered. The ruins of their city are scarce, as though much of it simply vanished.

Viridia: Goddess of the Clodian Empire. She governs nature and the sun, and her doctrine demands spreading the seeds of her practice to all lands.

Yuri Llaqta: An ever-changing land home to nomadic tribes. It lies to the east of the Empire, and has been in frequent conflict with their people.

ABOUT THE AUTHOR

Riley lives in the farmlands of Northern Alabama with her husband, two spoiled dogs, and her cockatiel named Seoras, who seems more like a toddler. Fitting, no?

LINKS

https://rileysknight.com
https://instagram.com/rileysknight/

SIGN UP FOR THE NEWSLETTER:

https://rileysknight.com/newsletter

www.ingramcontent.com/pod-product-compliance
Lightning Source LLC
Chambersburg PA
CBHW020650110726
47901CB00001B/127